SEASIDE CHRISTMAS

SEASIDE CHRISTMAS

WAYNE TURNER

Independently Published by Author: Wayne Turner

CONTENTS

Dedication ix
Acknowledgements x
Prelude xi

1	1
2	9
3	17
4	23
5	35
6	41
7	53
8	59
9	63
10	71
11	83
12	95
13	103
14	109
15	115

16	121
17	129
18	137
19	143
20	153
21	157
22	163
23	167
24	171
25	175
26	183
27	193
28	197
29	201
30	205
31	209
32	219
33	223
34	231
35	239
36	247
37	257
38	263
39	269

40	277
41	285
42	295
43	305
44	313
45	327
46	333
47	345
48	365
49	387
50	393
51	401
52	409
53	415
54	425
55	433
Epilogue	445
About The Author	446

Copyright © 2022 by WAYNE TURNER

The following is a work of fiction. A product of the author's imagination. Any resemblance to persons living or dead is purely coincidental, or used in the form or a parody.
All rights reserved. No part of this book may be reproduced in any manner whatsoever without written permission except in the case of brief quotations embodied in critical articles and reviews.

First Printing, 2022

Wayne and Elsie in Mahone Bay, Nova Scotia

This book is dedicated to the amazing readers I've met through the publication of my debut novel 'Seaside Glitter'. Through many interactions they have encouraged and nudged me towards writing a sequel. Through our combined efforts we have succeeded. 'Seaside Christmas' reenergized my love of writing. Fortunately, it also added zing and energy to a special bond I've shared with my amazing and loving wife Elsie over the past 54 years come December 2022. Needless to say, the dedication of 'Seaside Christmas' wouldn't be complete without shouting out, 'I love you!' and thanking my special lady for all she does in supporting my passions.

ACKNOWLEDGEMENTS

I would like to acknowledge three forces that combined to accelerate my journey beyond the written word and its storyline into the world of editing *Seaside Christmas*. First, I'll admit I resisted the efforts exerted to convince me to title the book *Seaside Christmas*. In the end, Elsie and Roxanna Boyd succeeded. Their efforts did not stop there. Both provided me with reviews and editing suggestions that smoothed out my storyline and energized its characters.

Combined with the efforts of our daughter Karen, the teacher, *Seaside Christmas* is now a fictional reality ready to carry its readers off on a romantic mystery filled with adventure in each page turned. Editing is a world of refinement every writer can and does benefit from. It's been a year or two since I last sat in a classroom as a student. Karen's editing set aside the red pen and went digital. Was it effective? Absolutely, and combined, with Roxanna and Elsie, mom's efforts Karen and her teammates refined my grammar and punctuation. Then nudged me towards closing out the editing process and publishing my second novel, *Seaside Christmas*.

Hoping you enjoy it and have a Merry Christmas reconnecting with Seaside Glitter's characters as they move forward in life and towards a *Seaside Christmas* celebrated in East River, on Nova Scotia's South Shore.

Front cover: Rights Purchased through istockphoto.com
Backcover: Photographer: Hannah Dominic on Unsplash.com

PRELUDE

Prelude: Where the action got underway in *Seaside Glitter*.

A family tragically loses their parents and grandparents in a horrific traffic accident. Reduced to a family of three, an ancient diary reconnects them to their true family roots. The families that greed once tore apart are drawn by curiosity and circumstance back to where their adventurous forebearers set out to build a new life in a new land 'New Scotland' today's Nova Scotia. Drawn by the diary's author and spirit they head out to the ominous floating islands out beyond the Tancook Islands on Mahone Bay. Does wealth and treasure await them on the island? A question worth pondering. Others have and continue to seek out wealth and treasure beyond mankind's wildest imaging's on sister islands. Is any of it really out there? Along the way childhood sweethearts reconnect. A wedding unfolds. Need more? Pick up a copy of *Seaside Glitter* and enjoy the adventure.

Prologue: Where will the action unfolding take us?

Seaside Glitter's newlyweds set off eager to create a new life together. Families torn apart 200 years past and recently reconnected, struggle with the distance separating their daily lives. Romance unfolds, touching unsuspecting hearts and setting them aglow. Chester's nemesis and force behind local criminal actions past and present begrudges the do-gooders and newly reconnected families. Recent probing's signal trouble could be afoot for the former school yard bully and criminal icon. Christmas calls out seeking to draw the

Ramsays and McClakens back together in a *Seaside Christmas* celebration. A young mother vanishes. Suspicion falls on the criminal icon's doorstep. He deflects it. Will the young mother be found, reunited with her family? Will past unpunished crimes finally see justice embrace their victims? Will a joyous Christmas unfold? Join our newlyweds in Chapter One. The action will unfold with each page turned in your copy of *Seaside Christmas*.

CHAPTER 1

Richard walked with Lyndsey hand in hand. Wedding guests eluded his gaze. Infatuated his eyes locked on the one who truly possessed his heart. An aura of love glowed freely off that owner's face and heart. Lyndsey gently treasured the hand in hers. Her peaceful aura rewarded her husband with a sigh of total satisfaction. If love blinded one to life's realities both would gladly suffer the consequences. The vows they had shared earlier cemented those committed to years earlier in countless sand boxes and childhood playgrounds. He'd never suffered the ickies of playground separations. Lyndsey had simply been a wann'a be tomboy, constantly at his side, until university had pulled them apart. Lyndsey attended the University of Toronto, Richard, Queens in Kingston. He blocked out memories of standing as John's best man at a wedding that never should have been. Replacing them with images of a South Shore beach. Memories where Lyndsey walked hand in hand with him barefoot in the sand. He sighed anew. The sigh echoed in Lyndsey as she paused and turned to Richard. In response to their cheering wedding guests the couple shared a passionate kiss that lingered. Time stood still feeding the rising wants in each of them. Their wants painted an image within and aroused wants anew within their bodies and hearts. Both sighed ending the passionate kiss, recalling how earlier inside while slipping out of their wedding attire a temptation had appeared on the opposite sides of the bed they'd stood beside. Richard had stood naked if one ignored the boxers he wore. Temptation won the day. Lyndsey hopped onto the bed. She scampered across its duvet, reached out and pulled her man to her body. Both sighed. A wedded first quickly unfolded on the bed. Short in duration their actions succeeded in satisfying their passions of the moment. They lay at each other's side savoring the pleasures they'd just shared. A kiss ensued. Then Lyndsey left Richard returning to the task of selecting her honeymoon outfit. Pink or purple she pondered. She turned to Richard and almost asked, *'which one should I wear?'* However, a third option won out and Lyndsey opted for a combo. She dressed herself in a compromise, a pink and purple dress. Richard eyed her throughout the procedure. Then responded to her chidings and dressed in a casual outfit topped with a suede sports jacket. On seeing the newlyweds return the band stopped playing. Richard and Lyndsey expressed their, thanks to their guests. Gilbert's catering received special notations. In departing both shared a smile that concealed recollections of the moments they'd shared earlier upstairs. In parting they waved adieus to the guests and walked to their vehicle. Wedding guests shouted out loud supportive farewells and applauded them with each step taken.

·······

Across town in Chester, Barnie raced his Buick through the Lobster Pot's parking lot. Frustrated he accelerated out onto the road cutting off a slow-moving pickup truck. An angry driver lay on the horn sharing rage with the idiot and nemesis they'd encountered in the Buick. Its driver an icon most locals avoided. Barnie acknowledged his new acquaintance by raising his left hand out the driver's window and flipping the slow driver a one fingered salute. He muttered a curse out the window, "Git a bus pass ya old fart! Make the roadways safer for real drivers." A glance in the rear-view mirror revealed the driver to be a silver haired woman. Barnie flipped another aggressive salute at the target of his aggression. A stop sign popped into view. Barnie hit the accelerator hard. An SUVs tires squealed in response to its driver slamming on the brakes. The cut off SUV skidded wildly-painting the road black with its tires' rubber. It narrowly avoided smashing into Barnie's Buick. The driver became the recipient of a Barnie salute. The Town of Chester faded in Barnie's rear-view mirror. The Lobster Pot Pub & Eatery's owner and self-appointed community icon grinned and basked in self-importance. He grabbed a can of beer off the passenger seat. A twist of the can's pull tab exposed its contents to Barnie. Guzzling the beer partially quenched his thirst and rising anger. Barnie let up on the accelerator a second or two then drove it to the floorboards.

Sales at the Lobster Pot Pub & Eatery were failing to meet Barnie's holiday weekend expectations. He cursed silently casting all blame on East River's McClakens and Ramsays. Eugette, the Pot's best waitress, had refused to work her Saturday shift. A car passed him headed back towards Chester. He recognized it as Eugette's vehicle. Barnie spotted his waitress in its passenger seat. His anger soared. He spotted the Lady-in-red's ex in the driver's seat. Barnie flung his empty beer can out the driver's window. He reached to the passenger seat and seized a fresh can of beer. An ugly snort drew a gob of mucus into his mouth. He turned and spit the gob out the driver's window. It swirled then, with poetic justice, flew in the open rear window and joined like kin infesting the back seat's headrest. East River Provincial Park flashed past to Barnie's right. The incompetence of Barnie's business associates fired up his oft diagnosed and ignored high blood pressure. Sweat dripped off his hands onto the Buick's steering wheel. Another snort and a second gob of mucus followed its predecessor.

Music sang out to his ears from the wedding reception at the McClakens. It drew a sarcastic snarl on Barnie's face. A quick gulp drained the beer can in his hand of its treasures and delivered all en route to a swollen bladder. Five then ten minutes flew past unimpeded. Barnie tossed another empty beer can out the driver's window. Local landmarks alerted Barnie to his where abouts. He slowed down a touch in anticipation of his turn off. Stones flew erratically in response to Barnie's high-speed turn onto his driveway. The Buick skidded to a stop beside a weather beaten mini-home. Barnie killed its engine. Anger still raged within its driver. A third can of beer called out to him. Its tab popped quicker than the second.

"You're dead bitch. Nobody fucks with Barnie. Just like your Daddy and your husband you're dead!" An extended chug-a-lug emptied the can's contents into Barnie's affluent belly. Faaauuut...plaaat! A loud extended fart echoed inside the Buick. Its juicy entrails soiled Barnie's pants and the driver's seat. Gasping for breath Barnie crushed the beer can held in his fist then tossed it out the driver's window. The driver's door flew open with a push from his shoulder and arm. On escaping the foul stench of the Buick, Barnie inhaled a series of desperate deep breaths. He closed the door with an angry slam. Barnie staggered away from the Buick towards his mini-home.

Inside he headed straight for the kitchen counter. There he poured himself a serving of rum from the open bottle sitting on the counter. The cigar ashes in the glass did not deter him from drinking its contents rum. Anger within Barnie flared up anew. He pulled his cell phone out of his shirt pocket. An attempt to access its list of contacts failed. In anger Barnie flung his cell phone across the room. It bounced off the wall and fell to the floor. "F...you!" Barnie screamed at his fallen phone. He avoided stumbling to the floor and staggered across to the living-room sofa. There he grabbed the landline and dialed a number from memory. It rang out announcing a connection. "Stupid bitch. She'd best learn to be keeping her nose out'ta the business of others. Lessen she be a want 'in to know the real truth. Ring, ring, ring, ri... the phone at the other end called out. Barnie almost slammed the receiver back into its cradle.

"Yo...Ned here. Who's calling?"

"It's Barnie. We've got problems me son.

"An S.O.B. I truly be! But never, never ag'in try ta destroy me proud Celtic blood lines by hinting we be kinfolks!"

"Right! Besides yer Mama was too ugly ta be a tempting me fore-fathers ta bed her! Har...har, me son."

The line fell silent. Barnie broke the silence. He asked, "Ya mentioned talking with Mike last week. Mike, our former mate and Chester's reborn bible thumper."

"I did."

"Did our doings out on the other Floating Island come up?"

"It might have."

"Might have? Either it did or it didn't you frigging idiot!"

"It did. But it wasn't me that brought it up! Mikie did."

"And?"

"I tolt him ta zipper his pie hole and not go blabbering about or confessing his past doings. I did!"

"Shit!"

"No. Mikie said he don't do that confessing ting to other folk! Why he claims to be connected. He talks straights up one on one ta that Jesus guy."

"Shit!"

"No. I actually have seen him doing it. Why he even promised to put in a good word or two for me. Say's he can be a saving me eternal soul."

"Damn! Was that Lamont bitch anywheres near you and Mikie?"

"No way. Mikie and I met up at my place. Now there was a time or two when Mikie, Martin, Slick and I met up out back of the Pot away from the parking lot! There wasn't nobody near that heard us a talking."

"Damn! Yer a certified batch of idjits! She goes out there to call her brats on her cell phone."

"That were a ways back. Early spring as I recall the timing."

The line fell silent again. A minute then two passed then Barnie swore, "There's no way to be sure she didn't overhear you idjits! I've been told she's been asking questions. I'll be a needing a favor, me son." Another prolonged silence ensued until Barnie broke it. "We can't be taking chances. Her Daddy and her husband went asking and we took care of them. They dug too deep and paid. They're dead."

Ned shouted back into Barnie's ear, "No way. I won't do it agin!"

"You will. If'fing the stupid bitch knows too much. She's dead! I won't have her prying into where her daddy stuck his nose. Listen up my friend. We need to put de fear of God in'ta both Eugee and Preacher Mikie. I will handle Eugee. Give her what she needs. A real man! Mikie I don't trust him and his preaching ways. He was there with us when you shot Martin and Rusty. Dead men don't talk."

"No. He's me Bud." Silently Ned rued his connection to Barnie. Deep within Ned heard his mother's chidings. She'd never approved of

Barnie. Her chidings struck a chord of truth in Ned's regrets of the moment.

"If'fing ya don't set things right. He could be a Dead Bud! I'm connected. I've heard the word circulating about town."

"No. I won't be a part of your doings, Barn…"

Barnie cut Ned off. He stated, "Git his woman. The reformed born ag'in bitch. She's not totally signed into Mikie and his Jesus Bud."

"No way. She's a true bless'in to our Mikie's new life! A kindred soul fer sure!"

The line went silent. Barnie pondered over the options open to selling Ned on his action plan. A sneer embraced his face. Confident, he broke the silence, "The fine lady has been asking about town fer passage out to de Islands."

"True. I overheard her asking Stu O'Grady and the Murphy lads."

"See? I told ya it was so." Barnie answered. Confident he added, "We'd be providing a needed service and passage. We'd be being right neighbourly to the Lady."

"And no harm befalls the lady?" Ned queried.

Barnie's sneer quickly turned into a confident grin. He suggested, "I'm getting a vibe my friend. The lady's bod is a delight. Would ye be hankering to be sampling our Mikie's play thingy?" The line fell dead on Ned's slamming the receiver into its cradle. Barnie snickered on recalling Mikie's wild introduction to the lady in red months past. His soul mate if one bought Ned's take on things would give Barnie a leg up on getting a handle on Mikie's actions aligning them with his needs. He also sensed he'd hit on a hunger buried deep in Ned's inner workings. He licked his lips while savoring the knowledge gained in his chat with Ned. Why, he pondered, would they include Martin and Slick in their babblings. Those two were definitely short a brick or two when it came to common sense. If needed he'd deal with them himself. Barnie sensed that a pathway to success was now afoot.

…….

Back at the wedding reception well-wishers gathered around the newlywed couple's vehicle. Their honeymoon departure was imminent as Richard opened the driver's door. He turned to Lyndsey and waited while she claimed the driver's seat. It took a minute at most for her to adjust the driver's seat and steering column to her needs. Once Lyndsey had secured her seat belt Richard stole a kiss then closed the driver's door. He walked around to the passenger side and entered the vehicle. Seated beside his bride Richard whispered, "Take me wherever your heart desires my love."

Lyndsey looked deep into Richard's eyes. She whispered back coyly, "Don't tempt me Ritchie. If I follow my heart's desire right this moment, there'd be a few shocked guests gathered about to see us off on our honeymoon adventure."

Richard grinned boldly then leaned over and the newlyweds kissed. The kiss lingered, its passion rising to match the roaring applause delivered by their wedding guests. Lyndsey fumbled with the ignition keys. On the third attempt the key slid into the ignition. A simple twist started the engine. Their lips parted. They smiled affectionately at each other. Melodies of songs they'd danced to earlier echoing in their ears and hearts. Lyndsey shifted into drive and touched the accelerator. The vehicle moved slowly away from the couple's gleeful supporters. Tin cans on strings sang out on hitting the paved road. Together the reunited childhood sweethearts set out on their true-life adventure. Lyndsey turned off at the Grave's Island Provincial Park entrance. She parked at the Gift and Antiques shop. Richard looked at Lyndsey with unasked questions on the tip of his tongue. They remained unasked. Lyndsey stepped out of the vehicle. She moved to the trunk, opened it and removed the broomstick with tins attached to long strings tied on. She gathered up the tins and tossed them along with the broomstick into the trunk. Satisfied, she flipped the trunk lid down. It snapped into place locked. She returned to the driver's seat. Richard remained silent. They headed out anew. In Chester Lyndsey broke the silence, "Souvenirs another ten clicks and our 'Just Married Tins' would have been history. We'll save them to share with Hope on her big day!"

Richard simply grinned and accepted the logic of Lyndsey's action. The ride to their booked Bed & Breakfast in Lunenburg passed in the blink of an eye. Once inside their room the newlyweds treated each other to pleasures they'd eagerly anticipated throughout the day.

CHAPTER 2

Music filled the air at the McClakens, homesteads in East River. Couples danced swaying to the music in the air. The newlyweds had headed off down the road eager to discover the magic each newlywed couple savors on their wedding night. The music faded on a song's slow romantic ending. Maria gazed into Jeffery's eyes. Flashbacks of childhood infatuations danced wildly in her mind. The glow in her dance partner's eyes stoked the embers of her memories.

The music stopped. Jeffery followed Maria off the dance floor. Together they walked away from the reception and its remaining guests. Their departure went unnoticed. Lyndsey and Richard ... bride and groom had slipped away earlier as had John and Eugette, and the wee ones, Megan and Taylor had headed home before the bride and groom's departure. Megan had displayed signs of burning out, while Taylor had become withdrawn, a true sign of his energy's departure. Hope stood her ground on the dance floor, while keeping a watchful eye on Gilbert. Unknown to Hope, Gilbert's eye followed her actions closely. He pondered the how and why of Hope's nudging John towards Eugette in shared conversations and dance floor actions. He reasoned Hope and Eugette's BFF status remained in full force. However, following the island caper he'd grown to accept a potential relationship at work between Hope and John. Hope's earlier words of excitement puzzled him, 'Look 'it them Uncle Gil. Eugette's enthralled with every word uttered by John. Her face is aglow in a joy I haven't seen since the tragedy. I can't imagine the hurt Maria and Eugette have endured. They lost their men to the sea. Two good men, Eugette's dad and her husband Rusty.

God! At times it's a gateway to paradise but at others the sea is a raging abomination. I love it but at times I totally fear it!' Biting his lower lip, he wondered if the thought of connecting with her sister's ex and brother-in-law had triggered hesitation in Hope? Every father's concerned dream raced through Gilbert's head. Would his Hope one day connect with a soul mate like he and Karyn, Lyndsey and Richard had? A smile released his lip from a prolonged nervous nibble encountered through his deep thoughts. His heart lightened on recalling the glow on Eugette's face as she and John had danced light footedly on the dance floor. Perhaps Hope was right and love's caress was once again embracing Eugette. A trip to the kitchen deprived Gilbert of catching Jeffery and Maria's departure. It would have added joy to his heart.

Maria walked hand in hand at Jeffery's side. Her eyes sparkled in anticipation of their destination. Walking towards the old Ramsay homestead the sounds of lively celebration faded with each step taken and pulled them closer to her heart's desire. Maria relished how the reunited couple had owned the dance floor. Waltzing in Jeffery's arms ignited many memories that had enchanted her childhood. Feeling the touch of Jeffery's body aroused her long-suppressed desires. Together they stepped onto the pathway to the homestead. Maria paused. She turned to Jeffery and gazed into the eyes of the soul mate out of her youth. Slowly their lips tentatively moved towards each other's. Maria paused. Tears streamed down her cheeks. Their salty essence accelerated her heartbeat. In her mind she rued life's bumps that had torn the once youthful toddlers and lovers to be apart. Tentatively their lips touched. Memories of childish stolen kisses she'd once savored cast all hesitation aside. The years of denial melted. A curio of hungry mosquitoes pulled them apart. Their pace quickened. They walked past the fish shed. On nearing the old Ramsay Homestead Maria stopped dead in her tracks. Jeffery followed her lead. The upgraded windows caught and held Maria's gaze. Though modern they retained the original look of the replaced windows. Anxious to recapture frozen moments out of their past, Maria walked up to the front door.

"She's open Maria. Give it a twist and we'll be safe inside out'ta the reach of these hungry skitters."

Maria followed Jeffery's tip. A twist of the doorknob and the door opened, swinging into the homestead. Maria stepped through the doorway. Jeffery followed her and, stepping inside the homestead, he closed the door. The home's fresh ambience drew an enchanted smile to Maria's face. The memories of encounters experienced in her youth vanished. Jeffery took her hands gently into his. Decades had slipped past since Maria had last stood inside the Ramsay homestead. Maria gazed in awe at the renovations that had unfolded since she'd last stepped through the homestead's doorway. She blinked and memories out of their past carried her decades back through time's never-ending window. *'Tears streamed down a young Maria's cheeks sitting at Jeffrey's bedside. She tenderly held his hand and longingly stared into his youthful fear filled eyes. Timidly she reached out and connected to her distant past.'*

A lively light hearted waltz sang out gently to Maria from the dance floor at Gilbert's. A second blink returned her to the moment and Jeffery's side. Her hips swayed gently to the music filling the air with a sweet energy. Maria's sway caught Jeffery's gaze. They came together and danced gently to the love song now echoing in both their hearts. They glided effortlessly across the kitchen and living-room floors, exchanging smiles with each other while swaying to the music. Jeffery paused. He stepped back away from Maria. His eyes locked on the hips gently swaying before him. A puzzled look exposed Jeffery's, thoughts. One moment he gazed longingly at his companion of the evening. The next moment a tiny red-haired Maria from the past added a youthful energy to the swaying hips in a white butterfly covered dress. Back and forth the images flipped. Each flip added joy to Jeffery's heart. A teen-aged Maria with a beau at her side quickly cast a shadow. Regret and remorse saddened Jeffery. In his youth he'd learned quickly to ignore the taunts of schoolmates that jested at his speech impediments and slow thought processing that had plagued him. The music stopped. Maria twisted about and beckoned Jeffery to her side.

Maria's mind carried her back to decades past. Back to a time when she had held Jeffery's tiny hands in hers and whispered a youthful lover's pledge. A pledge that time had erased following Jeffery's failed recovery from the effects of his island experience. Jeffery broke the enchanted lock that held their eyes in a loving gaze. "Welcome home Maria, I sure did miss you." Both savoured how Jeffery had overcome the setbacks that had torn them apart in their youth.

Maria countered, "Poppa, poppa demande...d"

Jeffery hushed Maria, "No not now Maria. He did what he thought best for you, his daughter. Trust me I grew to respect his fatherly fears and love that demanded he act on your behalf. Your momma and poppa were good people. Yes, they were stern but loving. Fear of the unknown drove them to forbid you from visiting our home. To most here abouts it was a place best avoided. My family became outcasts because of me, because of that long past adventure out on the Floating Islands. Tears touched Maria's cheeks. They flowed downward unabated until Jeffery's lips touched each of her cheeks in turn. Maria's eyes met Jeffery's. A smile touched both their lips. Jeffery stared lovingly into Maria's eyes, their lips touched, Maria's hesitation vanished. Their kisses again fed desires out of their youthful past. Maria frowned as Jeffery pulled away. She had wanted more. A sigh slipped past her parted lips. The homestead's interior caught her eye. Gone where its boxy squared off features that had boasted of its past. In awe of her surroundings, Maria stared at the open concept kitchen.

Jeffery proudly led Maria on a guided tour of the homestead. The kitchen he confessed to having objected to during its early planning stages. However regular weekend visits by Chef Gilbert had softened his objections then quickly erased them. Next, he stepped into his bedroom across from the kitchen. Maria hesitated briefly. Memories of past visits set her nerves on edge. A loving nudge from Jeffery relaxed Maria and they entered the bedroom. Maria sat down on the bed. Jeffery caught her nervous glances about the room. He sat at her side and applied a reassuring hug and whispered, "My wee one and I have parted ways.

Thanks to Lyndsey, Grace Ramsay my Good Neighbour Fairy now happily I'm told resides on the Floating Islands."

Maria shivered at the mention of Jeffery's wee one. He embraced her tighter and kissed her cheek. Maria relaxed. Their eyes connected. Jeffery's smile relaxed her more. He explained, "Grace we've learned is…was my great-great and somewhat greater great grandmother, no auntie that never lived long enough to take on her once assumed to be family roles. She foolishly drowned out there in the bay…East River Bay in pursuit of the Floating Islands."

Maria shivered anew then relaxed on sensing Jeffery's supportive aura.

"Trust me Maria that return to the islands showered my family with blessings. Something touched me. It was totally eerie. I could sense its presence and I swear it passed through me. The speech impediments and disruptive flow of thoughts I suffered following my first island visit simply vanished."

Silence befell the couple. Maria reached out and passionately embraced Jeffery. Their lips touched. Each in turn deepened the passion of their kiss. Maria released Jeffery. They eyed each other wantonly. Jeffery broke their connection as he stood up. Maria gazed up into his eyes then followed his lead and stood up. Together they walked out of the bedroom. Jeffery led their tour onward through Pappy's bedroom and the bathroom. Next, they walked side by side into the sunroom. A starlit night sky greeted them. Jeffery led Maria over to the loveseat and she sat down at his side. The twinkling night sky held their gazing eyes in check. Maria murmured, "Oh my lands Jeffie, it's absolutely beautiful."

Jeffery did not object to the childhood nickname Maria had shared with him many years past. Floating off Maria's lips it carried a loving touch. Except for their gentle breathing silence surrounded them. Off in the distance vehicles carried wedding guests away from the day of gala celebration. The sounds of their parting did not touch our reunited couple's ears.

"Oh Poppa," Maria whispered. She paused then continued, "You truly meant well. My life has been a good one. No regrets, my husband loved me and our Eugette. Poppa you absolutely adored Eugette and her twins Megan and Taylor, our grandbabies. And yes, regrettably, the sea stole you and our son-in-law Rusty from us too soon."

Jeffrey tried to silence Maria. He hugged her and said, "No need to sadden your soul, Maria. A rough and raging sea that day denied many of the friendship of two good men."

"No Jeff…y I need to say it. Life never denied me love. However, it did until this day deny me the love of the one, I truly treasured in my heart."

Jeffrey remained silent.

"The time that held us apart slipped past in a heartbeat. My Scottish and Acadian heritages combined and created a charming, hot blooded, red haired young lass, who stretched Momma and Poppa's parenting skills to their limits." Both Jeffrey and Maria chuckled lightly. She continued, "Many an East River and Chester heartthrob in pants arose in talks I overheard between Momma and Poppa. Hey! I was embracing my womanhood and simply needed to escape Poppa's restrictive controls." She giggled and stated, "I needed to experience life and expand my self-confidence."

Jeffery chuckled aloud. Maria poked him in the ribs. He jumped. Maria laughed and continued, "During March break back in junior high school many of us ended up battling a relentless spring flu. Most kids recovered in a mere four to six weeks." A giggle erupted from inside Maria. She recovered frowned momentarily then continued. "My battle lingered onward. Momma spotted the early signs of my condition. Once Doctor Rose confirmed my condition, Momma aligned with Poppa and his stricter set of controls."

Jeffery hugged Maria and kissed her cheek. Silence befell the reconnected childhood sweethearts. Maria snuggled closer to Jeffery on hearing him whisper, "No need to justify the past and its paths that pulled us apart Mari…"

Maria pulled free of Jeffery's embrace. She treated him to a warm joyful smile that displayed her dimples and concealed a look of determination. Determination that would treat Jeffery to her recollections of life that had pulled them apart, "I discovered my true friends and in the end dealt with the shame others tossed my way. My little Eugette truly outshone and showered me in life's blessings. December 21st will always wrap my heart in life's joys. Time has enriched those joys with the addition of my wee ones, my grandbabies, Eugette's Megan and Taylor."

Jeffery smiled and boasted, "Yes, Megan and Taylor definitely are a pair of energized blessings." He stood and walked towards the kitchen. Maria watched him walk away. Could and should she risk it all? Eugette's recent moods swings, frustrations and talk of their loved ones. Maria shivered on recalling the loss at sea of her husband Martin and Eugette's Russell...Rusty. The deaths of their loved ones had drawn mother and daughter closer. Eugette recently had claimed to have overheard the truth. She claimed Martin and Rusty's deaths had not been accidental. Jeffery quickly returned; he caught her shifting into a sitting stance on the loveseat on stepping back into the sunroom. A satisfied aura befell her person. She reached out and accepted the glass of bubbly frosty refreshment Jeffery offered. Raising her glass to her lips she sampled its contents with a sip. The tropical rum cooler added a glow to a rising smile offered to Jeffery. He sat down by her side. Together they gazed out into an enchanted star filled autumn night sky. No words were spoken. Each lost themselves in a sea of satisfying thoughts and possibilities.

CHAPTER 3

Back at the celebrations, Lenny nudged Pappy. He winked and glanced over at the Wright sisters. "Iff'in, we plays our cards right, me son, before the night be upon us we could be sampling the pleasures we savored in our youth." Pappy glanced questioningly back at Lenny. Lenny chuckled then boasted, "Don't be telling me your Family Tree no longer stands erect and ready to extend yer family's branches to places ye never imagined?" He smirked and added, "Take a good peek at them damsels. They sure have maintained their chassis in fine working condition. Lordie they both sure shook up and ignited the old dance floor at this here celebration."

Before Pappy could answer the band struck up another slow waltz. The Wright sisters walked coyly towards Lenny and Pappy with bold confident smiles on their faces. They smiled. Lenny greeted them, "You two sure are a delightful looking pair of sweet young things."

Both ladies giggled, fluffed their locks and added a sharper swing to the sway of their hips. Lenny eyed both ladies signalling his rising interest. Quickly they matched up and stepped smoothly over the dance floor. Other couples joined them in dance. The sun had set. Darkness claimed the night sky. Overhead lights switched on casting spotlights on the many dancing couples. Roger and Noreen slipped away from the dance floor as a Rap tune echoed over the dancers. They exchanged parting hugs with Gilbert, who invited both to return at morning's first light to his planned Kitchen Party Buffet. Both declined and reminded Gilbert they were booked on a morning flight home. Others remained oblivious to the music's genre, their bodies seeking to dance off the effects of one or two drinks too many. Both Lenny and Pappy never wandered far from the dance floor. The band's lead singer called out, "Last go at it my Lassies and Laddies, and those that'll admit they've aged once or twice over de years! Please join in and help us shut down this amazing day of celebration." All the remaining couples stepped out onto the dance floor. Gilbert joined them on being tugged out onto the dance floor by Hope. Everyone closed down the celebration in the arms of their companion. Gilbert in Hope's arms waltzed about to each other's delight, a father and daughter each lost in thoughts of their big dance yet to be.

They followed the last waltz to its last fading melody. Each parting couple declined Gilbert's invitation to return at sunrise. All expressed kudos for the amazing catering Gilbert had prepared for the reception. He accepted all compliments and the Kitchen Party plans faded out of sight.

Lenny worked his way towards his companions with an order of drinks from the bar in hand. He walked into a round of robust laughter. Aimee explained, "I just updated our young lad here on the happenings I suspect are unfolding down in the old Ramsay Homestead. I suggested his presence might not be appreciated! And then I suggested a welcome awaits him over at the Wright's in town."

Lenny joined in the laughter. Pappy stared silently into the eyes of his companions. A moment then two slipped by in silence. A tear's salty essence touched his lips. It triggered a flow of memories out of the past. The silence was broken when Pappy softly spoke, "It broke Helen's heart and mine, when that old fool Maria's father tore apart Maria and our Jeffery. Tis so seldom one discovers bonds with their true soul mate so early in life. Set our Jeff back beyond all the positive healing we had started to see in him. I'd gladly sleep aboard Rose Bud and git eaten alive by dem skitters iff'in it meant our two youthful soul mates out'ta the past reconnects and discovers the love they've been denied tills now."

....

The music had faded away on the band's closing out the last dance a slow waltz. Goodbyes and thanks for a great day of celebration had been exchanged. The dance floor and tented scene of celebration stood vacant. The band and all attendees had departed. Stacked crates held the rental dishes, glasses, mugs and tea cups from the wedding celebration. They awaited Steve and his cleanup crew come Sunday's predawn morning. Hope nudged then tugged Gilbert's hand convincing him to head inside. She succeeded. Back in the big house Gilbert sat at the kitchen table. Across from him Hope sat and refreshed Gilbert's memories of the day and its amazing festivities. Gilbert did not attempt to interrupt Hope. Instead, he relived Hope's recollections and at times exaggerated memories of the day. Hope paused for a second or two then her boasting continued, "A sister-in-law and auntie I'll surely be. Gads I'll be missing my Lyndsey and Richie too!"

Gilbert smiled and nodded his agreement back to Hope. He broke his silence, "Yes Hope, they will be missed." He paused then whispered, "But Richard hinted a Maritime Christmas could be..."

"What!" Hope shouted back at him. "Don't be a pulling me leg Dad. Lordie, just having rediscovered a sister I never knew existed and struggling to accept she's headed out to embrace life anew an excited bride with her childhood sweetheart in hand. Gads it will be fantastic to have them home for Christmas."

Gilbert smiled and replied, "No promises. But he did mention in passing concerns over how difficult it will be to celebrate the festive season at the Ramsay homestead without their parents and grandparents, especially with the knowledge that we'd be here celebrating a Seaside Christmas without them at our side."

Hope leaped up and bolted to the kitchen counter. There she grabbed her cell phone and attempted to start a text. Gilbert followed her lead. At the counter he embraced Hope and deftly took control and possession of the cell phone. Hope protested, "But I..."

Gilbert released her but retained possession of the phone. An unfamiliar sly smile accompanied his words, "They're honeymooners with other things on their mind."

"But!"

"But this, and trust me. One day your turn will come to be. Trust me like Lyndsey and Rich today you'll be preoccupied with them other tings."

Both Gilbert and Hope burst into uncontrolled laughter and embraced. On recovering they separated. Hope moved towards the counter piled high with the pots, pans, dishes, and utensils from Gilbert's catering of the celebration. She twisted about and returned to Gilbert's side on hearing him state, "Leave dems be. They'll wait till morning greets us anew."

A suppressed giggle escaped Hope's lips. Gilbert missed it. All certainty of Gilbert's non-sobriety freely expressed itself in his spoken words. An English Professor his spoken words and grammar seldom if ever included local linguistic twist and turns. Together they walked through the kitchen to the staircase. Walking up the staircase Hope added, "We'd best not be waiting too long. I suspect another celebration or two could be in the works."

"Yes. I saw a connection or two taking shape through the evening. John and Eugette were no strangers to the dance floor." Hope smiled adroitly while embracing silence. Gilbert continued, "Pappy put most of us to shame once he accepted Janella Wright's nudge-tug and joined the action. I suspect he might have danced himself sober before the band shut the party goers down with that Bryan Adams heart's delight waltz."

Hope stepped off the last step and joined Gilbert. She tapped his shoulder. With a glow beaming off her face she boasted, "True. Pappy demoed moves I haven't seen since Grammie pulled his heartstrings and owned him on the dance floor. So much has changed in such a short time. Pappy, John, Uncle Jeffery sure wish I'd been touched by some of that island's mag..."

"No! Don't ever wish that hellhole's life forces upon yer soul girl!" Gilbert shouted.

Hope stared bewildered at Gilbert. "But...bu..."

"No, don't go there, Hope!"

"Pappy's energy, John's grasp of life's positivity...Jeffery, his speech. All three totally changed since our island adventu..."

Gilbert faced Hope and placed his hands on her shoulders. "Hope my dearest daughter, niece...our Hope. I cannot go there. I cannot explain the outcomes that we are seeing in our loved ones. Please drop it and accept the blessings that have befallen our loved ones for what they are! Blessings! Pure and simple Blessings! Trust me blessings never have and never will be connected to that island and its evil!"

Hope's eyes closed. Images captured throughout the wedding flashed up randomly in her heart. Each embraced the others adding joy to her soul. Hope smiled on recalling the meals she'd helped Gilbert prepare. She boasted, "Your creative culinary delights captured and rewarded everyone in attendance Dad."

On hearing the word 'Dad' Gilbert's heart skipped a beat. A step took him to Hope. They smiled then Hope vanished in a trademark Gilbert hug. A second then two slipped by before Gilbert relaxed his hold on Hope. She stepped back from him and said, "Let it be Dad. I'll arise early and clean up, whilst you recharge yourself with an extended night of rest."

Gilbert simply nodded his approval. It had been a long day filled with embracing tasks lovingly taken on sunup through and beyond sunset. Together they walked along the hallway hugs and cheek kisses were exchanged. Hope stepped into her bedroom. A quick strip readied her for bed. Under the covers Hope felt totally alone without Lyndsey to chat up the day's activities with. Instead, she focused on another concern. A sigh enriched the thoughts bubbling energetically in her head. The glow bouncing off Eugette and John's faces added one to hers. Leading up to the wedding she'd sensed unease in her best friend's aura. However, Eugette's glow on the dance floor cast the fleeting concerns she felt aside. Sleep raced to her rescue and eased her free of the frustrations. The Sandman carried her off into a night filled with dreams fed by memories long buried in her past. Yes, thoughts of Norman accompanied Hope throughout a relaxed and recharging night. He had been that long ago older man, a boy really, in grade six that Hope had idolized. She was in grade two at the time. Mom's best friend Anya often brought her son Norman when visiting. A jovial storybook reader, the lad unknowingly had stolen wee Hope's heart with each storybook he'd entertained her with. Years later, Norman became Hope's Richard in dreamland. Down the hall in the master bedroom, Gilbert slipped into his blue and white Maple Leaf's pyjamas and crawled under the blankets. Sleep quickly stripped him of all stress. Relief embraced him. The day of celebration had been a total success. Drifting through the early stages of sleep the moniker 'Uncle' faded away. It was replaced by Hope's voice calling out, 'Dad, Dad, and Daddy!' No effort was required by the Sandman. Gilbert willingly slipped off into dreamland.

CHAPTER 4

At the Lamont residence Megan and Taylor reluctantly followed Mom's lead and headed off to bed. Eugette waved to John in response to Megan's plea. Once he arrived at the bedroom door both children knelt down to recite their bedtime prayers. Warmed by the childhood memories being played out, John placed his hand on Eugette's hip. She responded and snuggled up closer to him. Impish grins broke out on the praying children. "Lord please keeps our Mommie safe and thanks for giving us Mister Ramsay...John. Mommie likes him and he'll help keep her safe Amen."

Both adults sighed.

Megan and Taylor jumped up. They shouted in unison, "And Lord Mommie thinks he's cute!" Both bounced over the beds then down on the floor and over to Mommie and John. They gleefully hugged their thighs then released them ran over and jumped into bed. Together they whispered loudly, "Loves you Mommie." They pulled the covers up over their heads. The adults turned to leave. Both stopped dead in their tracks.

Megan boasted, "And Lord I think he's a cutie too."

Taylor grunted and corrected his sister, "Meg ... Guys and men aren't cute. They're Macho and cool!" Both John and Eugette snickered then chuckled as they walked down the hallway. Goodnights were exchanged between all.

They missed hearing Megan whisper, "Did ya see how Mommie lit up the dance floor in Johnny's arms?"

Taylor frowned but did not reply. In his heart he hungered to have his deepest prayers answered. He'd watched Mom and John on the dance floor throughout the wedding day. John had painted laughter and smiles on Mommy's face. He missed having a man figure in his family. Daddy had always lit up Mommy's face. Just like John had done earlier on the dancefloor. With those images in mind, Taylor gently tumbled off into dreamland with joy in his heart.

In the kitchen John accepted Eugette's offer of a Chai Tea with a Rye whisky chaser. Conversation shared recollections of the good times both had shared and enjoyed at the wedding. Time took flight. John glanced at his watch and smirked. Eugette caught the smirk. She asked, "Is there a problem?"

"No. Absolutely no. I've had a great time. But I should call a cab and head over to Gilbert's. It's after two in the morning!"

Eugette chuckled, "Catch a cab in Chester at 2:34 in the morning?" She shook her head sideways in the negative alluding that he had a better chance of catching flight out of Chester at 2:34 in the morning. "Stay the night." Eugette added. "I don't bite."

"But I."

"But Hope read you the riot act. Spilt the beans about us being BFFs since birth and connected at the hip?" John gulped. Eugette added, "She also suggested you not move in on me too soon and dropped a detail or two about my loss?" John nodded the affirmative. Eugette smiled boldly. "God, I love Hope a ton and more. In mom's eye and mine, she's simply my sister." She smirked, "Sad to say she's right. I'm not ready. I still hurt a ton. But we can compromise. You behave yourself and the sofa in the living-room is yours for the night. Then after breakfast I'll drive you over to Gilbert's. Is it a deal?"

"It's a deal." John answered.

Eugette strutted out of the kitchen. She called back, "Give me a minute or two and I'll get a sheet and some blankets on the couch for you."

John remained seated at the kitchen table. He sat in awe of the life changes he'd encountered since reconnecting with family out of his family's distant past. A special recollection tensioned his body and heart. Then just as quickly he sighed falling into a relaxed state of awe. Eugette interrupted John's thoughts as she called out to him, "In here John. It's all set up for you." John followed the voice. In the living-room he joined Eugette at the pulled-out sofa bed. They eyed each other. She rose up on her tip toes and stole a quick kiss. Goodnights were exchanged by both then they turned in. The early hour and high-octane day they'd shared quickly sent both off into deep sleep. John never uttered a single long rumored and famous snort throughout his early morning sleep.

The early morning playful antics of Megan and Taylor ended the relaxed dreamland adventures of Eugette and John. Over breakfast John shared the details of his scheduled flight back to Toronto and home to Newmarket.

....

A brilliant rising sun embraced East River Sunday morning. Post celebration cleanup was underway. Hope awoke on hearing Gilbert's voice belting out oft heard quotes from his beloved and famed Shakespearian masterpieces. Outside Steve's crew had arrived and departed. They'd almost beat the rising sun in arriving. The tents and rental equipment were quickly disassembled and packed onto their trucks. Earlier Gilbert had just managed to catch them before they departed, he settled up the billing and gratuities. He recalled with gusto for Steve and his crew memories of the gala event's success. Thanks were given for the tips received then Steve and his team departed. Gilbert gazed longingly out over the yard. All signs of the gala reception were gone. He smiled savoring the event's success then turned and walked back inside. There he frowned on spotting Hope up and gazing out the living-room window at a beautiful Scotian sunrise. A rare occurrence in their house as Hope was not an early riser of repute. Together they raced about cleaning the pots, pans, dishes, utensils from Gilbert's catering that had sated everyone's appetites at yesterday's wedding. With everything cleared Gilbert and Hope caught one last glance out the kitchen window eying the vacated site of the wedding celebration. In Hope's mind the altar scene echoed freely. In every fifth or sixth rerun the celebrants were replaced by her and a childhood heartthrob, Norman, lost in the throes of life's twists and turns. She truly longed to experience the love seen bubbling freely in Lyndsey and her husband, a companion that had stumbled under Lyndsey's domain long before the lad had come to discover his fate. A fate that had been predetermined by the woman he'd married yesterday. A destiny set in motion in a shared sandbox of their youth. A tingling in her hand reenergized the sensation of another's hand clasped in hers, Norman's, Hope's Normie and lost soul mate out'ta her past. A shiver ran down her spine. In truth Hope had long ago slipped free from Norman Trinity's youthful recollections. She'd been but a diversion on visits to Norman's home, where he'd been dragged off to the side and would read storybooks to his mom's best friend's daughter a toddler to hasten the passage of time during their visits. She'd quickly became infatuated with Norman.

In Hope's mind and heart her recollections centered on what ifs. In the blink of an eye, she returned to the reality of the moment. The glow on Gilbert's face heightened the joy dancing in her heart. Gilbert's thoughts centered on a longing to once again embrace and caress his wife Karyn whom he had lost to the perils of cancer. With reluctance he pulled himself away from the vacated scene of the previous day's celebration. Hope reluctantly followed his lead. Gilbert lost himself in the task of grading papers for his students. The tasks passed quietly adding confidence to Gilbert's opinion of his students and their talents-commitments.

Hope took the opportunity and lost herself in tending to Grammie's treasured rose beds. She busily snipped away filling a bucket that quickly approached its capacity with Hope's collection of brilliant orange-red rosehips destined to become another winter's source of rosehip tea. Time flew by unimpeded but also stood still. Hope easily avoided contact with the unexpected but the timely late season burst of new rose blossoms that had added a unique and special essence to the wedding scene just past. Hope lost herself in time's magic, recalling and lovingly reliving moments spent at Grammie's side tending to their treasured rose beds.

Gilbert freed Hope from time's grasp. He called out from the kitchen door, "It's a tad early for lunch but, soup and grilled apple-bacon cheese sandwiches are best served hot. Move it on in here girl. Your hunger pangs will thank you!"

Hope snipped one last rosehip and dropped it into the bucket. She whispered, "Gotta go Grammie. Yer Gillie's grilled apple-bacon cheese sandwiches are to die for!" A glance at her watch confirmed it to be a tad early for lunch. Their early morning rising had thrown their body clocks askew, it was 10:45 am. She picked up the bucket of rosehips off the ground then walked back towards Gilbert and the kitchen's aromas. A tiny voice called out softly in her heart, *'Catch you later sweetheart.'*

....

Finally, the hour arrived. The drive over to Gilbert's passed in a subdued silence. Except for Megan and Taylor in the back seat. They bantered back and forth over who would get to play with Bailey first. On their arrival Gilbert greeted them at the kitchen door. Megan and Taylor raced inside. On finding their Auntie Hope they pleaded, "You gotta make him, John stay. Our Mommie needs him. We prayed and God answered. You just gotta make him stay."

Hope crouched down joining them at their eye level. "I'd love to sweethearts. But Mr. Rams…"

"John!" Both corrected Auntie Hope.

"Ok. John has to fly home."

"But, bu…!"

"Sorry sweethearts he has to fly home. However, I know that he'll be back. Both John and your mom connected at the wedding yesterday."

"Yup and they kissed a lot!" Taylor declared.

Hope smiled warmly and hugged Taylor. Megan raced into the living-room shouting, "Bailey, Bailey come play with me!" Taylor squiggled free of Hope's hug and ran off in search of Bailey. A loud "meow, meow…meow," Sang out for rescue from the living-room. John returned from a quick upstairs run to gather up his luggage. He stopped dead in his tracks at the kitchen door. Bailey had cut him off racing to escape his two enthusiastic playmates.

Gilbert grabbed John's largest travel bag. He grinned and offered up, "It's been great having you here for the wedding. What time is your flight out?"

"Two-thirty. I got lucky and upgraded to a direct flight. No stopover in Montreal."

Gilbert glanced at his watch it read 11:45 am. He smiled and said, "Then if you're ready? I'd be happy to get you to the airport."

John and Eugette gazed tentatively at each other. Taylor chased Bailey wildly through the kitchen into the dining-room. Megan followed on his tail. They shouted out, "Bye John. See you soon. Ya best kiss Mommie goodbye!"

Eugette walked over and hugged John. Their kiss lingered. With hesitation she pulled away looked over to Gilbert and said, "If you're good heading to the airport, maybe I should stay and take charge of my crew?"

Gilbert replied, "I'm good. See you out at the truck John." He then headed out to the truck with John's luggage in hand. Hope joined Bailey and his friends in the living-room. A series of short pecks ended in another lingering kiss followed by a silent hug then John joined Gilbert outside. Eugette watched him leave. She pondered, I could have, I should have, but I'm just not quite ready to move on.

Taylor walked up to her and grabbed her hand. He nudged her towards the living-room protesting, "Meg won't let me play with Bailey."

The duties of motherhood swept away any thoughts of John. She joined everyone down on the floor entertaining Bailey. Outside the truck drove out of the yard. Everyone's focus centered on their current moment in the universe. A hungry heart savors the taste of love denied. The voices in the living-room faded. A troubled look cast away the excited glow that possessed Eugette's face on awakening that morning. Silently she rued, did my second chance at romance just walk out of my life? Who could possibly love a wreck like me and the baggage attached? Can I open up and reveal the wretch buried deep within my body and soul. Ugly is ugly. Men want women who can arouse them sexually and emotionally. I lose on both counts. A stream of tears free fell down her cheeks. A shadow befell Eugette. She glanced up into its essence and caught Hope crouching down to embrace her. She smirked nervously.

"What's up girlfriend?" Hope asked. They embraced. With Hope's urging both stood up. Hope suggested, "Bailey totally owns Meg and Tay. Let's step outside and chat." With reluctance Eugette followed Hope's nudging through the kitchen then out onto the side doorstep.

"Spill it girl! What's the problem? I'm not a fool and I'm sensing something is awry!" Eugette's fingers fidgeted. They revealed her nervous state. However, she refused to speak and refused to answer Hope's prying questions. She glanced at Hope. Their eyes connected and locked. Nervously she bit her lower lip. The words she'd overhear outside the Pot etched heartache deeply into her heart. So deep she had actually sought out and met up with Preacher Mikie. Eugette's body broke out in a bout of terrifying shivers. Hope reached out and secured Eugette in a hug. Tears tumbled off Eugette's cheeks onto Hope's exposed shoulders. She tensed. What could the problem be? Hope pondered a string of options. Could she be troubled by memories rekindled at the wedding? The loss of Rusty and her dad to the perils of the sea had broken Eugette's heart. However, that had happened two years ago. Did she feel rejected seeing her mom, Maria connecting romantically with Uncle Jeffery? A smile caressed Hope's face. She loved the new Uncle Jeffery that beamed so positively on being touched by Maria's love. What she silently asked herself could be terrifying Eugette? The shivers abated. They pulled slightly apart and gazed deep into each other's eyes. Neither spoke. Hope in desperation pulled Eugette into a tight embrace. Their cheeks touched connecting them. With a sigh both ended their moment of bonded connection.

Eugette sighed anew. Thanks, Hope I needed to connect. I needed to overcome doubts and fears that have arisen." Their hug deepened then they released each other.

Hope pleaded, "I only want you back, back to where we've been throughout life best friends, sisters forever!"

Eugette smiled and nodded a silent *'me too.'* The smile vanished. After a moment she spoke, "I've been shut out. Everybody that mattered, Mom, you, the community... everyone bought into the line peddled."

Guilt touched Hope's soul. She sensed the direction of Eugette's fears and doubts.

"It's been almost two years. Yes, life goes on. But seeing Mom basking in the love of a man who is not my dad. Damn it all, Hope it hurts. Not having Rusty at my side, in our bed, it hurts! Then to hear the words spoken that our men were not lost to the perils of the sea, but were murdered. It pisses me off. I was right all along. My instincts, my gut feelings I was bang on the numbers!" Eugette's eyes slammed shut. Her chin dropped onto her chest and a fresh set of shivers seized her body. Hope embraced her friend anew. Between deep caring sighs she rolled over the words Eugette had just spoken. Could they be true, she pondered. They'd always been connected. Hell, I even set Eugee up with Rusty way back when. Then I rewarded both of them by failing to connect or give credence to any of the dudes they'd tried to set me up with. Some friend I turned out to be? How can I fix it? How can I get my bud back?

"My babies saw me talking to him. Hell, they saw me slap him across his face along with their school bus full of their buds. My babies hate me!"

Hope answered, "Your babies Megan, Taylor they love their Mommy. We all love you! Hell, you even swept John off his feet at the wedding. And that is OK! Tell me what words did you hear? Why are you convinced Rusty and your Da..."

"Were murdered? Well, they were MURDERED! I stepped outside the Pot on a cell phone break, a call to my babies."

"And that's when you hear..."

"Heard Ned Stone, Martin and Slick were talking up a storm. It's not a rumour. I overheard them on more than one occasion. They were all involved. Ned expressed regrets, a lot of good that does my men. The others boasted how easy it went down."

"Who did you slap? Who did Meg and Taylor see you talking to?"
"Jesus!"
"What, Meg and Taylor saw you, their mom praying talking to Jesus? Every parent teaches their kids to pray, talk to Jesus, Eugette. There's nothing wrong with that."

Eugette frowned then shouted, "Not that Jesus, the new one. The Preacher Mikie...Michael Slivers!"

Both women fell silent each embraced themselves in a hug and pondered what to say next. Eugette took the lead. "I met up with Michael at the restaurant in Peggy's Cove."

"Really, you met up with Mikie Slivers? Was his new woman with him?" Hope questioned.

"Yes and no she wasn't with him. And trust me he's changed. He's not the repulsive sex fiend of repute from his past. He's changed. He told me to shut up in regards to talk about what happened to my Rusty and Dad. He told me what I heard was God's truth. Rusty and Dad were murdered!" He warned, no advised, me to pack up and git Mom and my babies away from here."

"Have you spoken to your mom since the meeting?"

"No, I'm afraid to. She believes like most, the story about them being lost to the perils of the sea. But I did try to talk to my Megan. She wouldn't listen. She slapped me said I made her look stupid in front of all her school chums! I tried talking to Meg. She just shut me out. God, it hurts!"

"Think back girl. We both had moments our wants locked us in battles with our moms. Admit it. Those moments passed in a flash. We were kids. They love you to the moon and back! The bottom line Eugette, what did you overhear out in the parking lot? What was said that's convinced you it wasn't a gaggle of local boys embellishing local rumors?"

"Ned Stone is the one. He clearly stated with regret that he pulled the trigger. He shot my Rusty and Dad. He's a murderer and walks free. Where's the jus..."

A truck door opened then slammed shut. Footsteps were heard walking towards them on the graveled driveway. A voice called out, "Hope, Eugette where's Gillie off to?"

Hope sternly whispered, "Not a word about our chat." She turned towards Uncle Jeffery with Maria at his side. A coy smile greeted the new arrivals. Hope looked to Eugette and chided, "Uncle Jeffery, is that lipstick on your neck?" Jeffery blushed and rubbed at his neck with determination. Eugette smiled at her mom and her companion. Hope answered Jeffery's question, "Oh, dad is driving John to the airport. Care for a coffee?"

Eugette walked over and hugged her mom. She cast a twinkling eye over to Jeffery. Then the four walked together back into the kitchen. Inside they were greeted by an unexpected silence. Hope started a fresh pot of coffee and Eugette headed off in search of her babies. She stopped dead in her tracks on spotting Megan and Taylor sitting side by side cuddling a relaxed and purring Bailey. She sighed then twisted about and returned to the kitchen. The captured moment stored safely away in her internal Mommy's photo album of precious life moments.

....

Off in Chester, Pappy awoke bright and alert late Sunday morning well past the morning's brilliant sunrise. Looking about the room's surroundings he surmised he hadn't bunked out at Lenny's. A quiet breathing alerted him to the presence of another. The arm wrapped around his chest slid down onto his stomach, then settled on his groin. A gaze downward towards his feet revealed an unfamiliar sight. He'd wakened free of the blankets piled up at the foot of the bed and he was stark naked. He spotted his family tree standing firm and erect. A totally unfamiliar sight since his Helen's passing. The image of a youthful Helen caught and held the focus of his mind. Guilt tugged at his heartstrings. Pappy relaxed. He embraced the images occupying his mind. A multitude of once shared passionate moments painted a gentle loving smile on his face. Guilt and sadness tugged at his heartstrings. The body beside him felt warm. It definitely was not his Helen. She'd passed on years past. Caught in a moment of indecision a voice spoke gentle words in Pappy's mind. His Helen spoke the words she'd often shared with him in life, *'Promise me Love you'll never stop loving should I be taken home first. Promise me you'll find another and love anew.'* Pappy shuddered. The words had carried him directly back to his Helen's side. They also eased him back into the grasp of dreamland. There he embraced the loving sweetness of the one he'd willingly shared life's magic with over the years.

CHAPTER 5

The drive to the airport passed quickly. Gilbert discovered that John that had not read Grace Ramsay's 1796 diary that had paved the road towards reuniting their families. He chatted up a storm in attempting to sell John on casting his eye upon the young lass's words. John nodded commitment to taking up Gilbert on his suggested reading. Flashbacks to their Island adventure restrained him from uttering a verbal commitment. A glance outside on hearing the clicking of the truck's turn signal confirmed the airport was close at hand. John declined Gilbert's offer to join him in the airport for a coffee. The truck slowed then stopped at the departures entrance. Gilbert unloaded John's luggage. John reached for the luggage. Gilbert embraced him in one of his trademark hugs. John surrendered himself to Gilbert's loving embrace. He broke their silence, "I'd best go Uncle Gilbert. Airport security can be a hassle at times." They separated. John took hold of his luggage.

Gilbert gazed in awe at John whose words, 'Uncle Gilbert,' echoed in his heart. He replied, "Have a safe flight home, John. And don't be a stranger. We are family after all." His eyes started to water up. They waved farewells and Gilbert turned and walked back to the truck. John turned towards the airport entrance. Gilbert shouted out. "Thanksgiving. Give it some thought. We'd love to have you join us for a Seaside Thanksgiving that'll totally sell you on the positives of life in our Maritimes."

John twisted about and shouted back, "I just might give it a go Uncle Gilbert. I'm already missing the call of your seaside and all it has to offer." Both men smiled then departed. Once inside John joined the travelers lined up at the airline check-in counter. To his surprise he quickly flowed through and walked away with his boarding pass in hand. The friendly airport staff whisked him through security and into the departures lounge. Seated at his boarding gate John relaxed and cast an eye over the mixed array of fellow travelers cued up at his flight's boarding gate. The mix stretched from business suited travelers through students and traveling families. On spotting a young mom with a pair of youngsters in tow the taste of another mom he'd left back in East River ignited a flavour burst on his lips. With pleasure he moistened his lips and savored the taste of Eugette's kiss. The youngsters across the way reminded him of Megan and Taylor. They freely tested the limits their mom would tolerate then pulled back before crossing that unspoken invisible line. On the mother's face John read a steady flow of unspoken communications that the youngsters had grasped and quickly complied with. The images of his mom and grandmother flashed warmly in his mind. Just as quickly they touched his heart. John sighed a warmth flowed through his body. Somehow it kindled recollection of a similar sensation he'd been touched by out on the island. The faces in his mind smiled and deepened the sensation in his heart. He pondered could it be? Had something, someone from life's other side reached out and touched his soul out on that island. A piercing pain shot through his body. John shuddered. In the moment he relived his island experience. The sensation hit his chest but somehow got deflected to his shoulder. John had turned his back on the religious upbringings of his youth. In that elongated moment he felt drawn back into the comfort of its callings. Had he been pulled away from death's doorway when touched out on that island? Mother and Grandmother smiled warmly in John's mind then they faded into a mist. A call out to his flight's passengers alerted him. He reacted with a nervous twitch. On breaking free of its hold, John stood then collected his senses and joined the passengers lined up for boarding. At his seat 16A he spotted the young mom and her youngsters seated in row 16. The daughter occupied 16B, Mom in 16C and the son across the aisle in 16D. John eyed his window seat 16A a frantic tug on his pantleg drew his attention to 16D. A smiling face gazed up at him. The lad inquired politely, "Would that window seat over there be your seat kind sir?"

John smiled down at the lad. The lad's energy reminded him of Taylor back in East River. He replied, "Yes, it is my seat."

"Well, it sure would be great if I got to sit in a window seat headed home."

Mom cut in apologetically, "Howard, apologize to the man. It is his seat." Young Howard frowned on hearing his mom's call for an apology.

Before he could comply, John stepped back nodded to Howard and his mom then said, "Not a problem. A family should be seated together. You're Howard, right?"

"I sure am mister."

"Then Howard, I insist you take that window seat." Howard flipped the release on his seat belt. He jumped up and hopped across the aisle. Grinning boldly at his mom, Howard boasted, "Excuse me Mom, I need to get past you to my window seat." Mom did not reply. She released her seatbelt and stood up. Howard eased himself in towards the window seat. On passing his sister a smile did not greet him. Once seated in his window seat with his seat belt fastened Howard grinned at his sister then stuck his tongue out at her. Then just as quickly, he turned towards the window and stared out through it. Mom turned to John and attempted to apologize. John waved it off. He assured her he was good with the seat swap.

Mom then seated herself. After John had claimed the vacated 16D seat he fastened his seatbelt. "Thank you, sir. I'm Stephanie. You've met Howard, the young lady beside me is my daughter, Rebeca. Again, thank you sir."

John smiled and replied, "Not a problem Stephanie, I'm John. John Ramsay and headed home to Newmarket. This seat works for me."

"A kind gesture John and one the I suspect made Howard's day."

John turned and smiled at the man seated beside him. The smile broadened once he recognized the man in his priestly garb. He replied, "I just need to get home. It's been a whirl wind action, packed visit, but I need to get home. Any seat will do." John sank back into his seat. Their stewardess presented the airline's standard introduction to the aircraft's safety features. Their aircraft started to taxi its way to the runway. Takeoff followed in short order.

Once airborne and cruising towards the Bay of Fundy and Toronto a stretch of quiet time embraced John. A myriad of thoughts raced through his head. Distant images of his deceased parents and grandparents eased a touch of rising tension. He cast aside the face of Tessa and rued the ill-fated affair he had with her. A hazel eyed Eugette with two youngsters in tow replaced the former mistress. A longing to be back with her arose within his heart. Quickly the first thirty minutes of their flight vanished. John stirred on hearing the refreshment cart stop by his seat. He accepted the offer of a fresh cup of coffee. The cart moved on past his seat. A sip of coffee cast aside the fogginess of John's hesitant visit to the edge of dreamland. The priest asked, "Would you by chance be related to Bill and William Ramsay out of Newmarket?"

The question drew a tear to John's eye. He brushed it away. He answered, "Yes, my dad and grandfather."

"Well talk about a meeting meant to be. I'm Father Lawrence Hardy. I believe I actually baptised you at Saint Mary's. I was a visiting priest to the parish at the time. What an amazing chance encounter. I'm returning from a missionary in Africa. To be truthful most of my time in the priesthood has been spent in Africa.

John injected, "Then you know the storied history of our parish. I can recall its details being fed to us in the Sunday School sessions of my youth."

"Yes, I recall the pride parishioners took in St Mary's past. Although only a visiting priest I was warmly welcomed into the lives of its parishioners. My brief layover in Halifax rekindled my love of the water. On hearing you introduce yourself to Stephanie, a flashback to my time in Newmarket prompted me to ask if you could be related to Bill and William. I can recall several outings with them out on Lake Simcoe. How are they doing?

A silence followed Father Lawrence's inquiry on the wellbeing of his dad and grandfather. With his thoughts gathered John replied, "Father I'm sorry to say my parents and grandparents, Mary, Bill, Maureen and William, have passed..."

Father Lawrence took John's hands in his. He expressed his sincere condolences. John accepted. Father Lawrence then whispered, "I'll add them to my daily prayers. I trust no one suffered a prolonged illness before their time of passing?"

"No." John hesitated then answered, "A fiery highway accident took them from us. We lost them all in a senseless accident." Tears flowed freely down John's cheeks.

Father Lawrence released John's hands. He embraced him in an emotional bearhug.

John whispered, "It happened right before my eyes. They vanished in a ball of fire." He sighed. Father Lawrence's embrace tightened.

"I'm so, so very sorry John." He released John from his embrace. Together John and Father Lawrence shared memories of the parents and grandparents lost in the horrific traffic accident. Time flew past unimpeded. Their pilot called for all passengers to secure their seatbelts, then announced their approach and decent onto the Toronto airport runway. John and Father Lawrence exchanged business cards. Inside the arrivals area they shook hands and committed to getting together. They parted. Stephanie walked over to John. She warmly embraced him and whispered, "Thanks for the seat swap, John. So sorry about the tragic loss of your parents and grandparents. Take care and blessings. She released him. John watched her and the children walk away. Thoughts of Eugette, Megan and Taylor popped into his head. John retrieved his luggage then headed home to Newmarket with a longing to inhale a fresh breath of sea air and be with the treasures tugging at his heartstrings.

CHAPTER 6

Sunday morning in Lunenburg, eluded the newlyweds. The Sandman entertained them beyond the last call for breakfast. A knock, knock on their door, followed by a friendly greeting by their hostess awakened them both. They snickered then kissed. Lyndsey shouted out, "We're up and about. Just need a minute or two to greet the day properly."

"Not a problem Mr. and Mrs. Ramsay. We'll see you downstairs shortly?"

"Yup! We'll see you shortly Mable." Lyndsey answered. Fifteen minutes later Richard and Lyndsey greeted Mable down in the reception area. They accepted the mugs of coffee sitting on the counter. Both declined the offer of a late breakfast with head shakes. Lyndsey added, "Oh no, we just can't impose on you."

Mable replied, "It'd be my pleasure and no trouble at all."

Though tempting, the offer was declined. Richard explained. "Our wedding reception meals, and I mean meals, leave no room for breakfast. I'll be lucky to polish off this amazing mug of coffee." Their decline of the late breakfast offer was accepted. Once they'd emptied their coffee mugs, Richard retrieved their luggage and loaded up the vehicle. Lyndsey chatted up a storm with Mable. She shared in detail recollections of their wedding celebration and reception. Both ladies laughed heartily over Lyndsey's retelling of Uncle Jeffery's adventure with the bridal garter. Richard stood off to the side taking in the memories being shared. Mable glanced towards him. Lyndsey picked up on the cue. She walked to Richard and treated him to a short but not too short kiss and hug. Richard settled their bill then farewells were exchanged. Back in the vehicle, Lyndsey again claimed driving rights. They completed a short drive about the Town of Lunenburg. Its brightly coloured homes and businesses had caught their fancy on their first visit to East River. The drive about simply added to those treasured memories. On driving past their Bed & Breakfast both glanced up towards the room they'd shared. Richard patted Lyndsey's thigh on recalling their late morning awakening. The recollection triggered renewed wants in his mind and body. The Bed & Breakfast faded from the rear-view mirror and they drove down the highway towards Bridgewater. On driving through Bridgewater Lyndsey signaled a right turn onto Hwy 10 the cross-country road to the Annapolis Valley. Richard looked questioningly at Lyndsey. He asked, "Why this road? It's shorter to go down through Liverpool, then cross country to the Valley and Digby."

Lyndsey smirked. She looked over at Richard and said, "Thought I'd best avoid Liverpool. It's just too close to our beach! Besides this road passes through New Germany, Hope says our dad's ancestors settled there on arriving in Canada."

"But the other route will get us to Digby and the Ocean Hillside B&B much quicker. It was straight ahead back before that turn. Besides ... McDonald is Scottish. Why would they have settled in New Germany?"

"Trust me. No, we must trust Hope. She did some deep digging to uncover their past. She claims they connected with a family from Germany and together purchased land in New Germany."

"But Gilbert said both your birth Mom and Dad, Sandy and Allan, both grew up under foster care. How did Hope…"

"Think about it Rich. We're talking about my sister Hope. If a way existed, trust me our Hope would find it."

"Is the land still connected to your family?"

"No. It exchanged hands numerous times over the years. However, Hope visited the current owners. I have the address and we're going to stop in for a visit." Lyndsey released the accelerator and braked lightly. She drove over onto the shoulder and stopped the vehicle. Tears flowed unabated down her cheeks. "My roots, Hope and I have roots and we're somebody. Our family has roots."

Richard released his seatbelt. He pulled Lyndsey into a full loving embrace. Initial attempts to kiss away Lyndsey's tears failed. Richard eased his embrace. Gently he rubbed Lyndsey's back. Time vanished. Eventually Lyndsey recovered. Richard grabbed a tissue and patted Lyndsey free of her tears. Richard gazed into Lyndsey's eyes he asked, "Want me to drive?"

Lyndsey nodded back in acceptance. Both stepped out of the vehicle. On meeting by the trunk, a soft sweet hug and kisses were exchanged. They returned to the vehicle, Richard waited a moment, then signaled and drove back onto the highway. Traffic was very light. Only an occasional vehicle passed them in the opposite direction. No vehicles had approached from behind. Lyndsey pulled a piece of paper out of her purse. It had an address and directions clearly detailed in hand written notes, along with a detailed map. She held it out and Richard glanced at it briefly. No words were spoken over the next stretch of highway. On spotting the Welcome to New Germany sign Richard touched the brake. The vehicle slowed down to the posted speed limit. Lyndsey stared at each house and barn they passed. She nodded on Richard signaling then turning left followed shortly by a right turn into a driveway. The vehicle stopped beside a large white house. They stepped out of the vehicle. Lyndsey stared in awe at the house. It had some upgraded windows but the overall look placed it in an era well beyond Lyndsey's comprehension. She pondered whether her dad's ancestors had actually built this house?

"Welcome home sweetheart! A home your ancestors once lived in!" An elderly couple walked eagerly towards Richard and Lyndsey. Smiles and joy highlighted both their faces. The gentleman stepped forward and offered his hand to Richard. A hearty handshake was exchanged. "I'm Hugh. Hugh Schreiber and this is my wife, Gisela."

Gisela dispensed with all formality. She strutted up to Lyndsey and embraced her in a welcoming hug. "Welcome home sweetheart.

Welcome home." She released Lyndsey. "Your sister Hope called and told us you'd be stopping in today."

Richard glanced at Hugh then Lyndsey. Hope slipped into the glance's vivid image displayed in his mind. They sure are look a-likes all three being blessed with de dimples."

Gisela moved to Richard and rewarded him with another welcoming hug. It felt like a homecoming to Richard.

Hugh commented, "Come, please come inside and look at the work of your forefathers. They sure knew how to build a house proper." Everyone walked together around to the front door. "It was built over a hundred and sixty years ago. Solid like a rock it is." Gisela and Hugh led Lyndsey and Richard on a tour of the house a three-bedroom home with many detailed wooden trimmings that reflected the time period of its construction. On stepping up the staircase to the second floor, Lyndsey casually slid her hand along the beautiful solid oak banister. A tingling sensation energized her fingers. It accelerated and shot up her arm. Frightened she tried to pull away from the banister. The effort failed. The sensations eased with each upward step taken. On reaching the second floor Lyndsey's hand slid off the banister. She flexed her fingers eyeing them with a questioning look on her face. Nobody commented. At each room's doorway touching the jabs and trim reignited the sensations. The tour ended up in the kitchen. A steeping pot of herbal tea awaited them, along with a plate of cherry scones freshly out of the oven. Although sated from Gilbert's amazing reception catering both indulged themselves with peppermint tea and cherry scones. Richard helped himself to a second one.

Lyndsey commented, "The woodwork throughout the house is amazing. I assume it is all original dating back to its period of construction?

Hugh answered, "Yes...yes. All the woodwork is original. It sealed the deal when Gisela and I bought the house. Hope tells me Allan McDonald was your..."

Excitedly Lyndsey cut in, "Yes, my, our dad and Hope claims he's related to the Brice McDonald that built this house."

"Yes, dear a Brice McDonald built this house with his partner Hans Black. They sure were men seasoned in the construction trade. The house is rock solid."

"Black...Hans Black?" Lyndsey asked.

"Yes," Hugh answered.

"Oh my God, Richard, could it be? Could my mom and her biological grandfather Hans Black be related to Brice McDonald's partner Hans Black?"

Gisela injected, "No. No sweetheart. The odds are just too great. It could never be."

"Yes Gisela." Lyndsey replied. Then added, "I was raised by adoptive parents Liam and Letitia...Lettie Melville nee Black. So, it could be?" Emotions grasped Lyndsey. An emotional gal by nature tears embraced her anew. An image of Lettie her adoptive mom, popped up in Lyndsey's head. Lettie had been proud of her ancestry and birthname Letitia Black. Richard went to Lyndsey's side. They embraced. Lyndsey dabbed away her tears. She added, "Yes, the odds are against it. But Hope confirmed our birth dad was Allan McDonald and that he was related to the Brice McDonald that built this house. But Hans Black, was my adoptive mom's biological grandfather and his ancestors were of German heritage. I could be twice related to the Brice and Hans who partnered up to buy this land and build this house on arriving in Halifax way back in..."

Gisela said, "I don't think it's possible, but please give me your address and I will send you a copy of our deed. It will allow you to track back through the various owners."

Lyndsey's head bobbed up and down. Richard pulled out a business card from his wallet and passed it to Hugh. He said, "Please send it. There may be no connection at all. However, Lyndsey sure would appreciate the chance to research it"

Silence befell the group. Richard helped himself to another cherry scone. He savored each bite while Gisela quietly bagged the remaining scones. Richard tried to decline the offering. His efforts fell on deaf ears. Gisela would have no part of it. Hugh and Lyndsey joined Richard and

Gisela. Outside the house parting hugs were exchanged. Hugh accepted Lyndsey's camera and snapped off a series of photos. They included Richard, Lyndsey and Gisela in front of the house. Richard snapped the final one. It included Lyndsey, Gisela and Hugh on the doorstep. During a final round of hugs Gisela whispered to Lyndsey, "Congratulations, sweetheart."

Lyndsey whispered back, "Thanks Gisela. We're off to Digby on our honeymoon. Got hitched up and married to my man yesterday."

"Yes, that too, but also congratulations on the gift growing within you my dear. You're aglow with the gift's tender touch."

Lyndsey did not answer. She rewarded Gisela with an all-encompassing hug. The hug totally expressed Lyndsey's feelings and thanks. Richard and Lyndsey exchanged parting thanks with the Schreibers then returned to their vehicle. Richard took the driver's seat. Parting waves were exchanged. Richard backed the vehicle onto the road. One final wave sent them on their way towards the Ocean Hillside Bed & Breakfast.

Over the first twenty minutes back on the road, Lyndsey absentmindedly massaged her fingers and hands. The sensations had parted. The recollection of their effect had not. Lyndsey turned to Richard and asked, "What if it's true? Could our birth father be connected to my adoptive mother? The woman who lovingly adopted and raised me at Dad's side, could it be?"

Richard did not answer. The question and possibilities raised amazing possibilities connecting near impossible time passages back together in the woman he'd loved intensely since they met in childhood. On departing New Germany, they turned off onto a cross country route that Richard claimed would connect to Hwy 8. The drive proved to be highly scenic. Both lost themselves in the captivating vistas driven through.

Lyndsey broke the silence. Coyly she questioned and toyed with her man, "When will we get there? I have a need that's calling out to me. I can almost picture in my mind that four poster bed I slept in last time.

It could fit my bill, provided someone doth not opt to spend the night on that soft cushiony chaise."

Richard took his eyes off the road. He gazed longingly at Lyndsey.

Lyndsey pouted, "I've got expectations that went unattended on our last stay."

"Trust me." Richard whispered. "I ravished you dusk till dawn in my mind on our last stay. Physically both of us were exhausted. We entered dreamland the moment our eyes closed and your head hit the pillow, mine the cushiony chaise's headrest."

"Then you'd best keep your eyes on the road. And I best rest up in anticipation of how we'll be bringing those dreamland passions and fantasies to life tonight."

Richard winked then turned his eyes back onto the road. On spotting the directional roadside sign, Richard slowed then came to a full stop. Traffic cleared and as directed he turned right onto Hwy 8 and followed it through to Annapolis Royal. From there the drive through to Digby passed quickly. Captured in the pleasures of a sleepy haze Lyndsey embraced herself in an emotional hug. With a casual sideways glance Richard noted that Lyndsey was in the Sandman's grasp. Their evening of anticipated pleasures added a skip to his heartbeat. Ahead of them their dinning destination returned his focus to the road. Richard spotted an open parking spot in front of the restaurant. He signaled and took possession of the spot. He quietly opened his driver's door and stepped outside into a pleasant fall evening then closed his door. At the sidewalk he stepped over to the passenger door and gazed in at Lyndsey. Seeing Lyndsey hug herself while staring out through a sleepy dreamland gaze, he smiled. With regrets Richard suppressed an urge to kiss Lyndsey on seeing her tongue glide slowly over her rosette lips. Silently Lyndsey's lips mouthed the words, 'I love you Ritch….ie.' The temptation soared in Richard's heart. He opened the door and moved with haste towards a treasured destination. Their lips touched. Lyndsey awoke. She reached out and embraced a shocked Richard. He stumbled and fell onto the awakened and aroused Lyndsey. Throughout Lyndsey's awakening their lips never parted. Touched by the refreshing fall air two sets of blue eyes opened. Their owner's lips parted and they burst into a friendly exchange of giggling. Richard broke the silence. He asked, "Are we hungry?" On receiving no reply, he boasted, "Wow! Nice pick. Looks like seafood delights await us at this unique little restaurant."

Through renewed giggling Lyndsey answered, "Am I hungry? Let me count the ways!" The lights of the restaurant distracted Lyndsey's thoughts from the evening through morning of pleasures awaiting their newlywed wants…desires. "Oh my God … we're here at the oasis of seafood delights"

Richard stole a quick kiss then stood and offered Lyndsey his hand.

"I'm starving sweetheart. I could eat a …"

Lyndsey released her seatbelt then Richard took her hand in his. A gentle tug and step back from the vehicle found the couple standing on the sidewalk and shifting glances between each other and the restaurant's window. They surrendered to the hungers of food. Richard closed the passenger door and together they walked into the restaurant.

Once seated their waitress approached and asked, "Would a coffee, tea, or an adult refreshment assist in selecting your meals?"

"Tea sounds perfect," Lyndsey replied. She glanced at Richard while he pondered the menu. Richard failed to respond. "I believe white rum on ice with cola will top off my Ritchie's day on the road." Richard remained focused on the menu selections.

Richard caught their waitress's name tag. He broke his silence, "I'm starving Mattie. Will the three-piece fish and chips fit on a single plate or is it served up on a platter?"

Mattie chuckled, "We'll add a side of slaw and yes it'll be close, but a plate will handle your seafood delight."

"Then I'm good. Lyndsey, have you spotted a delight or will a one-piece work for you?"

Lyndsey smirked, "Scallops Alfredo in a bowl not a platter I trust?"

"Excellent choice, will six, nine or twelve scallops quash you hunger pangs?"

"Are the delights one bites or a meal in themselves?"

"Let's start out with six, upgrades are optional should the need arise."

Lyndsey nodded her approval. Richard's grin expressed doubts on the extent of Lyndsey's hunger. Following a gleeful smile Lyndsey corrected her order, "I'd best go with nine. I'm hungry!"

Mattie set off with their orders in hand. In the blink of an eye, she returned with their refreshments. While Lyndsey's tea steeped in its mini pot, Richard sampled his rum. Both gazed lovingly at each other in silence. Time stood still until Mattie returned with their meals. Lyndsey giggled aloud on seeing their meals being carried to them by Mattie, her giggles turned to a chuckle on seeing the size of Richard's plate. Richard joined her on spotting Lyndsey's bowl of Scallops Alfredo. No words were spoken. Both Richard and Lyndsey lost themselves to their hunger pangs and the calls from their seafood meals. To Lyndsey's surprise she quickly found her bowl had emptied itself. Hunger had simply taken control and both meals vanished. Mattie returned to their table. Dessert offerings were declined. They chatted over Richard's rum and Lyndsey's tea post meal. Talk centered on their observations of others at their wedding celebration yesterday.

Lyndsey burst into laughter on recalling how her tossed bouquet had ended up in Megan's outstretched hands. "Megan. Oh, so sweet. I loved the glow on her tiny face on having my bouquet land in her hands"

Richard laughed in cheerful agreement.

"Then with all those disappointed single ladies watching her every move, she strutted boldly over to Hope and presented the bouquet to her. I'm so blessed." Lyndsey's face glowed. Richard reached over and took her hands in his. Time almost stood still.

"Jeffery, Maria." Richard boasted. "Together they owned the dance floor. There's a connection and a past between those two. So young to be a grandma, Megan and Taylor are truly blessed. Richard stood signaling it was time to go.

Lyndsey commented, "Seeing Maria with Megan and Taylor filled my heart with a flood of memories. Gads...I sure do miss Mom, Dad, Grampa and dear sweet Grandma." This time Richard's tears hit his cheeks big time. He did not attempt to stem their flow. Lyndsey rushed to Richard's side and embraced him. The hug buried his face into her shoulder. The hug endured until Richard gently pulled away. He stood and wrapped Lyndsey in a bear-hug embrace. A kiss broke the embrace. They separated and walked together towards the cash register. Richard paid their bill and they left the restaurant. The fresh cool sea air outside added zest to their steps as they walked along the waterfront. The evening lights and friendly faces they encountered painted smiles on their faces. Hand in hand they walked. Lyndsey caught sight of the gazebo. She steered Richard in its direction. Up on the gazebo's deck they stood side by side gazing out over the water and its star blazed sky. Lyndsey embraced Richard. Their lips touched igniting passions that raced through each of their hearts. Lyndsey released Richard. "We're home Richard. You and me, this is our new home. We may encircle the globe, but Nova Scotia will always be our true home." Richard acknowledged Lyndsey's words with a kiss. Together they returned to the vehicle.

Lyndsey's hand affectionately rubbed Richard's thigh as they drove out of Digby towards Shore Road and their destination. Light evening traffic quickly found them turning off Shore Drive and arriving at their destination the Ocean Hillside Bed & Breakfast. Warm greetings reconnected them with their hosts. Inside the Blue Room Lyndsey sighed, while Richard placed their overnight bags in the room. To both it was a homecoming filled with expectations. Richard opted to treat himself to a quick shower. Lyndsey passed on the option. She changed into a white cotton lobster covered nightie and crawled under the luxuriant bed's covers. Richard's lighthearted shower singing called out to Lyndsey's ears. She eluded the Sandman waiting for Richard's bedside arrival. Showered and dried Richard soon stood at the bed's side. He smiled gazing down at a coy Lyndsey and the contented aura she displayed. Once under the covers he snuggled up with Lyndsey. A passionate kiss aroused their bodies. Richard tossed the covers aside. No resistance arose as he freed Lynsey of her nighty. She returned the favor and slipped Richard's boxers free of his hips. He shifted and twisted aiding in Lyndsey's quest. The boxers quickly joined Lyndsey's nightie on the floor.

Each caress raised their wants and desires. Together they rolled over and settled with Richard atop Lyndsey. A wanton aah arose as he caressed her breasts taking each arisen nipple repeatedly and savoring its touch and taste. Both their lips and tongues sought out the other's body. Hands caressed and massaged the body in their grasp. Aroused Richard's passion touched Lyndsey's. She shifted and pulled his hips hard to hers. They became one. Their swaying bodies drove each other's closer to utopia. Each resisted an urge to relax and explode on each thrust and sway. They savored the pleasures and sensations delivered to each other. A gasp and sigh arouse Richard collapsed onto Lyndsey's body. Panting they lay together lost in the moment's pleasures. Recovered both kissed. Richard freed Lyndsey sliding off to her side. Time stood still. Hungry for more Lyndsey took Richard's passion in hand. The touch stirred new wants in her man. Each took turns in arousing the other into a night filled with the pleasures lovers crave in coming together. Gratified they embraced each other and drifted off into a deep sleep The wants and desires eagerly anticipated throughout the day fulfilled.

....

At sunrise Richard stirred and snuggled up with Lyndsey. Gazing at Lyndsey's relaxed state. Richard gently kissed her forehead then slowly arose stepping off the bed. He showered, shaved and dressed then walked down to the kitchen. Over a morning coffee he arranged an extended stay in the Blue Room and rescheduled their ferry booking to Saint John. A final sip polished off his morning serving of coffee. Richard returned to their suite. A perfect silence greeted his return. Quietly he undressed and returned to the bed and Lyndsey's side. Temptation overtook him. Snuggled up to Lyndsey Richard once again drifted off to sleep.

Richard and Lyndsey's extended stay treated them to a return visit to Port Royal and its Habitation. Needless to say, that visit nudged them off on a return visit to Delaps Cove Wilderness Trails. Day tripping to local points of interest filled their daytime hours. Evenings and early morning needs of our newlyweds embraced and sated them in loving embraces, driven by each other's needs and wants. Time's passage quickly found them back onboard the Princess of Acadia out on the Bay of Fundy. With no Bailey to distract them, they relaxed and lost themselves in each other's persona.

CHAPTER 7

Morning came early for Gilbert. A quick shower failed to erase his state of grogginess. Sleep had eluded him throughout the night. Dried off Gilbert headed down to the kitchen. The house was filled with silence. He grabbed a jacket and his truck keys and stepped outside. A short drive landed him at the local Café. In short order a Lobsterman's Breakfast arrived at Gilbert's table. He eyed it with pleasure. Halfway through his meal the peaceful solitude of the Café vanished. A familiar voice sang out in greeting, "How's she going me son?"

Before Gilbert could answer a hand landed on his shoulder with a smack, followed by Pappy McClaken grabbing a chair and joining Gilbert at the table. Several home fries took flight off Gilbert's plate. A voice called out, "We'll be having two more of dem Lobsterman's Breakfast over at that table. With coffees and be making mine with cream. Our ladies have been refining our dining habits!" Lenny joined Gilbert and Pappy at the table and greeted him, "Well fancy meeting the Professor outs and abouts so early in de morning. I'd be betting you've even beaten the cat out'ta de sack. But not your two best mates!"

Gilbert grinned warmly at his two breakfast companions. "It's great to see you Dad...Pappy and Lenny. What trouble have the pair of you been up to since we last met up. It's been a week, no it's closer to two, since we chatted it up."

Their waitress arrived with Lenny and Pappy's breakfast orders. All three men fell silent totally focused on the task at hand ... breakfast. An hour flashed by in the blink of a lobster's tail. Gail their waitress cleared away the empty breakfast plates and topped up their coffee mugs. Lenny finally answered Gilbert's question. "We've been occupied me son."

"With the Wright sisters I'll assume." Gilbert answered.

Lenny gazed at Pappy with a questioning frown. On turning towards Gilbert, he asked, "And just how did you come to know about our latest doings?"

Gilbert chuckled aloud. He replied, "The whole town's in on the latest escapades of you and my pappy, Lenny."

"Really, we're that high on the local gossip chatter?"

"Yes, you are. Don't forget my Hope keeps her dad informed."

"Dang it all and I thought she promised to keep it off the grid. Women. One needs dem but just can't trust dem to keep a secret."

Everyone laughed freely. Gilbert drained his coffee mug then excused himself. He had chores awaiting his attention. On standing he said, "You'd best be on good behavior Pappy, Lenny. There's ears and eyes out there eager to keep us up on all the latest happenings here and abouts." Friendly parting smiles and waves were exchanged. Gilbert once back in his truck sighed with relief. He felt confident news of Anya's return hadn't hit the full grid yet. He felt confident in the level of discretion Harley had applied to information centered on the case he'd shared over their recent phone conversations. Otherwise, he'd never have escaped breakfast without being subjected to a full interrogation and jesting by Pappy and Lenny. Anya, the third cog of the three amigos had often visited the McClaken homestead of his youth. Outside Gilbert allowed the past to cast anger on his soul. He recalled how Anya had bolted and vanished from the scene years past. The loss of Anya had deeply troubled and saddened Karyn. A short time later the first signs of Karyn's illness surfaced. The journey through to her passing Gilbert rued had been way too short. Although at times his ideals had clashed with Anya's, he'd have done anything to have had Anya at Karyn's side during her battle with cancer. A twist of the ignition key started the engine. Gilbert checked traffic then drove off towards the local grocery mart. Ten minutes later he signaled and turned into the mall's parking lot. Driving through the parking lot a face popped out of the past. Gilbert eased into an open spot. He gazed in wonder at the piece of his past walking towards his truck. Harley had been right in commenting about having spotted a long-lost soul back in town. In truth Gilbert admitted he'd been pondering how long he'd have to wait before Harley's comments would be certified as factual. She stopped and gazed at the words on the truck's passenger door. A myriad of memories flashed through his head. The true gifts one gains while time flies past unnoticed. Gilbert surrendered to the fact no escape route existed. In truth had there been one, he would have opted to avoid it. Gilbert smiled, seeking to conceal the anger and spite racing towards the tip of his tongue. He stepped out of the truck and walked around to where Anya Trinity stood. On gazing into Anya's eyes Gilbert recaptured a glimmer of the joy the woman had once added to his Karyn's life. The anger within faded. Both eyed each other and fought to restrain smiles fighting to break loose. "Anya? Anya Trinity?"

"Gillie...Gilbert? It's really you."

Gilbert supported himself with an arm on the truck's cab. Both continued to eye each other. Almost seventeen years and then some had flown past since they'd last bumped into each other. Karyn had still been at Gilbert's side. An image of the house they'd rented in Chester after their wedding flashed up then quickly vanished. Their high school days were also a faded memory of days gone by. Gilbert recalled images of his Hope and Anya's son in the living-room as the boy read storybooks to Hope. He fretted what was the boy's name? Nor... Norman! Or in Hope's toddler eyes Normie. Gilbert questioned Hope's behaviour and frame of mind of late. Did she know? Had word of Anya's return reached Hope? Had Norman also returned to Chester with his mom? Gilbert broke the silence. "It's me alright, a pound or two heavier and an inch or two taller."

Anya laughed aloud in response. "If only! I wish. I've been struggling to lose the pound or two that I just can't shake off my aging chassis. Maybe today's *Weight Watchers* meeting will reveal the magical formula?"

"You're looking good Anya. Welcome home. Is everything OK?"

Anya shrugged, "I'm surviving. Mom passed on."

"Our condolences, we planned to attend her services but…"

"It was kept private. I… I, couldn't bring myself to return at that time. Too mu…"

"No need to explain. Not sure what your plans are? If ever in need of a…"

Anya smiled, "Give us time. Norman is with me. He's finishing up his veterinarian studies and supporting his mom."

Gilbert grinned broadly. "What can I say? Your son always was sharp as a whip. If I recall the lad was a science and math wizard. On more than an odd occasion he helped our Hope out with her math."

Anya frowned slightly. Gilbert missed it. She asked "Then Hope didn't menti…"

"What my Hope knew? Knew you and Norman were back home and didn't tell menti…"

"She must be waiting for the perfect moment, just like most young women trend towards. Sadly, too often we learn the moment one's in is typically the sought-after perfect moment."

Gilbert started to cough. He covered off his mouth with an arm until the coughing subsided. He recalled Karyn laughing and suggesting, *'Wouldn't it be funny if one day our Hope and Anya's Norman…'* On lowering his arm, he smirked attempting to suppress an angst arising within on recalling Karyn's expressed thoughts and said, "It must be our generational thing. Each one has their way of embracing the world and its ilk's." Both chuckled lightly.

They eagerly fell into idle conversation sharing tidbits and highpoints in their lives. The separation life had delivered quickly slipped from both their minds. The conversation felt good. He sensed a connection back into his youth resurfacing. Yes, more than once their egos had clashed. Fondly he recalled how his Karyn had drawn them back together in friendship.

Anya looked away from Gilbert towards the mall entrance. She turned back to Gilbert and said, "I'd best get moving. My meeting starts shortly and my *Weight Watcher* chums will think I've abandoned them. I need their support"

Gilbert eyed Anya up and down. No excesses appeared in the image before his eyes.

Anya said, "We're at Mom and Dad's house. I couldn't bring myself to sell it after mom passed on. A situation arose and it worked out for the best. We've moved back home. And I'm good with it. I feel reconnected to my roots."

Gilbert gazed hopefully into Anya's eyes and asked, "Could we get together?"

"Yes, we should." A warm smile lit up her face.

Gilbert sighed. He asked, "A coffee or a tea perhaps?"

Anya accepted, "Ok. Both work for me." She paused then added, "Sorry to hear of Karyn's passing. It's never easy. Life that is."

Gilbert nodded his approval. "Call. Our number hasn't changed." They extended their hands and squeezed each other's then separated. Gilbert watched Anya walk away. A flood of emotions raced through his mind and body. Emotions he hadn't experienced in years. Racial bigotry had struck its angry arm out at Anya and her family. Gilbert could not recall her ever having had a heartthrob standing by her side. Each sway of her hips on walking away set off feelings he'd lost touch with years past. He watched her disappear into the building.

'Honk...honk!' Lenny's horn sang out to Gilbert as he and Pappy drove past Gilbert. Gilbert caught sight of them. He grinned on seeing Pappy in the back seat, with the Wright Sisters sitting beside him and Lenny.

Pappy's window rolled down. He extended himself out the through the window and shouted, "Got a bit of dirt in your eye my son? Or did yer Pappy just catch you eyeing that sweet young thing heading into the mall? Must be a newbie? I ain't seen that chassis strutting about town of late. Besides it's never too late fer a bit of de Loving." Pappy's companion ended the conversation. She grabbed him and hauled him back inside. Laughter echoed out of Lenny's SUV as it drove out of the parking lot.

Gilbert shook his head and chuckled. He walked around to the driver's door and reclaimed the driver's seat. All thought of grocery shopping vanished from his mind. The drive home passed quickly. Images and memories raced through his head. Many were treasured times out of the past. The image that pulled at his heartstrings was one of the three amigos Gilbert, Karyn, and Anya. They'd bonded in eighth grade. Karyn had been the glue that had kept them together. Gilbert reflected on how his views and Anya's had often conflicted. However, Karyn simply worked her magic and kept the amigos together. He pondered Harley's words, *'I need your help, Gil. Retirement is staring me in the face. Madison's connections busted my case against him. The bastard's a serial rapist and I want, no need to take him down before I'm forced out the door.'* On hearing Harley name Anya Trinity as one of the victims Gilbert's thoughts landed on the truth behind why she'd vanished years past. He recalled the image of the sweet young woman Pappy had caught him eyeing. Some were fretful tossing about concern over Anya and her safety. What had really drawn Anya back to Chester? Would she be safe back home? A resolve set in on Gilbert's heart. A tingle touched his lips. He recalled fondly the passionate teenage kisses shared in the embrace of Karyn's arms. Those recollections reminded him of thoughts he'd once pondered over, *'My God Anya's beautiful. Her lips. I love my Karyn, but think I'd like to taste another's no not just another, Anya's.'* In reflection he did not regret his failure to wander.

CHAPTER 8

A chill in the air signaled the approach of Thanksgiving. That chill drew two acquaintances from long past school days into the Café. Their eyes caught each other's in a random glance locked, and recognition slowly became reality. Both ladies smirked then broke into smiles. On being served Maria walked over towards the booth occupied by Anya.

Anya spotted the woman walking towards the seating area with a coffee in hand. She smiled and said, "Hi I'm, Anya Trinity if memory serves me right you are Maria Lamont?"

Maria replied, "That's me." Memories flashed rapidly through both their minds. Anya recalled a clipped newspaper article that spoke of a lobster boat lost to the perils of a ragging Atlantic storm. Its accompanying photo shared images of the father-in-law and son-in-law crew lost in the tragedy. Silently she asked herself could Martin have fathered Maria's child? Smiles of recognition connected the two. Anya raised her hand inviting Maria to share her booth. The invitation was accepted.

"Welcome home Anya. You're looking great. I'll bet you haven't gained a pound over the years." Maria said in greeting Anya.

"Thanks Maria. Glances in my mirror sing another song. You're looking good. Sorry about your husband. I should have got in touch but fell short."

"It hurts losing a loved one. How about you? Is there a man in your life?"

Anya frowned and replied, "There hasn't been. Life and just raising family has kept me busy."

They fell silent between sips of their coffees. Maria broke the silence. She asked with hesitation, "Back in the day. Our high school days did…"

"Did I hop into bed driven by my teenaged raging hormones?" Anya giggled then frowned and added, "I wish it had been so." Their eyes locked on each other. Anya's eyes betrayed a longing. A longing to taste the sweetness of love shared by two whose hearts were connected. The longings cast aside the realities that life had exposed her to in her youth. The longing in Maria eyes pined to cast aside the hurt suffered in the loss of Martin to a raging sea. The years of loving they'd shared in life had been special. Although special it offered no closure to her heart or soul. A long-suppressed question perched on both their lips. Throughout life rumors had suggested answers that remained unconfirmed. Both faces fell blank. Anya broke the silence. She asked, "I recall your first was a daughter. Did more follow over the years?"

Maria sighed, "No. My blessing is my Eugette and my grandbabies, Megan and Taylor. Along with Gilbert's, Hope. She's absolutely the next best thing to a second daughter."

Anya smiled and boasted lightly, "Yes children are true blessings. Normie my Norman moved back home with me. He's close to graduating with his veterinarian's degree. He's my God sent blessing and keeps me going."

Maria replied, "Yes, it's different raising a single child. You get to be parent and best bud until school days connect them to their world in the making."

Anya whispered, "I had a second child a daughter. August, a true God sent blessing." Suppressed sobs erupted deep within Anya. Her tears burst into a flood.

Maria reached out and clasped Anya's hands in hers. Neither woman spoke. Slowly the tears abated.

Anya revealed the heartache buried within. "August, my August passed on. Her love and life passions are memories I treasure more than life itself at times."

Shocked on hearing Anya speak of her daughter's passing, Maria pulled Anya's hands to her lips and kissed them. Both women sighed.

Time almost stood still; its passing confirmed only by the cooling of their coffee ladened mugs.

A loud joyful voice freed both from their frozen moment. "Well, what do we have here, one would be a pleasure. The two of you nothing short of a treasure!"

Maria released Anya's hands. She twisted around and was rewarded with a kiss. It ended and he sat at Maria side. He grinned boldly at Maria. "Could I be staring at a face out'ta me past?"

Anya smirked then nodded her head answering Jeffery with a positive confirmation.

"Don't be telling who you be, girl. Your name is right on the tip of me tongue. Lordie! If I weren't so old, I'd swear I'm staring at one beautiful Trinity Gal. Could I be right? The cat's got me tongue when it comes to yer name girl. But I know a Trinity when I see one!"

Anya beamed on hearing Jeffery's speech. The words spoken so clearly. The words and their clarity confirmed news of Jeffery's recovery she'd discovered while chatting with Gilbert. Anya stood and offered up an open armed hug. Jeffery dutifully obliged. She released him and chided, "And yes Jeffery, Gilbert and I bumped into each other. We had a quick chat."

"And...?" Jeffery asked.

Maria cut in, "Jeffery don't go prying into..."

Anya laughed heartily. "I'm good with-it Maria. Actually, we're getting together to catch up. Gilbert and I bumped into each other in the mall parking lot on Tuesday. It felt good."

To Jeffery's embarrassment the conversation shifted to recollections shared in their youth. Back in the day when a quarter swore a young Jeffery to secrecy. Gillie's brother sitting sessions often landed the teenage friends, Gillie, Karyn and Anya in a movie theatre with little Jeff in hand.

Laughter broke out on Jeffery declaring, "Not all of the action was on the screen. If you catch my drift?" Anya blushed then snickered and laughed aloud. It was a joyful laughter and the others joined in.

Anya confessed, "Yes. Gilbert and Karyn did tend to miss much of the on-screen action. On the other hand, we, you and me got to see some good movies." Anya glanced at her watch. Their laughter subsided. Maria picked up the signal. It was time to leave. Everyone agreed to get together again soon. Maria and Jeffery watched Anya walk out of the café. They followed headed back to Maria's home. The meet up had added energy and speculation to their day.

CHAPTER 9

"Gilbert, I bumped into Anya Trinity the other day. Well, I didn't really bump into her. However, I sure did recognize who she be! And I'm told you've already chatted with her in the mall parking lot." Jeffery awaited a reply from his brother. He wondered if Hope was also in the know. "She's still a looker. A right sharp lady Gillie and no silver streaks. A sweet young thing just like me!"

Gilbert laughed aloud then declared, "You're no longer a teenybopper Jeff. We're all a year or two beyond where we once were back in the day!"

"True!" Jeffery answered. "I recall back in the day, that there was no man in her life. At least not one I ever saw her with. And Maria tells me the same holds true. She sure has blossomed into one beautiful lady!"

Gilbert sighed. In that moment he was a million miles away. Jeffery's comments had hit home. Life had been good to him. Karyn, a treasure he missed more with each passing day. A sweetness touched his lips. Fired up by the memories of the sweet young thing he'd fallen head over heels in love with back in the day. He broke free of the youthful recollection tugging at his heartstrings. The sigh deepened. Gilbert confessed. "Yes, we shared some great times back in the day, Karyn, Anya and me. And yes, my Karyn was all the sweetness I needed. Sadly, I don't recall Anya having connected with anyone. Too bad. We tried to connect her up. But never got a match that gelled."

"Their loss." Jeffery commented. "She sure was a sweetheart. And fun to chat with. Never hesitated to give me a moment of attention regardless of how busy her day happened to be. My clock sure took a backwards leap when I bumped into Maria and Anya chatting it up over coffee at the Café. We had a good time chatting and sharing past memories. You know. Like movie theatres?"

Gilbert took on a glow in recapturing a moment out of his youth. Firmly he declared, "Karyn was my sweet young thing back in the day and straight through our shared lifetimes. I was never alone with my gal at my side. I miss her gentle touch and the alluring scent of my Karyn's body." Enjoying their brotherly chat Gilbert asked, "So you were checking her out, with Maria right there by your side? What Maria isn't enough of a woman for you? You need more than one? Trust me, Jeff. That woman of yours Maria has it bad! You'd best hold onto her and keep your eyes off other women."

Jeffery stared in awe at his brother. "Oh, my Maria, she's everything this lad needs or wants and a whole lot more. I just thought of you and days past on spotting Anya and my Maria over at the café chatting it up over coffees. And NO! I wasn't checking her out that way. I'm just saying. She's one pretty lady. And judging from the eyes turned her way in the café others liked what they were seeing. Why George's wife bopped him a good one for staring too long. Shouted out, 'Git yer eyes back in yer head Georgie!' Anyway, I'm just saying. I wonder if our Hope knows that Norman is back home?"

Gilbert nodded a positive response to Jeffery's question. Then confirmed, "Yes. Anya mentioned Norman and Hope had crossed paths. She knew before we did."

Jeffery grinned. With a smile he added, "Our Hope sure can hide a secret. Remember how Norman would entertain our Hope reading storybooks to her back in the day. Do you think they might connect? Mom thought little Hope had a crush on him back in the day. But always tsk, tsked it. Saying the boy way too old for our little Hope. Anya explained how the renters moved out of the old Trinity house last month and the timing was just right so they decided to move back home. That is the facts, Gillie. And there's still no man with her according to what Maria told me."

Gilbert fell silent. In his mind special moments out of the past flashed randomly through his thoughts. He sighed. Anya Trinity's lips had been the first he'd thought would fire up the needs and wants of a once youthful Gillie McClaken. However, that never came to be. Karyn, Anya's sidekick had quickly laid claim to her man. And the rest was history. A beautiful history filled with love up to the moment cancer had ripped sweet Karyn out of his arms. Anya Trinity and the thoughts he'd felt on bumping into her in the mall parking lot had raised an uneasy guilt in Gilbert's mind. Yes, maturity had definitely sweetened Anya's appeal. With question he pondered is it wrong to feel an attraction towards her? In a flash an angelic image of Karyn, his soul mate and wife lost to cancer replaced Anya's image. Gilbert's feelings of guilt deepened. It was short lived. Karyn's image eased Gilbert's inner thoughts. Moving towards the end, she'd urged him to embrace love should it come calling. He smiled at Jeffery and said, "Yes, I enjoyed chatting with Anya. And her son Norman did unknowingly hold a key to our little Hope's heart back in the day."

Jeffery nodded his agreement. He did not push the discussion. Thoughts of Maria in his mind set him to hoping Gillie and Anya might become an item.

The door swung open and Hope entered. She sensed an energy in Gilbert and Jeffery. The energy rekindled thoughts of Gilbert's Karyn, the mom…Aunt who'd raised Hope with an overabundance of loving care. A tingling shot up and down her spine. What could possibly be the trigger of the energies the brothers were sharing? She rewarded each with a hug then asked, "What's up? I feel energy in the air."

Jeffery smirked and said, "So you've already bumped into you know who!"

Hope smiled back boldly at Jeffery, "I, sure did bump into you know who." Jeffery fell into deep thought. A concerned frown overtook his face. Hope interrupted Jeffery's thoughts. She boasted, "We did a movie and dinner date!"

Gilbert looked to Hope and asked, "How was the dinner date? Before she could answer he looked to Jeffery and said, "Relax Jeff. Our Hope has dated once or twice. You'd best focus on Maria. She is aglow. It's so obvious the lady is in LOVE!" He started to walk out of the room. In leaving he called out, "I need time to reflect Jeff. Later." Gilbert headed into the living-room. In the living-room he paced tentatively back and forth glancing out the bay window. The hurt he'd suffered through Karyn's illness and death thrust arrows into his heart. With renewed guilt he admitted he'd once been infatuated with the idea of tasting Anya's lips. That reality never came to pass. Karyn had him wrapped snuggly about her baby finger. He recalled how wild rumours had circulated like wildfire once it became obvious that Anya was pregnant. Everyone speculated over who the father could be. Anya the daughter of a mixed marriage had racial slurs and bigotry cast her way. Proudly Gilbert recalled how Karyn, the Trinitys, McClakens and he had stood proudly at Anya's side throughout her pregnancy. He'd actually envied her as he and Karyn's efforts up to that point had failed to set them on the path towards parenthood.

On discovering the truth he'd cast that envy aside. Harley had made it clear that Anya had been raped. Karyn never got to feel a child growing inside her body. All their attempts at parenthood had failed. Then they'd been blessed. A tiny bundle of joy had entered their lives. Oh, how he and Karyn had embraced and loved their little Hope. Their special gift. Who'd been rescued at the scene of the tragic highway accident that had claimed her parent's lives. They adopted Hope, but raised her with her parent's surname, McDonald. Sandy and Allan were her biological parents. Karyn and Gilbert were her aunt and uncle, Mom and Dad. Their openness they believed had magnified the loved they shared. Gilbert shivered on recalling how they'd reacted to seeing their Hope entertained by Anya's Norman during their get togethers. Norman, a natural storyteller, spent many hours reading storybooks to the much younger Hope. Many a glance at wee Hope revealed she was totally infatuated with Norman and not the storylines.

Sensing a need for some alone time, Gilbert slipped out the front door unnoticed. Deep in thought he walked across the lawn. His destination was the boat dock and Karyn Anita the boat and lady who'd totally owned his heart. At the dock he gazed wantingly at the Karyn Anita. Temptation soared. Gilbert boarded his lobster boat. The inner hurt abated a touch. He checked the gas tank on finding it full Gilbert primed the gas line then released the vessel's docking lines. Karyn Anita drifted out onto East River. He grabbed the jacket off the cabin hook and donned it. The fall air carried a chill. A flick of the ignition fired up the engine. Its welcomed purr warmed Gilbert's heart. He shifted her into gear and touched the throttle. Karyn Anita responded. She carried her master out onto East River Bay with Mahone Bay set as her destination. Inside his heart skipped a hesitant beat. Throughout her illness she'd pleaded with Gilbert to accept love should it come calling after she slipped out of his life. Right up to the minute she collapsed in his arms, he'd never been able to answer her pleas with a yes.

Racing across Mahone Bay at full throttle Gilbert spoke freely with Karyn's spirit. Each word spoken lessened the anger he'd battled since losing the love of his life. Images out of their youthful three amigos past danced in Gilbert's head. The images faded into a haze. Racing past Pearl Island another image griped Gilbert's heart. Karyn's ashen deathbed face whispered, *'Promise me you'll accept love should it come calling after I'm gone.'* Through watery eyes Karyn's image vanished. Gilbert whisper, "I will my Love. I will." With Karyn's permission in hand, he now felt ready to seek out Anya and get the answers to questions that had gone unanswered throughout his and Karyn's lives. Ready to seek her out Gilbert gave the helm a twist and Karyn Anita responded. She carried him back home towards East River. Harley's comments hinted strongly towards knowing the identity of Norman's father, Anya's rapist. Gilbert felt a need to know the truth. Time slipped past unnoticed as he pondered the candidates. One ignited anger in Gilbert's heart. There'd never been an arrest or trial. He recalled his parents discussing the various candidates. One name arose often. It cast an icy pallor on Gilbert's mind.

An hour later Karen Anita arrived back at her dock. Refreshed and renewed Gilbert secured Karyn Anita to the dock and killed the engine. Back up on the dock Gilbert gazed at Karyn Anita's name plate. A sense of relief and need touched his soul and he headed back home. Outside the house he spotted Hope in the kitchen window. They acknowledged each other with waves. Awaiting Gilbert's return, Hope noticed the zip in Gilbert's step. It matched hers to a T. Hope slid her tongue over her lips in recalling the taste of Normie's lips on hers the other night. Inside Hope beamed on Gilbert joining her in the kitchen.

She boasted, "Dad, the dinner date and movie was fabulous." Gilbert frowned. The frown vanished on Hope embracing her dad in a loving hug. Jeffery rejoined them. During Gilbert's absence he'd stepped out to round up Maria and the twins, along with a supper offering. He entered the kitchen with Maria, Taylor and Megan in tow. The twins proudly carried Jeffery's meal contribution. Each carried a large pizza topped off with dessert offerings. Everyone moved towards the kitchen table then rerouted under Gilbert's directions into the dining-room. Maria joined Hope passing out plates, utensils and glasses. Gilbert filled the empty glasses with sodas of choice. He then topped off the two glasses Jeffery had treated to a serving of golden liquid over ice cubes with cola. He boasted, "I'm starving and have a need to recharge myself with a slab or two of these pizzas."

Hope opened the pizza boxes and passed servings of choice around the table. Silence befell the hungry dinners. The twins surprised everyone by each helping two large slices vanish. After mini-dessert pizzas had topped off the meal, Hope started to clear off the table. Jeffery stood and went to Maria's side. Before he could speak Maria stole a kiss then nudged Jeffery out of the dining-room. Hope and Maria worked together and cleared the table of the after dinner clean up. An easy mother-daughter like conversation flowed between them. A normal occurrence. To most folks here and abouts in East River and Chester, Hope was nothing short of Maria's second daughter. Adapted through the best friend relationship Hope shared with Maria's Eugette. On wrapping up the clean-up, Maria rounded up her grandbabies and signaled to Jeffery it was time to go. Megan and Taylor were summoned. Taylor smiled on hearing Meg whisper, "Let's work on Grampa Jeff on the way home for an ice cream treat." Friendly exchanges were shared as they departed. The kitchen fell silent with Gilbert left standing at Hope's side. Hope nibbled on her lower lip. She whispered, "I don't know your past Dad. But I really want to see who my Normie has become. I like what I've seen. I want more. But I just need to know."

Gilbert turned to Hope. He embraced her in a loving father-daughter embrace and placed a kiss on her cheek. "You will sweetheart, you will. Think I need to turn myself in early tonight." Their embrace ended. Smiles and goodnight cheek pecks were exchanged. Gilbert walked out of the kitchen and headed upstairs deep in thoughts garnered out on the waters of Mahone Bay earlier. Inside he sensed a troubled night's rest was in the works. Hope followed him up the stairs with a different destination in mind. A book's pages were calling out to its engaged reader. The early to bed sessions of late had ended in a series of frustrated book drops and failed attempts to reach a chapter's closing line. An experience most avid readers have experienced once or twice.

CHAPTER 10

The aroma of fresh coffee called out to Gilbert come morning. He quickly joined Hope in the kitchen. The coffee's aroma vanished in the blink of an eye. 'Phhffoop...oop.' Hope stared in disbelieve at the massive yellow fury ball that strutted with a hobble across the kitchen floor. A sour frown captured her face as the retched odor that accompanied Bailey's fart filled the air. "Oh my God, Bailey. You stink!"

Gilbert covered his face with a hand and fled from the kitchen. Hope reacted to Gilbert's suppressed laughter. "It's not funny. What are you feeding Bailey? He's definitely not on a healthy diet. Look at him! He's barely able to walk. Bailey ... sweetheart, it is diet time."

Gilbert returned to the kitchen. A grin plastered boldly across his face. "Jeffery, Uncle Jeff. He must have left some fish remnants lying about."

"Really, look at him. On arriving here, he was a big energized fluffy ball of fur. He barely topped the scales at twenty-five pounds."

"I only feed him the best."

"The best, followed by my feeding and topped off by Uncle Jeffery's"

"Ok. Bailey is a little overweight."

Hope walked over to Bailey. She knelt down at his side and lovingly patted the cat. Bailey responded by curling up to Hope's thigh. 'Mrrreow. Meeooow.' Hope attempted to scoop Bailey up into her arms. "It's time to visit the vet. We need a professional's opinion."

Bailey twisted about in Hope's arms. He stared at her and hissed in reaction to the V- word. "Oh, my not so little sweetie, Lyndsey will think you're Santa Claus when she sees you. Uncle Gilbert, we'd best add low-fat tuna to Bailey's treats." Hope stood up and carried Bailey into the living-room. Gilbert followed her. They both sat on sofa chairs across from each other. Gilbert eyed Bailey. In silence he agreed with Hope's diagnosis. The three unsupervised daily feedings along with Bailey's daily seaside struts that rewarded him with healthy servings snatched from the local sea gulls' clam hunts were creating a weight issue. He pondered; maybe a serving of liquid refreshment is needed? Memories of his first encounter with Bailey painted a smile on his face. The experience taught him to guard all servings of an alcoholic nature with greater caution than had been exercised back in Newmarket. Hope lovingly stroked and patted Bailey's head, back and chin. Bailey, in returned cuddled tighter up in Hope's lap.

Bailey eyed the pair of concerned cat sitters. In his mind faint images of a former long-term residence floated tauntingly. The images refreshed memories of good-times Bailey longed to relive. Days when the D word was a definite unknown. Besides diet is something better suited to Gilbert's expanding waistline. Bailey reasoned in his thoughts, a simple and slightly longer stroll along the shorelines and viola, I'm a fit, trim and slim pussy cat. If Big Boy Gillie adds low-fat tuna to the grocery list, it better not end up in my dish. Speaking of Bailey treats, what's happened to my liquid refreshments Grampa and Ritchie so lovingly slipped into my bowl? They're educated I'm told. Can't these Bluenosers read labels? Milk is extremely high in fat content. Hope abruptly stood up. Bailey's train of thought was jarred back into reality. A look of pure displeasure painted itself on Bailey's chunky face that had alerted Gilbert and Hope to the shift in Bailey's weight distribution. Mrreow...meeow! A little notice please! Hope shifted Bailey in her arm, then stooped down and placed him on the floor. A positive thought bounced about in Bailey's mind. It's din-din time. Yummy, yummy chow down time. The thought vanished in the blink of an eye. Bailey watched in frustration as Hope walked out of the room.

"Think I'll treat myself and freshen up with a relaxing bath."

"OK!" Gilbert answered. He added, "Lunch in an hour."

Bailey relaxed since the V word had not come up again. He sat in front of the sofa chair where Hope had placed him. The sound of running water echoed in his ears. Bailey stood and walked with determination towards its source. Halfway up the stairs he stopped. His heart raced in response to his activity. Between a series of deep panting breaths, he reluctantly admitted, ok … maybe I could shed a pound or two. Just don't stretch it into kilos. Feeling rejuvenated after a moment he continued up the stairs then strutted into the bathroom. Water was pouring into the tub. Steam rising off its surface called out to Bailey. He leaped up towards the tub's ledge. Ker plop Bailey failed to gain the required altitude. He slid unceremoniously back down onto the floor. Determination took control. A second extended reach and follow-up leap landed a smiling self-satisfied Bailey on the tub's ledge. He watched the water rising up in the tub and the wafts of steam floating up from its surface. A strange aromatic rose like scent kissed Bailey's nostrils. Memories long past painted a picture in his mind. Grampa Ramsay's mate Grammie relaxed and seated in her tub. The image vanished in a moment. It was replaced by one of Bailey seated on Grandpa's attic desk in Newmarket. With each lick of the clear enticing nectar in his saucer, Bailey's thoughts faded and grew foggier.

"Tis a beautiful, beautiful day it tis..." Hope's singing voice died. She had returned to the bathroom, closed its door and dropped the bath towel that was wrapped warmly around her body. Gazing into the mirror a rare envy arose within Hope's being. A gentle soul by nature Hope savored the energy Lyndsey exuded in expressing her passion. A frown appeared on Hope's face. It vanished as she touched both hands to her tummy. Motherhood the passion that possessed Lyndsey's life with every breath now held Hope captivated. Childhood recollections added to the envy. She whispered, "Sorry Sis. I envy you married and on the threshold of motherhood. Oh My GOD! Let it one day be me. Our bodies are magical. But to feel the sensation of a life growing within. She stared with awe into the mirror. "Norman, My Normie yes, we've barely reconnected. But I've walked at dad's side down that imaginary childhood aisle to your side a million times awake and sleeping. I like what we're becoming a couple. So very glad you're back home in Chester." Hope released her tummy and raised both hands to her hair. A twist and toss set her curls a twirl. She puckered up her lips and savored the taste of Norman's lips on hers. A playful smirk possessed her face. She whispered anew, "Look out Normie now you're my man." She turned towards the tub. On spotting Bailey, she smiled happily. A step then two took her to the tub's side. Reaching past Bailey Hope turned off the water. She patted Bailey then stepped into the tub. A hot tingling sensation race up her legs once she stood in the tub's hot steaming rosy waters. Gingerly Hope lowered herself into the tub's fragrant water. All frustration vanished. With eyes closed Hope focused on a savored memory of her sitting across from Norman in a restaurant. They were out on their movie night date. Normie stared lovingly into her eyes. She returned the stare tenfold. Hope whispered aloud, "Oh Normie, My Normie please love me."

Bailey walked gingerly along the tub's edge. On arriving at Hope's end of the tub he sat down on the ledge. Casting his eyes towards Hopes closed eyes Bailey focused his thoughts on convincing Hope a diet and trip to the veterinarian were uncalled for actions. He extended his neck carrying his head closer to Hope. Splash! Meow! Bailey slipped unceremoniously off the ledge into the tub. Its hot water engulfed Bailey fully. He sloshed about terrified. Hope's eyes flew open. She reached out and picked up a watery fully drenched Bailey. Holding him away from her body, Hope moved to a kneeling stance then stood up. She stepped out of the tub, grabbed her bath towel, and wrapped Bailey snuggly into its folds. Bailey tossed his head to and fro in response to the feel of the warm drying towel.

"Oh sweetie, my sweet little Bailey. What were you thinking? Let me dry you off, you poor thing."

Bailey relaxed in the comforts of the towel and Hope's massaging fingers. Yes! Yes, he thought. I've died, but it's only one life. Oh, so worth the anguish of the moment just past. His ears perked up in response to footsteps running up the stairs.

"Hope! Hope, are you Ok? Gilbert called out. He stopped outside the bathroom door. It was locked. Gilbert pounded on the door. "Hope! Are you OK?" He relaxed as Hope first giggled then broke out into laughter.

"I'm Ok Uncle Gilbert. It's nothing serious. It's Bailey. He slipped off the tub's ledge and joined me in the tub. He is perfectly okay now, aren't you sweetie?" Hope stared at a self-satisfied Bailey wrapped tightly in the bath towel.

"Are you sure Hope? Those thumps and bumps sounded serious!"

"We're perfectly ok. Relax. I'll let Bailey out after I get him dried off."

"Ok Sweetheart, lunch in a half an hour, thirty minutes."

"Make it forty-five. I really need that bath now, along with some fresh water."

"Take a shower."

"Nope, I want, no need, my bath!"

"That's No, Hope. Not nope, OK? Forty-five works for me,"

Hope sighed, pulled the tub's drain plug then relaxed. "Thanks Uncle Gilbert...Dad. Love you." Bailey purred away contentedly in the towel. While the water drained, she carried Bailey over to the tub. He squirmed nervously in anticipation of a repeat visit to the tub. Hope reach over and flipped on the shower fixture. She then spayed the tub vigorously. The tub quickly drained itself. Satisfied all traces of Bailey's golden yellow-orange fur had hit the drain she shut off the shower and returned its hand-held showerhead to its holder. She stooped down and engaged the tub drain then turned on the taps. Hot water gushed out of the taps into the tub. Bailey squirmed anew in Hope's arms. The squirming ceased once Hope stood and walked over to the vanity. There Bailey received a final rub down. Satisfied Bailey had fully recovered; Hope carried him over to the door. There she unlocked the door and released Bailey from the towel's clutches. On spotting an escape route, Bailey leaped through the doorway to freedom. Hope smiled watching Bailey float eagerly out into the hallway. She closed the door and twisted its lock into place. A sniff of the towel painted a smirk on her face.

Hope dropped the towel in the clothes hamper and retrieved a fresh one. Standing back in the tub she picked up the jar of bath bubbles and jiggered a healthy serving into the tub's waters. She then kneeled, returned the bath bubbles to the tub's ledge and turned off the taps. Satisfaction embraced Hope. A light giggle relaxed her spirits. A picture of Bailey soaking wet and squirming in the towel turned the giggle into laughter. A full lathering up, topped off with the added touch of an extended bath brush completed Hope's cleansing. Hope sat down and relaxed. Back in a relaxed place of reflection Hope closed her eyes. She teetered on the edge of dreamland. On that edge a youthful Hope walked away from the school and her grade two classroom. She held her lunch box in her left hand. Hope's right hand swung freely at her side. Her eyes glanced off to the side. They were fully engaged. The image captured was that of an older lad. Hope's storyteller. He stood surrounded by a gaggle of admiring friends. Friends little Hope envied. Especially the girls. They idolized the man of her dreams. Little Hope's heart savored the touch of Normie's hand. Although she'd only had hers held its grasp once or twice. She savoured the recollection of its touch. A school bus drove up and blocked Norman from her view. Together with his friends and fellow students Noman boarded the bus. He took a window seat falling right back into Hope's view. A minute at most passed by unnoticed. Then the school bus drove off stealing little Hope of her man's presence. Time almost stood still. The approach of Hope's school bus broke her free of the imaginary image of little Hope and Norman as they walked towards their school bus hand in hand.

Ker slash! Hope's head dropped down onto her chest and her body slipped unceremoniously into the tub's water. Awakened she splashed her way to safety and the reality of the moment. Grasping onto the tub's side Hope recovered quickly. The relaxing bath ended. On being released the tub's drain opened and its water drained. Stepping out of the tub Hope grabbed a towel and dried herself off and slipped into a bathrobe. On opening the bathroom door, the aroma of lunch in the making interrupted Hope on her way to the bedroom. She paused and inhaled the heavenly aromas. They distracted her train of thought.

Quickly she escaped their temptations. Another task arose. What to wear. A casual pants and top in matching hues of purple won the day. In gazing at herself in the wall mirror Hope fretted. Would Normie like it? She slipped into a trance reliving the dining experience they'd shared a day earlier.

Hope smiled hopelessly while recapturing the image of Norman seated in their booth across from her. Norman laughed heartily at Hope's refusal to eat the bite of his liver and onions he offered. Her head shook side to side and her lips sealed access to her mouth and taste buds. Memories of childhood exposures to similar offerings raised the intensity of her rejection of Norman's offering.

"Just try it, Hope. You'll love it once your taste buds touch it." Norman suggested. The suggestion fell on deaf ears. Defeated in his quest Norman demoed by example the dining pleasures she'd rejected.

A voice sang out, "Norman…Normie Trinity is it really you. My old bud?"

Norman and Hope turned towards the voice. Hope cringed on recognizing its source. Norman stared at the face out of his past. A face he'd been warned to avoid.

"It's me, your old bud, Garth!"

"Garth Stone?" Norman asked.

"Yes! It's me. Garth Stone aka Ned Stone's nephew. We sat side by side in our good old golden school days."

Hope stared down at her untouched food. Hunger had abandoned her once she'd recognized the voice calling out from her past. A sigh signalled her displeasure to both Norman and Garth. Both missed the darts flung their way. Eugette's words describing Mikie Slivers and Ned Stone's lewd actions and word games they subjected the Pot's waitresses to raised her ire. Hunger pangs called out to her. They went unheeded. Although recent rumors sang out of Mikie Sliver's born-again Christianity, Hope refused to put her faith in the rumors. True she'd seen him garbed in his pastoral white robes. But history prevented her from accepting his proclaimed conversion into Christianity's open arms. Their waitress walked over to their table. She asked, "Will you be joining the party, sir. Would you like a menu?" Invisible steam floated up off of Hope's body. Its presence went undetected by all but Hope.

"I'd love to sweetheart, but unfortunately work calls out to me. Would my takeout double burger and home fries order be ready?"

Mary twisted about and stepped away. She walked back to the counter. Hope's anger ebbed on hearing her call back. "Your order is ready to go sir." With each step away from their table that Garth took Hope's anger abated.

Norman waved an adieu to Garth as he stood by the counter. "Gads and wow! I haven't seen Garth in ages." Hope blocked out the excitement in Norman's voice. She focused her attention on Garth's interaction with their waitress. A thunderstorm raged inside driven by his attempts to connect with Mary. She started to stand up, ready to rescue their young waitress a girl of sixteen at best. Norman missed the action. He'd lost himself to his platter of liver and bacon. At the counter Garth grabbed his take-out order. He twisted about and nodded to Mary, "See ya, Sweetheart." His free hand swung towards Mary's butt. Hope arrived just in time. She grabbed his hand in flight and denied it the pleasure sought. She flung it into his face. Garth stared with contempt into Hope's eyes. No words were spoken. He left the restaurant. Mary cast her eyes downwards to the floor.

Hope whispered, "Don't be fooled. That one is bad news."

Mary frowned then smiled. She whispered back, "Thanks. He is creepy."

Hope nodded her agreement and headed back to join Norman at their table. On hearing her chair scrape the floor Norman looked up from his liver and bacon. He asked, "What's up?"

"Washroom break sweetheart. I'm back and hungry."

He asked, "Care for the last bite? It's great."

"No, I'll stick with my fish and salad. Much more to my liking."

"Ah! Spoken like a true fisherman's daughter."

Hope ignored Normie's jibe. She answered her rising hunger pangs. They vanished quickly. Over tea a second movie date was confirmed. Smiles between Mary and Hope were silently exchanged as they left the restaurant. On the drive home Hope listened as Norman chatted up recollections of times past spent with Garth and the boys. Back home at Gilbert's hugs and lingering kisses were freely tasted. On parting, Hope gazed with intent at Norman. She broke her silence. "You're a sweetie Norman. I think you'd best leave the G Man in your past if you want me!"

Norman's jaw dropped. Hope stepped out of the vehicle. "Trust me. He's not the Garth you once knew." Then she swung the car door shut and walked towards the house.

Norman fought off an urge to follow Hope inside. He had heard warnings since moving back home. Other buds out of his past had warned him about Garth when the name had arisen in conversations. The taste of Hope lingered on his lips. The taste sealed a wise decision. The driver's door opened and he chased down Hope. He took her hands in his and said, "Sorry Hope. You're right. I was foolishly grasping to my past. I've heard talk of Garth's bad life choices. You win." They kissed. Then separated and Hope, watched Norman drive away. Once the taillights vanished, she stepped inside.

Downstairs Gilbert's loud booming voice returned Hope to the present moment. He called out. "Lunch is on the table sweetheart! You'd best move it."

It freed Hope of her savoured moment of recollection, a flashback memory that had passed in mere minutes.

The first arrival in the kitchen was not dressed in purple. Aroused by Gilbert's lunch call, Bailey raced, not fast but trotted into the kitchen. Immediately he sought out the chef and entered plead mode. The move worked. On arriving Hope shook her head in disapproval. Bailey ignored the human body language being exchanged between his lady and the chef. The mackerel fillets set before the beast were the focus of his attention. The phone rang. Gilbert answered it. Hope watched him carry the conversation with a series of head nods. It ended on Gilbert saying. "Ok. I'll be there shortly." Then hang up the phone.

Lunch ended up a one person setting. Gilbert apologized, "Sorry Hope. The meeting's now a lunch meeting. I'll have to pass."

Hope shrugged and helped herself to a serving. As she ate Gilbert carried the conversation. It avoided touching on Chester's newest residents. Gilbert a seasoned parent had already spotted the zip in Hope steps in recent days. He wondered can she see it in me? He eyed Hope.

She protested "What? Did I do something?"

"No. Just admiring your outfit. It looks good on you. Purple always has been your colour."

Hope smiled back across the table. She struggled to remain low keyed. Afternoon plans called for a meet up and outing with her man. Her Norman. "Oh my God! I do like this outfit. However, dad, I dare you go pick one any one of the photo albums you and mom loaded up with photos over the years. The outfits I grew up wearing. Granted some were cute. But heck so was I. But the ugly ones. What were you and mom thinking?" Light laughter broke out. Both parties quickly drove it into fits of uncontrolled laughter.

Gilbert recovered first. He stumbled through a recollection, "You were four, no must have been five years old. Your birthday. Mom picked out your birthday gift. A purple, pink and orange jumper suit. It had yellow laced cuffs, neckline, and trimmings." A glow of joy flowed off his face. Gilbert boasted, "You loved it. Strutted about like a crowned princess."

Hope eyed her dad. She boasted, "I still do."

"Then before I head out for my meeting, I'll go dig it out of those boxes we stowed up in the attic. And one day my granddaughter to be can where it."

"I'm not pregnant!"

"Someday I trust. Sweetheart I'm in total envy of Maria. She's a grammie. I want' a be a grandpa I do." He paused. Then added, "No pressure sweetheart. But when the time and factors are right. That's the gift I'll savor."

Hope stared in wonder across the table at her dad. An image of her pregnant sister Lyndsey popped up in her head. It carried no heartache or envy. Only joy. The joy of soon becoming an auntie. She licked her lips and savored the taste of earlier kisses and the taste of Normie's lips.

Hope knew if abracadabra and snap of the fingers could grant that gift, she'd shoutout a double abracadabra in the blink of an eye. Instead, she sighed and smiled. After all dad had let the cat out'ta de bag. He had a meeting. A bonus that would leave her free to connect up with her man. A glance revealed her plate was empty. She suggested, "Leave the cleanup to me. You'd best get ready for your meeting."

Gilbert and Hope stood up. He walked around the table and hugged Hope. "Are you sure?"

"Yes Dad. Git out'ta here. I've got this. Catch you later."

Gilbert sighed. He walked out of the kitchen savoring the intentional slip of the tongue he'd let fly earlier. The results fit his plans perfectly. Ten minutes later he set off eager to be on his way.

CHAPTER 11

A quick run to Chester rewarded Gilbert. On arriving at Anya's, he parked the truck and headed to the porch and front door. The door opened and Anya greeted Gilbert. On stepping outside, she closed and locked the door. Back in the truck seatbelts were secured and they headed off to their lunch meeting. The truck filled itself with light conversation as it headed off to its destination the town of Hubbards. There Anya smiled on seeing the restaurant Gilbert had chosen. Inside their waitress walked them to a secluded booth. Seated Anya stared at Gilbert across the table of their booth. The cozy Hubbards restaurant added a relaxed feeling to their outing. The glow in Gilbert's eyes rekindled feelings she had savored on bumping into Gilbert as she headed to a recent *Weight Watchers* meeting. So much had happened. The horrors and nightmares had faded a bit over the years. Although she rued the call made years past, in her heart Anya believed she had made the right move. Yes, it had separated her from her roots. However, at times choices just had to be made.

Their waitress returned. Anya ordered a seafood salad, Gilbert opted for a Caesar Salad. They shared light conversation until their meals arrived. A quietness followed while they ate. On finishing their waitress cleared their table.

Gilbert broke Anya's train of thought. "I chatted with Norman while shopping on Saturday. He's a sharp young man." He gazed into Anya's eyes. Long suppressed infatuations stirred feelings in Gilbert's heart. He pondered Harley's most recent update. Anger bubbled beneath the surface of his persona. He suspected he now knew who Norman's father was and that explained away many of the actions that led up to Anya fleeing and cutting off all connections with family and friends. Especially Karyn and himself. Even though Karyn's passing had hastened in passage, the hurt he'd caught expressed on Karyn's face remained a difficult memory to cast aside. Afterall, they had been the three amigos. Images of the best friend connection between Karyn and Anya restrained Gilbert's rising affection for the beautiful woman seated across from him in their booth. In reflection he realized they'd almost become an item back in the day. However, it never came to be. Karyn made the first move. A confident composed young lady, she liked what she saw and quickly lay claim to it. Had she been less confident perhaps things would have worked out differently. But Gilbert knew he would never have traded what had been, his Karyn, for what could have been? He sadly recalled how racial bigotry had crushed Anya's self-confidence over the years. She'd never admit it but those close to Anya saw more potential in her than she believed existed. In glancing across the table, Gilbert smiled at the glow and self-confidence expressed on Anya's face. He had felt no sexual desires since Karyn's passing. An image of Gail his office administrator reminded him of opportunities he'd worked diligently to avoid. What potentially could there be for an old dog like himself? A glance downward at his belly revealed a physical attribute that he'd lacked in his youth. Questions raced freely through his mind. Would any woman be attracted to him today? He peeked across the table. A sigh escaped his lips. A stirring signalled life where none had existed in ages. Gilbert pondered their previous encounter and asked himself, could the *Weight Watchers* thingy work with the likes of me?

    Anya broke his line of concentration. She smiled and boasted, "Yes, Norman was quite excited about bumping into Hope at work. He beamed with pride and boasted how great it felt to chat with her." She paused and a glow radiated from her face. She continued, "Claimed he'd never been hit on by a hot babe before! I believe the direct quote was, 'Mom. I've never been hit on by a such a hot babe before!'"

They both laughed lightly. Gilbert added, "Yes, after our chat Hope explained how earlier she'd bumped into him while grabbing a quick lunch at the store deli. On spotting him she did a double take. Then they struck up a conversation. Hope hinted it felt like there'd never been a break in their connection. She lit up like a thunderbolt in telling me how they'd reconnected! It confirmed that she actually knew about your return before I did. And I'm told you chatted with Maria and Jeff the other day."

"I did and I was amazed how he beat out his is speech impediment".

Gilbert nodded. "Just this summer past, it was a totally unexpected blessing."

Anya smiled warmly. She replied, "Sorry it took so long. I hated how he suffered through the ignorance of so many locals. I'm glad he finally broke through."

Gilbert nodded his head in agreement. Yes, it has been a total blessing, being able to reconnect with Jeff and share the feelings we'd been denied earlier."

Anya smiled and asked, "Are Jeff and Maria an item?"

"Yes."

"I'm not surprised. Actually, I'm glad. Back in the day they were a matched set. Until that…"

"It really broke Jeff's heart. Kids can be honest in their words. Back then their parents simply fed on and spread vicious rumours about Jeffery and us McClakens. Whatever it was, he just struggled in trying to express himself. He was always a good kid. Mom always called our Jeffery a special brother and son." Gilbert relaxed chuckled then added, "Yup! I can fondly recall a time or two we were glad he couldn't express himself. It kept Karyn and my actions and hidden from Mom."

Anya giggled softly. Their eyes locked on each other's. She stopped then suggested, "I can recall thinking that you and Karyn had never fooled your mom. It's a woman thing. Not all communication is via the spoken word."

Gilbert chuckled on thinking back and recalling a fast one or two he'd savored as having fooled his mom. Both relaxed. Their thoughts focused on recollections of how Hope had been totally infatuated by Norman. Get togethers at their home or the Trinity's home had often found Norman assigned storytelling times with little Hope as his audience. Norman, he recalled had developed amazing oral skills through those storytelling sessions. Hope on the other hand had simply become infatuated with the older man in her life.

Anya broke the silence, "It's different seeing your own kids living through the life stages you think you aced. Suffice to say Normie keeps his mom up to date on his doings. In truth he always did. Thinking back, I can see some of me in Hope. Oops! Sorry but before Karyn laid claim to you, I too liked what the two of us saw in you. Thanks to God, and Karyn our three amigos relationship survived. My pregnancy? Simply stated it wasn't planned. Thanks to God, mom, dad, Karyn, you and your family I survived. And yes, the racial bigotry and slurs cut like a knife. But again, I never had to stand alone." Anya and Gilbert fell silent as both savored images out of their past. In them they were bonded together with Karyn the three amigos stuck together and committed to each other like peanut butter to a toasted midnight snack.

In a flash the Gilbert and Karyn recollections vanished from Anya's thoughts. A teary-eyed university Norman stood at his mother's side. Earth to earth ... Dust to Dust. Anya shivered recalling how the dirt had hit her daughter's coffin. Yes, Norman stood at Anya's side. She silently recalled the tears she'd shed staring out into a world of emptiness. August, their August did not. The shared mother-daughter moments lingered in a broken heart. Planned Parenthood had never been a factor in the creation of Anya's tight knit family unit. A single Mom, the love of her son and daughter had been an endless blessing in her life. Endless until her beautiful August had discovered the truth. They had drifted off into a deep sleep. A mother and daughter, asleep, embraced in each other's arms. Anya had been wiped, tired, drained from working an unexpected double twelve-hour shift at work. August had been struggling through a nasty ongoing bullying session at her school. A brother is a brother. A mother is a mother. August had needed her mother and Anya rued how she'd agreed to work the extra shift. They had needed the money. It bought August her graduation dress. A dress her baby would wear through eternity.

"Anya what's wrong. Are you OK?" Gilbert asked. Tears flowed freely down Anya's cheeks. Gilbert reached across the table feeling helpless. He took Anya's hands in his. Staring helplessly at Anya he wanted to kiss away her tears. Propriety stopped him dead in his tracks. The warmth of Anya's hands in his felt right. Gilbert saddened inside on feeling Anya pull free of his grasp.

"Sorry. I'm so sorry Gillie...Gilbert. I should never have returned." She picked up a serviette and wiped her face free of its tears. "I've felt the questioning looks of locals out of my past. Their stares confirm my worst fears. However, I just ha..."

"I, I could never, would never..."

"I know. Gilbert. I know. Through it all you, Karyn, Jeffery, Grammie, Pappy, were there and supported us. Mom, Dad, as you know, they've passed on. Our families were connected. Not kin folk but family all the same." Both sat in silence staring down at their table. Anya broke the silence. "After Dad's funeral service and gathering at the church, Mom spent the night at Monica Felton's home. They were lifelong best friends and companions. Monica's husband had passed on two years earlier. I was alone at home that evening with my Normie. He returned! The bastard returned. Once wasn't enough! That's why I fled. On awakening from that assault, I knew what had to be done. One look in the mirror, I survived. The bastard believed I was dea..."

"Oh my GOD, Anya you should have run to us. Karyn, me. We would have..."

"No. I couldn't I just had to escape. I believed, I still believe Norman, my little Normie saw what happened! He's never asked why we moved away. He may not remember. It could be he has blocked it out."

"Anya!"

"No. Let me finish. I had to return. It had been in the works for several years. After Mom passed on, I kept the family home. I rented it out through a property manager. I wasn't ready to return. It's said tragedy strikes in threes. The third strike was the killer for me. From that second assault a blessing arose. A daughter my August rose up out of the horrors I'd been exposed to. My God oh how, I miss my dear sweet August."

Gilbert took Anya's hands anew into his. Their faces lifted upwards and stared blindly into each other's. "I'm a personal care worker. It pays our bills It has supported us over the years. August struggled through mean-hearted bullying sessions at school. We're not of a pure-blooded African Nova Scotian heritage. Dad was and had the audacity to fall in love with a white woman. August was thirteen, a sweetheart and a spitting image of me at that age. My God, but my baby was beautiful. Her skin just like mine, my August professed proudly of our heritage. Our generation has failed. Racial bigotry still exists. Its evil and hatred lives on."

Gilbert squeezed Anya's hands. In his heart images of Anya at thirteen flashed through his mind. At her side stood a fifteen-year-old, love smitten Gilbert with Karyn's arm wrapped about his waist. He nervously bit his lower lip.

"What happened to your August?"

Anya sobbed. "The day we'd fallen asleep embraced in each other's arms, I was physically wiped. I must have relived my horrific past through one of my endless nightmares. My August heard me shouting out pleading for mercy. She shook me free of my terrified sleep. She asked. In error I foolishly confessed." Anya's sorrow broke free. She sobbed. Gilbert released her hands. He ran around the table and embraced Anya. Anger arose within Gilbert. "I killed my sweet August! I murdered my baby!"

Gilbert tightened his embrace of Anya. The heat of her body drew memories of what it felt like to have another's body touch yours. Anya's hot tears soaked through Gilbert's shirt then flowed down his chest. He felt totally helpless. An image leaped to the forefront on his mind. The face of Anya's tormentor, the face of one never charged or fully investigated a nemesis to most law-abiding locals. Sadly, Gilbert knew a regime of feigns addicted to the benefits of loyalty to the nemesis still existed.

Anya whispered, "My August blamed herself. The bullying had destroyed her bubbly personality and confidence. His hand reached out from my vile past and murdered my baby … my August committed suicide."

Their waitress walked up to the booth. On catching them in a private moment she walked away from the booth. Ten then fifteen minutes vanished. The tears abated. Gilbert released Anya from his embrace. Both sat silently waiting for the right words to be spoken. Anya broke the silence. "I'm sorry Gillie…Gilbert. I should never have returned. Norman is working to complete his veterinarian's program. I got laid off from my position. Corporate restructuring, they called it. We needed a roof over our heads and decided to move back home to where all my miseries and joys started. Talk about stupid! One need not look any further than me!"

Gilbert, he held Anya tight to himself. In an embrace he'd not shared with anyone since the passing of his Karyn. Their waitress returned Gilbert nodded as he whispered, "Our bill please. We are ready to leave." On receiving their bill Gilbert paid at the bar. They walked out of the restaurant bar together. Several locals caught their departure. All-knowing sneers wiped earlier smiles from their faces. Conversations turned into an abyss of negativity. It failed to touch the ears of Gilbert or Anya. Emotionally distraught Anya remained silent through their drive home. On arriving at her home Gilbert parked in the driveway. A multitude of youthful memories flashed through his head. The pregnancy that resulted from Anya's first assault had at times raised envy in both Karyn and his hearts. Their efforts had continually failed to impregnate Karyn. However, their envy never turned into anger. Gilbert recalled how Anya had embraced motherhood. On Hope's arrival in their lives, they'd strived to walk in Anya's footsteps. In that aspect they had totally succeeded in their goal. The only hurt had arisen on Anya's fleeing Chester and cutting off all connections with that world. Karyn missed and needed Anya on her journey to life's end. The absence had fired up anger and hurt in Gilbert. Given what he now knew Gilbert's soul unburdened itself. He understood the actions taken and the whys behind them. He felt a need to nurture and love the lady out of his past who fate had brought into his life once again.

Could he consider leaping into Anya's arms and love's call? What would his family, his Hope say? Would Norman let a man anywhere near his mother? A multitude of questions flashed through Gilbert's mind. None of the questions concerned Gilbert. His heart and mind had bonded on supporting Anya and her emotional needs.

"Thanks Gilbert. I never meant to dump all my life's tragedies on your lap. Karyn was so right for you and you for her, back then. Back when hard choices had to be mad..."

"Yes and no, we, Karyn and I lived a magical loving life together. I'll never regret the love that magic caressed us with. But..."

"No. No buts, If I can recall a steadfast rule of grammar that was always your trademark. I need time to heal. I need time to rationalize all my emotional upheavals. Being with you feels so right yet so wrong, I don't want my garbage to mess up the good life you've lived. I don't wa..."

"But I wan..."

"No buts Gillie...Gilbert. No buts. Please give me some time. Give yourself some space."

"But I nee..."

"I better go. Norman will be home shortly."

Gilbert gazed questioningly into Anya eyes. She touched her fingers to her lips kissed them, then passed the kiss to Gilbert's lips. With reluctance Anya opened the passenger door and stepped out of Gilbert's truck. She closed the door. A smile broke out on her face on reading the lettering on the truck's door. 'LOBSTER CAPITAL OF THE WORLD ... WE CATCHES THEM ... WE COOKS THEM ... WE EATS THEM' She waved to Gilbert then walked up to the porch and front door of her home. On retrieving her keys, she unlocked the door, then turned back to Gilbert and waved goodbye. He returned the wave. Anya opened the door and stepped inside. Once the door closed Gilbert backed out of the driveway and drove home. Both parties struggled to focus on the moment at hand.

Anya felt alone in the empty house. Inside a struggle played itself out. She'd avoided attempts by men to enter and share their life with her. Gilbert's plea had touched several heartstrings. A sense of horror and lost joy reminded Anya that her August had been conceived in the house through the terrifying assault she'd endured. The love she'd treasured growing up in the house kissed her soul. She rued that August would never feel that love buried deep in every part of the home she, August's mother had been raised in. Anya felt an unearthly sensation touch her soul. No, it went beyond a touch. It caressed her soul. She whispered, "Mom, Dad is it you? Thanks, I love ya." Anya rested her back against the hall wall. Each of her parents had spent a lifetime professing their love to Anya. The front door opened Anya froze on sensing the presence of another love, her son, Norman. She pulled herself free of the wall and turned towards the door. Mother and son smiled on catching sight of each other.

"It's OK, Mom. Sorry I'm late. Traffic was heavy. I'm here now. I love you." Norman's words softened the pain in Anya's heart, but not the ache felt deep in her soul. Norman stopped on catching sight of his mom's watery eyes. A hug ensued. He asked, "You ok, Mom?" He released her on feeling her lips touch his cheek.

"I'm good, Normie. I'm good. Just got caught up in a shared moment with our August."

"Hope you told her I miss and love her bunches, Mom."

"I did and she knows."

Norman hugged Anya anew. Then released her and walked off towards the kitchen. He called back, "Good! I'm hungry, Mom. See you in a bit."

Anya walked into the living-room and claimed the sofa. On feeling comfortable and snug on the sofa, she gazed out the room's window into a starlit sky. In the distance the glimmer of a bright light flickered. In a flash she felt embraced by a warmth. Slowly Anya felt the warmth of her August's spirit touch her body. Time stood still. Its passage impeded by callings of two connected souls. Anya's heart skipped a beat. She sensed the presence of the love that had been ripped from her side.

Lightheaded Anya stared off towards the glowing light's trail. She felt a light touch her face. She pondered is this a reality or heartache racing through my mind? A voice out of the past sang sweetly in Anya's ears. She savored its sweetness. It was the voice of August and it warmed her heart. Its words echoing in Anya's mind. She whispered, "August, August is that you? Please don't leave me, I ... I love you."

"And I love you." The voice whispered back softly.

Anya stared in wonder at the vision that held her captivated. The familiar sight emerging painted a loving glow on Anya's face. Cloaked in a light golden flowing gown that kissed the sweet beige skin within its folds, Anya immediately recognized her daughter. A gladdened heart carried Anya forward. With arms outstretched she reached to embrace her daughter. But her arms simply passed through the image embraced in her heart. She whispered, "I love you so much ... So very, very much."

"And I love you too Mom." In Anya's heart August swooped down and their lips touched each other's cheeks. The touch of August's lips on her cheek felt warm, but hesitant. Anya pulled herself away and frowned. Concerned Anya asked, "What's wrong August? Your kiss ... you hesitated. What's wrong?" Anya looked deep into her daughter's eyes then pouted when a tear trickled down her cheek. Anya repeated her question. "What is wrong sweetheart?"

August frowned. To Anya she whispered, "It's time for me to move on. Embrace life mom its sweetness awaits your touch. I love you."

"No. No sweetheart. Don't go. I don't want to lose you again!"

"Mom, where's the peanut butter?" Norman shouted out to his mother.

"In the pantry Normie. It's in the pantry." August faded out of sight. Anya pondered had she just experienced a true blessing? Had her August come home? Had she just blessed their move back to Chester?

Norman touched her shoulder. Anya sighed then settled with ease deep into the sofa. Norman sat beside her and wrapped his mom in a panicked embraced. His heart raced wildly in his chest. "Mom, Mom, are you ok?" Anya shivered lightly then her eyes fluttered nervously. Norman sighed. He tightened his hold on Anya. Her eyes popped open, both mother and son gasped, then relaxed. Each eyed the other. Anya pulled free of Norman. She sat up then stood. Norman joined her. They embraced.

Anya kissed her son and whispered, "I'm ok. She's with us. Did you see her?"

Norman frowned and stared with questioning eyes at his mother. She broke free and walked off into the kitchen. "Your toast is burnt Normie. I'll put more on." Norman walked cautiously into the kitchen with his cell phone in hand. Anya greeted him, "I'm good. Don't worry."

CHAPTER 12

A brilliant late November Sunday morning's sunshine greeted everyone stepping out of the church. Hearty greetings and friendly chats broke out. Maria glowed standing by Eugette's side seeing her daughter bask in the attention of her coworkers from the Lobster Pot Pub & Eatery. She smiled at them. Each greeted Eugette with an all knowing and approving twinkle in their eyes. The twinkles vanished as they spotted an old Buick moving slowly past the church. Its driver a nemesis to most that watched it drive past. Tensions eased once the Buick turned at the corner and vanish. Megan and Taylor tugged at Grammie's coat sleeves. With hints of mischief in their eyes they pointed at their mom and her friends. Maria set her parental ears into total alert. She focused on the twins but stole and occasional glance towards her daughter and her entourage. All eyes were locked on Eugette. A glow lit up Eugette's cheeks. Her audience grew impatient. Following a sigh she answered, "Oh! John is the brother of the groom. Nice but not from here. A true CFW Come from Away." Chuckling broke out in mass.

Tara shouted out, "Saw ya down by the ferry with him. With Johnnie and must say the lad's got a nice butt!" Laughter broke out in full force. Tara added, "Amazing lips too! Iff'in what I saw them a doing with yours was fer real!" The laughter deepened. Eugette nervously nibbled on her lower lip. Tara asked anew, "Well? We're all ears!"

Jennifer grabbed Eugette's purse. She retrieved its cell phone. On flipping it open she selected recent calls. A solid list revealed one number. It wasn't a local one. Eugette grinned and reached out to her phone held by Jennifer. She stated. "Ok! I'm into him. My phone please." Jennifer smiled and boldly pressed call on a link to Eugette's man. She held the phone to her ear. An inquisitive grin owned her face. The called line sang out at the line's other end.

"Hey Sweet Thing How's my special hug?"

Jennifer held the phone out offering it to Eugette. She boasted, "It's your man, Sweet Thing. He's asking for his special hug."

Eugette replied. "Ok! I'm into him." Deep inside Eugette savored the taste of John's lips and a shiver raced through her body on sensing her Rusty's eyes taking in the scene from on high. The sensation triggered by guilt buried deep in her heart. Mikie Slivers and Ned's words whispered in the back of her mind. She wondered could John be trusted? Would he believe, could he believe? No one else had bought into the questions that continued to feed the anxiety that troubled Eugette. She smiled and declared, "Ok! We did kiss. Once or twice. My phone please." With her phone in hand, she coyly greeted her man, "Hi Johnnie. Gads, I sure do miss you."

All coworkers sang out together, "Your sweet thing misses you too Johnnie!" Laughter broke out. Each of them squeezed Eugette's hand with care in parting. Jennifer and Tara treated themselves to a hug before stepping away from their treasured co-worker and schoolmate out of the past.

Eugette joined her mom and twins. She kissed the cell phone and whispered, "Hello? I'm still here Sweet Thing. Sorry. My coworkers are stringing me along. Dying to dig up some good stuff on you and me. If you know what I mean?"

"Oh! Trust me I know. Tell you what cell phone kisses are ok. But lack the taste of a real kiss."

"Don't I know it!"

John sighed then suggested, "Want a real one? We're but two hours apart. Hop on a plane. I'll book it. We'll be in each other's arms before tomorrow's sun rises."

"Oh my God! Don't tempt me, Johnnie. I can almost taste your lips on mine."

"Then let's do it!"

"Sorry. I can't I've never flown in a plane. Just thinking about it scares me."

"Ok! But if an irresistible urge hits. Call me. We'll make it happen!"

Eugette walked over and joined her mom and twins. She kissed the cell phone and whispered, "Later sweet thing." Quickly the church parking lot emptied. Together they walked over to their vehicle. Once inside her vehicle a twist of the ignition key started the engine. She gazed at her cell phone's screen displaying a listing of her recent calls. She blanked the screen and returned the phone to her purse. They drove out of the church lot and headed home. On arrival the car emptied and the twins raced each other up to the front porch. Maria joined them. Quickly Eugette headed to the house. At the front door she released a sigh of satisfaction. The door was locked. It appeared her cautionary words were getting through to mom? Eugette just felt better and secure inside the house with the doors locked. A smile rewarded Jeffery in his absence with thanks. Eugette suspected he'd convinced mom to lock up the house when not home. Another positive entered Eugette's thoughts, as she recalled how with each passing day the growing glow that bloomed in her mom confirmed love was afoot in her life. Eugette savored a hunger to experience feelings akin to those currently caressing her mom's heartstrings.

Once the door was unlocked the twins ran inside and headed into the living-room. A flick of the remote switched on the television. Maria ended up in the kitchen after freeing herself of coat and scarf. Eugette ended up in her bedroom. A glance connected her with her late husband. Their bedside photo spoke of much happier times. She slid a guilty tongue over her lips. A voice in her heart spoke gently to Eugette's heartstrings. *'Our promise my love. Embrace it. We promised each other we'd always savor and welcome love's gifts in our lives. I miss you and the love we shared. Its sweetness lingers to this day on my lips. Sadly, my life has ended. Stolen in the heat of our youthful passions. Please allow love to touch and caress your heartstrings throughout the adventures yet to be. Embrace it. It'll touch our babies and you. I truly miss you love always*

Rusty. The photo blurred through tear-stained eyes. Eugette dabbed the tears away with a tissue then stood up. Recollection of the exchange with coworkers at the church drew a hiccup followed by a coy smile to her face. Cartoon voices called out to her from the living-room. Eugette walked out of the bedroom. She called out, "Mom."

"I'm in the kitchen love. Our babies are in TV land."

"I'll be right with you mom." In the kitchen a cup of steamy tea awaited her arrival. Seated at the table Eugette wrapped her hands about the mug of tea. She said, "Thanks mom. I really need this."

"I know. How'd you find our church service. The message really touched me today."

"Yes, it was a good one. I felt myself slowly recapturing my faith and its life

values."

Maria smiled across the table to Eugette. "Me too Love. Never lost mine. But have questioned many things of late. Like you it also touched me."

"Where's your man Mom?"

Maria smirked then replied, "Gerry Jones called yesterday and needs help on an engine repair. Men, they can't resist the opportunity to play with something mechanical. Said he needed to get an early start."

Eugette raised her mug and sipped at its hot peppermint tea. On returning the mug to the table she answered. "I'm glad Jeffery is in your life."

"Thanks sweetheart. It just feels so right. I'm so glad you convinced me to join you at the wedding."

Eugette chuckled and boasted, "It wasn't me, mom. It was Hope's doings."

"Really?"

"Really mom. And don't worry. She filled me in on the details."

"Details? What details?" Maria asked.

Mother and daughter locked eyes. A moment then two slipped by. Eugette answered, "You were inseparable. Schoolyard sweethearts is what Hope told me."

"Yes. We went to school together. It was an age thing."

"Yup! That's what Hope told me. Walked hand in hand to and from the bus stop. And someone I'm told was spotted on numerous occasions stealing kisses from her embarrassed schoolmate."

Maria sighed. A glow radiated from her face. She whispered, "I loved him back then sweetheart. I loved your dad and married him. Our love was special and rewarding. But right now, I need and want Jeffery in my life."

Eugette stood. She walked to her mom, knelt down and the two women hugged. No words were spoken. They released each other and Eugette stood up. She retrieved her mug of tea and walked off to join the twins in TV land. Maria remained seated at the table. A myriad of cherished childhood memories raced through her head. Each memory relived tugged warmly on her heartstrings.

Later that evening, Eugette found herself curled up under warm bedcovers. Reflections of the day pulled at her emotionally. In many ways she envied her mother who had a man at her side. Laughter rising out of the kitchen carried mom and Jeffery's voices to Eugette's ears and heart. A sigh confirmed the wants astir deep within. Eugette flipped from her cell phone e-book to phone mode. One number dominated her recent calls. A photo of its owner deepened Eugette's sigh. Work had kept them apart at Thanksgiving. Hope assured her their efforts to entice Richard, Lyndsey and John into a Seaside Christmas adventure were on track. Lyndsey had commented that John's cell bill of late would easily cover his travel expenses. Staring at the photo displayed beside John's number she set her dial fingertip in motion and speed-dialed the number. A satisfied smirk crossed her face as the phone called out to its desired connection. Each unanswered ring tempted Eugette to disconnect.

On the third ring John answered, "Hi Babe. Everything ok? Loves ya!"

A series of soft kisses sailed over the airwaves. Each warmed its recipient's heartstrings. John felt strange on first asking how the twins were fairing. But as each of the twin's updated adventures was shared

John grew hungry to be back at their side with their mom. A relaxed sigh sang out to John's ear. He grinned on being asked, "Christmas, do you do turkey?" The line fell quiet. One end pondered an answer. The other eagerly awaited an answer. An option was offered up, "We could do lobster? But Christmas down here in Chester tends to be turkey."

"Is this an invite?"

Eugette sighed. She answered, "If it gets you down here consider it an order. I need and want you in my life." Eugette rued, had she over committed? Recollections of the good times shared at the wedding on the dancefloor kept drawing her back wanting more from the relationship. Rusty had lit up her heart and life. She missed that feeling. Seeing mom embracing love anew added fuel to Eugette's wants. It wasn't jealousy. But a need to feel a semblance of the love lost with Russel stolen from her side, her family's side. A series of short sobs leaped past Eugette's lips. She fought to suppress them. The encounter with Barnie two days past flashed wildly in her head. It angered Eugette. The man exuded evil pure and simple.

John cautiously asked, "Are you ok? Is there a problem Love? Was that a sob I heard?"

John's words, cleared all recollections of Barnie from Eugette's mind. Her heart savored the word, 'Love?' Favorite tunes called out to her heartstrings. With each beat Eugette floated about the wedding dance floor in John's arms. Time had gained speed since the wedding. An event she'd almost considered not attending. A smiling image of Hope popped up in her heart. It vanished. Recollections of swirling about the dance floor with John eased her guilt. Whether lost at sea or otherwise, Eugette knew Rusty was gone. His return was not an option. Hope had nudged John and Eugette towards each other with resolve. Could their relationship survive the pressures of separation? Separation deepened by the miles that stood between them and kept them apart?

John broke the silence, "Turkey ... Luv. Turkey, we do turkey. And I luv turkey stuffing."

"Yes!" Eugette shouted into the phone.

"I could fly in the week of Christmas, let's say early well before the big day and stay over bu..."

"Mmm... the sooner the better." Eugette cooed into the phone. "This distance thing sucks," she added. They both chuckled coyly.

"I'll talk with Rich in the morning. I've been worked on by Lyndsey. Work is busy but let me bounce some options off him and I'll get back to you. It would be great to be with family over Christmas. Actually, no I'll be there come Christmas. But I'll be flying. Rich and Lyndsey are leaning towards flying down the rails with VIA Rail. This will be our first without mom, dad, and our grandparents." The line fell silent.

Eugette pondered a reply. The thought of losing her mom weighed heavy on her heart. She'd already lost her dad and Rusty. Eugette knew the pain and heartache death delivered to its survivors. She paused then replied, "Sold! Book your flight. We'll make it work." A glance over to the photo of her and Rusty on the bedside table drew a tear to Eugette's eyes. In her mind she heard Rusty's words echoing, *'Promise me love. If something happens? Promise you'll love anew. Our babies need to be touched constantly by love's treasured touch.'*

The silence bothered John. He asked, "Everything OK? Are you still there?"

"I'm here John. Your loss just rekindled the pain of my loss, dad and Rusty. It hurts!"

"It does." John replied. He struggled to change the direction of their conversation. Finally, he asked, "How are Megan and Taylor? Oh, from the tidbits of downeast happenings I've gathered from Lyndsey and Hope I gotta ask, has Jeffery popped the question yet?"

Eugette took the bait. Sadness lost its grasp on her thoughts. She replied, "They're great. School and Jeffery are keeping them going non-stop." Eugette stopped speaking. She reflected on the reality that Jeffery could-would soon become more than just mom's man. He'd be family. She grinned and pondered, would that make Hope and me cousins? The sound of John's lips on his cell phone signaled a caress was flying along the phone lines to Eugette's cheek. She returned the welcomed caress. Idle chit chatting ensued. The call reluctantly ending with the exchange of goodnight kisses an hour later. Both parties quickly turned in for the night. Pleasant thoughts eased them both off into dreamland.

CHAPTER 13

With winter knocking on the door many savored memories out of the past quickened winter's pace. Life embraced reality. Back in the lecture halls of higher learning, Professor Gilbert McClaken lost himself in the needs of his students. Hope savored the excitement of her new position with Social Services. Some of the cases she was assigned ripped at heartstrings unaccustomed to the realities of domestic violence. Most rewarded her efforts to align her name with the clients' needs and give them hope in moving forward. The opening had popped up unexpectedly. Most days the successes far exceeded failures and setbacks encountered. The old McClaken homestead stood empty on many an occasion. Its owner off in Chester recapturing stolen moments out of his youth. Where Jeffery's heart continuously skipped a beat and more.

With Jeffery's presence at her mother's side and the twins back in school, Eugette sought out truths denied her heart and soul. John Ramsay had ignited feelings once reserved for her late husband. Those feelings still tugged at her heartstrings. A deep desire to uncover the truth behind the loss; deaths of Rusty and her dad tempered the want John offered up so willingly. The community and family nudged Eugette towards accepting the loss to the official line that proclaimed her men had been lost to the perils of a ravaging Atlantic storm. Had remnants of their lobster fishing vessel been recovered; perhaps she'd have allowed herself to reluctantly accept the line as an unwelcomed truth. In her heart, she knew her men were no fools. They'd never have ventured out given the storm forecast that had been broadcast leading up to their disappearance.

Waitressing at the Lobster Pot Pub & Eatery had exposed her ears to words that tended to choked the truths out of the official storyline. Words overheard out behind the Eatery fired up a need to uncover the truth. The need of an income tempered her anger. A glance across the kitchen caught Megan and Taylor up in a Rock, Paper, Scissors game with Grammie and Jeffrey. She blew kisses across the room to them then left the house. Work called.

Outside Eugette stepped into her vehicle then drove with regret towards work. The Lobster Pot Pub & Eatery jumped into view. She signaled then drove into the Lobster Pot's parking lot. Hesitation overpowered her. Following the conversations, she'd overheard recently she now truly believed her dad and Rusty had been murdered. With Eugette's resolve solidified, she quickly lost her sense of comfort in working at the Pot under the controls of its owner. She sighed on catching Rusty's hazel eyes in her mind. A shiver ran through her body. Had Rusty witnessed her stepping out and connecting with John at the wedding? If believed all actions playing out on earth were visible through the eyes of those gazing down from on high ... from heaven. A guilty head waved side to side acknowledging the sinful ways she'd flaunted her body on the dance floor. Even their babies Megan and Taylor had witnessed their mother's lewd behaviour. With a sigh she asked herself, "Am I an unfit mother?" A fist banging on the driver's window broke Eugette free from her condemning thoughts. A twist of her head drew her eye to eye with the screaming face of her boss.

"Git your whore's ass in'ta de Pot Girlie! I won't pay to have your useless ass sitting out here in the parking lot!" Barnie grunted and drew a goober up out of his throat. In anger he spit it out onto the driver's window. Eugette cringed. Her eyes slammed shut hiding Barnie from her line of sight. Loud slamming of his fist on the car's roof cast Eugette into an abyss of fear. She sobbed. Barnie stepped back from the door and tossed his arms skyward in frustration. A blue car drove into the parking lot. Its occupants glanced over at Barnie, then exited the vehicle and entered the Lobster Pot. Barnie huffed and puffed then turned and walked over to the front entrance. Eugette nervously watched the man she hated enter the Pot's front door. Nervously she nibbled at her lip. Should she give credence to Mikie Slivers and Ned's overheard conversations? Had she stuck her nose and ears too far into places best avoided at all costs? A moment then two slipped by. Eugette consoled herself in the knowledge that they needed the money, the pay checks and tips she earned to support their meager lives and lifestyles. She retrieved a fistful of tissues then stepped out of the car. On locking the door, she vigorously wiped up the slimy goober Barnie had hurled onto the driver's window. A glance over at the entrance deepened her pent-up resolve. Eugette whispered, "I can do this. The bastard can't beat me. I'll do it but there are other options. Hell, I can flip burgers. Did it once and I can do it again?" A co-worker waved from across the parking lot. Eugette joined her and they entered the Pot together.

Inside they continued chatting up greetings with their co-workers then walked off to the employees changing room. Everyone had expressed eager interest in gaining more minute details on how the big wedding had played out. Time failed to temper interest in the lore of the event. Topping off their priorities, who was the stud Eugette had been spotted driving about town with? Were they still connected despite the distance separating the rumored couple? Once changed into their work clothes the ladies stepped out of the employees' room.

In the hallway Barnie stepped out of his office. He eyed Eugette up and down and waved her into his office. She obeyed with reluctance. Inside the office Barnie closed and locked the door. Eugette cringed. He spat out, "Take a seat. We need to talk sweetheart!"

All Eugette's womanly cravings for the opposite sex vanished in the blink of an eye. She glanced over to the door.

"It's locked!" Barnie boasted. "We need to have a serious one-on-one talk." He sat on his desk and waved Eugette over to an empty chair. She refused to take it. "You've been hobnobbing where's you should never be at girl. Those McClakens don't walk on water. They're trouble.

"They're God fearing and honourable people! Nothing like the trash I'm looking at!"

Barnie leaped off his desk. Eugette froze where she stood. He grabbed her blouse then in rage viciously slapped Eugette's face in anger. Her body swayed back and forth reacting to the vicious slaps Barnie delivered. They stopped. Barnie angrily yanked then released his grasp on Eugette's blouse tearing it and exposing her body. She tumbled to the floor curled up in a ball. Barnie stared in disgust at Eugette a curled-up ball. "Shut it bitch!"

The sobs turned silent but continued. Through tear-stained eyes Eugette stared at her aggressor. Red hot burning sensations leaped off her cheeks seeking refuge in Eugette's soul. Seething with anger the aggressor walked around the source of his enraged anger. First, he drew his right foot back then in anger delivered a volley of kicks to her back. He then stooped down and pulled her upright. The aggressor and victim's eyes locked onto each other's. Barnie blinked. Eugette shivered inside. She rued the day she'd boasted about being hired by Barnie. She eyed a trophy sitting on a wall shelf. Anger almost won out. In her heart she wanted the man dead. Images of her babies called out to her from deep within. The trophy remained on the shelf. She glared at Barnie. He retrieved a new waitress's blouse from a cabinet. "You'd best change you look a mess."

Eugette eased over to the door and grabbed the door handle. The door refused to budge. Their eyes locked again. Barnie stated, "You're safe. It's dead bolted. Now change. Or I'll do it for you!"

Terrified Eugette broke into a bout of deep shivers. On Barnie reaching towards her she started to unbutton her blouse then twisted her back around so it faced Barnie's eyes. He grabbed her shoulder and pulled her back around. "We'd best be making sure you're not hurt." He ripped the blouse off her body. It dropped to the floor when released. Barnie eyed Eugette's breasts. Drool dripped from his mouth. He grinned and sneered, "Lassie you've been too long without the services of a real man."

Fear gripped Eugette's body and soul. Quickly she slipped into the new blouse and started buttoning it up. Barnie interrupted her actions. He grabbed her by the shoulders and forced her to stare into his flushed anger ridden face. Aroused he whipped his fly open and fumbled to retrieve the beast inside his boxer shorts. Disgusted, Eugette clenched her fists together and drove both with vengeance up into Barnie's groin. He gasped and dropped to the floor clutching his crotch with both hands. Eugette twisted away from the fiery red blazing eyes that held her frozen in their grasps. A cell phone sang out from her purse. It distracted her aggressor and she ran away from him. She spotted a clutch of keys on the desk and grabbed them. At the door a series of keys failed to unlock the keyed deadbolt. Finally, one succeeded! Eugette pulled the door open and ran free of her aggressor. In the hall she turned right. Then ran into the employees' room and retrieved her purse. Terrified Eugette ran out the back door unnoticed. Once outside she ran to her car. Inside she fumbled with the car's keys. A pause followed by a deep breath restored her sense of being. A twist of the key and the engine stuttered then started.

Words failed to fly out past her lips. She drove out of the Pot's parking lot. A sense of relief embraced her. However, fear continued to hold Eugette in its grasp. Outside Chester she continued to drive with no destination in mind.

Back at the Pot Barnie relocked the door. A loud knock called out from outside the office door. He shouted out, "What is it? I'm busy!" Nobody answered. Silence befell the office. He grabbed his cell phone and called Ned who answered on the second ring.

Barnie whispered, "The little bitch stuck her nose in where it doesn't belong. She knows what happened."

"Really?" Ned asked. He added, "Don't look at me. My lips are sealed!"

Barnie sneered and answered, "Not likely. I warned you. I told you to zip it up in her presence. She's bad news. If she talks in the wrong places we could be in trouble!"

Ned continued to stare blankly out his apartment window. Disbelieve arose within his mind. None of the options unfolding hinted at positive outcomes. He knew what options existed in Barnie's world.

"Look Ned. None of this had to happen. If you idiots had only kept your mouths shut about past doings. Look she stepped out. Keep an eye out for her car. Hell! You'd best haul ass on over to the Lamont house. If she headed home and spills her guts we could be in trouble! Move it my son. Haul ass!" Barnie disconnected the call. He locked-up the office and headed out front where he helped tend to the Pot's bar and cash register. He announced to the staff that their co-worker had requested a shift change. Most staff frowned with disappointment. They assumed he referred to Eugette and rued on losing access to another update on the status of their pal's love life. Deeper regret and anger flowed like poisoned darts from the eyes of several staff members. Barnie's continued success as owner and the driving force behind the Lobster Pot Pub & Eatery's financial success angered them beyond comprehension. They knew his successes varied greatly dependent on which set of books one based their views on. Outside a select group of insiders and those unwillingly caught up in the actions the illicit activities driving Barnie's wealth into overdrive were unseen. Out of sight out of mind. Unfortunately staff desperate to taste a little of life's sweetness became pawns hungry to climb the ladder towards financial success. The moral and personal cost they endured in all cases quickly skyrocketed beyond everyone's control.

Finally, the Pot closed down for the night. Barnie locked the doors and joined the last staffer outside. First, he drove past the Lamont house. The bitch's car was not there. Slightly relieved he headed over to Ned Stone's apartment. In his mind the time for action had arisen.

CHAPTER 14

Gilbert walked into the Halifax restaurant. He glanced around and spotted his lunch partner. A waitress approached him. He pointed towards his destination and said, "Thanks, but I'm with Inspector Kingston." The waitress nodded agreement and waved him on. At the booth Harley Kingston stood up. The two friends shared a handshake followed by a jovial hug. Gilbert released and eyed Harley. He boasted, "I see you're slim as ever. I wish! But good dining is my downfall. Always has been."

"It's just me. Never could put on the weight my doctor swore I needed. It's more in kind to be my Bev's fault. God, I miss my lady."

Gilbert nodded agreement. I'm with you on that one Harley. Miss my Karyn big time. And time's passage hasn't eased the hurt one iota." The two friends sat down across from each other in their booth.

Harley shook his head in distain. He muttered, "So the son of a bitch is still walking the streets a free man. And I use that term loosely. He frowned. Bastard's guilty as sin, but just too connected in the wrong places. Correction, the right places from his viewpoint."

"The bastard is no friend of mine."

"Damned right or mine. We could have had him dead to rights. But as I've repeated often my investigation was shut down. Lack of credible evidence they said. Drop it or there'll be regrettable consequences."

Gilbert frowned acknowledging the frustrations Harley encountered working to nail shut the cases involving Chester's Barnie. His career in teaching had exposed him to many obstructions and career bumps over the years. Money and connections talked. Like Harley, Gilbert had never regretted his station in life and the values they'd been raised with.

Harley grinned all knowingly. He whispered. "I never shut it down, my friend. I will nail that sorry son of a bitch." He snickered, "My basement office is filled with boxes of records compiled over the years on those cases. Keep on working with me and we'll nail him and his band of well-placed cohorts."

Their waitress arrived and they ordered. Gilbert surprised himself. He followed Harley's led and ordered a vegetarian offering. Harley asked, "Have you seen Anya Trinity of late?"

Gilbert frowned. He answered with a negative nod of his head. However, the question drew fresh recollections to mind from his long past love smitten days of youth. Along with his recent reconnect with Anya. Recently through Harley, he'd come to know the truths behind several East River youthful broken hearts. Anya's beautiful smiling face called out to his heart. Its ebony-ivory skin held him captivated. Gilbert struggled to suppress the truth from Harley. He suspected the task was a mission impossible.

Harley recognized the hidden truth in Gilbert's response. He interrupted Gilbert's captivated state. "He got her twice my friend. And she wasn't the only one. When the truth is out, he'll be doing big time. I'm working on the side with a young lad posted to Chester. He's clean. He sends me copies of investigations that could be linked to my investigation."

"Then there is substance to young Eugette's beliefs?"

"Damned right there is. And it goes beyond that. We won't nail him and his on most of the doings. Sadly, in many cases victims are reluctant to move forward with charges. The passage of time only builds on their reluctance to take action. It reflects the sad state of our legal system. Gilbert, do you know many of the staff at the Lobster Pot Pub & Eatery in Chester?"

"One personally. Eugette Walker, Maria Lamont's daughter, and a number just to see them. A number of the women are connected. They are friends and chummy within their circles."

"I'd like to talk to them on the sly. I'll need you to connect me. Do you think Eugette would be willing to talk. I believe she can help in building up my investigation?"

Gilbert nodded then answered, "I do. I will talk to both Eugette and her mom, Maria."

"I'm with you there Gil. I believe she can help me."

Gilbert paused. Then added, "Give me a day or two. I'll talk to her mom, Maria. She knows a number of Eugette's coworkers personally. They grew up with Eugette over the years and have stuck it out I hear."

Their waitress returned with their meals. Conversation centered on Gilbert's enjoyment of the vegan meal he'd ordered. It busted his preconceived leanings towards a meat and taters dining preference. Harley chuckled over Gilbert's positive comments extolling the great taste of his vegan meal. He recalled how Bev had after years of effort finally succeeded in nudging her man towards a diet that leaned heavily towards the vegan offerings. Both men savored recollections of special times shared with the women in their lives. Harley towards Beverly and Gilbert definitely savoring his Karyn. Harley hinted once or twice that he suspected Gilbert could be seeing someone. Both times Gilbert denied the suggestions.

Their waitress returned and cleared off the booth's table. Both men refused the coffees offered. Quickly she departed then returned with the bill. Gilbert reached out and accepted the bill and said, "I'll touch base with Hope and we'll talk to the Pot's waitresses on the side. I'm sure they'll gladly agree to meet up with you."

"Great!" Harley answered. Here's some of my cards. I'll touch base in a day or two." He stood and reached for his wallet and said, "Seeing you chow down on vegan fare was worth the expense. Please let me pay."

Gilbert brushed him off. "No! This one's on me my friend. It's been great getting together. And that veggie thing wasn't bad." Gilbert smirked then admitted, "Actually I really liked it. A refreshing shift in my dining."

Harley grinned boldly. He replied, "It's a Greek dish. I highly recommend you try more." The men exchanged a hearty handshake. Harley braced himself for an expected hug. They separated and walked out of the restaurant. Gilbert's stride flowed with confidence. He savored the recollections that had arisen on mention of Anya. He cautiously savored the feel of her body embraced in his arms back at the Hubbards restaurant. He'd not been with a woman since Karyn's passing. He frowned. An ire arose within him. Cancer had hit them hard. Ripped their lives apart. Denying access to the golden years they'd planned for and savored throughout their time together. He surmised that Harley's mention of Anya held meaning and confirmed she also suffered like the others. An angry reaction arose in Gilbert's soul. He entered the university building. On entering his office, a friendly smile greeted him.

Gail, his assistant smiled. She updated him, "Hope and Maria called. Oh! Three English 101 students stopped in. They all pleaded to see you asap. That Elise Rose with her blue eyes locked so onto you? She needs, an extension on her paper. Oh! Your meeting set for 5:30 p.m. today has been rescheduled to Friday morning at 10:00 a.m. I confirmed you were good with that." Gail's admiration of Professor Gilbert McClaken glowed on her face. A youthful spinster she had seen her Gillie through his wife Karyn's illness and passing. Gilbert nodded his thanks and walked into his office. Gail ran a wet tongue over her lips. It raised her inner cravings. Her eyes closed and she sighed. Brrring...ring! The office phone called out and tore Gail free of her inner desires. The afternoon flew past unimpeded. Throughout its passing gnawing bits of information shared with Harley over lunch fired up a hungry need to know in Gilbert's soul. He cut his day at the office short. On the drive home to East River, images of Anya Trinity pulled him closer to her. In some, a teenaged Anya taunted his once raging youthful hormones to vistas never imagined possible. One cut deep. It portrayed sadness beyond comprehension. The look he'd captured on her face back in the restaurant embraced in his arms. Her words etched sorrow in his heart, *'I killed my sweet August! I murdered my baby!'* Recent ones fired up a wanting and desire to reconnect with a love arising for one connected deeply to the days of his youth. In East River Gilbert ignored the turn-off to his home. Another destination called out to him. In Chester he slowed to a crawl on approaching the Trinity house. The driveway was empty. He parked on the street in front of the house. Up at the front door he pressed the doorbell. It failed to call out. Gilbert knocked on the door. He gazed down at his feet. Seconds turned into hours. He pondered should I leave? Will I be turned away anew? Light footsteps disturbed his thoughts. He looked upwards through the door's glass and caught sight of Anya approaching. He sighed. The door opened.

"Gillie!" Anya said with a smile. Somebody's heart skipped a beat. Or did both their hearts skip a beat? "Please come in. I'd say join me for supper but its only macaroni cheesed up with a side of sausages."

"Sounds great." Gilbert replied as he stepped inside. He closed the door behind him and followed Anya back into the kitchen. She directed him to the table and prepared a plate for him. Over supper they shared a light chit chat and exchange of thoughts. Gilbert learned Norman was otherwise occupied. The details were not revealed. Most of the chatting flowed from Anya's lips. He dried the dishes while she washed. Afterwards they made their way into the living-room. The room carried Gilbert back a decade or two. Sitting on the sofa their eyes floated about the room recapturing lost moments out of their youth. On returning from their adventures their eyes locked on each other's. Each wanted more of the temptation presented. Anya faltered first. She reached out and embraced her want. Eager lips discovered pleasures never before tasted. Sighing gained intensity. Instinct and desires soared. Long unfulfilled sexual cravings savored the pleasures offered up and willingly served to the soon to be lovers. The moment passed quickly. Sated their naked bodies bonded with each breath taken. Sleep befell Gilbert and Anya. Early morning's sunrise treated them to a morning both savored then tumbled back under the guiding hand of the sandman. Eleven o'clock arrived quicker than either had anticipated. A snuggle and morning kiss fully awoke the couple. Anya gathered up her clothes and ran off to her bedroom. Gilbert sheepishly got dressed.

Anya called out, "Would coffee and toast work?"

Gilbert joined her in the kitchen. The coffee and toast answered their needs. After they'd committed to dining out later that day Gilbert headed homeward. In driving back to East River Gilbert's focus struggled to remain locked onto the road and traffic. Back at the house he grabbed a quick shower and wandered about the house in search of Hope. The search failed. Gilbert treated himself to an unexpected daytime rum and cola. Sitting on a sofa chair in the living-room he relived memories of the evening he'd shared with Anya.

CHAPTER 15

September's newlyweds were enjoying a little Saturday morning alone time at home. Though a confirmed Mommie-to-be, their honeymoon continued to extend itself even though they had been back home a stretch. Lyndsey had also been nudging herself forward in response to a desired shift in her career. A shift she'd embraced over the summer spent in East River. Earlier inquiries had garnered positive responses over the summer. Standing in the kitchen gazing out the window she rued her failure to lock down a letter of acceptance in this year's Bachelor of Education program at the University of Toronto. Frustrated, she pouted in the privacy of the kitchen, while silently thanking Grandma Ramsay for the love and treasures she'd added to the kitchen throughout life. Treasures that today enriched Lyndsey's life. The short pout vanished with Lyndsey recalling the amazing love of Grandma Ramsay.

However, her disappointment did not vanish under the watchful eye of Grandma Ramsay. Lyndsey's passion towards the teaching profession had been ignited by her tutoring experience over an amazing summer in East River. Not to mention or disregard the occasional personal sales pitch by Uncle Gilbert. She wanted it. Licking her lips, she recalled several wants she'd savored and actually tasted of late. Lyndsey gazed out the kitchen window. A beach scene held her captive. The salty tang of sea air stole her heart. Grandma-Lyndsey's kitchen vanished. Sea breezes recharged her body in her mind and carried her back to a savored beach moment shared with her Richard. The recollections popped her dimples free on a smiling face. Joyfully they stepped Lyndsey through each stage of their shared day on the beach then treated her to a replay of their wedding day. Time patiently stood still. Lyndsey savored moments of passion lived in Richard's arms on their honeymoon. A longing touched Lyndsey. Visions of their B&B 'Manor Room' held her captive. An amorous Richard smiled up at Lyndsey crouched atop his hips. Both of their enamored eyes locked on each other. Her sheer lace negligee revealed a scantily clad body yet hid its aroused needs from Richard's eyes. He tentatively reached out to her. Lyndsey rose up on her knees. She coyly wet two rosette-coloured lips with her tongue. Richard stared in awe. Lyndsey reached out grabbed Richard and pulled him towards her. He sighed. Their lips touched. Under Lyndsey's control the kiss exploded the needs of the newlyweds. Time stood still yet raced by unimpeded. Lyndsey pulled away from Richard. He attempted to embrace her anew. His advances were rejected. Richard submitted himself to Lyndsey's lead. Slowly she proceeded to free her man from his imprisoning clothing. Each item removed landed warm inviting kisses on the exposed body revealed to her eyes. Excitedly she pulled the last item free expos...

"I'm home my love." Richard's greeting and footsteps fell on deaf ears. On entering the kitchen, he stopped short at the sight of his wife. Slowly he walked up to her and sighed.

Lyndsey responded with a gasping sigh. She whispered, "Now Richie, let this be another passionate moment we'll savor throughout our lives. I need you. I want you now."

Richard wrapped Lyndsey in his arms then released her. She twisted about and sighed anew with closed eyes. He embraced her pulling her hips closer to his. He whispered back, "Gads I loves all of ya Lyds."

Lyndsey broke free of his embrace. She frowned and shouted, "All of me. But there is not enough of me Richie. I still don't show enough! Nobody knows I'm pregnant. I still don't have my bump...my baby belly!"

"Yes!' Richard shouted back. "I love it when your dimples pop out. Give her a week or two, she'll have you..."

"She is not a given Richie! She could be a he or he could be a she!"

Richard reached out and embraced Lyndsey. They hugged. "She or he, Lynds a bundle of love we'll have." Lyndsey giggled. Richard pulled her tighter. Foolishly he shared a recollection of a gender overseer's session with their neighbour Dolly. "Lyndsey let's give Dolly the credit she claims. Remember she performed a number of dangling threaded needle sessions. Each session predicted our first to be a daughter." Lyndsey did not reply. She did giggle anew.

Both pulled apart and twisted about to the sound of the front door opening. They raced each other out of the kitchen on hearing Roger call out, "Rich, Lyndsey, anyone home?"

Richard stood aside and Lyndsey embraced Roger briefly. On spotting Noreen, Lyndsey abandoned Roger and greeted Noreen with a mother-daughter embrace. Roger and Richard simply stood back and observed their ladies connecting. In silence they watched Lyndsey urge Noreen to walk with her to the den. Both men smiled. Richard asked, "When Noreen was pregnant?"

"Oh, I see. It's about the baby thing and memories of Noreen being pregnant with our boys?" Roger quickly answered. He grinned and added, "I sense a father-son session in the works Richard. She is frustrated, wants her status to proclaim itself to the world. Wants her baby belly to pop out and shout, "Hey look at me I'm pregnant!" Go ahead Richard tell me I'm right. I see that puzzled look on your face. Besides I've been there twice."

"No. No Roger, we're good. Besides Dolly MacGill..."

Roger chuckled in cutting Richard off short. He responded, "Rich! Forget Dolly MacGillicutty and her dangling needles. Had she been right Noreen and I would be the proud parents of two sets of twins, with both sets being girls." He shook his head in amused jest. "Richard, relax. I will speak to Noreen and have her reveal the magic of the birds and bees, along with that special nine-month journey you and Lyndsey have embraced." His belly jiggled with the laughter that escaped his lips. "Trust me Rich. I will not dare to explain the magic of a woman's body and pregnancy. In ten, twenty years' time, you'll laugh boldly in recalling this moment and my wise choice. You'll be in the companionship of the amazing creations the love you and Lyndsey share created. They'll look at you with the question and bewilderment I see on your face. Trust me. Noreen is the source of knowledge you need." He chucked anew and boasted, "I'd only totally confuse you. Their bodies are different. Their minds no, trust me I'll set you up for a chat with my lady, Noreen. I suspect Lyndsey is chatting up a storm with her now." Together they walked into the kitchen.

Roger grinned on spotting a full pot of coffee on the counter. Richard beat him to the pot and served up mugs of Lyndsey's freshly brewed coffee. Seated at the table after several servings from his mug, Roger raised the topic that had drawn him and Noreen to the Ramsay homestead in search of Richard and Lyndsey.

"Thanks for stepping in and settling up your parents and grand-parents' insurance with John. He called my office yesterday and updated me on his situation. And yes, he is still hungering to get back down east with Eugette. From our talk I gather credit goes out to both you and John along with Hope's interventions."

"It felt good Rog, Earlier all the frustrations and stresses that we found ourselves struggling to navigate were just too much. However, since our East River adventure and visits we are connected anew. Our working relationship is amazing. We sure need our new John at the office and boatyards. In truth I actually believe our parents and grand-parents somehow reached out and touched our shattered relationship." Richard paused then asked, "Any hints on John's thoughts moving forward?"

Roger laughed heartily then a look of deep thought covered his face. Richard missed it. Roger replied, "I agree Richard. John's actions and involvement with Tessa caught everyone off guard. I cannot confirm or deny participation from above, however I agree with your feelings regarding today's John. Had William, Bill, Maureen and Mary been privy to my phone chat with John today, John would have ignited pride in all their hearts."

"Had I only known, I could hav…"

"No Richard. I confess to having been blind to the affair. The rage and anger he exposed us to at the office during the probate of the wills. I suspect he ended up entrapped in the refutability of the eldest sibling's rights and entitlements. Add to that the insurance issue. It's good to see you boys reconnected. I won't ask you to detail the turn around that unfolded down east. We'll simply call the outcome a true blessing to all parties."

"Well put Roger. A blessing all around and it's great to be reconnected with my brother."

"Speaking of John, Eugette sur..."

"Eugette, Megan and Taylor's Mom, yes, she is Hope's best friend forever. They're a pair of friends connected at the hip."

"Great. She is the focus of John's leaning towards an extended Christmas absence from the office. He talked about heading down east for a Seaside Christmas with you know who at his side."

"Away with you Rog, John is itching to head off to East River for a Christmas with Eugette?"

"Yes. And little Megan and Taylor are adding a positive mix to John's itch."

Lyndsey walked into the kitchen with Noreen at her side. In surprise she shouted, "Oh My Gads ... Did I hear correct, our John's is planning to head down east for a Seaside Christmas with Eugette? I bet Hope is involved and nudging John towards booking and confirming his travel plans"

Roger spotted Lyndsey. He jumped up raced over and treated her to a trademark Roger all-embracing hug. Lyndsey slowly managed to wiggle partially free and asked, "We're going with him, right? I've never celebrated a Christmas with my baby sister. God! I can't wait to head off down east."

"No. John simply hinted that he's thinking about it. He remained committed to being here for and working through the heavy workload at the boat yard. But he sure lit up in chatting about Eugette."

"But..."

"Sorry Lyndsey. We're really busy. Maybe early in the New Year?"

A look of determination planted itself on Lyndsey's face. Noreen smiled on spotting it. Both Roger and Richard frowned. Noreen walked over to the counter and plugged in the kettle. She opened a cupboard and eyed the assorted packages of herbal teas. Lyndsey joined her. She said, "I'll take a mint tea. Its calming essence will help me gather together my thoughts." Noreen opted to follow Lyndsey's suggestion. She prepared two mugs of peppermint tea, and then joined everyone at the kitchen table. Lyndsey's eyes glazed with question looked over at Noreen. Words they'd shared in the den bounced around in her mind and heart. *Could it be she pondered? How could their passionate beach moments not be the magical moment of her child's conception? Efforts to recall the feeling she'd identified as the moment failed.* A sip of tea returned Lyndsey to the kitchen table and her companions of the moment; Richard, Roger and Noreen. On locking her gaze onto Richard, Lyndsey's thoughts and focus shifted towards convincing hubby and John that a Seaside Christmas eagerly awaited them down in East River.

CHAPTER 16

Driving towards Halifax Eugette slowly sold herself on the only option she saw open to herself. The drawing card pulling her away from home added a skip to her heartbeat. Safety was of paramount importance. Chester had lost its warm security blanket feel. The feelings felt foreign. Throughout life it had provided Eugette and her family a home and blanketed them in an unquestionable sense of comfort and safety. That blanket had been shredded and tossed aside less than an hour ago. Fears raced through her head. Had she reached the point of no return? Images of mom, Megan and Taylor struggled to pull daughter and mother back home. Home to Chester. Fear drove Eugette to stay the course. In wiping away the on and off again teary-eyed sessions personal resolve took hold. Eugette believed staying alive was the best route to guarantee her family's safety. Mom would be good once updated on the whys of her fleeing Chester. Traffic on the 102 slowed to accommodate the rush hour volumes. On passing the Sackville – Annapolis Valley exit volumes dropped and speeds picked up. Suddenly the moment of decision stared at Eugette. Exit 6 Halifax Airport. Yes, or no? In a split second Eugette flipped on her right turn signal. On spotting the sign 'Halifax Airport Park'N Fly she slowed then followed the directional signs. She almost turned around on sighting the Park-N Fly entrance. She pulled over to the curb and stopped. Being a widow sucked. The only positives surfaced recently on connecting with John Ramsay at the wedding. Eugette cursed, "Damn you Hope. Why did you nudge me towards John? He's aroused needs in me I buried in motherhood and the self-pity of my widowhood.

Eugette's resolve tipped the scales. She released the brake and drove into the lot. Once parked Eugette texted John and stated her intentions. His reply was immediate. She then replied with a promise to text once a flight was confirmed. Determined to follow through Eugette stepped out of her car. Outside the car she noted the lot's coordinates she'd parked in then walked back to the Park'N Fly entrance. Throughout the stroll her determination drove her forward. The actions unfolding would initiate Eugette into the world of the jet setter and accelerated travel aboard an aircraft. A nervous itch set her on edge. However, determination and a longing soothed the itch. Once inside the airport she opted to try one of the least busy Airline booths.

To her surprise and supressed joy, the agent asked, "Would a direct flight to Toronto with a 7:20 pm departure work for you Eugette?"

A smile broke out on her face. She blurted out, "Yes! And thanks for the great service."

"Are there and bags to be checked in?"

"No. It's a last-minute thing. No time to pack. Just gotta go!"

The lady agent and Eugette smiled lightly confirming agreement on her last-minute flight plans. With her ticket and boarding pass in hand Eugette headed to the food court. After she'd polished off a burger & fries a calmness touched Eugette's being. Foolishly she'd pushed the limits. However, she did not regret solidifying the truth behind her beliefs. In a sense she felt Rusty nudging her towards safety. On tossing her waste into the trash dispenser she wandered aimlessly through the airport. A quick text updated John with her flight details. On every second pass she eyed the entrance to the departure gates and security. Bright red signage drew her to a vendor's shop. There without hesitation she purchased three cooked lobsters. A treat to be shared at her destination. A nervous itch started to rise up inside Eugette each time she approached the security entrance. Finally on the third approach she succeeded. On eying her boarding pass the security woman waved her on through. She smiled and said, "Enjoy those seafood delights. I envy your intended diners. Have a safe flight."

Eugette twisted about and called back, "Thanks, I will."

On clearing through the security area and its scanners, Eugette headed off to her departure gate upstairs. Each step deepened her resolve. With an hour left to kill she wandered over to a book vendor and purchased a mystery novel. The first choice had been a love story. But she opted to avoid that subject until securely in her man's arms. She then headed back to her departure gate and started reading the novel. Her cell phone buzzed. Quickly she retrieved it from her purse. A series of taps opened messenger. There she eyed John's reply to her earlier text giving him her flight details. 'I'll be there, Love. Is everything OK?' Eugette quickly replied, 'Can't wait. Need and want you TOO!' She then powered off the cell phone. John's reply set her at ease. In a flash Eugette lost herself inside the novel's fictional world. A loud call out for passengers to board her flight landed Eugette back in the reality of the moment. Once aboard and seated she relaxed.

On surviving their aircraft's take off Eugette quickly dove back into her novel. The only interruption to her reading came in the form of a welcomed cup of coffee offered up by the crew. The flight arrived early in Toronto. Eugette followed the passengers in disembarking from the aircraft. Inside the airport she spotted John. Her pace quickened. She ran eagerly towards him and vanished inside John's welcoming embrace. A long lingering kiss ensued. Finally, she dared to pull away from John's body.

He eyed the box covered in red lobster prints. "For me? You shouldn't have. But I've developed a love for lobster. Well let's say a liking. The love part I'll save for you. They walked towards the baggage area. Glancing at Eugette, John spotted the awe in her eyes. Their surroundings were second nature to him, he refrained from making any comments. Beep...beep the luggage carrousel called out announcing the arrival of her flight's luggage. Eugette nodded a negative.

She added, "What you see is what you get. No baggage. Just me." Twenty, minutes later they arrived at John's SUV. Seated in the passenger seat Eugette watched John load the lobsters in the back seat. The drive to their destination passed quickly. The miles upon miles of businesses and housing intrigued Eugette. She did not harbour feelings of envy towards those that lived their daily lives in the fast-paced surroundings they drove through. In Newmarket, John touched the brake. The SUV slowed and then turned into the parking lot of the Blue Buzzard. The familiar surrounding eased John's thoughts. He'd avoided earlier dinning options. In truth the Blue Buzzard just felt right. Inside Eugette felt strangely at home. Her years of work in the food and dining trades contributed to the feeling. John waved to the bar and pointed towards his booth of choice. His intentions were acknowledged by a return wave from the bar staff. Seated in the booth their waitress approached and offered them menus. She commented, "It's been a stretch since we've seen you about John. Welcome home. The specials are chilli and a sandwich of your choice or all you can eat wings."

John replied "I'm hungry but not up for a feed of wings or chilli, make mine a hot hamburger sandwich."

Eugette pondered then said, "I'd love a grilled chicken wrap with a chef's salad I'm not up for chips at the moment."

John confirmed both orders then Caroline their waitress walked away from the cozy corner booth John and Eugette sat in facing each other across the table. Eugette took his hands in hers. Both gazed into the other's eyes. John struggled over the details that had been revealed to him by Eugette. Her mom had alluded to them while he'd been in Chester. Hearing Eugette confirm them as real deepened his dislike of Barnie into a hatred. In his heart he felt Hope nudging him towards the dance floor and Eugette at Richard and Lyndsey's wedding celebration. They had connected. Hesitant at first, Hope's assurances that she approved had drawn John willingly to Eugette's side. Images of her energized twins Megan and Taylor painted a smile on his face. Silently he pondered over how quickly one's life could change in the blink of an eye. Fear of parenthood, coupled with Tessa's sexual powers had led him to destroy his marriage. A marriage that he now knew never should have been. Connected eye to eye and through an energy flowing between their joined fingers their silence drew them closer together.

"Yes. Barnie my boss, manager...abuser, destroyed our lives. Mom, my precious Megan and Tay..."

John whispered, "Damn the bastard." He squeezed Eugette's hands tightly. In his mind he recalled his encounter with Barnie at Chester's Lobster Pot Pub & Eatery. Barnie grinned and stared at him. He held a bloodied fish bonker club in his hand. The image caused John's forehead to tingle. 'Bam, bam... two gunshots rang out in John's mind. A stinging sensation grazed his cheek. Crumpled in a stunned heap he pondered what comes next. The image of Tessa's face contorted with extreme hatred burned itself into his mind. Darkness closed in around him. He pondered could death be calling out to him? Faint voices bounced randomly through his thoughts. He whispered, "Mom is it my time? Are you coming to take me home?"

Next a vision of a fading island captured his mind, fed by the roar of a marine engine. Could it be that time's passage was calling out to him? Lives were drastically altered over the summer past. The ills of time's serving of evil drove a shiver through his body's core.

Eugette released John's hands. She reached out and grabbed his forearms. John's frozen face frightened her All colour had drained from his face. She shouted, "John, John what's wrong? Are you Ok?"

John snapped out of his mind's replay of its summer experiences. A smile across to Eugette relaxed her fears and grasp of his forearms.

Their waitress returned with both meals in hand. "Hope you're both hungry."

Both turned and eyed the huge plates of food. Eugette claimed the grilled chicken wrap, John the hot hamburger.

"Bon appetite," Caroline said then turned and walked away from their booth.

Over their meals Eugette updated John on news from East River. Both smiled over the fast-tracking relationship that appeared to be pulling Maria and Jeffery together. Eugette recalled a glance she cast their way back at the house. She'd spotted a look in both their eyes and faces. A look that had vanished on her dad's death. Silently she hoped she'd also come to share a similar glow. John gazed into Eugette's eyes. He laughed on hearing Eugette mimic Megan and Taylor greeting Jeffery. "Grampie Jeffy, Grampie Jeffy!"

He pondered will they connect to me with the love they're sharing with Jeffery? In his heart John felt a pang of jealousy towards Jeffery's connection with Eugette's twins. It quickly faded with recollections of Jeffery's positivity. Their East River experiences had definitely been an adventure. However, the outcomes had enriched the lives of all parties. In glancing over to Eugette John found himself caught up in the simple beauty radiating from her face. He suppressed an urge to kiss the peachy lips his eyes and mind had locked onto. Contented he sat and listened to Eugette's ongoing positive news updates from home. Most of it a mother's boasting of her children's classroom achievements. Both declined Caroline's teasing efforts with the dessert menu. On settling the bill, they exited the restaurant. On the drive back to his apartment John stopped in at the office. There he grabbed the file folder of his latest proposal and quickly returned to his SUV and Eugette.

At the apartment John followed Eugette's lead after he'd placed the lobsters in the fridge. He joined her and sat on the loveseat at her side. Smiles were exchanged. John placed his arm on her shoulders. Eugette flinched and pain reflected itself on her face. His arm pulled away from her shoulder. "Are you..."

Eugette cut him off, "I'm OK! It's a pulled muscle. I must have cramped up on my flight. It's nothing. Stupid me I fell asleep on take-off."

"I have some muscle relaxant rub. It's great stuff. A massage with my rub will work wonders on your shoulder."

Eugette frowned. How would John react to the truth? Had she erred in turning to him? The man's presence aroused her sexually. His touch connected them in ways she had not felt since the loss of Rusty. Relaxed and aroused she did not object to her top sliding upwards. Its progress froze. John cringed on seeing the purple, blue-green bruises that covered most Eugette's back. Sensing his shock-repulsion she shivered fearing rejection.

"Oh my God, who did this to you?" John stared mouth agape at her bruised back.

Eugette reached out and embraced John burying her tear smeared face in his chest. Time stood still frozen in the shock and fears of the embraced pair. John recovered first. He remained silent. He lifted her arm off his shoulders and raised both slowly up towards the ceiling. The purplish-blue bruises stood vivid in his mind. He slowly lifted the top up over her head and off. He took her hands in his, stood then guided her to follow his lead. Silently they walked together into the bedroom. At the bed's side she stooped and removed her shoes. Then stretched out on the bed lying face down on the bed. Shame froze her tongue. In silence she rued the ugliness of her body. John slipped back into the bathroom then returned with his tube of muscle rub. Gently he applied it to Eugette's bruised back. No words were spoken. The rub on penetrating the bruised flesh erased the ache from her nerve endings. His fingers accelerated Eugette's journey into a relaxed state. Her fears vanished. Sleep called Eugette to the escape of dreamland. There deep desires sent glowing warmth throughout her body. John retrieved a quilt from the walk-in closet. He smiled on hearing a series of light snorts escape from the Sandman's captive. The quilt settled over Eugette's sleep bound body. John walked out of the bedroom.

The bruising he reasoned had been inflicted very recently. Who he pondered fighting hard to suppress anger had beaten her so savagely? Prior to the wedding he'd only encountered Eugette while at the Lobster Pot Pub & Eatery. A face popped into John's mind. It snarled and cursed at him. Had the Lobster Pot's Barnie attacked Eugette? John recalled being served by their waitress Eugette at the Lobster Pot Pub & Eatery. His clenched fist and restrained an urge to curse aloud back at the mocking face in his head. In the kitchen he fixed himself up with a batch of peanut butter cookies and a glass of milk. Deep thoughts raced questioningly through his head. With all but one cookie gone John stood up and walked to the bedroom door. He gazed with wonder and admiration at Eugette asleep on the bed. The options open to catch a good night's sleep appeared scant. John retrieved a second quilt from the closet. He kicked off his shoes and lay down next to Eugette on the bed. A flick then two more covered him over under his quilt and added more cover to Eugette. Silence surrounded them. In time John worked through his pondering and drifted off into a deep sleep

CHAPTER 17

Sleep eluded Maria. Motherly instincts had held her a bay from the sandman's beckoning calls. Over the years her ears attuned themselves to the sound of footsteps on the front porch and the twist of a door knob. A teenaged daughter's comings and goings tended to sharpen her mothers' ears to those late-night sounds. Once trained, a mother's ears never failed to trigger alerts to missed detections. Maria opted to escape the turmoil of her restless night's sleep. It had not been her companion throughout the night into the early morning hours. The bedside clock read 5:32 am. She tossed the covers aside, crawled out of bed, stood and rushed into Eugette's bedroom. On stepping into the room, she stopped dead in her tracks. The bed had not been slept in. Panic set in. She turned and rushed off to the twin's bedroom clinging to the hope her daughter had spent the night curled up with her babies. That hope vanished. Inside the bedroom she spotted Megan and Taylor curled up under their covers fast asleep. She scanned the room, desperate to spot a sign of Eugette's presence. Maria twisted about and walked back down the hallway. She listened impatiently straining to hear any sign of her daughter's presence in the house. The house phone called out. Maria grabbed its receiver and shouted into it, "Eugette, where are you?"

A rued voice answered, "She's not with you? I've been working with the staff to track down Eugette all night. She never showed up for her shift. The girls tried to track her down but couldn't. We called 911 and reported her missing."

Maria breathed in deep fearful sighs on recognizing the voice. It was a voice she'd shied away from throughout life. Maria recovered, "No. She's not at the house. If you hear anything from my Eugette's coworkers please have them call back." With that said Maria slammed the receiver down onto its base. Shivers racing throughout her body triggered by Eugette's absence and more by the voice out of the past. She walked angrily off into the kitchen. There she grabbed her purse and retrieved her cell phone. On sitting in a chair, she dialed Eugette's phone number. The line sang out at its destination then went straight into voice mail. Frustrated she waited for the beep and said, "Sweetheart, it's mom here. Give me a call. Love ya and miss ya. Mom." With a sigh she disconnected the call. The process repeated itself this time Jeffery's line sang out on being speed dialed. The ringing line went unanswered. Maria sobbed. She called out, "God please! Where's my baby? Help me find her!" Maria collapsed onto the table into her arms. Tears ran freely down her cheeks. A desperate mother's tears soaked her cotton nightgown covered arms.

Megan had awakened to the commotion Grammie had set in motion. Running first into Grammie's bedroom, then into the kitchen she spotted Grammie at the table. She bolted and ran to Grammie's side on hearing her heart retching sobs. Megan reached out and hugged her Grammie. She cried out, "Please, don't cry, grammie. I'm here and loves ya."

Maria froze. She'd heard Megan shouting out again in fear, "Please Gram...Grammie, please don't cry!" Megan pleaded while embracing her Grammie. Maria silently pleaded for Jeffery to answer her call. A defeated Maria sagged; Megan released Maria from her embrace. She slid down onto the floor. Sad eyes stared up at a weeping grandmother. Grammie's face collapsed again into her arms on the tabletop. Life lost all meaning in that moment. Time stood still locked in a mother's worst fears. The line continued to call out to Jeffery. He had no voice mail options.

Suddenly a welcomed voice answered the line, "Hello. Jeffery her..."

"Oh, thank God! Jeffery you're home! Please Jeff...Jeffery, please come right away I need you. We need your help."

Panic hit Jeffery square in his chest. He almost stuttered in attempting to answer Maria's plea. The sobs the receiver delivered to his ear shook his heart. It raced inside his chest. He inhaled a deep calming breath. Then spoke in reply to Maria's plea, "I'm on my way Love. I'll be at the house in the shake of a kitty cat's tail. Maria, are you, Eugette and the twins, ok?"

"We're at the house. Megan and Taylor are with me. Please we need you. Eugette is missing!"

"Wait, could she be with Hope?" Hearing no response Jeffery shouted, "Ok. I'll call Hope then I'll head over. Ok. I'll be there in a jiffy. I'm on my way."

"Oh please! Please we need you now Jeffery." The phone line disconnected. Jeffery had hung up at his end of the line.

Jeffery in a panic speed dialed a number locked in his head.It sang out at the other end of the line. The call to Gilbert's house line went unanswered. He disconnected the line unaware that Gilbert had turned the ringer off to focus on his paper gradings a day earlier. A quick trip into his bedroom and Jeffery had himself dressed. He ran out of the house towards his truck. Inside the truck he fired up its engine. On driving out of the yard he opted to make a quick stop at Gilbert's. A third sense told him Hope's presence would be a blessing for Maria. He almost froze on spotting Hope walking away from the lit-up kitchen window at Gilbert's. On parking, he killed the engine and ran off towards the house.

....

Hope had dressed earlier then wandered downstairs into the kitchen. An unrestful night's sleep had kept her awake and fretful. Her energies depleted she'd opted to escape the bed. The silence that embraced the house tickled her curiosity. She pondered, where is Dad? Hope walked down to his bedroom. A peek inside revealed his bed unoccupied and undisturbed. Could it be? she wondered. Had his connection with

Anya overpowered his regular routine? She walked downstairs into the kitchen. At the counter she fired up the kettle. For some unknown reason the allure of herbal tea called out to her. Distracted from the task at hand, the unwatched kettle quickly burst into a full boil. A glance out the window treated her to a star filled sky. With her mug of tea in hand Hope strolled over to the table and sat down. Recollections of yesterday's outing with Norman filled her mind. Hope jumped out of the chair on hearing her cell phone call out from the living-room. She stood then ran towards the cell phone's beckoning call. The action robbed her of Uncle Jeffery's arrival. On grabbing the phone off the coffee table panic hit on spotting Maria Lamont's number and ID on the cell's screen. Hope swiped the screen answering the call. She shouted "Hi, Eugette? What's up? Why you calling me in the middle of the night?"

"She's not with you?" Maria shouted back into the phone."

"No. Why would she be?"

A moment of silence passed then she whispered, "Help me, Hope. Help me find my baby!"

Hope froze on hearing the kitchen door open then slam shut. Panicked footsteps deepened her frozen state. Maria's words echoed in her head, *'Help me Hope. Help me find my baby!'*

Jeffery ran through the kitchen. He'd heard her voice in the living room. On spotting her he shouted, "Where's Eugette? She's with you right?"

Hope stared in shock at Jeffery on hearing Maria's voice calling out from her cell phone, he grabbed it from Hope's hand and interrupted Maria, "She's not here Love. We're on our way. Hope is with me." Jeffery sighed. To Hope he said, Let's go girl. Maria and Eugette need us. He passed Hope's phone back to her, "Here, please talk to Maria she, needs you! Where's Gilbert?"

Hope jumped up and took her phone from Jeffery. She answered, "Don't know uncle, dad never came home last night." Hope slipped into her jacket and shoes and together they ran out to Jeffery's truck. All the while Hope kept up a steady encouraging conversation with Maria. She'd next to grown up a second daughter to Maria. The words flowed easily. At the other end of the line Maria's fears eased with each encouraging word Hope uttered.

Off in Chester, Maria rested against the kitchen table with the cell phone in her hand. She sat up in the chair. Megan jumped up and embraced Grammie anew. With her face buried in Maria's bosom she shouted out, "Please don't cry Grammie. Please!" Her muffled plea reached the ears of Taylor. In panic he ran into the kitchen to Megan's side and embraced her. He released her then joined Megan in protecting their grammie in a loving embrace.

Maria grasped the cell phone tightly in her hand. She embraced Megan and Taylor. Her heartbeat slowed. Time stood still in Maria's mind while Jeffery raced on driving towards Maria. Hope's voice and stream of supportive reassuring words eased Maria and the twins' fears. She released Megan and Taylor then stood up. Both looked up into their Grammie's eyes seeking reassurance that all was well. Maria stooped down. Kneeling on the floor she hugged them both. Her action worked. They relaxed in her embrace. Maria whispered, "We're ok. We're ok. Jeffery and Hope are on their way." Their embraces endured. They missed the crunch of gravel in the driveway. It went unnoticed.

Outside Jeffery drove up the driveway. His foot hit the brake and the truck stopped with the bumper only inches from the front porch. A twist of his wrist killed the engine. He withdrew the keys and held them in his hand. Neither action slowed him or Hope, down. In mere seconds they stood on the front porch. Anxious and concerned Jeffery knocked twice on the door, then unlocked it and ran inside. A glance into the living-room, then dining-room did not locate his quest. He entered the hallway and gazed into the kitchen and spotted Maria embracing Megan and Taylor. Maria gazed up and her eyes connected with Jeffery's. The threesome jumped up and ran to Jeffery and Hope, who stood in the hallway. The threesome quickly became a fivesome. Maria wrapped Jeffery in a love starved hug. The twins sobbing each grabbed onto Hope. Several, moments passed then Jeffery released Maria. The twins released Hope and turned to Jeffrey. They hugged his thighs. On catching sight of Hope again, Jeffery was released. Megan and Taylor twisted about and leaped into Hope's arms. Fear pasted itself on their faces. Both shouted out to Hope their version of their dilemma. Mom had gone to work and never got there. She'd vanished! Mom's car had vanished into thin air. Hope rubbed their backs and whispered a constant string of reassurances that their Mommie was ok. And Auntie Hope with Jeffery and Gilbert's help would find her and get her back home.

Taylor shouted out. "Call Johnny, Auntie Hope. He likes Mommie and will find her!"

"Don't be stupid Taylor, "John is far, far away and wouldn't know where to look for Mommie." She paused then stated, "We'd best get Poppa Jeffy and Mister Gilbert to help get Mommie back home!"

Maria slowly gained control of her fears. Secure in Jeffery's embrace Maria's sobbing abated. She whispered to Jeffery, "Let's go to the living-room." She turned to Hope and nodded. Hope responded and took control on the twins.

Once in the living-room they sat. Maria's face paled. She blurted, "I didn't believe her

Jeff! I failed my daughter. She's gone. I didn't believe..."

Jeffery tightened his embrace of Maria. "Gone where Maria? What didn't you believe?"

"I don't know what she overheard. I know she believes every word. Oh my God Jeffery,

She is right! I didn't believe her. I can recall both our men being secretive before the sea stole them from us. God forgive me I'm a lousy mother." Maria sobbed into Jeffery's chest. Jeffery slowly rubbed Maria's back. She relaxed in response to Jeffery's caring massaging of her back. Both fell silent. Internally she prayed Eugette's beliefs were not true. In desperation she suppressed the word, 'Murdered'.

Jeffery recalled the sadness that had befallen East River and its residents with the loss at sea of Martin and Rusty. A rogue wave had been the final ruling.

Maria stated, "Barnie called the house just before I called you. I was up and pacing the house fretting over Eugette's absence. It's just not her style. Where can my baby be Jeffery. Barnie said she never showed up for her shift. He put on his smiling nice guy mask and expressed concern about Eugette. Said her coworkers claimed she didn't show up at the Lobster Pot for her shift. Claimed he'd been working with the Pot's staff trying to locate her. There's no sign of her car here or anywhere. He claimed he called 911 and reported her missing. There was never a roque wave. My Eugette knew the truth and nobody would listen! I should have known then Jeffery. I know now. And my Eugette has vanished. My baby is missing! She's fled in fear Jeffery and don't ask me how, but that bastard Barnie is involved in it somehow! I just know!"

Jeffery wrapped Maria in an all-embracing hug. He whispered in her ear. "Stay here with Hope and the wee ones. I'm heading over to the Pot and I will get answers. We'll get your Eugette home safe and sound. Trust me love. Hold tight. Let's go to the kitchen. We're needed." He stood Maria joined him. They walked tentatively back into the kitchen. The aroma of fresh brewing coffee greeted them. Megan and Taylor smiled on spotting their grammie at Jeffery's side. The adults chuckled then burst into laughter on spotting the youngster's faces covered in cookie crumbs. Hope shrugged admitting her guilt in the cookie caper. Talk around the table centered on reassuring the children that all was well. Jeffery quickly polished off his mug of coffee. He stood. Maria joined him. They walked to the front door. Jeffery asked, "Could she have been hungry for a taste of John. You know. Just caught up in the moment and flown up to Toronto?"

Maria shook her head in an affirmation no. She declared, "My baby has never been in an airplane. She's often gazed up at them and shuddered in fear at the thought of being way up there in the sky. No that's not an option." They shared a reassuring kiss. Then Jeffery headed out to his truck. Maria stood inside the open door and watched him drive away. Hope, Megan and Taylor came to her side.

Taylor boasted, "It's ok grammie. Jeffery will find Mommie."

Hope closed the door. Together they walked back into the kitchen.

"They kissed. Grammie and Jeffery kissed." Megan jumped up and with a smirk declared to Taylor. Then added, "Grammie kissed him!"

"She did not!" Taylor shouted back. Then added, "He kissed her."

"She did so!" Megan shouted back at Taylor. She snickered and declared; "Besides girls are better kissers!"

"They are not!" Taylor shouted out and moved towards Megan with his lips puckered up.

Megan braced herself preparing to fend off her amorous twin brother. Maria pulled both Megan and Taylor tight to her side. Outside Jeffery smiled back at Maria and the twins, then got in his truck. Jeffery back out onto the street. Parting waves were exchanged. Then Maria closed and locked the front door. Megan and Taylor followed Maria back into the kitchen. Seated at the table everyone's head struggled to fight off sleep. Hope nudged Megan and Taylor out of their chairs. Maria followed her lead. They all ended up snuggled together on Maria's bed. Sleep eased them all free of the fears that had earlier ended their night of slumber.

CHAPTER 18

Jeffery drove into the Lobster Pot Pub & Eatery lot and eyed its lit-up interior. He slammed on the brakes. Once stopped he killed the engine jumped out of the truck and ran to the Pot's front door. There he angrily yanked open the door to the Lobster Pot Pub & Eatery. He walked inside and stared down Barnie standing behind the eatery's bar. The look on Jeffery's face alerted Barnie to a confrontation about to erupt. He grabbed his fish bonker and leaped over the bar and ran towards his foe. The Eatery fell silent. All early morning diners' eyes were locked on the two men. Several clicks sang out as their cell phones entered video mode. Jeffery shouted, "Where is she Barn, Where's our Eugette? If anything happens to her I, we'll…"

"Hold down Bugs… Jeffery my friend, I've been asking the same thing since Eugee failed to show for her shift yesterday." Jeffery pulled back from Barnie.

Several more clicks sang out. A couple entered the Pot. On spotting Barnie and Jeffery confronting each other they stopped dead in their tracks.

"Get yourselves seated. Jeff and I are having a private conversation."

The couple stood frozen in their tracks. Barnie glared at them. The forced smile on his face vanished. A snarl replaced it. The snarl took on a bright pink then an angry red glow appeared on Barnie's face and the screens of countless cell phones locked onto the scene unfolding. Barnie turned from Jeffery. He glared into the dining area. Connie and Debbie, the Pot's on duty hostesses leaped to the forefront of Barnie's eyes. Move yer asses, girlies. I ain't paying you to stand abouts looking dumber than Bugshit McClaken here!"

Jeffery reached out and grabbed Barnie by his shirt. Jarred back into the conversation at hand, Barnie turned back to Jeffery. His scarlet red face faded to a red, then pinkish hue. He smiled at Jeffery. "My apologies Jeff, my sordid past is sadly hard to cast aside. I'm working on it"

Jeffery released his grasp on Barnie's shirt. He stared down Barnie, "You'd best be losing it. Or I'll beat it out'ta yer soon to be sorry carcass." Silence engulfed the Pot its engaged combatants, frozen hostesses and patrons. The pause provided Barnie an opportunity. He slipped his famed fish bonker out of sight. He placed it in his jean's tool pocket. "My apologies, Connie, Debs please assist these patrons to a table." He avoided eye contact with all the patrons, eyes and cell phone cameras locked on him. "Jeffery, let's go to my office. We're all worried sick over Eugette's failure to show up at the Pot. Look at Connie she's working double shifts to cover for Eugee." Jeffery did not speak. A thousand and one feared scenarios raced through his mind. Images of Maria's tear-stained face kept him focused on the why of his encounter with Barnie. A glance deeper into his mind caught Megan and Taylor clutching Maria's thigh in fear. Resolve calmed Jeffery. He had promised Maria and the wee ones he'd get the answers they hungered after. A solid left itched to be released on the stupefied smiling face of Barnie he stared into. The itch never escaped Jeffery's restraints.

"Trust me, Jeffery! Everyone here at the Pot is worried sick over where our Eugee has gotten herself to."

With reluctance he listened to Barnie's words. He sensed many of the Lobster Pot Pub & Eatery's staff felt akin to the way Barnie had expressed their concerns. However, in the faces of several he detected fear and concern.

"Let's go to my office. Let these good folk get back to eating and searching thar brains. Maybe one of them will recall something overheard or a passing glimpse of Eugee they've forgotten? We do care about her!"

Jeffery nervously chewed on his lower lip. With reluctance he agreed. "Ok, your office works." He followed Barnie who'd turned and started to walk towards the bar.

At the bar, Barnie waved to Debbie. She ran to his side. "Debbie dearest, please be a sweetheart and cover off the bar and cash for me." Debbie nodded her acceptance of Barnie's request.

Jeffery smiled at Debbie. She reached over and squeezed Jeffery's forearm. The touch acknowledged Debbie and her coworkers' concern over Eugette's whereabouts. Jeffery gazed at Debbie. He stiffened on spotting tears on Debbie's cheeks. They nodded thanks to each other. Most of the girls at the Pot had been E's classmates over the years. He'd seen them growing up together. Jeffery held no doubt that Eugette's chums, like himself were worried sick over the where and whys that surrounded her sudden disappearance. Debbie's solidified his confidence in their support.

"Debbie whispered, "We'll find our Eugee. We'll find her."

Jeffery then followed Barnie past the bar into the hallway that led to the kitchen. They entered Barnie's office off the left wall. All eyes in the Pot's dining area returned to their immediate surroundings. Conversations pondered the substance of the meeting unfolding in Barnie's office.

"If a hair is out'ta place on E's hair I'll..."

"Relax Jeff. I tried calling both Maria's and you. All my calls went to voice mail. Except my last one. We're all concerned, just like you."

"I haven't had time to check my cell messages."

"I can totally appreciate that. Eugette's been our most reliable hostess since day one. Our staff and patrons love her. Barb and Terri have been checking out all Eugee's hang outs since she failed to show up. Our girls thrive on her. Eugee's tips top all the other hostesses combined."

"Maria, Megan and Taylor are worried sick."

"Have you reported her missing to the cops? I did. Each call in will escalate their response."

Jeffery pulled out his cell phone. Its voice messaging indicator blinked nonstop. His fingers flew over the cell's screen. The line called sang out once then was answered. "Chester Detachment Constable Olmstead, how can I be of service?"

"Hi Anna, it's Jeffery McClaken. I'm calling to report Eugett..."

"We're with you Jeff. A dozen, no two, have called in reporting Eugette missing. Barnie was the first call. It felt out of place. However, the calls that followed red flagged everyone's concerns. I just ended a call with her mom, Maria."

"What are you doing?

"We've set all our resources in motion. I have E's cell number. Double called all her contacts. If anyone has clues or tips on her regular, or out of the ordinary hang outs, please get them to us. We'll pull every string in our arsenal. We will find her. We'll find Eugette"

Jeffery bit his lower lip nervously.

"Call all her contacts. Talking to a friend can free up a misplaced memory or image. Is there a beau?"

"Sort 'a."

"Call him!"

"He's out'ta town. Up in Ontario."

"Would she be with hi..."

"No way, Anna ... she'd never leave Megan and Taylor home with Maria and not say a word about plans to travel. No. That's a no brainer. Eugette just wouldn't. Besides I'm told she's never flown anywhere before."

The line fell silent. Time stood still. Frustrated Jeffery nervously squeezed the cell phone in his grasp. "Jeff...Jeffery are you still with me?"

"I'm here!"

"I've got your number, Maria's and a host of others that have called in. We've fast tracked this one into action. We'll find Eugette and get her home safely."

"What can we do?"

"I've asked Maria and others. What is Eugette's vehicle plate number? What make, model and colour is her vehicle?

"I should know. But don't! I'm drawing a blank!"

"Go to Maria. She's frantic. Help her check Eugette's papers at the house."

Jeffery stared blankly over at Barnie. He answered, "Ok. I'm heading over there now."

"Thanks Jeffery. I'll keep you updated." Both parties terminated their call.

Barnie stood. He walked over to Jeffery. "We're with you Jeffery. Ned and the boys all swore they'd go all out not stop until she's…"

Jeffery stared into Barnie's eyes. His stare reached deep into the soul of Barnie. A nemesis of Jeffery's throughout their lifetimes. "If you've don…"

"You, Maria and the cops are on my speed dials! Ned talked to Mikie…Mikie Slivers. Mikie swore him and his lady would be a praying fer Eugee!"

Jeffery stood up. He inhaled and exhaled a series of long deep breaths.

Barnie read Jeffery's body language. "I'd never touch Eugee. We've had our differences, Jeff. But please give me a break. I'm not a monster. We'll find her! We will." No, handshakes were exchanged. Jeffery nodded his closure and turned towards the office door. Barnie followed his lead. The bar and dining patrons fell silent on spotting Jeffery and Barnie walking towards the Pot's main entrance.

Jeffery refrained from shaking Barnie's extended hand. The rejected handshake caught everyone's attention. Barnie stood silently. The sneer on his face followed Jeffery one of his foes as he opened and walked out through the doorway. The door closed Jeffery returned to his truck. Back inside the Pot, Barnie returned to his office. Inside it he slammed the door shut. Anger and frustration itched away at his soul. He pondered, just who do those fucking McClakens think they're fooling? My connections and business associates will take the bastards down off their lofty perches quicker than Satan could torch out the refund of an errant fool's soul. A deeper concern surfaced. I wonder who's seen Chester's newest home comer? The nerve of her. Who did that Trinity bitch think she was moving back into Barnie's digs? Had she reconnected with Maria? Both, Barnie reasoned, had aged with grace. They'd best not be talking up the past. History, Barnie grinned, more often than not repeats itself. He grabbed his cell phone. A double click and tap set Ned Stone's phone to ringing. Ring, ring, rin..., "Answer my biding now, asshole!"

Ned Stone eyed the ringing cell phone in his palm. Its display revealed the caller. Ned's committed resolve teetered. Both threatened outcomes terrified him. Barnie's threat could land him in prison. Barnie's threat would erase the fears of imprisonment. Ned trembled. Dead men don't do time. Their time is eternal. The cell fell silent. Thirty seconds later its ringing started up anew. Reluctantly Ned answered it summons. The caller had not changed. "Ned...Ned Stone here."

"Right, you're a tad slack in answering, my son. Have you been back out to check on my absentee staff?"

"Yes! But there's no sign of her anywhere, Barn. Simply stated, she's vanished into thin air."

"Shit. Where the hell is the bitch? You're a good man me son find her and I'll take care of you.

CHAPTER 19

A day later Maria fretted over the continued missing status of her Eugette, her baby. Miles away in a Newmarket apartment a couple stirred, then cast sleep aside. A warm arousing kiss did the trick. John cut it short. He sighed and inside embraced the new John, Eugette was creating. He asked, "Are we hungry? I'm a bachelor but can cook. Would eggs scrambled up with bacon work?"

"I like mine sunny side up. They add a little sunshine to my day, even on a cloudy day."

"Ok! Sunny side up it will be. The bathroom is down the hall. Grab a quick shower and I'll fire up the stove. Breakfast in fifteen?"

"Sounds good by me. Then I will need to hit a Walmart or Lady's Shop. I need something fresh to slip into." In walking past John, Eugette teased him with a sexually arousing kiss. Their tongues touched and their internal fireworks exploded. The kiss ended. Eugette pouted and said, "Care to check out the shower?"

John eyed her amorously. To his shock, he declined the offer. "No. I'd best get breakfast fired up."

She shrugged and walked off to the shower. On awakening and through their kissing session she'd felt John's desires stirring against her body. It felt good and she felt ready to commit herself physically to both their needs. The shower passed quickly. In shampooing her hair, Eugette felt reenergized. She shut down the shower, toweled herself dry, and got dressed. The aroma of coffee and breakfast called out from the kitchen. On arrival she took a seat and smiled as John served up his breakfast offering. Once they'd finished breakfast, John refilled their coffee mugs and they headed off into the living-room. Seated side by side on the loveseat, John suggested, "Should you call your mom? She'll be worried sick."

Eugette frowned. But inside she knew it had to be done. She pondered then said, "Ok. But let's use your phone. I don't want to turn mine on."

John nodded his agreement. John retrieved his cell phone and returned to the loveseat. He asked, "Does she have a cell phone?"

Off in Chester, Maria sat on the sofa. Jeffery quickly followed her with two fresh coffee filled mugs in hand. He set her mug down before her on the coffee table. He smiled she smirked.

Jeffery suggested, "We'll find her. We won't stop until she's safely back home with us."

"When Jeffery? This is totally out of character for my Eugee! I need to know she's ok!"

"Then join me and enjoy your coffee."

"Men they just don't get the mother-daughter thing!"

"No, we don't. Most hold it in an envious state of wonder. Me hopefully one day I'll get to treasure the envy!"

"Jeffery, is there someone you're planning on holding in that to be state of envious wonder?" Their eyes locked on each other. Jeffery leaned over and kissed Maria. The kiss lingered. Maria pondered. Oh my God. Could we? Motherhood came early as did my joy of embracing my grandbabies. Could my clock still be ticking? Their lips parted. Jeffery slid off the sofa. In the blink of an eye, he knelt at Maria's side. She cut him off before he could speak, "Let's recapture and share a touch of the love we were denied in our youth. I need to savor the flavor of its sweetness a bit."

The joy radiating from both their faces answered the unasked unanswered question. Jeffery rose up to her side and a hug ensued. Following a light kiss, they separated and Jeffery returned to his coffee. Unlike the couple, it had cooled off. Jeffery took both their mugs into the kitchen. There he placed Maria's in the microwave. Following its beep Jeffery's mug replaced Maria's in the microwave. Ring, ring, ring … the house phone sang out to both their ears. Jeffery twitched; Maria bolted off the sofa and ran into the kitchen to the phone. On picking up the receiver she smiled and burst into tears on hearing Eugette's voice call out, "Mom, Jeffery are you there?" Both sighed.

Maria answered, "I'm here sweetheart. Where are you. My God. Everyone is out searching for you. Why didn't you call sooner? God! I've been worried sick."

"I couldn't mom. I had to do something. I wanted to call. But I couldn't!"

"Where are you sweetheart?" Maria asked.

A pause ensued. Eugette broke the silence. She said, "Mom, I'm in Newmarket with John."

"You're where?"

"I'm in Newmarket with John Ramsay. You know Richard's brother. I flew up yesterday."

Maria sighed. She pondered were all her fears misplaced? Was it just a lovesick urge that landed her daughter in Newmarket? She firmly stated, "Eugette, we've been worried sick! A simple phone call. Or at least a hint towards your intentions! I'm not blind to love's beckoning calls."

The line fell silent. Then Eugette answered sharply, "I couldn't call MOM. And it wasn't a HOT FLASH that sent me scurrying to John's side."

Maria listened frozen with each word Eugette spoke.

"I asked too many questions Mom. I had to get away!"

Maria gasped and asked, "It's all about our disagreement over dad and Rusty's deaths. Isn't it?"

"Yes! It is Mom."

"Are we safe sweetheart"

"Don't trust Bar…"

"The BASTARD!" Maria's face paled. She added, "I won't. We won't. But I need to know you're safe. I need to just talk to my daughter like I could yesterday."

"Then talk mom. Just talk. I'm listening and Love YOU."

"Ok sweetheart. I'll try." The line fell silent briefly. Then Maria broke the silence, "But you've never flown before sweetheart. How was your flight? I take it all went well. What do you think of the big city?"

"How are my babies? Can I speak to them?"

The line fell silent. Eugette asked anew, "Can I spe…"

"No." Maria answered. "They spent the night with Hope and Gilbert."

"And you Mother?"

Again, patient silence touched the line. Then Maria answered, "I'm enjoying a coffee with Jeffery."

Eugette snickered then replied, "OK Mom. And yes, I had a good flight."

Maria smiled on hearing John comment, "She claims to have slept straight through most of it!"

"Did not," Eugette protested.

Maria laughed lightheartedly aloud. Eugette joined her. The minute passed. "Mom, I'm sorry for scaring the bejesus out'ta you and everyone else. Causing you all this worry. But something came up, something happened and I just had to get away. And YES, it's related to all of the chaos that has consumed my world of late."

Maria avoided acknowledging Eugette's comment. She continued her mother-daughter conversation, "You needed the break sweetheart? OK, I get it? What is the plan? How long will you be strutting about in the big city?"

"We're in Newmarket Mom. Not TO. I only flew into TO."

"OK. So, what are the plans now?"

Eugette snickered lightly. John took the receiver from her. He motioned with his free hand a need for more coffee. Eugette caught the motion and headed to the kitchen after catching a short sweet kiss. John waited until she was out of sight. Then he asked, "Mrs. Lamont did yo…"

"Maria please Maria works for me, John."

"Ok. Maria." The line fell silent. John broke the silence. He asked, "Maria, what happened to Eugette's back?"

Maria froze. Flashbacks to her grandbabies pleading calls for her to answer the fears revealed in a conversation she'd shared with them etched a shocked fear on her face. Ruefully she bit hard on her lower lip. The bite drew a taste of blood to her senses. She pondered, *'Why didn't I listen, believe my grandbabies. Grandbabies don't lie.'*

"Maria? Maria is everything OK?"

"Yes. I'm good John. Eugette's bac..."

"Yes. On the couch yesterday, she flinched on my massaging her neck and back. Against her protest I removed her top and..."

Maria frowned at the thought of her baby's nakedness in John's presence.

"E's back, Maria, what happened?" John asked. He fell silent on Eugette's return to the room.

Maria sighed on hearing John's question. She fell silent and her mind flashed back to the scene of her conversation with Megan and Taylor that she'd brushed aside. *'Megan had pleaded with Taylor, 'But we got to Tay. Grammie said if we ever needed a kind ear to shares a fear, we'd best be going to her. That's what Grammies is all abouts...' Taylor had responded, 'No Meg. We Can't. We'd be rat'ing on Mommy!' Taylor had then crunched up his face in an attempt to drive home his determined stance against squealing on Mommy. She'd seen that it just didn't cut water in his books. Taylor's growly snarly deepened. Megan had shrugged it off. 'You saw it. We saw it. And we both know the reason Mommy is so ugly and unpredictable is because of what we saw!' Taylor had then whispered back, 'What if it's really true? What if he really is what people say he is? Since summer he sure looks like he could be him!'* Taylor had then rolled his eyes in an all-knowing fashion that had irked Megan to the nth degree. Maria smirked on recalling how Megan had tried in vain to cast a look over at Taylor. A look she'd said Mommy had been casting her way of late. Little Megan had explained how she'd felt something was not right and had resolved to uncover the source of Mom's troubles. Until this week she had felt bonded in a rewarding sibling kinship with Taylor. Boys she had fretted aloud, *'It's true Grammie they're so slow. If it doesn't make excessive noise, generate offensive odors, boast of their superior body strength it's unworthy of open discussion.' Megan had revealed that her Mommy had slapped her harshly on the face just the day before. Not once but twice.'* Tears freely flowed down Maria's cheeks. She fretted and questioned why hadn't she listened?

Jeffery spotted the tears. He dropped to his knees and embraced Maria, neither one answered John's call out, "Maria, Maria, Jeff, Jeffery are you there?" Eugette walked back into the room. John smiled and whispered, "Maria I'll call back later, Eugette is ok. We're heading over to Richard and Lyndsey's shortly. Trust me I'll call back. Please don't mention we called. She really needs to chat with the twins. Give them hugs from us and use this number it's my cell line." He disconnected the line. He turned to Eugette and lied, "Your Mom will call back. They're headed over to Gilbert's to get Megan and Taylor. Eugette accepted John's words. She sat down next to him on the sofa picked up his coffee mug off the coffee table and passed it to him. They smiled and exchanged a kiss. John asked, "What happened to your bac…"

Eugette frowned and pulled away. She did not answer John. Her stance faltered under John's renewed efforts to discover the truth behind Eugette's battered and heavily bruised back. "First, you've gotta promise not a word goes beyond us!"

"Agreed."

Eugette snuggled up to John. He nervously fought off an emotional sensation that hit him full blast. Tears flowed freely down his cheeks. Deep within himself John felt reconnected to love and its world of caring that he'd been raised in. He listened in silence as Eugette revealed the truth behind her injuries and why she'd sought out refuge in him.

…….

Maria sobbed. Jeffery tightened his embrace. Maria wiped away her tears on Jeffery's shirt. She pulled away from him then stood. Their eyes locked and Jeffery stood listening intently to Maria's words.

"I need my grandbabies. We gotta go to Gilbert's now. I need to talk to my grandbabies!" Her body trembled. She suppressed the nervous edge and bolted towards the front door. Jeffery followed her lead. Once inside Jeffery's truck they drove over to East River. The truck pulled up beside Gilbert's truck and stopped. They both jumped out and both ran up to the kitchen door. At the door a smile broke out on Maria's face on spotting Megan and Taylor in Gilbert's kitchen window. The twins disappeared then suddenly the kitchen door flew open. Maria dropped to her knees and embraced her grandbabies who had raced to Maria eager to hug their Grammie. The hugs lingered. Hope and Gilbert joined the gathering on the porch. Smiles abounded in all gathered together.

"Grammie, grammie, did Mommie call? Where is she?"

A Grammie kiss landed on Megan's cheek. "Mommie is safe. Mommie is in Newmarket with John. She flew up to Toronto yesterday and is safe and sound. Now they're in Newmarket where Auntie Hope's sister lives."

"I like Lyndsey!" Megan boasted.

"We all do sweetheart. We all do." Maria sighed. She looked up at the adults gathered with them on the porch. Her face turned firm. She asked, "Could we be excused? I need to chat up a Grammie session with my Grandbabies?"

Taylor boasted, "But I'm the man of the house Grammie. You said I was!"

"You are Tay, you are. But first we need to sit down and have a Grammie chat."

"Ok." Both Megan and Taylor answered together.

Maria stood. Jeffery received a kiss. "Can we hold our Grammie chat at the homestead Jeff?"

Jeffery nodded indicating his approval. Maria rewarded Jeffery with a follow up kiss. She then walked off towards his home with Megan and Taylor each joyfully claiming one of Grammie's hands. Jeffery accepted Hope's offer of a hungry man's breakfast. He walked inside and joined Gilbert and Hope in the kitchen. He listened while Gilbert talked on the phone. The one-sided conversation piqued his interest.

"I agree Harley, and we've just learned Eugette is safe. She flew up to Toronto and is now up in Newmarket." Gilbert paused and listened. He answered, "Yes, in Ontario, with family. Yes, I'm eating my words. My friend, you were right from the get go. We need your help. Anya needs your help." On getting two sets of eyes and ears locked on him, Gilbert fell silent. He nodded silent responses to words that touched only his ears.

'What about Mary, Marie no Maria is anyone wise to her situation. She suffered the same atrocity that Anya did.'

"Oh my God! How many victims were there?" Gilbert asked with a deep sigh. Jeffery's ears perked up. Gilbert added, "I'd best go and call you back on my cell phone Harley." He glanced over at Hope and Jeffery. Both cast fixed stares at Gilbert. With a sigh he hung up the phone then walked out of the room.

Hope turned to Jeffery and cast silent questions his way. She had caught the signs of intrigue that had glowed on Jeffery's face. She broke the silence, "Uncle Jeffery, do you know what dad is talking about?"

Jeffery did not answer. Recollections from the past puzzled him. He did recall hushed up conversations that mom and pappy had discussed in great detail, but he was always shooed away before they'd openly talk it out. Sort 'a like how Gilbert's phone conversation had flowed. Mom and pappy's talks had mentioned Anya. Jeffery recalled how beautiful young Anya's ebony-ivory skin had been. It did not surprise him to see what a beautiful woman she was today. Eventually he'd discovered what the private conversations were all about. Anya had been pregnant and talk about town had been very derogatory towards her condition. He liked how his family had stood strong in support of Anya and her family.

Gilbert and Karyn had always supported Anya. They'd doted over her baby boy and the young lad he became. Eventually Gilbert married Karyn, a kindred soul and lifelong friend of Anya's. Both women had always treated Jeffery kindly with a gentle caring hand. Then the accident and little Hope arrived. Jeffery cast an eye Hope's way. Sadly, Jeffery recalled how Karyn had been lost to cancer. That recollection tugged at Jeffery's heartstrings. At some point he recalled how Anya had disappeared and slowly faded from his thoughts. That is until she had recently moved back home to Chester. Had time stood still or simply carried Jeffery through a rapid heart rendering flashback?

They ended with Hope shaking Jeffery free and back into the kitchen. She pleaded, "Uncle Jeffery, do you know what dad is talking about?" Hope fell silent.

CHAPTER 20

At the homestead Maria released both tiny hands she'd held on their walk from Gilbert's. She opened the door and the threesome stepped inside. Both children bit at their lower lips. They followed Grammie over to the living-room sofa and sat beside her. Maria embraced them both in a loving Grammie hug and all three relaxed.

"Nobody is in trouble, sweethearts. But your Grammie is so, so terribly sorry she didn't listen to you when you came to me for help. I'm truly sorry." A follow up Grammie hug ensued. Maria released her grandbabies. She asked, "Can we go back and visit that call for help? Grammie is so very, very eager to help make everything right."

Megan bit her lower lip on recalling the terrifying moments that had led up to their seeking out Grammie's help. A prickly stinging sensation added reality to her recollection. Mommy had always...always been nothing but love before that day. Megan's tiny teeth pressed harder intensifying their bite on a numbing lower lip.

Taylor shouted out, "Don't tell Meg. Mommie will hate us!"

Maria embraced both frightened grandchildren anew. The embrace lingered and assured both they need not be afraid.

Megan thought, what can I do to get through to Taylor? He was there with me. If he won't believe me who will? Not Mommy, that's for sure. She recalled the stinging sensations from Mommy's slaps on her face. Tiny tears started to tumble freely down Megan's cheeks.

Taylor blurted out, "Megan we should take Grammie and go talk to Jesus. He knows the truth."

Megan cast a perfect womanly glare at her brother. She sensed the tears and in frustration wiped them away with both hands clenched into tight ball like fists. Fear and love raced unabated though Megan's heart. She relived in her mind the moments that had ignited those fears along with the feelings Mommy had shared after they'd recommitted to their mother...daughter love connection. The connection had faltered after they'd seen mommy slap Jesus in front of his house, both Taylor and she'd become the subjects of bigtime bullying at school. All their mates on the school bus had seen what their mommy did. She ruefully recalled the day she'd avoided mommy out of fear. *'The front door of their home had swung open. Both children tensed on hearing harsh footsteps walk across the hallway floor. Megan stared down at the floor in fear. The tingling in her face accelerated. She jumped up and readied herself to flee from the one who'd been nothing but a bubbling source of love before yesterday. Taylor had spotted Eugette...Mommy walking into the living-room just missing Megan's dash out of the room. Taylor had jumped up and ran with open arms towards his Mommy. Eugette had stooped down onto her knees and embraced Taylor lovingly.*

"*I love ya Mommy!*" *Taylor boasted.* "*I love ya a whole lot.*"

"*And Mommy loves you twice around the moon and back again sweetheart. Where's Megan, Taylor? Is she with Grammie?*" *Crouched safely behind her bedroom door Megan overheard their conversation.*

Taylor had twisted himself free of Mommy's hug. He pointed over to where Megan had been. "*No Mommy she right there.*" *Both Mommy and Taylor stared at the empty room. Megan had successfully fled on Mommy's arrival.* "*Must have had some 'ting to do Mommy. She was right here with me a minute ago.*"

Eugette had stood up. A gaze around the room confirmed Megan's absence. A burning sensation froze Eugette's hand. It confirmed the reality of the confrontation she's had with Megan yesterday. She exhaled a series of long regretful sighs. A fear bit into her heart. She asked herself in dread. 'Does Megan now hate me? Did she now hate her mom, me?'

Taylor picked up the bag at Eugette's feet. A peek inside revealed package of cookies on top of the groceries inside the bag, he chirped, "Can I? Can I have a cookie Mommy?"

"Yes Taylor. You can have two cookies. Where is Grammie?"

"Grammie fell asleep reading her book in bed."

"OK. Thanks Taylor. Please take two cookies and put the groceries on the kitchen table. Oh. Please put the milk in the fridge."

Taylor picked up the bag and half carried half dragged it out into the kitchen. In the kitchen he quickly put the milk and cheese in the refrigerator. Once the groceries were all on the table he eyed, then opened the package of cookies and claimed his two. Taylor quickly became blind to his surroundings. His whole world focused on the two chocolate chip cookies and how to eat them. Following the first crunch Taylor's world vanished.

Eugette walked past the master-bedroom door. Inside she caught sight of Maria...Grammie fast asleep with a soft covered book on her chest. Next the door to her bedroom stood closed. She walked past it then stopped outside Megan and Taylor's closed bedroom door. Silently she resolved to somehow arranging separate sleeping quarters for Megan and Taylor. Megan had clearly expressed an interest, no a need to have a girl's only bedroom. Memories of her childhood girls only bedroom flashed up in her mind. She reasoned yes; I was an only child. But I'm not a fool. Every girl needs the privacy and privilege of a bedroom filled with personal things intended strictly for one person's eyes. That being Daddy's little princess, oh my God, Eugette rued. I miss you Daddy, Rusty. I love you both to pieces and miss you both to the moon and back. God I'd trade a lifetime for just one more of your kisses Rusty. I can almost taste them. She reached out and grabbed the bedroom door's knob. A twist and gentle push opened the door. Eugette walked into the room. On spotting Megan curled up in a fetal ball sucking on a thumb with tear-stained eyes her heart shattered. She ran to the bed. Jumped onto it and embraced her daughter. Both sobbed unfettered and loudly.

Megan whispered, "I'm sorry Mommy. I'm so sorry. Please love me again."

Eugette tightened her embrace of Megan. In response she simply burst into tears. "Megan, my Megan please forgive and love me. I love you more than life itself. Please don't hate your Mommy. I'm so, so sorry sweetheart." Megan twisted around and faced Eugette. Through tear-stained eyes and cheeks the mother and daughter's lips touched. Both believed a peck on the cheek would not suffice. The kiss intensified. In a flash it ended. Their embrace of each other grew tighter. The tears abated. Each patted then run their fingers through the others hair. Broken hearts healed. They sat up on the bed's edge. Their embrace of each other continued. Both mother and daughter disconnected from the tiff that had arisen just the day before. Instead, all focus centered on rekindling their love of each other.

Taylor's call out to Megan, drew a frown to Maria face, "Megan we should take Grammie and go talk to Jesus." An image of Chester's newest preacher popped up in Maria's mind. Past images and recollections of interactions with Mikie, Michael Slivers, aka Chester's version of Jesus reincarnate sent icy shivers racing through Maria's body and mind. She pulled her grandbabies into a warm loving Grammie hug. She whispered, "I talked to your Mommy. She's safe with John at his home. And your mommy loves you two beyond the moon and back." She missed her Eugette but felt relief with her daughter off in Newmarket with John, Richard and Lyndsey. Megan took Grammie's hand in hers. Coyly she presented her best pretty please face and pleaded, "Let's go Grammie, back to Mister McClakens house. Bailey needs company." Maria nodded agreement and stood up. Together they walked outside and back to Gilbert's home. A feeling of belonging embraced Maria and her heart. Martin's request out of their wedded past echoed in her heart, *'Promise me Love, if something happens, you'll find another and embrace love anew.'* A tingling sensation raced through her body. It added energy to her step and a glow to her face on seeing Jeffery in the kitchen window at Gilbert's. Yes. Home was taking on a new meaning and Maria loved its touch.

CHAPTER 21

Action quickly unfolded in response to John's call to Richard. Once aware of the situation Richard ordered John to haul ass over to the homestead with Eugette at his side. No other option was offered up. John agreed, then drove over to Richard and Lyndsey's with Eugette. He'd attempted at first to convince Rich to meet up with him at a café downtown. Lyndsey had intercepted their plans and insisted he head straight to the homestead. Along the way he called Rich back and updated him on the news and picked Richard's brain for supportive action items to move forward on. The call ended with Richard suggesting then stating he would call Roger and ask for his input and support. Their call ended on John turning off the road and heading up to the homestead. At the door Lyndsey greeted him. John recognized the look. A coy innocent but inquisitive pose. He smiled internally, feeling concern for his brother. It appeared obvious that Lyndsey had Richard totally wrapped around her baby finger and subservient to her every beckoning call along with her every whimsical wish and desire. Another glance up to Lyndsey and their eyes connected. John swore to himself the lady could draw a confession out of a stone-dead block of concrete. He steadied himself up to withstand her pleasant but inquisitive nature.

"Hi Lyndsey. You're looking good. That glow has taken hold."

"Johnathan Ramsay, are you calling your sister-in-law fat."

John smirked; Lyndsey giggled. At the door he gently hugged her. He defended his words. "Never, I would never insinuate such a thought. But growing up I was there through mom's pregnancy and gained first-hand experience at a strategic stage in my development. I..."

Lyndsey pulled away from John. She retorted, "Really. You were what two or was it three and you already knew all there was to know about the birds and the bees?"

They laughed together. Lyndsey nudged John off to the side. Actually, she pulled him through the door and declared. "Follow your nose. Richard and fresh coffee await you in the kitchen." On spotting Eugette who'd been standing behind John, Lyndsey beamed. A welcoming smile burst out on her face along with her trademark dimples. Eugette sighed and Lyndsey pulled themselves together in a welcoming hug. Eugette flinched. Lyndsey released her. "Sorry I just couldn't resist a welcoming hug. Git in here, girl and welcome to our home. Together they joined John and Richard in the kitchen. Lyndsey asked, "Care to join me with a peppermint tea? It's my favorite?" Eugette took in the entire kitchen. Compared to hers it was a dream kitchen. It went beyond her wildest dreams or expectations. Lyndsey caught the awe on Eugette's face. She said, "Yes, it's a dream kitchen. Not of my doing. This is the old Ramsay Homestead. If Grandma Ramsay blinked or simply hinted, that she wanted something, well as you can see, Grampa Ramsay delivered."

Richard, throughout the conversation edged himself up beside Eugette. He restrained himself from embracing her in a hug. Smiles were exchanged. Richard turned to the table and said, "Please make yourself at home. Here this chair is calling out your name. Please be seated." The tea kettle whistle screamed out. Lyndsey quickly topped up two mugs then added a peppermint tea bag to each mug. Once everyone was sitting John attempted to defend his earlier comments. With a glance around the table, he gathered his thoughts. Locking eyes with Lyndsey he commented, "You're looking great Lyndsey. Mom and grandma must be tickled pink up there. Each glimpse would fill them with pride seeing you with Ritchie at your side. Dad and grampa too. And like me, they'd all boast up the glow of your mother-to-be's aura."

Lyndsey got Eugette in a sidewise glance. Both smiled then giggled aloud. On recovering they turned and faced John. Richard remained silent. Although aware of grandma's ways he'd learned early in life to heed grampa's wisdom.

John sensing, he was on a roll added, "Grandpa was no fool either. He wisely gave grandma free reign. So, I guess it wasn't really grandma's fault. She doted on mom throughout the pregnancy. If mom so much as sneezed or dared to pick up something? The Lord had to be there at her side. Grandma was a sweetheart. However, I quickly learned though experience and I quote, 'Only a fool would dare to question or test Grandma Ramsay's knowledge of life and its magical journeys."

Lyndsey frowned at John. She declared, "Grandma Ramsay was an absolute sweetheart!"

"I that she truly was. However, I was there. Grandpa Ramsay, God bless him, often had to pull mom or dad aside and coach them on pathways and opinions best not crossed or tested."

Richard continued to skid the conversation's boundaries. Finally, he boasted, "I agree, Lynds, Grandma was an absolute sweetheart."

John grinned and retorted, "I totally agree. However, I lived through mom's second pregnancy. I could quote her till the cows come home. The first one. AKA Moi, was not but a cakewalk. The nine months slipped by in the blink of an eye. No issues arose. The delivery, a simple one-time drive to the hospital. Others I've heard weren't so fortunate. The delivery? Or should I say my arrival. No shouting. No screaming. No pain. I was ready and simply popped out."

Richard, Lyndsey and Eugette staring their eyes locked on John. "No way!" Richard retorted.

John simply replied, "I was there throughout yours, start to finish brother. I possess first-hand knowledge! Beside that's not why I'm here. Can I have a coffee top up?"

Lyndsey nodded an affirmation to John. She topped up the two mugs of coffee and eyed the tea mugs. They had barely been touched. She returned to the table.

Once Lyndsey was seated John looked to Eugette and said, "I feel like I'm in heaven since you texted me yesterday. Having you here feels so right. So good! Your, mom in chatting with me said you made the right move. We'll help make things right. Just ask and we're there.

Richard nodded agreement. He added, "Whatever needs doing. I did call Roger. Simply stated, he's on board and is a gateway to some great resources."

Eugette listened to the pledges of support. A series of sniffles burst free then she reached out and took John's hands into hers. Their eyes locked. Lyndsey and Richard stood and gently embraced Eugette. She whispered, "Only when you're ready. You're not alone." She looked over to Richard then turned to Eugette and suggested, "Let's have a girl talk. Rich, maybe it would make sense for you and John to head over and see Roger. You can call Maria if needed. I will take care of Eugette."

John eased himself free of Eugette's grasp. He stood and walked to her side they kissed. He whispered, "See you in a bit Love. You're in good hands with Lyndsey." Richard stood and together he headed out with John. On hearing John's vehicle driving away, Lyndsey nudged Eugette up and they made their way into the den.

Once seated on the loveseat, Eugette opened up. "I can't. I will never go back to the Pot. It's all centered on the reported loss of my dad and husband to the perils of the sea. I never bought into that official storyline. And yes, it has been a cause of friction between me and my mom. Simply stated, I have overheard conversations over the past year and more. I know my dad and husband were murdered and that bastard Barnie Madison made it happen."

Lyndsey gasped, "Oh my God! It can't be!"

Eugette shook her head in the negative. She continued, "I did some digging and the results only sharpened my resolve and convictions. Did you cross paths with the owner of the Lobster Pot Pub & Eatery when down home? I'm here because of that bastard. Yesterday he accosted me in the parking lot. I was in my car. He flung a goober onto the driver's window and slimmed it. Called me a sorry assed whore. I should have left then." Eugette paused briefly then continued, "The fool I am I reported in for my shift. We need the money to survive since we lost dad and my Rusty. The bastard called me into the office. I was terrified. But too naïve to run. Too stupid!"

Lyndsey gently embraced Eugette. Both women gazed at each other. Somehow Eugette felt bonded. She sensed the essence of her best friend Hope in Lyndsey? They were sisters. Could one's DNA carry one's aura within a sibling?

Eugette broke the silence. "I had believed one of Barnie's cohorts Ned Stone had fired the shots that killed dad and my Rusty. To make the story shorter so did Ned. Last week I met up with Mikie Slivers, the lobsterman that rescued Tessa from the island. He was Ned's partner and fellow lobsterman. Since the island debacle he's living a Christian rebirth. Around Chester he's the second coming. Local kids refer to Mikie as Jesus. Well Jesus set the record straight. Barnie fired the shots! And he definitely framed Ned Stone for the murders. Stupid me. I kept up my inquiries. Word of my actions got back to the wrong person."

Lyndsey listened intently. She gently rubbed Eugette's shoulders.

"In the office I panicked and tried to escape. He attacked me. Slapped and punched my face and body, tore off my blouse and knocked me down onto the floor. He viciously kicked my back, legs and hip, I honestly believed it was over. I almost blacked out. My babies flashed up randomly in my head. The bastard exposed himself to me!" Eugette sighed. Tears poured down her cheeks. "In a desperate move I clenched my fists together and drove them hard up and smashed the bastard's balls! He dropped to the floor groaning in agony. I grabbed keys off his desk and fled after unlocking the office's double keyed deadbolt locks. After driving around town aimlessly for a while. I headed out of town. On passing the turnoff to the McClakens I hit the on ramp to Hwy 101. On spotting the highway sign for Halifax, I pondered hitting the airport and disappearing. With each sign I passed my resolve grew. And here I am. Mom said I should stay the course if possible? Damn I miss my babies, my mom. I'm a real dumb bitch. Don't know when to…"

Lyndsey hugged Eugette avoiding her back. She whispered, "No. No you're not. You're a woman who's been to hell and back! Thank God you saw that sign, connected with our John at the wedding and broke free. God! Thank you. Eugette we're here for and with you. How's your back?"

"Sore. I might have a broken rib or two."

"Then let's get you taken care of girl."

Eugette looked at Lyndsey with a questioning gaze on her face.

Lyndsey stood and stated, "Before this and this." Tapping her wedding ring and baby belly, "I worked at a Retirement Villa. They have the resources to get your body right. Relax and I'll give them a call. Roger is a God sent blessing. And a damn good attorney. He'll set the wheels of justice in motion. That bastard will rue the day he messed with you!" Eugette stood and followed Lyndsey back into the kitchen. Minutes later a short phone call ended. Together they walked outside. Lyndsey locked the door. They entered Richard's SUV and headed off to the retirement villa.

CHAPTER 22

Barnie eased his old Buick slowly past the Lamont house in Chester. He frowned and cursed on not spotting Eugee's car in the driveway. "Son of a bitch! Where can she be? Ned checked out East River and the McClakens. They're locals and, other than Gilbert's, they never go anywhere beyond the South Shore. Time to call in a favor or two. On pulling into the Pot's parking lot Barnie uttered, "Stupid bitch. You're just like your Mama. Neither one of you has an inkling or a clue to the breadth of the Barnster's resource network. Little girlie, you crossed the line the other day. Once I'm finished with you, you'll savor the option death offers up!" Barnie parked then stepped out of the Buick. Staff and customers gathered together outside the Pot's entrance rushed over to Barnie.

A chorus of varied shouted out questions sang out to Barnie. "Any word on Eugette? Has anyone, the searchers and rescuers, the police anybody reported a positive sighting or communication with our Eugee?"

Barnie looked sadly out to each of their pleading faces. He bit his lower lip and dabbed away pretend tears from his eyes and cheeks. He addressed them, "I'm so, so very sorry. Along with many more and her family we've been searching throughout the night. Still no sightings or contact has been reported. I wish I had better news. We all miss our dear sweet Eugee. I swear we'll find her and get her safely back home. Dear God, Maria Lamont her mom is worried sick. The sadness is etched right into her face and entire body; no parent should ever have to go through what Maria Lamont is facing. The look on Eugee's babies faces. They want their Mommie back home with them." Barnie bowed his head and erupted into a bout of sobbing. He excused himself, "I'm sorry I'm beat and totally drained. I need to get inside and grab a bite to eat and a quick energy nap." He started to walk towards the Pot's door.

Tara, a staffer, shouted out, "Will scrambled eggs work boss? I'll get the chef to fire up a quick order."

"Thanks, Tara, that would be nice. No coffee. Perhaps an orange juice. Oh! Please ensure all searchers and police are taken care of on the house. It's the least we can do for these people dedicated to helping us get our Eugee back." The gathering broke up. Staffers followed Barnie back inside the Pot. Customers finished their dining and departed while others entered the Pot and its dining area. Inside, Barnie acknowledged his inquisitive staffers then headed straight to his office. Within minutes Tara delivered his steaming hot breakfast tray. On setting it down on the desk she turned about and walked back out of the office. Barnie called out to her, "Thanks, Tara. Much appreciated. Please no visitors to my office. I need to grab a short energy nap then head back out." Tara closed the door on entering the hallway.

Once the door closed, Barnie shoveled the scrambled eggs through his piehole in a fit of rage. The orange juice disappeared in a single gulping swallow. On finishing, Barnie expelled a loud obnoxious belch. Remnants of partially chewed scrambled egg flew out of his mouth onto the tray and desktop. Barnie grinned as a second belch added more to the tray and desktop. He wiped most of it away with both of his sleeved arms. On retrieving his cell phone, Barnie speed dialed Ned Stone. The call went unanswered until the fifth ring when Ned rescued it from his voice mail.

Seeing the caller id Ned shouted, "No sign of her yet, Barnie. I just drove past the house and saw Maria and Jeffery heading out in his truck."

"Where were they headed?"

"I don't know. Just out I guess."

"Just out you guess? You stupid son of a bitch. What if she contacted them? They could be heading out to meet up with Eugee! You stupid frigging idiot. I'm guessing God ain't perfect. In handing out the fucking brains he completely missed you! Find out where they're headed to. I need to know." Barnie disconnected the call. Frustrated he hulked up a goober and flung it out towards the goober bucket sitting over by the far wall. Like most others it missed the bucket catching its side. A slow slide added it to the foul gathering on the floor. He pulled a drawer open an eyed the revolver sitting inside a plastic bag. Resolve set in. Barnie realized in that moment the desired results were calling on him to take action and set things right. In acknowledgement, Barnie slammed the drawer shut. He shoved the breakfast tray aside then relaxed with his head down on the desktop. Quickly he lapsed into a deep sleep. A random volley of snorts confirmed his sleep state. Tara returned and remove the tray. She exited the office quickly. It was not a place that staffers looked forward to visiting.

CHAPTER 23

Maria sat deep in thought beside Jeffery as they drove towards East River. Ring, Ring Jeffery's cell phone sang out from his shirt pocket. In a flash Maria's hand reached out and retrieved the cell phone. On spotting the 905-area code she swiped the cell answering the call. The area code matched the one from Eugette's earlier call. "Eugee?" A short silent pause ensued. She broke it, "Hello. Maria here. Is everything ok John? Please can I speak to my Eugette?"

"Mom it's me. I'd really love ta hug you but I can't. Will a kiss do? Ppppeet."

"And a million more back at you sweetheart. I'm just so ecstatic that you're ok. My baby is safe."

Eugette replied with a grin, "I'm a woman Mom. Not a baby."

"You'll always be my baby. My treasure. And yes, you are a woman. A special one. You're the Mommie of my grandbabies! How are you? What's happening?"

Eugette sighed. She replied, "I'm fine. Really, I am. Guess where I'm at?"

Maria giggled. The question carried her years into the past. Back to when a much young Eugette would call from a friend's home and ask, *'Guess where I'm at Mom?'*

"I'm with Lyndsey at the place where she worked before the big day. I'm at Daylily Meadows Retirement Villas. It's an amazing retirement resort and I'm being spoiled rotten Mom. And I love it. They started me off with a full body massage that was totally amazing. And, they used body oils. Oh my God. You gotta get one Mom. Right this moment I'm getting a manicure to be followed up with a pedicure. I think I've died and gone to heaven!"

Maria sniffled then sobbed and replied, "Please, please sweetheart don't mention the D-word. Not after what we went through searching madly high and low for you. Please don't mention that D-word. I'm so happy to hear that joy singing out in each word you speak."

"Mom, I won't ever use it again. I'm so sorry. Forgive me?"

"A million times over. I'll always forgive you, sweetheart, no matter what you do! I totally love and miss you."

"I miss and love you too Mom. How are my babies?"

"They're good. They're still with Hope and Gilbert. We're driving over to East River now."

"Tell, them Mommie loves them. Give them both hugs from Mommie. Oh! Mom here's Lyndsey she wants to say hi."

The line fell silent until Lyndsey said, "Hi, Mrs. Lamont."

"Hi Lyndsey. And please call me Maria. And Lyndsey, God bless you and your family. I don't know what hauled you down to East River and Nova Scotia. I just so grateful my baby had a destination she could call out to. I'm scared for my baby. I'm ashamed because I didn't listen to her. I put her life in danger. That BASTARD is behind all of this." Maria took into loud sobbing. Tears flowed wildly down both her cheeks.

Lyndsey called out "Mrs. Lamont, Maria are you ok?"

Jeffery took the cell phone from Maria's hand. With a touch of the brake and a twist of the steering wheel he turned into Gilbert's and parked beside his truck. He answered Lyndsey, "We're ok Lyndsey. Just arrived at Gilbert's. Give us some time and call back. No! I'll call back. Megan and Taylor gotta talk to their mom. They gotta hear her voice."

Lyndsey replied, "We'll be anxiously awaiting your call. Thank you. And whatever needs doing. Trust me we will do it. We'll keep Eugette safe! Oh! One more thingy. On Roger's suggestion, I took Eugette's car keys along with her Park'N Fly parking stub and sent them to Hope. Could you…"

"Consider it done Lyndsey, it would be best to get that vehicle out'ta sight. And thanks Lyndsey. I'd better go. Here come the wee ones! Bye." Jeffery disconnected the call and returned the cell phone to his shirt pocket. He hugged then released Maria. They both stepped out of the truck. Megan and Taylor embraced their grammie. Kisses were exchanged. Once the greetings settled-down they all walked into Gilbert's kitchen. Hope jumped up and ran over to Maria. The two embraced each other in a loving embrace.

Maria whispered, "Just hung up from chatting with our Eugette. She's OK. She's being spoiled and thanks be to God, she's got the joy back in her voice." Maria pulled away from Hope's embrace. She immediately fell into Gilbert's all-encompassing hug. Jeffery eyed them with envy.

In jest he retorted, "Iff'in my brother doesn't let go of my gal, I just might have to lay a bigtime hugging onto his gal!"

Gilbert released Maria. She went to Jeffery and they shared a lingering kiss. Jeffery ended the kiss. He stepped back from Maria and asked Megan and Taylor, "Would you two like to chat with you mom?"

The both started to bounce up and down shouting. "Yes! Yes, we want to talk with Mommie!"

Jeffery pulled out his cell phone and walked into the living-room. Megan and Taylor followed on his heels. At the loveseat, Jeffery said, "Ok. Sit down here. Side by side. No fighting." They obeyed. A childish hug was shared. Jeffery said, "OK! I'll call your mom and put the phone on speaker. Talk as long as you want. OK?" Two smiling faces beamed agreement up to Jeffery. He speed-dialed Lyndsey's cell phone.

Eugette answered, "Hello."

Tears flowed freely down both of the children's cheeks. Together they shouted, "Mommie!" Mommie picked up the conversation. Jeffery turned and walked off into the kitchen. On hearing Megan, Taylor and Eugette's voices tears freely flowed down Jeffery's cheeks. He fought to wipe them away with both sleeved arms. Maria rescued him with a loving hug. They then joined Gilbert and Hope seated at the kitchen table. A sense of total wellbeing befell the household. Life's true blessing sang out to all present.

CHAPTER 24

Time's passage added an edge of finality and fear to most Chester residents as weeks passed without word about Eugette. Her former coworkers lost the edge they'd added to the experience customers embraced in dining at the Pot. Many had been schoolmates of Eugette's. An unspoken fear gnawed at their heartstrings. Over the weeks leading up to Christmas many tables and booths stood empty at the Pot's peak hours of business. Rumours swirled about town and the surrounding area. In an effort to parlay those rumours, Barnie offered up a reward for information leading to Eugette's safe return to Chester, her family and friends. The action led to an array of information hitting the Chester detachment's workload. That being the nature of the public's response to rewards. Barnie's reward had been announced at ten thousand dollars. That amount quickly gained momentum with locals adding personal guarantees to the total. Then Barnie's caring nature kicked in. He placed a 'Reward Donations' box on the bar cash register countertop. Tracking of the donations was overseen by Barnie. On the reward doubling up its opening amount, Barnie graciously appeared on local media radio, television and print editions. Each appearance added to the reward. The honesty and sincerity Barnie portrayed led to lineups forming at the Pot's peak hours of operation. All these local contributions personal and monetary, added a steady higher demand to the Chester detachment's workload and ran up a heavy overtime tab. Maria and the McClakens maintained a steady line of communications with the investigating officers. Over the weeks leading up to Christmas the media's coverage soared then ebbed with each of Barnie's appearances.

To their credit, with ongoing coaching by grammie, Jeffrey and the McClakens, Megan and Taylor maintained the states of mind expected by their schoolmates and teachers. They outwardly appeared to be grief stricken without their mom. However, their resolve stayed the course nurtured by regular phone chats shared with their Mommie. Both children accepted their mother's assurances that she was safe, and would be coming home. Jeffery advanced beyond Grampa Jeffy to simply being designated as Grampie. Expectations leading towards Christmas hinted that the title would soon become official. Their status quickly turned into a respected couple about town that most couldn't recall a time they hadn't been an item about Chester.

....

The old Ramsay homestead in Newmarket became a busy hive of activity. Its vehicle count jumped to three plus a steady flow of visitors. On Roger's suggestion Eugette took up residence there. She connected and bonded with Lyndsey who shared many fun filled family idioms she been privy to as a result of growing up glued to Richard's side. John benefited from Lyndsey's choice to leave ilk's out of the past buried where they belonged deep and out of sight. Like Richard, she treasured the new John and the positive influence Eugette had on him.

One week in mid-November work pulled Richard and John out of town. It was also the week that Lyndsey shared Grace Ramsay's 1796 Diary with Eugette. The first five pages captured Eugette's heart, soul and imaginative spirit. She was eager to delve deeper into the young Scottish lass's world of intrigue. Together they burned a bounty of midnight oils. Once Lyndsey knew she had Eugette hooked, she shared recollections of the Ramsay – MacClakens island adventure out on the storied Floating Islands of repute. Following several early morning harrowing escapes from nightmarish dreams fired up by the diary and Lyndsey's words, the women took to sharing a bed. Both felt safer in the other's physical presence. On the return of their men neither one revealed the adventures and magical moments that had bonded them together almost like sisters.

Eugette's days kept her busy. She'd gained employment with Lyndsey's former employer. The Daylily Meadows Retirement Villas. Residents took a shining to their new dining room attendee. Quickly, Eugette's thoughts of work back home faded out of her mind. She simply embraced her new way in life. The most important bonds that being family and friends back home - stood the test of time. Mom and Eugette's babies. They continued to own all rights to Eugette's heart even as her relationship with John developed and they grew closer.

Come the middle of December Eugette managed with backup from home, to swear Megan and Taylor to an oath of secrecy. If they zipped their lips and remained saddened children longing to reconnect with their Mommie, then a surprise Christmas adventure could be afoot.

Megan picked up on the clue first. She asked, "Mommie? Does that mean we will get to see you? And hugs you?"

"Oh please! Pretty please Mommie. We miss you so much!" Taylor shouted out. "And we've been good. Really good, Mommie."

"Surprising as it may seem Mom, he really has." Megan professed in backing up her brother's claim.

Eugette felt elated and energized chatting with her twins. Being away from home, she felt guilty on having run away from home and ending up in Newmarket with the Ramsays. She dropped a hint, "I would love to hug both of you to pieces Sweethearts. After Mommie chats with Auntie Hope, she will tell you about Mommie's surprise."

Taylor asked, "Mom iff'in Grampa Jeffy and Grammie became like, you know your Daddy and Grammie were, what would that make Auntie Hope? Would she be my Great Auntie Hope?"

Eugette pondered Taylor's questions. How would she feel if Mom were to remarry? A glance back in time and she found herself savoring with relish the glow on her mom's face when at Jeffery's side. A silence befell the line. Eugette recalled the morning's early awakening at John's side she embraced the love that bubbled up inside her heart and mind.

She broke the silence, "Why no. And yes. Auntie Hope has always been a Great Auntie. And she always will be. But if what you said happens, she'd also be a cousin."

"Really? What's a cousin?" Taylor asked.

Megan jumped in, "That's someone whose mom and or dad is related to your mom or dad?"

Eugette paused in thought. Then answered, "That's something Auntie Hope can best answer. Can you get her for me?"

"Can we leave the phone on speaker?" Megan and Taylor shouted out.

"No. It's best I speak to Auntie Hope. Then she'll know what my surprise is going to be."

"OK, if we have too." Megan answered with a touch of disappointment. At times in the past, she recalled attempts made to avoid mom talks. In the moment Megan clutched lovingly to each word Mom spoke. On spotting Auntie Hope walking into the living-room she frowned then said, "OK Mom here's Auntie Hope. Loves ya."

"Loves ya too, Mommie." Taylor shouted out. Both twins embraced each other. In a whisper they exchanged a warm, "Mommie loves ya and so do I."

Auntie Hope took the phone and switched off the speaker. Megan and Taylor walked side by side throughout the house. On spotting Bailey up at the top of the stairs, they bolted and raced up the stairs. To their chagrin, Bailey caught the thumpity thumps of his pursuers. He bolted down the hallway in search of solitude. A commodity that never stood the test of time. In his heart the old cat loved the attention and pampering his pursuers loved to lavish on him.

CHAPTER 25

Maria stood and smiled on Gilbert entering the homestead with Harley right behind him. "Welcome. Jeffery's grabbing a quick bath. Could I offer up a fresh coffee?"

"Yes!" Gilbert replied. Harley nodded agreement. Both men claimed chairs at the kitchen table. Once they'd been served theirs, Maria poured herself a mug of coffee and joined them at the table.

She asked, "Are there any new updates since our phone chat the other day?"

"Yes." Harley answered. He explained, "With your daughter determined to be home for Christmas I've been bouncing options off Gilbert, Roger and his associate Walter Lizards. They connected me to a local attorney Parker Rose, who will be working with us. Our absolute foremost priority is her safety and that of everyone in her companionship."

Maria smiled in agreement. She glanced at the bathroom door and Jeffery who had just stepped through it. "Coffee dear? Come join us. We're discussing how best to safely get my Eugette home for Christmas."

Jeffery walked over to Maria and they kissed. He then headed to the counter and poured himself a mug of coffee. With mug in hand, he claimed the chair next to Maria.

Harley continued with his update. "Roger suggested and it's only a suggestion-that a diversion would work."

"A diversion? What kind?" Jeffery asked.

Harley smiled and answered, "He suggested inviting a relative or friend to join the Christmas gathering. Someone with a jovial flare who would distract from Eugette's presence home. Someone out of your past. They'd be a definite type A extrovert that simply draws all the attention to themselves. Harley paused reflecting on the truth behind Roger's request. Research had paid dividends revealing a history known only to a select few. He asked does anyone come to mind?"

The table fell silent. A moment or two slipped pasts then a smile burst out on Maria's face. She said, "Yes. If she'll come, I believe dad's sister Auntie Delilah O'Malley would be perfect. Auntie hasn't been back home in Chester in a dog's age. She lives in Murray River PEI. My God, Auntie Delilah is a definite type A and extroverted to the max."

"Sounds like we have a livewire," Harley injected. He added, "Could it be Eugette had simply been visiting her Auntie? No. We'd best not go that route."

"And then some!" Maria boasted. She added, "Auntie Delilah, Lila, as she prefers, is a definite livewire. If not for Lila my Eugee would have been put out for adoption at birth. She backed my wishes and convinced dad and mom that I should keep my baby. Auntie's opinion held sway over dad. I recall back in the day Auntie was a nurse. A maternity nurse. Yes. She would be a perfect fit to what you're asking as a diversion."

"Are you sure?" Jeffery asked.

"Absolutely. Auntie Lila will kick up many past recollections in the minds of those of her generation. According to dad, Auntie Lila tested Grammie and Grampa Lamont's wits to the max. I could spill the beans on her, but I'm thinking it would be best if we left that task to her."

"Great! Sounds like she'll fit the bill." Harley pulled out a business card and passed it to Maria. He added, "Maria, please call your Auntie Lila and explain our need, our plan and tell her I will give her line a buzz." Harley paused briefly then added, "Another update. We've advised close locals involved in the search for Eugette that she is ok. They've agreed to keep that status under tabs. We don't want word of it to land where it could do some harm." Maria frowned. Harley nodded and added, "Not to worry. We have all aspects under control, Maria. Everyone will be safe from harm." Silently he savoured Maria's suggestion. Delilah O'Malley had been the one Roger's research had centered on.

Maria nodded and replied, "Ok. I will Harley." She added. "I haven't seen Auntie in ages. Her hubby passed on several years past. It'll be great to have her back home over Christmas."

Jeffery asked, "Wow! I always looked at your Lamont family as steadfast die in the wool folks. It sounds like your Auntie Lila sure don't fit that image."

Maria grinned ear to ear. She boasted, "You'll love her, Jeffie. You'll love Auntie Lila. She's just what we need and what Roger suggested!" With that declaration out in the open and Harley's suggestion addressed, conversation shifted to sharing past childhood memories that the foursome had experienced. All four were die-in-the-wool East River-Chester lifers. The gathering broke up on Gilbert and Harley's departure. Maria asked Jeffery to drive her back to Chester to retrieve Auntie Lila's phone number from an old family address book. He heartily agreed. After a stop in at Gilbert's to hug Megan and Taylor they headed off to Chester and Maria's house.

....

Back at her home Maria tracked down the old family address book off a living-room bookshelf. On flipping through it she found Auntie's address and phone number. A quick dial energized the line in Murray River. It sang out to Lila's ears. She answered on the third ring. On hearing Maria's voice, tears of joy hit Auntie Lila full force. She recovered quickly and asked, "What's wrong sweetheart? Why are you calling. Who died?"

"Nobody died, Auntie. What are your plans for Christmas? We'd love to have you here in Chester for Christmas. Please say..."

"Oh, my Gads! I haven't been back home in ages. Yer Grammie and Grampa will be rolling over in their graves when I roll back into town!"

"Then you'll come?"

"Danged totting I'll be there. With all the bells and whistles in full blast. Why I can't wait to see the looks on old Petunia Fargus's face when she sees me strutting about town. Oh! And Eddy Jarvis. The bugger jilted me fer that prim and prissy Monica Delannie. Whoa! I can't wait to get there, sweetheart."

"And we're just as excited to have you back home Auntie." Maria replied. She added, "Auntie I have another question not a request to ask."

Lila replied, "Fire away sweetheart."

Maria with hesitation updated Auntie Lila with all the going ons that were afoot in Chester. On learning that her big brother Martin and Eugette's husband Rusty's deaths were being investigated as murders she tensed up. However, once the full plate of going ons was fully laid out, Auntie Lila bought into the plan hook, line and sinker. Maria glanced at Harley's business card and gave Auntie his phone number and advised her that Inspector Harley Kingston would be calling her shortly. Afterwards conversation simply shifted into Auntie and niece catching up on each other's life happenings. On hanging up and ending the call Maria sighed, grateful that they were on a five-cents a minute long distance calling plan. In reflection later it came as no surprise to Maria on learning Auntie had called Harley immediately upon their call ending.

....

With travel plans and modes of travel secured with confirmed bookings, everyone's focus centered on Eugette's safe return to Nova Scotia. A sadness befell the Daylily Meadows Retirement Villas. News that their newest beloved staff member was headed home painted a sadness on the faces of residents and staff. However, everyone bought into the commitments to stay in touch. Eugette had won their hearts just as they had hers. She enjoyed chatting with the resort's administrator and Roger's brother, Jack, its bookkeeper. On learning of the plans to fly Eugette and John into Charlottetown to connect with her aunt on her father's side of the family, the jovial Delilah O'Malley of Murray River PEI, Eugette, John, Lyndsey and Richard totally endorsed the plan. Laughter arose on learning how Delilah, a once young Scottish lass, had dared to fall in love with an Irish lad an O'Malley and dared to move off to PEI with her husband. They believed having the lively Auntie Lila back home in Chester for Christmas would help distract concerns centered on Eugette safety. Auntie Lila was simply back home to support her niece Maria and her grandchildren. Many locals had come to believe Eugette's fate held dire consequences and she'd never again walk the streets of Chester. Eugette, at times, struggled with the thought of being back home in Chester with Barnie aware of her presence. Details of their travel plans were altered with a highly scattered series of wee-whitish-fibs. Fibs told to protect Eugette but mostly to conceal the truth from well-intentioned wagging tongues within the resort's residents. Rest assured good times were shared by all at the resort leading up to Christmas. Eugette had easily won the hearts of the retirement resort's residents.

Over tea Lyndsey giggled then teased, "I'm guessing Auntie Lila is a lively one. She'll add a fiery distraction or should I say energy to the town of Chester over Christmas. You are one special Mom, Eugette. Rest assured I'd walk the same path you are about to walk. God! I cannot imagine your feelings being away from your amazing twins!"

"In a heartbeat I'd do it a thousand times over and never blink an eye. Gads! Thinking back to what I put Mom and Dad through! They were amazing. Now that I'm a mom, all those gasps and loving sidewise smirks I triggered on their faces ... I get it a million times over. I so miss my babies. Each night laying upstairs in bed with them a thousand miles away. I hug them to pieces and cry myself to sleep. And to think in a few days I'll get to hug my babies for real. Lynds iff'in I died tomorrow trust me this motherhood adventure treated me to a glimpse of what heaven is all about!"

Lyndsey and Eugette clasped hands and arms seated across the table from each other. They bonded. Their short time together under the same roof bonded their heartstrings into a melody most mothers come to treasure throughout their lifetimes.

……..

The sound of crunching gravel in the driveway snapped the ladies back into a world of reality. The front door opened. John entered first with two large luggage units with matching carry-on bags in tow. Richard followed. He boasted, "I tried to limit the lad's shopping but he wouldn't listen to a word I said."

John defended himself. He declared, "Most of it is Christmas gifts. I just couldn't stop myself."

The women went to their men. Lyndsey stopped at John. She embraced him. Before she released him to Eugette she stated, "Thank you, John. We love the new you." A second hug ensued. Then Lyndsey released John to Eugette.

Richard quickly welcomed Lyndsey with a hug and a lingering kiss. The kiss ended on a growl from Richard's stomach. He shyly grinned.

Lyndsey asked, "Are we hungry?"

"I'm starving!" Richard proclaimed.

John added, "Me too. We got tied up on a job and foolishly skipped lunch." On realizing Lyndsey had packed lunches for them both he grinned and said, "I know. Richard popped the lunches you packed in the office fridge. And they'll be in good hands. Once Billy spots them they'll be gone!" Eugette remained silent. She watched the brothers try to justify their dining actions with Lyndsey. The look on both their faces and Lyndsey's declared a winner. The friendly banter between the Ramsays endeared them to Eugette.

Richard broke the silence. He asked, "Are your bags packed, Love?"

Lyndsey giggled then grinned. She boasted, "I've been packed since the day we booked our Via Rail tickets. Say the word and I'll let you load them up. Oh! Are you packed, Sweetheart?"

Richard frowned then gulped, "I could be. It'll only take me ten, well maybe fifteen, minutes at most, Love."

"Trust me, Love. Dad's big old blue luggage bag. It's upstairs in our bedroom and it's packed!"

"Ok! Then I shall assume Eugette is packed and John's bags are over there. Give me a hand, John, and we'll load up my SUV. We can deliver everything to the Union Station in Toronto, then we'll treat ourselves to a great meal out at that Greek Restaurant down near the station. OK?"

John retorted, "Sounds like a great plan. Let's get moving, Richie. I will assume you two are still sold on flying down the rails to Nova Scotia, while the wise soar through the wild blue yonder, in the blink on an eye?"

Lyndsey smirked, "We're sold. We'll glide down the rails on a romantic adventure. The clickity clack of our silver chariot will be an experience you'll envy in its retelling over the years yet to be."

No one replied to Lyndsey's boast. Richard teamed up with John and they quickly had the SUV loaded up and ready to go. Both men waited outside for the ladies to join them. On stepping outside Eugette watched Lyndsey lock the door. Together they joined their men at the SUV. Toying with her purse, Lyndsey pulled out the Via Rail tickets. She waved them at the men. "See, I've got them. And the bonus being except for the special Daylily Meadows Retirement Villas carryall bag you two won't have anything to check in at the airport." Lyndsey opened the back door and Eugette climbed inside. John tried but Lyndsey ceded the front passenger seat to him. She joined Eugette in the back seat. The drive to Toronto and its Union Station passed quickly once they were on the Hwy 404. The front seat focused on work talk and the TODOs that needed attention. Richard double talked John and succeeded in committing him to entering holiday mode and letting Bill and the staff handle the work end of things during their absence. John nodded agreement.

The backseat chatting centered on calming down Eugette's nerves. Under Gilbert's direction that followed Inspector Harley Kingston's recommendation, John and Eugette were flying into Charlottetown, PEI then meeting up with Delilah O'Malley, Eugette's auntie who had agreed to accompany them onward to East River and Chester. It was felt her presence would assist in adding an energized Christmas distraction to Chester. A dinner out at the Lobster Pot Pub & Eatery was planned with the Auntie in attendance, thus selling locals on her long overdue visit back home to Chester from Murray River a visit triggered by a desire to be back home with her family celebrating Eugette's return home. On hitting the Don Valley Parkway traffic slowed down. That did not deter Richard. He took an exit, then worked his magic in weaving their way through Toronto to the Union Station. The task at hand there flowed smoothly. Lyndsey handed Richard their tickets and the men off loaded and checked in all the luggage. On returning to the SUV Richard's shoulder got a tap, tap. He twisted around smiled at Lyndsey and returned the tickets and their baggage claim tags to her. She nodded her thanks.

Next stop took them to a Downtown Toronto Greek Restaurant that Richard and Lyndsey adored. They'd arrived just after seven pm and were ushered into their reserved table. The men followed their lady's lead. Everyone ordered non-alcoholic refreshments. Lyndsey ordered the Spanakopita, a Greek Spinach Pie, Eugette, the Mediterranean Tuna Salad with Dijon Dressing, John, a Mediterranean Baked Red Snapper with Bell Peppers, and Richard closed out the ordering with the Mozzarella and Feta Pita Grilled Cheese. Needless to say, on heading home the gentlemen carried their lady's doggie bags. The meals had been large and no desserts were ordered. Throughout the drive home traffic was light. On hitting Hwy 404 light but frequent snorts floated up out of the back seat. Back home at the homestead everyone opted to turn in early. Quickly the house fell silent. Sugar plums and excited Christmas travelers' minds and hearts were gently nudged off into dreamland by the Sandman.

CHAPTER 26

Everyone awoke refreshed and excited. None more than Lyndsey. In an effort to calm her down Richard took on breakfast duties. It passed quickly. Both ladies opted for fruit salads. John and Richard simply had eggs cooked sunny side up, no bacon, no toast. The Greek meals nudged everyone into a light breakfast. John accepted the keys to Richard's SUV and they headed out to the Go Train Station. He attempted one last sales pitch on the benefits of flying to one's destination. "You'll be cooped together in a wheeled sardine can over 24 hours. It'll be agony beyo..."

"It'll be delightful. It will give us time to focus on life's joys." Lyndsey hugged Richard.

John accepted the answer written on the faces of Richard and Lyndsey. Eugette hugged both then kissed Lyndsey's cheek. She whispered, "Thanks, Sis. Safe travels and we'll see you real soon. A second hug ensued. Overhead, the boarding announcement for their Go Train called out, *'Passengers boarding the Toronto Go Train proceed to your boarding gate.'* John exchanged parting hugs with Richard and Lyndsey. With Eugette at his side he watched them walk off towards the boarding gate. Watching Richard struggle to keep pace with Lyndsey added a smile to his face. The three overnight bags were packed to the max and appeared to be testing the staying power of their zippers. The bags also were slowing down Richard's pace. He caught a quick wave from Lyndsey as she passed through the gate well ahead of Richard and their overnight bags. John waved back then turned and headed towards Richard's

SUV. The hassles of airport check-ins and security faded from John's thoughts. On driving out of the parking area he relaxed; tomorrow's flights and travel plans definitely beat out a 24 hours train ride. He suspected Richard was feeling relieved at having delivered their travel luggage and boxes of Christmas gifts to the Union Station in Toronto yesterday evening. The option had also benefited John's travel plans. With both his and Eugette's baggage and gifts traveling by rail, their flight tomorrow would go much smoother.

Richard called out, "Lyndsey, please slow down. There's seating aboard for everyone."

Lyndsey stopped, twisted around, and smiled at Richard. Once he'd caught up, she rewarded him with a kiss. Richard panted. He then worked at switching his hands to balance the weight of their overnight bags. "Give me my makeup bag, it's light."

"Your what bag?"

"My makeup and personal bag."

"No."

"It is light. I can handle..."

"No."

"Men! Why are they so...!

A passing grandmotherly passenger answered Lyndsey's plea, "They think we're all damsels in distress. And they're our knights in shining armour."

Lyndsey giggled and replied, "Really?"

"Really, let him spoil you. Come the postpartum blues you'll treasure his every misguided effort. Your mood swings, negative, positive, wild, sometimes joyful mood swings and bouts of tearfulness will drive him crazy."

"Surely you jest?"

"An only child, I assume. No siblings, brothers, sisters?"

"Mmm...yes. I was a solo act."

Richard avoided the conversation Lyndsey had entered into. With the assistance of a fellow traveller, he managed to load all their baggage onto the Go Train. He returned to the entrance and offered a hand to

Lyndsey who continued to chat up a storm with her newfound companion. Inwardly Richard hoped the companion wasn't headed to the Maritimes on Via Rail.

Lyndsey's companion tapped her shoulder and pointed to Richard at the entrance. She advised, "We'd best get ourselves onboard. I spotted your luggage tags and wouldn't want you to miss your connection to Halifax. Which East River are you headed to dear?"

Lyndsey answered with a question, "There's more than one?"

"That's right. There's East River up New Glasgow way, East River Sheet Harbour, then East River down on the South Shore, nears ta Chester."

"That's the one!" Lyndsey exclaimed. East River down by Chester!" With the question resolved Lyndsey and her companion boarded the Go Train with assistance from Richard. Together the trio took seating arrangements that would accommodate easy conversation throughout their run to Toronto. On being formally introduced to Zerlina Wildes, Lyndsey's newfound companion, Richard took a liking to her friendly chit chatty nature and grandmotherly appearance. Silently, he recalled the passing of his parents and grandparents. The lively conversation rekindled memories of woman talk he'd been shooed from over the years. He allowed the memories to surface in a smile on recalling the chidings of his Grandfather William Ramsay. *'Lad you would be best served not listening to the idle chattering of the ladies. Come sit with your men folk and learn well of the tales of valor we've lived!'* The clickety-clack of the Go Train's wheels combined with the brilliant sunshine slipping through the window, soon sent Richard off into a relaxed semiconscious sleep, or in Lyndsey's words, 'A Ritchie Nappy Nap.' Either way, Richard escaped the conversation being shared between Zerli and Lyndsey. Had Richard escaped an urge to nap, he'd have learned of Zerli's travel plans. His earlier concern would have been validated. Moncton, New Brunswick awaited Zerli at the end of her Christmas travels. Memories of John's description of the woes of rail travel in a wheeled sardine can over 24 hours, would echo in Richard's head then melt into an abyss once Zerli's unique nature and storytelling skills drew him in and shifted the conversations into three-way often animated laughter filled sessions.

Richard expelled a light snort. Lyndsey chucked, leaned over, and kissed his cheek. Turning back to Zerli she boasted, "My man claims he doth not snore."

"And recorded proof of the allegation has never surfaced, I'm sure."

"Ritchie's protests and denials are too sweet to erase."

"Aye, I bantered about many an accusation while chuckling off my Thomas's denials! Those denials still echo in my heart. My Tom has moved on, passed on over."

"You're a Maritimer?"

"What gave me away?"

"A year ago, on hearing your accent and witticisms, I would have chucked them off as comical personality traits. Since then, we've re-connected with kinfolk from Nova Scotia's South Shore. Yer pleasant outgoing nature and expressions! Gads! Maritimer just sings out from yer soul Zerli."

Both Lyndsey and Zerli burst into fits of uncontrolled laughter. Richard stirred then nodded back off into dreamland. Reining her laughter in, Zerli chuckled then boasted, "Lyndsey my dear, for a young married lass you've been well schooled." On spotting tears rolling down Lyndsey's cheeks, Zerli passed her a tissue. Lyndsey held the tissue, but allowed the tears to flow freely. The laughter had triggered recollections of losses suffered. In Lyndsey's mind and heart those tragedies and their consequences raced about unimpeded. Neither woman spoke. The sudden loss of her dad, and Leti, her adoptive Mom's, battle with cancer had triggered the tears. The terror of witnessing the accident and deaths of her in-laws, both parental and grandparents switched the flow into unabated waterfalls. Zerli stood. She reached across and knelt at Lyndsey's side. Her welcoming arms embraced Lyndsey. On retrieving tissues from her pocket Zerli dabbed away at Lyndsey's tears. Time stood still.

Overhead speakers in their Go Train called out, "Please remain seated. We will be arriving at Union Station shortly."

Lyndsey shivered, then recovered and opened her eyes. Zerli kissed her cheek, then released Lyndsey and stood up. "I'd best git myself seated we'll be arriving at the station shortly."

Both ladies chuckled anew on hearing Richard's series of loud snorts sing out for everyone to hear. The Go Train slowed, followed by a series of rumbling clickety-clacks. It then stopped and passengers stood making ready to disembark. Richard returned to the land of reality. Smiling, he gazed at Lyndsey's face. A smile embraced her excited pink cheeks and glowing blue eyes. Unable to resist, Richard kissed Lyndsey. The kiss lingered. Disembarking passengers smiled warmly at the couple's declaration of love.

Lyndsey pulled away. She declared, "It is happening, Richie! We're on our way home for Christmas!"

Richard watched in agreement as Lyndsey picked up her makeup bag. He frowned at the smirk Lyndsey targeted him with. The frown vanished on seeing Zerli take the bag from Lyndsey then disembark ahead of her. Seeing Zerli's hand proffered to Lyndsey to assist her stepping off the Go Train raised concerns in Richard's mind. He pondered, 'Could she be traveling beyond Toronto? Would their travel arrangement now become a threesome?'

....

Inside Union Station, Lyndsey and Richard accepted Zerli's offer to join them in the restaurant for a bite to eat. Outside the restaurant Richard stopped. He advised, "Go ahead, Lynds. I will put these bags in a locker and grab a book to read on the train. Should I grab one for you?" Richard asked and politely smiled.

"No. I have one. Besides Zerli and I will have plenty to chat about on the train." He kissed Lyndsey then headed off to find a locker for their overnight bags. With their bags safely stored in a station locker, Richard hit a bookstore. The choices were plentiful and crossed all genres. In the end, Richard stepped out of the store with a Stephen King novel he had on his wish list. A walk about the station and he spotted the restaurant entrance. On stepping through the doors, Zerli boldly waved a hand catching Richard's attention. A short walk to their table reconnected him with Lyndsey and Zerli, whose loud joyful voice had also called out to him. Richard quickly learned that Zerli would be traveling through to Moncton. He smiled and nodded his pleasure. Inside his head John's parting words echoed reenergized anew. *'You'll be cooped together in a wheeled sardine can over 24 hours. It'll be agony beyo...'* Their light meals passed quickly with their table alive with energized conversations. Their waitress cleared the table and Richard took the bill. While he paid the tab. Lyndsey and Zerli found a vacant bench and claimed it. On sitting down beside Lyndsey, a frown followed by a kiss greeted him. The frown did not deter him from flipping the book open to its preface. Both knew the other's reading preferences and respected them. Quickly he lost himself inside the tale unfolding before his eyes. Inside his mind he stood on the edge of a forest in a fictional world. A poke in the ribs by Lyndsey and Richard shouted, "Yeow!" A twist of his head caught sight of Lyndsey's smile. They kissed.

Lyndsey announced, "They'll be boarding in ten minutes. You'd best go get our bags."

On retrieving their bags Richard joined up with the ladies. The boarding call sang out and quickly the passengers boarded the train for their stretch run through to Montreal. Again, they managed to claim seats facing each other. Everyone settled in comfortably in their seats. A train whistle sang out, Then, their car jerked softy several times. Quickly the ride gained sped. Clickity-clack ... clickety-clack the train's wheels sang out to its passengers and crew. Richard settled back and lost himself in the pages of the Stephen King novel he'd found in the Union Station bookstore. It like the others in his collection were page turners that quickly carried Richard off on another reading adventure.

Lyndsey and Zerli smiled on watching Richard vanish into his book. Zerli said, "I envy you and your destination. East River, Chester and Nova Scotia's South Shore. Absolutely beautiful country. But a true misnomer if I ever heard one."

Lyndsey looked at Zerli in puzzlement.

"It's a 'South Shore' thing lassie. Have you ever looked at Nova Scotia on a large-scale map?"

"No."

"The east, west, north and south of it just don't make a scrap of sense to the average tourist who comes from away. The locals try to help. But the fools putting together the tourist guides, Lordie, they don't have a clue to share amongst the lot of them."

"It's a skip and a hop east or north of Chester. The river runs into East River Bay, then on out into Mahone Bay. A town I simply fell in love with on our first visits."

"With good cause, I'll swear. Have you been there, Mahone Bay, in December?"

"No, just late spring, early summer and fall."

"Then you'd best be marking Mahone Bay and its 'Father Christmas Festival' on yer TODOs and gotta-git-to lists. It's an amazing little town, especially come Christmas."

Lyndsey struggled to conceal her dimples and a smirk fighting to break free on her face. The unique linguistic twists many locals freely slipped into their friendly banter amused her. Lyndsey's smirk broke free into an uncontrolled burst of laughter. Zerli smiled at her newfound friend locked in uncontrolled fits of laughter. A questioning gaze slipped past Zerli's smile. Lyndsey reached out and pulled Zerli into a welcoming embrace. Her fits of laughter spread to Zerli. Both ladies surrendered to the peals of laughter. Lyndsey sighed, almost gained control of herself then rejoined Zerli in her rollicking laughter. Richard stirred restlessly. An energized series of snorts escaped his gaping jaw. The fits of laughter escalated. A silver haired conductor walking through their coach car stopped on reaching their seats.

"Tickets me laddie and ladies. And for a share ov'en yer laughter I'd be pleased to double stamps yer rite of passage on this flying silver bullet that be a whisking us all to our destinations."

"Oh, my Gads ... Another Maritimer has joined our merry band of holiday travelers."

"Young lady, we'd be preferring the title of Homeward Bound Christmas Maritimers. Ye'll not be finding no Holiday Trees down in our stretch of the land byes the sea."

Lyndsey dug furiously inside her purse. "Aha! I's got them. Here's be our tickets sir. My hubby Ritchie...Richard will be in the upper bunk out of Montreal. I'm Lyndsey and I'll be taking the lower bunk." She extended her hand towards the conductor offering up their tickets for inspection and validation. He accepted the tickets, eyed them once over and punched validation holes in the tickets.

"Thank you, Lyndsey. You'll be with us straight through to Halifax after we stop for a short four-hour layover in Montreal. I see you've booked sleepers. A smart choice I assure ye. Is this yer first trip to our Maritimes on de rails?

"Yippers, but not my first train ride. Mom and Dad took me all the way to Ottawa back when I was but knee high to a grasshopper."

"Well, you'll be in fer a new experience on this trip. These days we refer to it as flying down de rails. And iff'in one's headed to our Maritimes we say flying down de rails ta Paradise." He passed the validated tickets back to Lyndsey. "Enjoy your flight, Lyndsey. If you need any assistance simply press that buzzer and we'll bees taking care of you. And byes the way, you've lucked out this trip."

"How so?" Lyndsey asked.

"You'll be flying first class all de way to Halifax with me Vernon Gunn and like you I'm head 'ng home to be with my kin folk over the Christmas Holidays. I'll be your conductor of choice on our flight home."

Lyndsey returned the tickets to her purse. She smiled and asked. "Where's home?"

"God's Country me Lass, I'm heading home to God's Country. I'll be catching a bus out of Halifax, then my folks will drive me de last stretch of my journey home ta Cape Breton, and Orangedale in the heart of Inverness County."

"Then I'll look forward to your company all the way to Halifax. Where we will meet family and drive down to East River."

"Have a great visit. Enjoy the South Shore. Out Chester way I assume. Being as you'll be heading down to East River. Iff'in you were to be heading north you'd land up in East River by New Glasgow."

Lyndsey smiled. Zerli held out her ticket for their conductor. He took the ticket and quickly punched out Zerli's validation holes in the ticket. "I see you'll be leaving us in Moncton. Is it yer final destination?"

"No sir. Like you, Lyndsey and Richard my final leg of the journey is with family and a ride home to Hillsborough."

"Up there in railway-land home to the Rail Museum."

"So, you've been there?"

"I've been up yer way once or twice. Took the Dining Rail Excursion run both times. Hillsborough is one cute little town."

"Then you're one and two up on me. To my grandpa's chagrin I've never taken the excursion. Grandpa and a string of family behind him were die in the wool railwaymen."

"Ye'd best be booking an excursion then young lady. Tis never too late to put a sparkle in a Grandpappy's eye! Enjoy your flights lassies." The conductor walked away and greeted their fellow travellers.

"What a charming and chatty chap. Looks like we got lucky and will be entertained a time or two, straight through to Halifax, and Moncton for you Zerli."

"Lordie yes and he'd best have some coworkers on board, if he expects to get every ticket validate before we hit Montreal. Capers…Cape Bretoners they sure can talk up a storm and then some."

Both Lyndsey and Zerli laughed lightly. Lyndsey reached over and retrieved her travel bag. On seeing Lyndsey pull out her knitting from the bag, Zerli followed suit. Both ladies lost themselves in their knitting. An occasional rip and snort out of their napping companion, Richard added all-knowing smirks to their faces. Each recalled how their man vehemently when informed of his alleged snoring would deny it to the nth degree. The train slowed on approaching the heart of Montreal.

Their conductor entered their coach. Walking briskly along he called out, "Montreal Station in twenty minutes. Montreal Station in twenty minutes. Please remain seated until we come to full stop at the station. Anyone requiring assistance, please remain seated." He stopped on spotting the knitters. "Beautiful ladies, and I'm totally amazed. How did ye know I needed a pair of socks?"

Lyndsey pouted. She answered, "Mine's a pair of baby booties. They'll never fits you."

"And mine's the makings of a loveable sock monkey," Zerli added.

Richard stirred then with a wild yawn escaped the grasp of the Sandman.

"Welcome back to the land of the living, me son. Iff'in you and yer lassies need assistance remain seated and I'll lend ye a hand."

Richard rubbed his face vigorously. The train slowed to a near crawl and the coach darkened as it entered the covered approaches to the Montreal station. Ching, ding, drrrrup, silence. The train came to a full stop. Passengers scurried about gathering up the baggage. Once the coach had cleared out, our travelers stood up. They stretched. Richard and Zerli took possession of their bags. Lyndsey followed Richard's lead and exited the coach. Zerli followed. They exchanged parting farewells with their conductor and followed other passengers towards the station's escalators.

"Enjoy yer stopover. We'll be seeing you once we're heading out on our final leg, Home to de Maritimes."

CHAPTER 27

Back in East River, Barnie stomped and paced aimlessly about his living-room. Anger raged inside him and loud verbal cursing bounced off the walls. Where the fuck was his man and why hadn't they found the bitch's body? He'd directed his connections to find her vehicle. But like local law enforcement, they had failed to locate it. A man of action, Barnie tossed back the last of his rum on ice soother. On stepping outside his house, he staggered over to his Buick. Seated inside behind the wheel, Barnie raged on in a nonsensical dialog unheard by anyone. Had the words reached another's ears they'd have fled on hearing the murderous gibberish. Stones flew wildly on Barnie nailing the Buick's accelerator. The car shot out onto the road. A strip of black rubber enhanced a growing stretch of it already painted on the roadway. Curses prevailed throughout the highspeed ride. The brunt of it all landed on Ned Stone and his Mama. "You son of a bitch, Ned. You're useless. All I asked you to do was find the bitch or her vehicle. You'd best not be fucking with the Barnster. I've seen you eyeing her up and down on being served at the Pot! Fuck with me and you're a dead man! No body fucks with Barnie and lives to tell the tale. Absolutely nobody." The Buick skidded on veering off the street into the Lobster Pot Pub & Eatery's parking lot. It painted a strip of burnt rubber on the pavement.

He parked then walked up to the Pot's entrance and stepped inside. Fretting over an array of answers to his questions the truth hit him. He exhaled a deep sigh of relief. After all, he roused, the old Nedster always had an eye and a sweet spot for Eugee. The old fox had simply found her and was simply sampling the goods. Barnie had always suspected that the lass had a sex drive that matched her Daddy's good looks and shagging powers. In his head, flashbacks served up glances he'd enjoyed of her body in setting her straight back in the office. A stiffness arose down in his crotch. He savored the images of her tits and ass. He felt reassured that he'd solved the unanswered question, 'Where is Eugee. Is she safe?' Barnie relaxed. In the office, he wished Ned well. In his mind he pondered, did the girl have an ass like her Mama? He whispered, "Enjoy yourself, me son. But leave something for me and our paying clients. They demand nothing but the best." He paused then added, "And the suckers will pay the price tag I demand."

A rap on the door interrupted Barnie. He opened the door. Chad a cook stared at him. Chad asked, "Has Eugee surfaced, boss? God! Everybody's worried sick over her safety. We're getting concerned with the lack of any positive updates."

Barnie glanced down at the floor before looking Chad straight in the eyes. He replied, "Sorry, son. Everybody has been searching high and low. Like her family, everyone involved is sickened with grief. But hold tight. We will find her. We will get our Eugee back home safely!"

Chad nodded agreement with Barnie's words. He stuttered in replying, "Yes, we will boss. She's so lucky to have so many people working so hard to bring her home. Her family must be eternally gratified to have you leading the all-out efforts to find their, our Eugee."

Barnie nodded agreement. "We will get our Eugee back home safe Chad. Trust me, we will." He patted Chad on the shoulder then turned back into the office, closed and locked the door. There he reflected on the words shared with Chad. A smirk popped out on his face. He frowned confirming there was no way on earth that the little bitch would work another shift at the Lobster Pot Pub & Eatery. She was just too valuable an asset to Barnie's other business enterprises. After all, the big boys would gladly drop big bucks and their drawers to have a go at what sweet little Eugee had to offer up. Frustration set in. Barnie speed-dialed Ned's cell number. Once again it flew directly into voice mail. He disconnected, then lost himself in reviewing the Pot's books. They were enjoying a good haul considering the absence of their most productive and highest tipped waitress. One number warmed Barnie's heart. The Eugette reward fund continued to grow with each passing day. He pondered how can I best put that money to work. Where will it work best for me? In a flash the morning flew by without an interruption.

Another pounding on the office door pulled Barnie out of a fretful nap. He'd dozed off in reviewing the books. "Be right with you. Give me a second or two." The pounding continued. At the door Barnie released its lock. He pulled the door open. A frantic Anna starred at Barnie their eyes locked. Barnie broke the connection. He asked, "What is it, Anna. What's the problem?" Anna remained wordless. Barnie looked Anna straight in the eyes. He said, "No, sadly they have not yet found our Eugee. I'm so very sorry. But right this minute. No. I cannot say that she's home safe." Barnie paused then added with a stern facial expression, "Sorry, wish I could but I can't, Anna. Please get control of yourself."

Anna babbled expressing her inner fears, "Oh no! I know you can't sir. We're just so worried. But that's not why I disturbed you sir."

"Then what the hell is it, girl? Spit it out, damn you to hell and back. Just spit it out, girly!"

Anna pulled herself together. She pointed down towards the dining area. "It's him. It's Pastor Mikie, Jesus. Mister Stone, Ned's partner. Oh my God. You'd best come see him. He's preaching to all the diners. Urging them to git off their arses and git out there and bring our Eugee home ... Dead or alive! Please, she just can't be dead. Not our Eugee!" Anna burst into tears. She sobbed and pointed towards the dining area. Barnie shoved Anna aside and stomped off down the hallway. Spotting Mikie spewing out his salvation rhetoric inflamed Barnie's anger. He grabbed hold of Mikie's pastoral garb and fought to suppress a growing sneer from becoming a snicker. Barnie dragged Mikie off towards the Pot's entrance. There he forced the door open and tossed Mikie outside. Barnie's booted foot added speed to Mikie's exit as it landed forcefully on his butt.

Rage overtook Barnie. He glared out at the stumbling Mikie. A police officer stepped out through the door and walked up to Barnie's side. He stated, "Leave him to me sir, I will address his inappropriate behaviour. Our teams and volunteers don't need his crude goings on while we work to get our Eugee home for Christmas?"

Barnie suggested, "Sergeant Stafford perhaps you could drag his sorry arse off to your office and lock him up. The fool thinks he's the second coming of you know who!"

The sergeant replied, "Don't tempt me, Barnie. But if push comes to shove, I may act on your suggestion." He paused and glanced around the parking lot. On seeing nobody else close at hand he added, "The crazy son-of-a-bitch should be locked up. Unfit for a jail cell. But should be locked up all the same!"

"So true! This town doesn't need a born-again wacko loose on its streets!" Barnie answered.

The sergeant made ready to step away. Barnie coaxed him to hold on a second or two. Then two staffers appeared bearing take-out coffee trays loaded to the max, along with two boxes of assorted sweets. They offered them to the sergeant, who gracefully accepted the goods. Barnie and the staffers received hearty thanks then the sergeant walked away. Staffers cast a warm thanks Barnie's way. He walked back inside and headed back to his office. Word spread quickly through the customers in the dining area. Tips accelerated along with donations towards the search and rescue efforts.

Back in the office, Barnie sat at his desk. Frustration ate away at his inner soul. Could he now be facing not only the loss of his top waitress, but access to the money her body would have generated through other revenue sources. He pounded the desktop with his fist. Could it possibly get any worse he pondered?

CHAPTER 28

John's cell phone called out announcing an incoming call. He eyed the 902-area code displayed on the cell's display and casually answered it. "Hello."

"Oh my God! It's you. It's my little niece Eugette. I can't wait to get home fer Christmas sweetheart."

John smiled and recovered. He replied, Sorry Auntie Lila. This is John, John Ramsay. Hold on and I'll get Eugette for you. Just a second. Hold on." John smiled at Eugette and passed the phone to her.

Eugette took the phone from John. In moving it towards her ear a steady chatter of conversation flowed out of the phone's speaker. "Thank you, thank you. Oh, my Lordie I feel so blessed. Are you there, sweetheart? Oh lands. I'm truly blessed I am." To Eugette the voice sounded vaguely familiar. Weaker but somehow familiar. A warm memory flashed up in Eugette's mind. In it a beautiful blonde toddler strutted through her thoughts. The toddler's attire nailed down the occasion. Eugette gazed internally at the rosy cheeks and blue eyes out of her past. The beautiful pink sweater now sat in a hope chest back in Chester in her bedroom along with the matching pink slippers on the toddler's feet. God! She thought, were my legs ever chunky and fat! I was a fat kid. Ugh! She shouted into the receiver, "Auntie Lila? Auntie Lila is it really you? Oh my God. It's really you."

"It's me, sweetheart. Oh, I'm so excited. You'll be here with me tomorrow. I can't wait to wrap you up in my arms and hugs that little sweetheart I ain't seen fer years. Too many years."

"I know. It took the recollection your voice triggered in my mind. It was Easter way back in the day. You and Uncle Joshua were visiting I was what two maybe two and a half? God! I love that beautiful pink knitted outfit you made for me. My Megan wore it and one day her daughter will too."

"You still, have it?"

"Yup! It's in Megan's hope chest in my bedroom back home."

Parker Rose interrupted the conversation. "What beautiful memories ladies. Are we ready to make fresh ones starting tomorrow? Say, yes!"

"Yup!" Answers sang out first from Auntie Lila then from Eugette.

Auntie Lila added, "I can't thank you enough Mister Rose. Maria called me and explained what was happening. First, I got that number from yer mom, sweetheart and I called it. That nice inspector, I like his voice. It's sexy!"

"Auntie!"

"Can't help myself girlie. The man's got a sexy voice in my opinion."

Eugette and Parker chuckled over Lila's lively demeanor and spoken views,

Auntie Lila broke into the laughter, "Then you called Parker and confirmed everything was a go. And that nobody was pulling me leg. Us seniors gotta be careful. If Parker had called me before your mom. Lands sake! I'd never have answered the phone. There's just too many crazy scammers out there today. Timmy was a tad leery when I first explain our planned adventure. Then he settled down on learning where I'd be heading to fer Christmas. I'm there for you, sweetheart, your mom and your babies. Joshua would be too but he'll have to watch over everything from heaven. My Joshua passed on years back. Lord, I miss my man. My squeeze. You must too. Rusty was a good man. You must miss him."

"I do, Auntie."

"And your mom misses her Martin. Another good man. But something tells me she has eyes on another one these days, a Jeffery I believe. I never could then I never really looked. But good for your mom. She's still a young one. Suspect she has a mile or two left on her chassis." Eugette giggled. Auntie added, "And if I hear right, so do you, sweetheart. Have a new man in your life, that is. I look forward to hooking up with both of my nieces and checking out the new men in their lives. However, I'm only seventy-two you know and my wits are still as sharp as ever. The lad giving us all this trouble. He got it straight from his gene pool you know. His Mama never was a sharp one. However, she was a good Mama. She tried to raise the boy right. But iff'in his daddy was who rumour said he be. Well, she never did get married. Which tells me the girl had some sense about her."

"The bastard!" Eugette uttered.

"Aye, that he was and is to the full definition of the word. A bastard at birth and a bastard through his actions. Or so I'm told. Oh! Sweetheart, you get in at 3:20 pm. Shall I meet you at the airport? It's but a short run from Murray River to Charlottetown.

"No! Auntie. John has rented a vehicle. We're good and can't wait to see you tomorrow. Loves ya, Auntie."

"Me too Eugee. Sorry! I know you don't like that nickname. But I love it. Oh! My neighbour Timmy will be here tomorrow. He wouldn't take no for an answer. Supper will be off the grill. The old bugger loves to barbecue amongst other things."

Eugette asked, "So you do have a man in your life Auntie?"

"Well, sort of. He's a retire railway man. Not that he's ever very far from a train. No, I stand corrected, Timmy's never very far away from a model railway train set up. But I'm sure he'll tell you all about it. Just a great neighbour to have in the neighbourhood. And sweetie, he gives great hugs on occasion."

Eugette took the cue from John. She smiled and said, "Gotta go, Auntie. Love ya. See you tomorrow."

Bye, bye, sweetheart. Oh! I'm thinking, no never mind. See you both tomorrow."

Eugette disconnected the call. She cuddled up into John's arms savoring his body heat. Smiles burst out on both their faces. Both wondered if they'd get a word in edgewise on arriving at Auntie Lila's in Murray River, PEI. Eugette pulled free of John. She asked, "Supper, what would you like?"

John stood up at her side. They kissed. He suggested they hit the Blue Buzzard in Downtown Newmarket. With no objections voiced, they stepped outside, locked up, then headed off to the Blue Buzzard. A sense of anticipation embraced their thoughts.

CHAPTER 29

Megan and Taylor sat cuddled up on Auntie Hope's lap. Like Hope, they gazed about the living-room and sipped at their mugs of hot chocolate. Mister Gilbert had ceded to Auntie Hope's nudges and allowed them to add a little Christmas cheer to the house. Both had hesitated and shied away from getting excited about Christmas this year. Neither had bothered with writing and posting their letter to Santa. Their Christmas list matched each other's to a T. They reinforced the passions behind their list nightly and frequently throughout the day in fervent prayers for their mom and her safe passage home for Christmas. Great sorrow and regrets were expressed in those prayers and they pleaded for forgiveness for the odd occasion when they might have misbehaved once or twice.

Taylor broke the silence in the room. He asked, "So Mommie is flying to Murray River to get our Great Auntie Lila? I thought you were our only Auntie, Auntie Hope. You're a Great Auntie in my books fer sure."

"Mine too!" Megan added. "I can't wait to hugs her and bury my face in Mommie. Smell her and know she is really my Mommy."

"Me too, sweethearts. You know why Auntie Lila is coming this Christmas?"

Megan answered, "Yes. Somebody is afraid of what Mommie knows. And Mommie ran away from home to stay safe."

"Ya!" Taylor added. "Roger and Mister Rose, you know a friend of the ones who helped Lyndsey and Richard get married, and Inspector

Harley think Great Auntie Lila will add a distraction and energy to Christmas in Chester. Take thoughts away from Mom and what's happened to her. What is Great Auntie Lila like? Is she really a distraction?"

Megan frowned and said, "Will she stink, you know smell? Will she smell like that old teacher, Miss Rumple? Boy, she stinks sometimes."

Hope took the empty mugs from the twins and placed them on the coffee table. She then hugged them both while blowing bubbles onto their bellies. She asked, "Does your Grammie smell nice?"

"Well, yes. Grammie smells really nice. Ask Grampa Jeffy. He's always sniffing Grammie and telling her how beautiful she smells." Taylor answered.

Megan added, "He sure wouldn't be telling Miss Rumple how nice she smells."

"Let's not be too harsh on Miss Rumple." Hope injected.

"Well, Billy Samples said, 'She taught his dad in grade six. And she was stinky way back then. His dad claims she could clear the classroom with just one fart.'" Megan boasted.

Hope sensed it was time for a topic change. She lifted Taylor off her lap and set him down next to Megan who had slid of Auntie Hope's lap. On standing up, Hope grinned and boasted, "First one into the kitchen gets the last of the Peppermint Candy cane ice-cream!" The twins bolted towards the kitchen then stopped dead in their tracks. At the kitchen entrance they stood and smiled back at Auntie Hope. She obliged and walked around them into the kitchen. The twins raced after her over to the table and sat. They eyed Hope's every move. Hope asked, "Cones or bowls?"

"Cones, please!" Both twins shouted back with glee. They intently watched Hope scoop the ice-cream into three cones. The task emptied the ice-cream bucket and the box of cones. Smiles greeted Hope on her arrival at the table. She sat and joined Megan and Taylor in helping their treats vanish.

Taylor boasted, "Grampa Jeffy, likes his in a bowl. Likes it better in a big bowl. But I like mine in a cone." He licked his fingers free of ice-cream left on both hands."

Hope asked, "What's next?"

Megan frowned then asked, "We're really, really excited about getting our Christmas wish and don't care if Santa overshoots our house. Cause we know what we're getting. What do you want from Santa, Auntie Hope?"

Hope cast herself into a look of deep thought and reflection. Several moments dragged past. Then a glimmer ignited and sparks flew out of her eyes. She announced, "I'm getting more than I asked Santa for. Right this minute Lyndsey my sister is in Montreal waiting to get on a train to come join up with us for Christmas."

"Wow! She's really on a train. A train like we saw in Halifax with Grampa Jeffy?"

"Yes! And she will be here tomorrow along with her husband Richard."

"I like him." Megan boasted. "He's cute!"

"Oh, please." Taylor moaned. "Men aren't cute."

"He is too. And so is Dwayne Maxwell. I like him!" Megan boasted.

Taylor shivered, "Girls. You've all got one track minds."

Hope doubled over in laughter taking in the twin's banter. In glancing at Taylor, she spotted the makings of a future heartthrob. One that would set many a young lass's heart into skipping a beat or two. She nudged the conversation a touch sideways. "Say, wouldn't it be cool to ride the rails like Lyndsey and Richard are right now? We could climb aboard the train in Halifax and head to Truro or even further like Moncton?"

"Could I ride up front with the engineer?" Taylor asked.

Hope frowned and signaled a negative with a swinging sidewise of her head. Taylor asked, "Why not? I'd be good."

The crunch of gravel in the driveway distracted the conversations. Taylor raced to the door then ran outside on spotting Grammie and Grampa Jeffy. Megan and Hope followed. All were chided and chased back inside. The chiding wasn't challenged. Megan and Taylor knew shoes, boots and coats were the order of the day outside in December. Hope shrugged knowing slippers and a sweater didn't count. Taylor and

Megan ran back inside. The adults followed. Hope fired up the kettle after having offered up a round of tea. Taylor boasted, "Grammie, guess what? We're going on a train ride with Auntie Hope just like Richard and Lyndsey are right this minute."

Hope gulped then smiled across the table at the twins each sitting on an adult's lap. The kettle's whistle sang out loudly and rescued her. No explanations were needed or expected. It was the Christmas Season and wishful dreaming ruled everyone's day sun up to sun down. Gazing into the twins faces their energy stole her heart and a wish list gained focus.

CHAPTER 30

Harley Kingston stood and waved on spotting Gilbert enter the restaurant. A grin broke out on his face on recognizing Parker Rose at Gilbert's side. On their arrival at the booth his grin expanded. He jovially proclaimed, "This really cements the deal bringing in a legal gun slinger of noted repute. Smart move, Gillie."

"Good to see you, Harley. Good to be on the same team for once." Parker boasted. "It's been years since we worked the same case. Mind you, after I refocused my practice and expertise your success rate must have soared."

"Right! But trust me, getting you on our side means the pleasure's all mine, Parker. I just want to nail this bastard for all the hurt he's inflicted on good people."

Parker nodded in agreement. They all took seats at the booth. "I take it you're not retired, Harley?"

"Not a chance. I've got unfinished business on the table. I almost feel like that British detective of fame. God! What was his name? Just one more clue and I'll nail the bastard to the wall." He bowed his head and chuckled. "Maybe on hearing the judge render a JUSTIFIED verdict, I could give it some thought. I want to close this one out big time."

Their waitress appeared at the booth. Drinks were ordered and she left giving them time to review the menu. Parker commented on the menu's unique structure, "I like the choices. Have you gone vegan on me, Harley? Not that it's a bad thing! But I'll confess the little darling strutting about at my side these days is totally vegan. And she's sold me on it too!"

Harley chuckled. He replied first, "My Beverley, Sweet Bev, worked on me for years. Hell, I would take the lunches she lovingly made and lose them in the office fridge. Then I'd hit the fast-food outlets. I tried to fool my Lass. But she knew and God bless her she never stopped loving me. By the Jess! I miss my Bev."

"She was a sweetheart, Harley. Just like my Karyn. When it came to the finer sex, we sure knew how to pick them."

Harley roared in laughter. He boasted, "We knew, my friend. We didn't have a clue. Our ladies knew what they wanted and once they caught sight of us our days on the singles scene were numbered!" The table fell silent. Their waitress returned with three tumblers of liquid refreshments. They ordered their meals off the daily specials.

Parker commented, "So, are you also on board with the vegan scene, Gilbert?"

Harley injected, "Not likely! But the lad has shed a pound or two since I last saw him."

"No. I'm towing the line. Walking the straight and narrow line." Gilbert boasted in self-defence.

Harley cut in, "If I might note, I've detected a swagger of late in our chats and definitely in the aura you're projecting, Gilbert. Could there also be a lady on your scene of late?"

"No!" Gilbert replied.

Harley chuckled and added, "Don't be denying it now, Gillie. I called your place once or twice and Jeffery and little Hope have been keeping me up to date."

Their meals were delivered. Conversation switched from male bonding into ums and aahs, as the men savored their food. With their plates emptied they were cleared and a second round of refreshments were ordered. Harley asked, "So, Parker, what inspired you to come up with the hairbrained idea to bring Eugette's Aunt Delilah home for Christmas? I know you're creative. Your firm has busted several of my cases, that I believed were air tight, wide open. You should have stuck with your notoriety and not shifted your focus onto wedded domestic terminations. Or, as a number of my fellow officers would say, domestic annihilations. But really, do you think Auntie will deliver the distraction we need? Most thoughts will be centered on Christmas. Christmas will also stir up longings. Never mind. I get it! Bringing her home will sweeten Christmas in the hearts of the many locals that have worked and volunteered diligently towards finding and bringing Eugette home safe to her family and friends. I've chatted with Auntie. And yes, I did occasionally get a word in edgewise." The three chuckled aloud over Harley's declaration. He injected, "I'm an old generation cop. I still hold a cautious hesitancy as to whether a feeble old senior Auntie can really distract attention and thoughts away from Maria Lamont's daughter?"

Parker grinned boastfully. "Yes! As you noted Harley, I got my start in criminal law. I'm sure you're aware, Harley, research is a big part of every case worked. Roger's team dug deep into the facts. They uncovered an eye opener. I want to nail the bastard! Criminal law has always held a soft spot in my preferences. But back onto your question. After working with Roger, on several related cases that both our firms were working, I attended a theatre fundraiser. Key backers got to head backstage and hob nobble with the directors, crews, actors and actresses. The leading lady took a shining to Moi! Recognized a prime catch the minute our eyes caught sight of each other."

"Really? Being a notorious legal eagle, you'd never bullshit me?"

"Furthest thing from my mind, Harley. But after the Ramsays called on Roger. Let's just say the challenge intrigued me. Not to mention the opportunity to get back working on a criminal case and teaming up with you. And, as you know, everyone involved bounced ideas around the table. I bounced the distraction concept off my leading lady, Fantine, and she suggested it would work. They use it on the stage with ease. More than you could imagine. I touched base with Gilbert. It's like the magical workings of a magician. Cast the deflection coyly and with ease. Its effect will work magically in our favor. Gilbert, you bought in with just a little hesitation. Harley, you hummed and hawed over the plus minuses involved. But with Gilbert's nudging you bought in. Although you did state clearly, *'Parker you're crazier than a shit house rat.'*" Parker chuckled aloud. He continued, "After you and Gilbert chatted with Maria Lamont, she bought into the idea! And Auntie called you directly."

Harley injected, "I just don't want any harm to come to anyone involved!"

"It won't," Parker replied. He added, "But after she'd contacted Auntie, Maria did experience a touch of uncertainty. At that point I asked her to speak with my Fantine. The ladies hit it off. Fantine sold Maria on the idea after both had talked with Eugette. Then you must recall, Maria connected me up with her Auntie Dalilah...Lila over in PEI. Murray River to be precise." Parker paused. Then added, "Wait till ya meet up with Auntie Lila. Why, like you, I too was lucky to get a word in edgewise in all of our chats. What a sweetheart. Couldn't thank me enough. Hasn't been home in a dog's age. Then the topper, my Fantine is an Islander! Knows several families living down the road from Lila. Trust me! Christmas will be a blast. Jeffery said Fantine and I could bunk out at the old McClaken Homestead, but I insisted on taking a room at a nearby Bed & Breakfast. I suspect some of Chester's mature residents will recall Auntie should they bump into her over Christmas. A homecoming Christmas for sure! Trust me, Auntie isn't feeble!" Their waitress appeared with the bill in hand. Parker reached first and retrieved the bill. "My treat boys. I can't wait to get together in East River for Christmas."

Harley and Gilbert thanked Parker. Then Harley asked, "Have you got room for homeboy over Christmas Gil? I'd hate to be stuck up here in the city all on my lonesome."

Gilbert stood and shook Parker's hand. He turned to Harley and nodded a positive then added, "What's one more? We'll find a spot to put you up, good friend."

The three men exited the restaurant. Outside they separated and headed off back into their workaday worlds.

CHAPTER 31

Lyndsey stepped off the escalator, steadied by her hand in Zerli's. Richard followed them. Both shuffled off of the massive flow of hurried travellers. They stood in awe of the station's aura. It was huge. To Zerli, it was old hat. She'd traveled the rails on countless rides back home and in returning to her home in Newmarket. Richard eyed their baggage. He suggested, "Four hours is a stretch. I will find a locker then catch up with you, Lyndsey. Is there a spot I should head to after I snag a locker?"

Zerli nudged Lyndsey, "Let's hit the amazing underground shops. They've got absolutely everything a mom-to-be could want." Lyndsey nodded a yes reply. She stood gazing in awe of their surroundings.

Zerli looked to Richard and answered. "We'll be there. In the maternity shops. They're easy to find Richard, there are signs everywhere." The women walked off.

Richard watched them disappear around a corner. He shrugged. A quick glance located the station's lockers. He headed straight to them. With their baggage stowed away safely, he started to meander about the station. The constant flow of people amazed him. Newmarket and East River remained his first choices in the realm of best places to live. He pondered. If Lyndsey's career took her here, could/would he follow? The question went unanswered. The truth won out. Where Lyndsey went, Richard would follow. A huge burger pit caught his eye. Actually, the aromas wafting from its grills did the trick. With no sign of the ladies, Richard opted to tend to a rising hunger within. The wait at his table was short. The server delivered Richard's order on a tray, a monster cheese burger, fries and a tall frosty beer. He lost himself in the pleasures set before him.

Down below in the shops, Lyndsey and Zerli were lost inside a Baby Clothing Boutique. They had visited a series of ladies and baby boutiques. This one's size and vast product lines amazed Lyndsey. She grimaced, maybe we should have gone for that ultrasound testing that the doctor had suggested to know whether our baby was a boy or a girl. The outfits Zerli held pulled Lyndsey in opposite directions. She fretted. Could Dolly be right? If yes, pink was the one to take. However, Noreen had warned her not to put too much credence into Dolly's needle works. And she had not been referring to Dolly's knitting. Dolly's readings on Noreen during both pregnancies had missed the target. If the same held true now, blue was the way to go.

Zerli interrupted her thoughts. "I'm twisted too, Lyndsey. Go with the pink. I'm sensing a daughter will be your first."

"Gads! My first? How many am I carrying?"

Zerli broke out in laughter. Lyndsey walked up to her and retrieved both outfits from her friend. She walked towards the cash. Along the way she paused in areas she'd visited earlier. In each one she snapped up outfits that had caught her eye earlier. A positive swagger energized Lyndsey's step. Zerli simply smiled in feeling the energies her new friend and mother-to-be exuded. In her mind she savored recollections of her pregnancies. All seven had been blessings. Blessings that had earned her Grandmother Status. On exiting the boutique, they spotted Richard in a Ladies Boutique. Zerli sneaked a peek catching him at the cash. He earned her respect. Lyndsey looked away, secure in her belief that Christmas magic worked best if discovered Christmas morning under the tree. Richard stepped out of the boutique and quickly spotted them. Together the trio made their way back up to the station's arrivals/departures area. Time had slipped by faster than anticipated. Line ups had formed starting at the boarding gate for their train. A voice boomed out over the station's speakers, "Sleeping car passengers for the Ocean Limited, please proceed to your boarding gate."

Richard rushed off and retrieved their travel bags. He quickly returned and joined Lyndsey and Zerli in the line that had formed. Another voice called out on the speakers, "Passengers requiring boarding assistance please identify yourself to the boarding assistants."

One could feel the energy and excitement building. A friendly but familiar voice greeted them. "Laddie, it would be my pleasure to assist you, your lady and the expectant grandmother in boarding. Please follow me. Oh! Let me take those parcels." Their charming conductor freed Lyndsey and Zerli of their shopping bags. They followed him with Richard in tow. Down below, the excitement escalated on arriving at the entrance to their sleeper car. Once aboard, they made their way to the seat assigned on their tickets. To Lyndsey and Zerli's pleasure they were again traveling together. Zerli's seat directly across from Richard and Lyndsey. Richard had barely stowed and arranged their baggage and packages filled with boutique purchases when the flood gates opened up. Sleeping car and coach passengers stepped lively in seeking out their assigned cars. To Richard and Lyndsey's surprise the boarding went quickly. Other than three stragglers, boarding was completed in under fifteen minutes. They had expected longer based on the cued passengers awaiting the general boarding call. Zerli simply settled in then boasted, "You'll learn in no time. There's no stopping a Maritimer headed back home on these pre-Christmas flights. It's pure bedlam. But fear not. We've got a personal guide a Caper, Cape Bretoner, our Conductor Vernon. I suspect this is a going to be one wing dinger of a flight down the rails?

Both Lyndsey and Richard stared with questioning looks on their faces at Zerli. They wondered, what did we get ourselves into?

Zerli chuckled. "You've never been on a Holiday Run, have ye?" Neither replied. "Well, ye'd best just sit back and relax. I'm guessing the party will break out well before midnight." Train whistles bleated out their song. Their sleeper car jerked softly once, then twice. It then smoothed out into a relaxing gait. Zerli lost herself in her knitting. Both Lyndsey and Richard stared out their window at the scenery flying past.

A grin broke out on Lyndsey's face on recognizing Vernon's voice in conversation with another group of travellers.

"Well, looks like we'll all be blessed once de celebrating breaks out me son. Oyez, it'll be a grand one! I be taking it ta be that ye lads have yer instruments with ye? And would ye be let' in a Fellow Caper with his harmonica joins up wit ya? That being me."

"Wouldn't have it any other way me, son."

"And what enticed ya to fly home down de rails, me son, and not soar above de clouds in a sardine can?"

"Oyez, we just wrapped up our tour. Needing a little recuperation time. Ya knows, some good old down time. Haven't flown down de rails since I was but knee high to a grasshopper and on me grandpa's knee. And that weren't yesterday, Vernon, me son."

"Oh my God, Richie. Who is that person, Vernon's chatting with? I know that voice!"

"Tickets, Laddies and Lasses. And welcome aboard the Ocean Limited Christmas Express. Vernon Gunn, your conductor, at your service."

Beaming, Lyndsey handed their tickets to Vernon. He quickly snipped, snapped, punched and verified their rights of passage along with Zerli's.

"I see a wee bit of shopping was seen to in Montreal. A fine place to be adding to a ladies' finery. Iff'in, you catch me drift. Oh! Jest so you're not shocked, I'll be performing wit our celebrity band of renown at our Christmas Jammer a wee bit later. Ye'd best be rested and well fed. De dining car is straight back that away. I suggest de fillet of sole." Everyone's faces lit up on hearing Vernon's announcement.

Zerli piped up, "And where's de party ta be, Vernon?"

"Same place you're headed fer supper. De dining car. Comes prepared to rock de night aways! Tickets, tickets. Please have your tickets ready for your charming Conductor Vernon Gunn."

Before anyone could ask another question, Vernon had moved on to the next sleeper car.

....

On arriving in the dining car our trio seated themselves at the table they'd been led to. All the items fired up their hunger. However, three orders of fileted sole were placed, along with two white wines and a diet ginger ale. Darkness had overtaken the landscape outside. Friendly chitter chatter flowed between the dining friends. Once the orders arrived, they lost themselves in their dining delights. With the meal plates cleared they settled in on their teas. Lyndsey's eyes floated in awe about the dining car. In her mind's setting she was carried off into dining venues set in movies once filmed in; *The Orient Express, The Titanic, Tiffany's* along with a favorite venue, the Royal York in Toronto where her adoptive parents took her with them to celebrate their anniversaries. No aspect of their travels had invoked John's images of flying down the rails in a silver sardine can. She savored the friendly banter of Vernon their conductor. Deep within herself Lyndsey struggled to place the voice she'd heard in conversation with Vernon earlier in their sleeper car. Suddenly it hit. A weekend filled with rising bands while attending the U of Toronto. She knew the band and its lead singer. They'd gone on to tour globally. Alice, a fellow student, claimed he'd hit on her. But in her mind Lyndsey knew the truth. He'd hit on Lyndsey! She stared, google eyed, off into the dining car. His name remained on the tip of her tongue but it eluded her efforts to recall the name.

Richard called out, "Hello! Lynds, earth to Lyndsey, where are you, my Love?"

Lyndsey snapped back into the dining cars reality. She smiled with charm at Richard and Zerli. They both bust out in laughter. With their teas empty all three stood and made their way back to their sleeper car. Images of the Christmas Jammer soon-to-be energized their minds.

....

Ring, ring...rin. Eugette reached into her purse and retrieved the new cell phone John had gifted in advance of Santa's arrival. On seeing the caller's ID, a smile broke out on her face. A swipe of its face answered the call.

"Hi, sweetheart. I sure am looking forward to seeing ya at the airport. It's been way too long since we last got together. Oh, you were such a sweetie pie."

"Hi, Auntie Lila. We're looking forward to seeing you too. It's been a stretch since we last got together. I can't chat too long, Auntie. We're driving to the airport now and traffic is really heavy."

"Oh, I won't keep you long. Just wanted to touch base. And say how excited I am to have my great-niece and her man visit me in Murray River. Say, Eugee, how in the dickens do you manage to drive those crazy highways up on the mainland and survive. I've been told those Toronto drivers are absolutely crazy. They want to get to where they're going before they pull out'ta their driveways. Now you be sure your young man drives safely. Would you like to say hi to my neighbour Timmy? He's right her..."

"I better not, Auntie Lila. The airport is just up ahead. I best let you go and stay safe."

"Well then, we'll be seeing you and yer man real soon. Oh! I'll call your mom and tell her all's Ok. OK?"

"Ok Auntie. See you soon." Eugette disconnected the call.

John glanced over her way. A smile filled his face. "I take it that was a great call. Your Auntie sure is a lady with a tale or two to tell. I'm looking forward to meeting her. I never had anyone like her in my life."

Eugette grinned, then broke into laughter. She boasted, "Then you're in for a treat. But she is a sweetheart. Never missed a birthday. If you were family the card was in your mailbox on the big day."

"I wish. Other than close family I never did get many cards." They fell silent. John maneuvered his way into a spot in an off-site airport parking lot. Together they stepped out into a bright sunny afternoon. Overhead a brilliant blue sky greeted our travellers. Upon being dropped at the airport's departures entrance their adventure gained momentum and took on a reality of its own. On approaching the check-in agent, Eugette totally relaxed. The reality of the moment hit her on hearing the agent ask for their tickets, John stepped up and passed their tickets to the agent.

"Any baggage to check in?" Their agent asked.

"No." John replied. He added, "Got lucky and my brother took it on their trip to Halifax. Not to worry, they're flying down the rails to Halifax. Left yesterday and should get there today."

"Sounds romantic," the agent replied with a smile.

John chuckled and said, "No. Think I'll stick with the highway in the sky. Have a good day. Merry Christmas." The agent passed their tickets and boarding passes to John. Their check-in had flowed very quickly. John retained their one piece of luggage a carryon sports bag and passed Eugette her ticket and boarding pass.

Eugette asked, "Was she hitting on you?" John chuckled turned to Eugette and they kissed.

He pulled away and added., "No way. Besides, this boy is taken." Eugette rewarded him with a quick kiss. They wandered through several shops but quickly tired of the endless array of goods encountered. Shopping just didn't energize the moment for either one. Together, they presented their boarding passes and entered the preboarding security cue. Gazing at the long lineup Eugette was in awe and intimidated by the huge numbers of airline passengers. The feeling eased. With only a small carryon sports bag they quickly cleared security. Once through security with their boarding passes in hand Eugette felt at ease with her hand in John's.

On passing a book shop, a book cover caught Eugette's eye. Several coworkers had been reading it. They swore it to be a must read. John followed her lead. On seeing Eugette reach out towards the book John picked it off the shelf. The title failed to ring a bell for him. In eying it John commented, "An interesting take on religion. I've never really seen it weaved into a fictional storyline. In our home the word was taken seriously. No jesting down that path."

"Me too," Eugette commented. But several coworkers dealing with serious life issues have been reading it. They suggested it to anyone who'd listen. It may sound strange but it wasn't their words of suggestion that piqued my interest. It was their persona, their aura. I can't explain. But it just called out to me. Does that make me weird?"

John stared at the book's cover. In a flash he felt the aura of his earlier island adventure touch his inner soul. An icy but warm feeling overcame him. He pulled Eugette to his body. They kissed. On releasing her he said, "No, you're not weird. Life is strange at times. It's yours, the book, and it's on me."

"Really?"

"Yes, really. Give it a go. If you take on the glow of your coworkers, you just might sell me on giving it a try." John led the way to the cash. Together they made their way to a coffee shop and settled on two teas. From there they headed to their boarding gate. Seated Eugette lost herself in the pages of her book. John sat beside her, lost in his own thoughts. So much had changed in his life since the accident. The latest twist had come about on his flight home after the wedding at Gilbert's. He been coerced into trading his window seat with young Howard for an aisle seat. The trade had landed him beside Father Lawrence Hardy, the priest he discovered who had actually baptized John years earlier. The recollection had warmed John's heart anew to a distant religious upbringing. A chuckle almost escaped his lips as he recalled meeting up with Father Lawrence at the Blue Buzzard. It had been a good meet up and the first he could recall ever seeing a member of the clergy hoisting a frosty beer.

The general boarding call caught their attention. Once seated and buckled up their aircraft started to taxi towards the runway. John glanced sideways towards Eugette as their aircraft raced down the runway. In the blink of an eye, they were airborne and had leveled off on reaching their cruising altitude. He gazed over at Eugette. She stared at the pages of the book held in her hands. Tears streamed down her cheeks. John leaned in for a kiss. The book dropped. They kissed. Eugette whispered, "I'm ok. They're tears of joy. I'm going home. Home to my babies, home to mom." A second kiss followed. John pulled away. They smiled at each other. Eugette slipped back into her book. John relaxed and settled back into his seat. He missed the coffee delivery having slipped off into a light nap. The aircraft's decent and approach to the landing runway awoke

John. A glance downwards and he caught sight of his hands clasped in Eugette's right hand. Although he'd never been to the Island somehow, at the moment, they touched down and PEI just felt right.

Deboarding unfolded quickly. On walking towards the baggage area, a loud sharp but welcoming voice shouted out, "Over here, sweetie, over here sweetheart. It's me, your Auntie Lila. Welcome to PEI, and you too, sweet cheeks!" They glanced towards the voice. A short four foot-eleven thunderbolt raced towards them. Eugette opened up her arms. Niece and Auntie buried themselves in a long overdue embrace. John stood aside and watched the reunion unfold. The energy Auntie exuded bounced outward and caressed John. He relaxed. Auntie Lila's energy somehow eased his concerns. The fears vanished once Auntie Lila extended her greeting to John. The lady's warmth stole his heart. Somehow, he felt at home. Next up, Lila introduced them to her neighbour and chauffeur Timmy. John declined the offer of a ride. He explained that they had prebooked an SUV. At the rental vehicle Timmy thought aloud, "That's strange. They gave you one with Nova Scotia plates."

John declined to mention it had been arranged by Parker Rose. Once they had stepped into their vehicle, John followed Timmy and Lila's SUV through to Murray River. The drive passed quickly. Both John and Eugette were taken aback by the deep shades of green the grassy fields exalted in areas not covered in snow. After all, it was December. Inside Lila's home, after a short chat up, a homemade dinner centered around Timmy's barbecued cedar planked salmon steaks awaited them. Needless to say, we don't need to reveal who chattered the most. Both sighed on grasping the magnitude of the meal. However, no protests were raised. Timmy connected easily with John. After super Lila chased the two men out of her house. Timmy did not object. Excitedly, he lassoed John and dragged him three doors down the street to his house. Once inside, Timmy proudly shared his model railroad O scale layouts with John. The layouts fully occupied the home's two smaller bedrooms through a multitude of layered layouts. Had Auntie Lila not scurried over to retrieve John his entire vacation may have ended up inside

Timmy's railway wonderland. On returning to Lila's a warm embrace awaited John. Over late-night teas John listened and the ladies' shared memories of days past.

Tired eyes revealed themselves to Auntie Lila. She led her guests off to their bedroom. Standing outside the room she boasted, "Do nae be bashful, sweetheart. Yer Auntie ain't an old prude! Have yourselves a goodnights rest and whatever else might arise." Giggling Auntie Lila hugged each of her guests then strutted off to her own bedroom. The house fell silent. Stripped to the bare essentials, Eugette climbed under the covers. John eyed her exposed body and back. The healing had fast tracked and the yellow bruising was almost gone. He joined her under the covers. Committed to each other they snuggled up and exchanged a heated round of caressing. They'd yet to reach the next level in their relationship. Eugette not quite ready and John afraid to destroy the good thing they'd been building together. Physically they were ready. Physiologically they were getting closer. The sandman eased both off into his nighttime wonderland. Neither resisted his gentle nudges.

CHAPTER 32

Back at Gilbert's house in East River, Hope helped unload their massive Christmas grocery order. Jeffery had responded to her call for help. He loaded many bags of frozen produce into his truck, then drove home and placed them in his deep chest freezer. Afterwards he drove back over to Gilbert's. Hope had managed to stow away all of Gilbert's shopping spree that had remained under her watch. The noticeable missing item being the headliner of the Christmas Dinner set to feed everyone at Gilbert's this Christmas. She giggled in recalling past journey's up onto Buzzard Mountain for their Christmas trees and turkeys. It would be an adventure she looked forward to sharing with members of their reconnected family. Especially Lyndsey, her sister. With the task at hand completed, only the mug of green tea and Maria's arrival with the twins stood between her and the next task. Jeffery had passed control of his home, the old homestead to Hope. Together with Maria and the twins she would be adorning the home in its Christmas finery. The last task currently unfolding had the twins searching for the star attraction a Christmas Tree. This one coming from a local tree farm. Suddenly Hope was jarred free of her thoughts. The stomping of feet across the side deck announced the arrival of company. Before she could stand the kitchen door flew open. Megan ran inside with Taylor close behind.

"You gotta come right now Auntie Hope. Grampa Jeff is setting up the tree!" Taylor shouted.

"It's a big one!" Megan added.

Hope stood and retrieved her coat, hat, mitts and slipped into her winter boots. Together the trio stepped outside into a snowy winter wonderland. A light ten-centimeter snowfall had added a touch of Christmas Spirit to East River overnight. She walked across the yard towards the old homestead with an eager hand in each of hers. On passing the shed Megan and Taylor broke free and raced towards the front door. They shouted out. "Common Auntie Hope, Grammie and Grampa Jeff will be all done before we gits inside!"

Hope ran the last thirty feet and caught up with them at the front door. On stepping inside they found Jeffery stretched out on the floor under the tree. Grammie stood near the kitchen calling out instructions, "No! It needs to go right. It's leaning too far to the left. Or is that the other ways around?" On spotting the new arrivals she added, "We're almost ready. We'll need some decorations soon."

"I'll get them. They're in Pappy's bedroom closet. Let's go, Meg, Tay, I'll be needing some help." In the bedroom Hope retrieved the Christmas decorations from the closet. The smaller boxes were assigned to the twins. Hope stooped down and picked up one of the big boxes. A second trip to the bedroom and she joined everyone in the living-room. Jeffery and Maria stood side by side. Each nodded and tilted their heads several times. Once Maria gave the good to go, Jeffery started to string the led lights onto the tree. Hope assisted by untangling the stringed lights and handing them to Jeffery. In no time at all the tree was glowing with a multitude of coloured led lights.

Hope stooped down onto the floor and opened up the boxes. She announced the rules, "No jumping ups and downs. If you can't reach a branch leave it for an adult. Got it?"

"Got it, Auntie Hope." Megan answered.

Taylor shouted, "Can we do it now?"

"Yes. But be careful." Hope answered. She turned to Maria and Jeffery and asked, "Would hot chocolate work for both of you? I know it will for Meg, Taylor and me."

Silent nods approved the suggestion. Jeffery joined the twins in decorating the tree. In the kitchen, Hope spotted Maria looking faint. She rushed to her side. "Are you ok? Here, sit down and rest." Once Maria sat down, Hope set the kettle into action and prepared five mugs with chocolate and the extras. On retrieving the milk from the fridge, she eyed Maria anew. Concerned, Hope pulled a seat up next to Maria. She asked, "Is it a bug you've picked up? That sucks this time of the year." She reached out and touched Maria's forehead. There was no fever. "Did you just start feeling off, Maria? Can I get you something for it?"

Maria reached out and took Hope's hands in hers. Their eyes connected. She shivered and confessed, "I've only felt this way once before. If you know what I mean."

Hope's face lit up. Maria nibbled at her lower lip. She confirmed Hope's thoughts, "My clock is still running. I believe I'm pregnant."

Hope embraced Maria. She whispered, "Congratulations, Maria, does Uncle Jeff…" The kettle's whistle shouted out its readiness. Hope tightened the embrace then released Maria. She ran to the counter and tended to their hot chocolate drinks. Both gazed at each other. With the drinks ready she set them on the table along with the cookie jar. A glance over at the tree surprised Hope. It was almost fully decorated. Only its topper was missing. She sat down at Maria's side. "Are you sure?"

"Absolutely! Please not a word beyond me. I will talk to Jeffery and my Eugette after my doctor's appointment. But come the new year there'll be no hiding the truth." They embraced anew.

Hope committed to zipping her lips. She called out, "The tree looks great. Are we ready for some hot chocolate?"

Quickly the table filled up. The subject of conversation centered on the beautiful job they'd done in decorating the tree. Just as the last cookie disappeared from the cookie jar, the door opened and Gilbert stepped inside. On spotting the tree he nodded approval. Then asked, "Where's the angel Jeff? The job's not done till the angel sits atop the tree!"

Jeffery answered, "We're saving that for Grammie, Gil. Are you ready Love? Another Angel awaits your touch."

Maria answered, "Could I beg off, Love. I'm really tired. Hope, would you do us the honours, please?"

Without hesitation, Hope stood and walked over to the tree. Jeffery handed her the angel. After eyeing the tree from several angles, Hope set the beautiful angel atop the tree. Everyone, smiled signaling their approval. Gilbert pulled out his cell phone. He shouted, "Photo op. Everyone in front of the tree. Once they'd all gathered Gilbert fired off a ridiculous number of digital shots of the tree and the team that had decorated it. Satisfied, they took chairs in the living-room. All eyes taking in the tree's beauty. All but Hope. She busied herself about the kitchen cleaning up the remains of their hot chocolate Christmas treats. Jeffery switched on the stereo and soothing Christmas music filled the room. Each head filled with magical Christmas wishes along with eager hearts to see all their anticipated Christmas guests gathered at their sides. On completing her cleanup, Hope joined them. In walking into the living-room Maria's eyes caught hers. They smiled and nodded. Agreeing some Christmas cheer needed perfect timing.

CHAPTER 33

Off in Eastern Quebec the Via Rail's Christmas Express dining car was filling up with eager guests and fellow travelers. Chairs were arranged to allow the maximum number of guests to partake in the party about to get underway. The band set itself up. A last-minute special band guest stepped up to the microphone. "Welcome to our Via Rail Christmas Special, dear friends. I'm your Emcee tonight. And iff'in ya didn't catch it earlier the name is Vernon. Vernon Gunn with a G. Please relax. And iff'in ye knows de words feels free to join in and sing along with the band. Oh! I'd best introduce the lads. They're here with us flying de rails back home to God's Country, that being Cape Breton. Please join me in welcoming the D..."

Loud boisterous cheering and applause broke out. Vernon stepped aside. A fiddler took the stage and a Christmas reel broke out. Feet started stomping, hands clapping keeping beat with the fiddler. Two guitarists and a banjo picker joined in on the festivities. The clickity clack of the train's wheels vanished, overtaken by the music bursting forth throughout the night. A pause befell the dining car. The bands lead guitarist and singer waved to his audience, "Mademoiselles, monsieurs, ladies, gentlemen, please join me in welcoming a special guest. Our very own accomplished harmonicist, Vernon Gunn with a G."

Loud applause reverberated throughout the car. The music started up anew with a lively foot stomping Vernon on the harmonica. Then the band joined in along with the guests. Time definitely did not stand still. When Lyndsey glanced at her watch it was 1:00 a.m. and she suspected a time shift to Atlantic Time was now the official time. The music and friendly chatter amongst guests were in full form. Once, no twice, no definitely at least six times, she'd jumped up and taken to dancing in step to the music. The lead guitarist and singer caught her eye countless times. Richard had missed it. Not Zerli. She had her eye constantly on all the action playing out. Guests left randomly but were quickly replaced by others waiting in the cued lineups. Around 1:35 a.m. the fiddler and Vernon performed a duet together. The lead guitarist singer strolled over to where Lyndsey and Richard sat. He introduced himself, "Hi I'm Danny... by chance did you attend the U of T back in 19...? I had to ask. You look vaguely familiar. Well actually to tell the truth, my wife Alice has photos of her roommate from back in the day. And I could swear you're that roommate!"

Lyndsey stared at him in amazement, "She shouted, "You married my roomie, Alice? Oh my God."

"Sure did. Love her to pieces. We have two daughters and a son. Meredith, Agnes and Daniel after me of course."

"That's amazing! I'd love to get back in touch with Alice. Is she on the train?"

"No! Alice is back home in Cape Breton. That's where we're heading. Back home fer Christmas." Danny searched through his pockets but failed to find a pen, piece of paper, or a band business card.

Richard retrieved his wallet and pulled out several business cards. He wrote Lyndsey Ramsay-Black on the back of one. Danny accepted them, then with Richard's pen scribbled a phone number on the back of a card and passed it and the pen to Lyndsey who stared at him in awe.

Danny shouted. "I'm up next. I'll be sure to tell my Alice we bumped into you and Richard. Is this your first? Sorry had to ask. Besides our three, Alice is also like you. Doctor claims this time it could be twins. Take care. Enjoy your Christmas, My God! Can't wait to tell my Alice."

Lyndsey extended their stay. Memories of special moments once shared with Alice back in the day at the U of T flashed musically through her head. However around 2:00 a.m. Richard caught Lyndsey nodding off into short Dreamland visits. He tapped her shoulder and after the bands next song they made the way back to their sleeper car. The berths were made up. Lyndsey hit the bathroom. She washed and changed into a nightgown before she kissed Richard then crawled under the blankets in her lower berth. On returning from the bathroom Richard followed Lyndsey's lead. They exchanged goodnight sweetheart kisses and quickly fell asleep, gently rocked by the train's motions. Come morning, they both awoke on hearing the call to breakfast. Oddly, both awoke up in Lyndsey's lower berth.

....

Breakfast was enjoyed. The coffee top ups helped both to add an edge to their state of alertness. The late night/early morning music jam denied them of their normal sleep needs. Both Lyndsey and Zerli lost themselves in their knitting. But not before Zerli had retrieved her needle of choice and treated Lyndsey to Zerli's needle and thread test. With the needle suspended on its thread over Lyndsey's right hand Zerli became adamantly excited. First the needle entered a swirling circular motion, the kicker? Suddenly it stopped dead in its tracks, then took to swinging about in an elongated oval that could have been mistaken for a ragged straight line. After a moment it came to a rest. Zerli bubbled over with excitement. She shouted out., "Oh, my lands girlie. You are going to have twins. Yes, you are. A girl and a boy."

Richard glanced up from his book. On several occasions he'd heard their neighbour Dolly predict a girl, then two weeks later somehow their child to be had became a boy. He opted to dive back inside the mystery adventure underway inside the pages of his book. Suddenly he was rustled back out of those pages.

Their charming conductor Vernon Gunn stepped sharply through their car calling out, "Next stop, Moncton, Moncton is our next stop ladies and gentlemen. If disembarking please remain seated until our train comes to a full stop at the station." On spotting Zerli he asked, "Will you need any assistance madam?"

"I'm good Vernon. Thank you so much for an amazing flight down the rails back home for Christmas. And a Merry Christmas to you and yours! Hope I catch you on my return flight home to Newmarket." The train slowed right down. Several bumpety bumps followed then it came to a full stop. Richard and Lyndsey joined together in exchanging Merry Christmas wishes with Zerli. After she'd stepped off the car Richard strangely missed her bubbly energy. They waved as she met up with family. Minutes later their ride took flight and started off anew down the tracks. Both relaxed. Their journey was closing in on its destination. Lyndsey stowed away her knitting, Richard his book. They gazed out the window at the vistas in view. Neither one really heard the call out for Truro. However, on hearing Vernon announce they were passing through Bedford they became excited. Home was but a skip, a hop and a jump away. Suddenly the train slowed down to a crawl. They passed freight cars and strings of passenger cars sitting idly on adjacent lines of railway tracks. A series of bumps ended with the train coming to a full stop. Richard gathered up their baggage and shopping bags from Montreal. Charming Vernon appeared out of nowhere. He assisted Lyndsey and Richard in deboarding. Then he focused on the other passengers after hearty Christmas Wishes and Greetings were exchanged. Lyndsey took the shopping bags from Richard. Together they walked beside the train's cars towards the station. Both felt excited to be back home for Christmas.

....

Hope sighed on finally nudging Lenny's SUV into the last available parking spot at the Halifax *VIA RAIL* Train Station. Internal images of Pappy running about town with Lenny at the wheel drew a smirk to her face. *WHY,* she pondered, must men of all ages possess the biggest, noisiest, and most powerful vehicle on the planet? They were easy to love. But whoa, at times their manhood buttons were best left untouched. On walking over into the station, Hope savored the Christmas lights and garland outside and throughout the station's interior. She focused her attention on spotting Lyndsey and Richard. Inside the station families were reuniting, lovers embracing. Eagerly, Hope glanced around the chaos of arriving passengers being greeted and welcomed home. Where's my Big Sister? Panic almost set in. She called out, "Lyndsey, Richard, it's me, Hope! Where the heck are you two? Lyndsey, Richard, it's me, Hope! Where are you at?"

An unfamiliar voice roared out, "Over here's, Hope! It's me Vernon Gunn, VIA RAIL Conductor and I got what's you're looking fer girl!" Hope darted her eyes fully about the station in panic. "Don't be worrying, girl. I see you. Over here. Off ta yer right. All is OK! I'm just a giving yer folks a proper welcome. Git yourself over here, young lady."

Hope's jaw dropped on seeing a very pregnant Lyndsey fast stepping it towards her. They met and welcoming embraces and tears of joy broke loose. Richard ran over to join them. Vernon stuck to his side. Finally, Hope and Lyndsey released each other. Vernon shouted, "I see what ya means, Richard. Those two could be twins, excepting fer the short one's strawberry blonde topper."

Richard braced himself Hope had spotted him. He received a Merry Christmas, and a family reunion embrace, from his sister-in-law. It ended. Hope glanced over at Lyndsey chatting up a storm with the man in uniform. She called over, "Vernon, Vernon Gunn. The *VIA RAIL* Conductor wit de Charm!" She grinned and added, "Sis has been texting me throughout the trip. Welcome home, Vernon, and thanks fer getting my folks back home!"

"Ah its but a perk of the job, meeting all these amazing people while flying down de rails. Merry Christmas All and welcome home fer de holidays. Gotta heads off and catch me bus up to Orangedale, where my folks are awaiting my arrival. Agin, it's been a blast. Catch ya later."

They watched Vernon walk away. Hope stared at Lyndsey and Richard puzzled, then asked, "Where's yer luggage. Surely that's not all you brought with you? It is Christmas?"

Richard grinned. He boasted, "No there's more. Sure, hope you brought Gilbert's truck."

"Went one better. Hit up Lenny and borrowed his SUV. It's got lots of room."

"Good!" Richard replied. "Let's load up our traveling and shopping bags then you and I can get our checked in baggage while Lyndsey relaxes in Lenny's SUV." Thanks to a baggage cart and the helping hand of a porter the retrieval and load up quickly passed with all baggage accounted for. Richard tipped their helper and Christmas greetings were exchanged.

Hope dangled the keys at Richard. She taunted, "Care to drive, brother-in-law. It's a real man's vehicle. Totally loaded!"

"And you will be?" Richard replied.

"Chatting up a storm with my sister!" Hope tossed the keys over to Richard. She joined Lyndsey on the SUV's back seat. Richard opened the driver's door and climbed in behind the wheel. He commented, "It's got GPS!"

"Yup! Just hit home as your destination. I preprogramed, it." Hope called out.

A twist of the key started their run back home to East River. The train had been slightly behind schedule in arriving. On the upside, the day's heaviest traffic had already passed through the city. After their 24-hour ride home on the train, the steering wheel felt great in Richard's hands. Christmas music added seasonal cheer to their ears. Richard enjoyed the music. Hope and Lyndsey never really noticed it. They'd lost themselves in sisterly chatter throughout the run to East River. At exit seven on Hwy 103 Richard flipped the signal light on and took the exit. From there the GPS wasn't needed. He knew the route well. At Gilbert's he pulled in and parked beside the purple truck of East River Fame. He stepped out of the SUV. The kitchen door flew open. A race ensued by the welcoming home party. Hope and Lyndsey joined Richard. Christmas took on its true meaning. Good folk welcomed each other with blessings and love into their worlds. Megan and Taylor stole the show. They buried Richard and Lyndsey in hugs enhanced with tears of joy, that had been trigger by a touch of their mom's aura that floated off both Richard and Lyndsey. They shouted repeatedly almost word for word, "Thank you oh so much fer coming home and you know what. We're just so excited cause you're both here. And it's Christmas! Megan nudged up to Lyndsey. She pressed her face onto

Lyndsey's belly and inhaled. Quickly she stepped back and whispered, "You've been with our mom. I smelt mom's perfume floating off of you and needed more. Sorry."

Lyndsey stooped down and embraced Megan. Taylor nudged in and joined the group hug. Lyndsey whispered, "It's totally ok sweethearts. Yes, we have shared some good times with your mom. They drove Richard and me to the train station in Newmarket. And..."

And Mommie and Johnny with be here real soon!" Megan and Taylor whispered."

Lyndsey stood up the twins grinned and proclaimed, "And iff'in we are good we'll git the tings we want fer Christmas. And trusts, me we've been good." They paused a second then Taylor asked, "Lyndsey, is that a baby in yer belly? Grammie said you were in a motherly way is how she put it. But I know what she means. My buddy Billy's mom has de same thing as you've got."

Chuckling broke out amongst the greeters and welcomers. After Jeffery and Gilbert both received their highly anticipated hugs and embraces, they started to disentangle themselves and worked their way into the house. Freed up Lyndsey spotted Maria. They hugged and Lyndsey whispered, "Total sweethearts. They must keep you going 24/7 while stealing yer heart with every breath they take."

Maria sighed, "Your day will come. Parenting is awesome. But grandbabies trust me, they take you to another level. Yup, grandparenting is an amazing, joy filled world." They pulled apart with shared smiles. They followed Hope and the twins as they headed into the living-room. The men set to work unloading Lenny's SUV. The task passed quickly. Inside, Gilbert directed traffic. Richard and Lyndsey had been assigned the same room they'd stayed in on their earlier visits. This time a warm homey feeling touched Richard on delivering their assorted luggage up into their assigned bedroom. The men rejoined the women. Hope took anew to preparing the hot chocolates and Jeffery tended to the men's wants. The crunch of gravel outside signaled another arrival. Hope raced outside. There she was greeted by Pappy and Lenny. Only slightly disappointed, she treated the men to hugs and Christmas pecks on their cheeks. She returned to the house and accepted the keys to Jeffery's truck from Lenny. She gave him the keys to his SUV.

He grinned at Hope and asked, "So I take it you'll be a wanting one jest like it now, Lassie?"

Hope simply smiled in return. She returned to the task at hand. The living-room's energy and conversations soared. Inside, she felt a kinship drawing closer. The magic of Christmas caressed her heart.

CHAPTER 34

Fresh island breezes greeted Auntie Lila's guests on one of their awakenings. On glancing at her watch Eugette almost panicked. It read 12:24! She'd slept through to noon. She relaxed then snuggled up anew to John's warm body. Loud friendly voices rose up from downstairs and energized her day. With reluctance Eugette slipped out of the bed. A quick search in their bag retrieved a fresh set of clothing along with some personal items and products. John received a morning peck on his cheek, then Eugette made her way to the bathroom. Once the hot water hit her body, Eugette sighed and embraced its warmth. Throughout the shower she managed to escape the realities of a world she'd never expected to be living in three years past. However, reality has a habit of opening one's eyes and mind to unimaginable twists and turns never considered possible. Twenty minutes after stepping into the shower Eugette stepped out into a steam filled bathroom. At the sink she toweled and cleared the mist covered mirror. Then she started to towel dry her body. A cool draft hit as the door opened then quickly closed. A switch flicked and a ceiling fan powered up. Gazing into the mirror she caught John eyeing her naked body. Eugette concealed her reaction. In truth, his eyes felt good as they slid slowly over their target. John walked over and Eugette twisted about. They embraced. Although of short duration, she felt good pressed against his aroused body.

A voice called out, "Breakfast in five. Best move it iff'in we're to catch the next ferry!"

John released Eugette. A short kiss was shared. He whispered, "Nice. Very nice. But we'd best move it." John dropped his boxers and stepped into the shower. Eugette dressed and dry fluffed her hair. On leaving the bathroom a glance back caught a tempting glimpse of her man. The aromas of breakfast floating through the air killed all of her romantic thoughts. Back in the bedroom she did a quick walk about to make the bed and stowed all their soiled clothing. Breakfast pulled a hungry Eugette downstairs. There she was warmly greeted. An aproned Timmy stood by the counter working away on several omelettes. Auntie Lila nudged Eugette into a chair and delivered a fresh mug of coffee. Two sips into the coffee and an omelette was delivered garnished with home fries and bacon. John joined the breakfast gang. He received the same treatment.

On clearing the table, Timmy asked, "Are we clear on the ride to the ferry? Wouldn't want you to miss it."

Auntie Lila chided Timmy, "No fear of that, me son. Delilah will be their navigator. And trust me! I know every short cut to our destination. Oh! Timmy. You'd best take Mittens over to your house whilst I'm off to my Homecoming Christmas in Chester. Lordie, folks out'ta me past will be thinking they're seeing a ghost. Why, I ain't been back home in a dog's age and more."

Everyone burst into light laughter. Timmy added, "I'd venture to say once they bump in'ta you they'll know who they're dealing with. But iff'in ya want to yank their chains Lila, just let them get a word or two into your chats."

"Well! You wouldn't be suggesting little Lila talks too much, TIMOTHY?"

"God, Lordie, NO, Lila. I'd never be doing such a thing. And yes, I will take Mittens home with me after I clean up the house here."

Lively chatter broke out around the breakfast table. Then Timmy announced, "I don't mean to be rushing you folk out the door. But your ferry does keep to its schedule."

Everyone stood. Lila hugged Timmy. In turn he hugged both Eugette and Lila, then shared a hearty handshake with John. At the front door he watched them drive out of the driveway and head out to the ferry. Parting waves were exchanged. Before leaving Murray River, Lila directed John to pull in at the local Home Plate Bakery. He obeyed. Auntie Lila slipped quickly into the bakery and back out to the SUV. With her baked treats in hand John followed Auntie's directions and the built-in GPS in heading over to the Woods Island Ferry Terminal. To Lila's credit and claim they arrived on time for their booked ferry passage over to Caribou, Nova Scotia and another much anticipated step closer to home, for both Eugette and Lila. John fed off the positive energies of the ladies. He was unsure of the relationship Auntie Lila shared with Timmy, but believed from his short observations they knew each other well.

....

In driving off the ferry at Caribou John simply followed the flow of traffic. Shortly after Pictou they hit Hwy 106 and connected up to Hwy 104 headed west. John learned quickly not to refuse a treat offered up by Auntie Lila. He deferred to sitting back behind the wheel and observing and listening to the chatting going on between auntie and niece. The lady's vibrant energies amazed him. To nobody's surprise, Lila had claimed the front passenger seat. A great deal of family history was revealed to him. Throughout the run, beyond chuckling and shared laughter, Eugette got very few words in. That fact did not create tension, it merely endeared Auntie Lila to both her traveling companions. Lila alerted John to the Truro/Halifax turn off up ahead. He nodded thanks while catching a glimpse of the directions on the GPS screen. Lila's energies never abated. Before they hit the turnoff for Stewiacke, Eugette had nodded off to sleep. In doing so she'd snuggled down and stretched herself out on the SUV's back seat. Dusk started to befall them. Quickly night's darkness set in. On passing through Halifax, John followed Lila's suggested diversion. They exited Hwy 102 and took Rte. 333 West. Although darkness had set in, the multitude of varied Christmas light displays added a magic to their journey. On hearing John confess he'd never been to Peggy's Cove, Lila insisted they make a brief stopover to grab a peek at the lighthouse. On arriving, John was surprised by the number of visitors still at the sight after nightfall. Eugette stirred but did not awaken. Lila strutted along at John's side. He received a non-stop verbal guided tour of the rocks and a sighting of the Peggy's Cove lighthouse all lit up. Although a touch chilly, John enjoyed the tour and the company of Auntie Lila. The sea air invigorated him. They returned to the vehicle. Their Christmas Homecoming now stood a short run down the road. Several times Lila chided him for speeding. John eased off on the accelerator each time. He surmised, if I'm anxious to be home, I imagine Eugette is walking on air. Thoughts bouncing through his head constantly twisted his thoughts into calling their destination home, his new home. The Christmas lights passed added to the magical tugs and energizing his heartstrings.

....

On departing Peggy's Cove, Eugette gave in to a tiredness that had been tugging her in and out of dreamland. She remained snuggled down on the backseat and rested her head on the bundle of blankets Auntie Lila had retrieved out of the cargo area on returning to the vehicle after touring the rocks at Peggy's Cove. Auntie's directions kept them on the old highway. She'd expressed a need to see more of the homes lit up in their Christmas regalia. The last stretch of the trip home felt like eons in its passing. On entering dreamland, it passed in the blink of an eye. The SUV's headlights hit the roadside sign *'Welcome to East River'*. John eased off on the accelerator. Without a cue, Eugette reached out and embraced her blanket pillow. Auntie's hand slid back and shook Eugette's hip nudging her away from sleep's grasp. Suddenly the vehicle came to a full stop. John waved to the kitchen window and caught Hope's attention. He said, "OK! Auntie Delilah, we're home. In East River that is."

The house emptied except for Maria and the twins. With great restraint they awaited their Christmas package inside, in the living-room. Outside Auntie Lila released her seatbelt and opened her door. She stepped out onto the snowy graveled driveway. One glance over at Gilbert and Jeffery and she boasted, "Lordie, Lordie, is that really Helen's boys? Let me see now ye were both but knee high to a grasshopper back in the day! I'd say you've packed on a pound or two since I last laid eyes onto you Gillie. And Jeffery, what a fine young man you've become. So sorry about yer Helen's passing on, Robbie. She was a real sweetheart."

Pappy slid up to Delilah and wrapped her up in a welcoming hug. He whispered loudly, "Ah! Pappy works fer me here's and abouts. However, an occasional Robert, just might restore a smidgin of me youth, Lovey Lila." He released Lila. All eyes turned to the SUV. Santa's special delivery stepped out and a hush greeted her. Gingerly, Eugette walked into the welcoming party. Hope rushed forward. She boasted, "Git yourself over here girlfriend!" She buried Eugette in an all-encompassing embrace. They sobbed whilst muttering apologies and greetings into each other's ears. Eugette whispered aloud, "My mom, my babies?"

Hope replied, "Inside. Let's get there too!" Everyone followed Hope and Eugette into the house. The kitchen door slammed shut on catching a gust of frosty December wind. Two bullets raced out of the living room. Eugette dropped to her knees and embraced her twins. Tears flowed freely. No words just deep joyful sighs of joy. The embraced family savored the scent and reality of the ones in their grasps. The circle surrounding them widened. Maria had been standing in the kitchen entrance. Once her daughter and grandbabies had hugged for a few minutes, she raced over, dropped to her knees and embraced her family. Everyone in the circle except Jeffery stepped off into the living-room. Minutes later he joined the family he'd learned to love in their embrace. With hesitation, Jeffery stood up. Maria followed his lead. Eugette struggled at first but with a nudge or two convinced her twins to join their mom with Grammie and Papa Jeffery. Jeffery got treated to a hug from Eugette. Together the five joined the action unfolding in the living-room.

Eugette gazed about the room. On not spotting a Christmas Tree she frowned and asked, "Where's the Christmas Tree? My God, Hope, what would your Grammie say if she were here? Your home always had the most beautiful Christmas Trees going or coming."

Hope responded, "So true. And to be totally truthful, the few Christmas decorations seen here abouts are the workings of Megan,

Taylor and me. We kind 'a twisted Dad's arm into letting us add a hint of Christmas to the house. Those trees of legend are CFWs Come from Aways, but not too Fars Aways, I assure you. Unlike Uncle Jeffery's tree, ours requires an expedition into the Bad Lands of Nova Scotia. Way up onto a mountain of notoriety. That being Buzzard' Mountain, home to the Buzzard Mountain Free Range Turkey Ranch and its sister entities, one being their amazing Christmas Tree Farm." Hope smirked and winked at the two enraptured twins.

"Really, Auntie Hope? Your Christmas tree is waiting for us up on a mountain?" Taylor asked inquisitively.

Megan giggled then added, "She's pulling yer leg Tay, Christmas trees come from tree lots. Like the one Grampa Jeff took us to get his tree! Right, Auntie Hope?" Both Megan and Taylor twisted around and gazed up into their mom's face. They asked, "Right Mom?"

Mom reached out and embraced her twins. With them snuggled up to her bosom she claimed, "I haven't seen Grampa Jeff's Christmas tree. It could be big. But look over there in that corner. See how wide open and empty it is? That's because that's where Auntie Hope's Dad, Gilbert, puts up their tree. See how big Gilbert is compared to Grampa Jeff? Well picture the tree you decorated at Grampa Jeff's house and Gilbert's tree will be way bigger and bushier than the one at Grampa Jeff's. I know. I've seen many trees in that corner. And they were huge!"

"Bigger than you, Mommie?" Taylor asked.

"Yes! If we're lucky we won't have to cut a hole in the ceiling so the tree will fit!"

"Really?" Megan asked with a questioning look on her face.

"Really!" Grampa Jeff confirmed. "And I think we'll be heading out in search of that tree tomorrow."

"Can we go?" Megan and Taylor shouted out. "Pretty please. We'll be good!"

"Maybe. If you're really good and there's room for everyone in the big van we rented." Jeffery teased in replying.

"No way! Look at all the trucks and SUVs outside. Mister Lenny's SUV is the biggest one ever made, or at least that's what he said!"

Jeffery grinned, "Well sometimes Mister Lenny likes to stretch out the truth."

"I'd never do such a ting, me son. Never! It's not in me! My Momma would tan me iff'in I did." Lenny protested. All eyes turned to Lenny. He corrected himself, "What I mean to say is Momma never had a need to tans me. Because every word out'ta me mouth is the Lord's truth. So, helps me God. They tried to make a bigger one. But it was too big fer de road. Till the day comes when the roads get bigger. I've got the biggest SUV out there."

Jeffery chuckled. He added, "That being the case, Mister Lenny, Gilbert rented the biggest van out there just so we could fit everyone inside it and also leave room for our Christmas Turkey inside the van. He wouldn't fit onto the roof because of the size of Gilbert's Christmas Tree."

Laughter broke out throughout the living room. The sound of Gilbert's return broke up the laughter. He had slipped away to Hubbards to pick up the hefty order of pizzas and a side of crispy chicken wraps ordered for the mother-to-be. Hope jumped up, followed by Jeffery. They ran back and forth between the kitchen and dining-room setting up the table for everyone. On completing the tasks Hope called out, "Come and get it. Before it's gone. I'm starving!"

Pappy and Gilbert cast an eye at each other. Tears trickled down both their cheeks. They'd not seen the dining-room so full at Christmas since Grammie, Helen McClaken, had passed. Even without a Christmas Tree the Spirit of Christmas filled the house. A tall tales and more floated freely about the dining-room with the most mature stretching truth's reality beyond its limits. Each tale secured a spot in the minds and hearts of the youthful and were set aside for future growth in their retelling. Auntie Lila quickly caught the eye of Lenny. With the table cleared away most drifted back into the living-room.

Two pairs of droopy eyes signaled the approach of bedtime. On finding their hand tucked in one of Mom's hands neither twin objected to being led off to bed. Once upstairs, Eugette stepped into a familiar room - Hope's. She pulled the blankets back and crawled in under them. Megan and Taylor followed her lead. Each claimed a side. Within minutes the sounds of celebration rising up from below vanished as the reunited family drifted off to sleep in the security of each other's persona. Visions of sugar plums danced through each of their heads.

Evening slid into early morning and the celebrations settled down to a mild roar from a boastful rumble. Lenny and Pappy were the first to leave. Jeffery, Maria, Hope and Auntie Lila headed off to the old homestead next with Maria driving the truck. She'd avoid the free-flowing alcohol, as had Lyndsey. Shortly after they had departed, Gilbert set John up for the night on the living-room sofa bed. Then, Gilbert, Hope, Lyndsey and Richard turned in for the night. The howling winds outside abated. A calmness befell the night. Snuggled in bed at Jeffery's side Maria's face glowed with joy throughout the night. Her baby had returned and her family though growing was once again back together. Christmas in her heart was a done deal. The glow's richness energized Maria's dreamland wanderings that night. And come morning greeted all she came in contact with. Though days away the Spirit of Christmas thrived in everyone's heart.

CHAPTER 35

Come morning a loud banging on the kitchen door disturbed everyone at Gilbert's. He was the first to arrive at the door. Richard followed on his heels. A sigh of relief relaxed Gilbert on spotting Harley Kingston and Parker Rose on the doorstep. He unlocked the door. Both visitors stepped inside. Greetings were exchanged and Richard, Harley and Parker were introduced. Richard took to firing up the drip coffee maker. He received nods of approval from the others.

Harley winked at Parker and announced, "I received a similar awakening much earlier this morning. Parker came a calling with a suggestion. Burns me arse to admit it, Gillie, but for a pencil pushing lawman the lad is a sharp one. But don't go quoting me on it."

"And I won't let on that you're a hard knock detective who doesn't follow rumours but sticks to the facts and follows the evidence. More than I can say for some of the younger ones following in your footsteps" Parker fired back in jest.

Gilbert cut in, "OK! What's the plan? I thought everything was right on track."

Harley grinned than replied, "Parker suggested we might not be able to nail him on certain past actions. But we could set a candle aglow that'll set him into action. Which could trigger him to stumble and open doorways to nail him bigtime!"

Gilbert swore, "But he..."

"Not one of the women at the Pot are willing to open up. I tried!" Harley announced. He added, "Two recently gave birth and are devoted single moms. Neither one is willing to speak out. Three, according to a source, have had abortions in the last eight months. But they will not open up to me! Damn it all. I've tried. With that being said, I like what Parker has suggested." Harley glanced over at Parker. Gilbert followed his lead. "Explain the plan, Parker." Harley stated.

"Would a fresh shot of coffee help?" Richard asked. On receiving a chorus of yeses, Richard set up four mugs of coffee on the kitchen table. Everyone claimed a chair.

Parker explained, "Now that Eugette is back home and safe amongst family and friends, I believe we should make her presence known."

"No way!" Shouted Eugette from the kitchen entrance. All eyes turned to her. She headed to the table and grabbed a chair. "That Bastard murdered my dad and husband. They're gone for ever. He has to pay the price. Lives have been destroyed. I'm here, because somehow, I one upped him and then managed to escape. The bastard has to pay. He just has too..." Eugette collapsed onto the table in tears. John ran into the kitchen to her side and enfolded her in an embrace. Lyndsey followed on John's heels.

....

Beyond Eugette's sobbing a silence befell the room. Lyndsey released Eugette then headed to the counter and fired up the kettle. Minutes later she joined the others at the table with two peppermint teas in hand. Eugette stared through tear-stained eyes around the table.

Parker broke the silence. He said, "I agree Eugette. But please hear me out. There's been an outpouring of support for you in this community. A reward was established and set up to hasten your safe return home. And yes, it was set up by the Lobster Pot Pub & Eatery's owner."

Eugette shook her head in distain. She whispered with a hateful vent, "That bastard!"

"Agreed." Parker answered. "But let me continue. The reward has built up into a tidy sum. According to Inspector Kingston, no valid leads have been called in, other than your car being located at a mall parking lot in Moncton. And the rumour is hinting that a proper accounting of the reward's funds has not been forthcoming. If you agree to having your return announced publicly that accounting would be demanded by the public. That alone would free you of his attention. Family, friends and officials will ensure your safety. We will keep you safe and he will pay. Once the pins start to tumble his network of connections will fall apart. Several have already talked."

"Really? Eugette asked.

"Yes! And their words are being taken seriously. Right Harley?"

The kitchen door opened Jeffery, Maria, Hope and Auntie Lila walked inside. On spotting Harley, Auntie Lila shot over to his side and ordered, "Git yer self-up here, laddie. Auntie Lila needs a hugging!"

Harley stood and both grinned boldly at each other. Then Harley vanished in Lila's welcoming embrace. She released him and asked, "How's Barb, no Bren, no, gives me a second. Bev, Beverly. How's yer little lady?"

Harley grimaced. Then said, "Sorry to say, my sweet Bev has passed on."

Harley vanished anew in a loving embrace. On releasing him Lila said, "I'm so very sorry. You must miss her. She was such a sweetheart. And a looker too!"

"Aye, that my Bev was, Lila. I was so blessed to have been gifted a lifetime of her love'in."

With that said, Lila walked over to the counter. Harley sat back down. He reconnected

with Eugette's eyes and nodded a positive response. "Eugette, I have been in contact with locals throughout my investigation. This case is standing between me and my retirement. Trust me I'm ready to go. He'll not stop me this time around."

"Who talked?" Eugette asked.

"I cannot tell you at this point." Harley answered.

"Then I cannot, will not expose myself!" Eugette declared.

Harley looked to Parker. Both nodded. Harley stood up and walked towards the living-room, John released, Eugette. She stood and followed Harley into the living-room. Fifteen minutes later they returned to the kitchen. Eugette announced, "I'm Ok! I'm back home and ready to let the world know!" Cautious sighs escaped around the room. Maria stepped up to Eugette and embraced her daughter in a loving hug. Megan and Taylor ran back into the kitchen and stared about at the full house. Auntie Hope dragged Eugette away from the crowd. She boasted, "Let's go get you dressed up for a public appearance. My closet is overflowing." Together they headed upstairs. The twins curious, followed in their footsteps. Twenty minutes later Hope reappeared with Eugette at her side. The twins had been distracted by Bailey and had followed their best bud into the den. Harley announced, "I've contacted the local detachment. We're to head over and reporters will be there to learn of your safe return. It's scheduled for 1:00 pm, are you good to go?"

"Yes. Home is home. No more guilt. I did nothing wrong."

A full round of supportive embraces ensued. Followed by the women taking over control of the kitchen. In short order everyone sat in the dining room with a full breakfast plate demanding their full attention. Over time the plates emptied. Jovial seasonal conversations flowed freely between everyone. Maria expressed her sadness on learning Parker's Fantine would not be joining them in celebration of Christmas. She'd looked forward to actually sitting down and chatting with a real live theatre actress. Parker promised he'd arrange a get together for them. But Fantine, being the lead lady in a Gala Christmas fund raiser in Halifax had a full schedule with no open slots. He then advised everyone that he would be heading back to Halifax, later that day, explaining that his caseload had doubled. It required his attention. "Rest assured, my main priority is focused on closing out our Chester cases. I will be back."

Eugette stood and walked over to Parker. She signaled and he followed. Out in the kitchen she received Parker's full commitment to her concerns and fears. Once convinced, they returned to the dining-room. Cleanup had been set in motion. All but Gilbert and Jeffery headed into the living-room.

·······

Rumour spreads quickly in small towns. Word hit the street that an update on Eugette's whereabouts would be announced at 1:00 pm. A nervous energy raced throughout the town. At the Lobster Pot Pub & Eatery, staff carried out their duties with a nervous edge to their every move. Diners were quick to notice the nervousness in their servers. They held off on temptations nudging them towards asking questions. Most added a string of whispered prayers before raising utensil to their meals. With Christmas Eve just around the corner most thoughts tethered on hopes for a positive announcement. All eyes turned to the Pot's owner as he strutted quickly from his office over to the main entrance. Barnie's presence drew harsh looks from both staff and diners.

Tara whispered to Anna, "Our Eugee's gotta be OK. She's been there for us since our schooldays. Our best bud, always there when needed. I couldn't handle it if she's not, OK?"

"I drove pass her house this morning. Not a sign of any life. Oh my God. I'm so sorry. But the house looked totally empty - no vehicles and no lights. Tara, you're close to her. Did she seem ok on that day when she arrived then disappeared after he hauled her into his office? If I didn't need the money to raise my son, I'd be out'ta here so fast. He gives me the creeps."

"Best keep your mouth zipped and not mention him. Word gets around and the consequences can bear ill tidings."

"Really?"

"Yes. Trust me, Anna. We'd best zip it. Here's a couple, please get them seated." Anna followed Tara's suggestion. Dealing directly with customers helped lessen her nervous edge. The Pot's dining area quickly filled up to capacity. Many of the patrons wore media id cards. They ordered lite fare and cleared out well before the scheduled news update set for 1 pm.

Tara watched the last diner exit the Pot. She turned to Anna and said, "Cover for me. I gotta know. I gotta hear the update straight out'ta their mouths. I'll be back in a flash." They hugged briefly then Tara raced out to her car. On arriving close to the detachment, she noticed a number of off duty coworkers' vehicles parked on the street. To her surprise she found a rare open parking spot and claimed it. Tara slowed on walking past Gilbert McClaken's purple truck. A silent prayer slipped past her lips. She seized onto the hope that his presence signaled a positive outcome. Constable Olmstead greeted her at the entrance. Her presence was not challenged. Both new and respected each other. Constable Anna Olmstead directed Tara towards the scheduled news update. A buzz of murmured chatter filled the room. Tara stared through watery eyes towards the front of the room.

At 1 pm sharp Sergeant Robert Stratford addressed the gathered media. "Ladies and gentlemen, it is with great…"

Tears flowed wildly down Tara's cheeks triggered by the first words out of Sergeant Robert Stratford's mouth. Those that followed were lost to her internal thought processing. All hope vanished from Tara's heart. She sobbed while staring aghast towards the front of the room. Life ceased to make sense. Eugee, her childhood schoolmate since they'd met in kindergarten, was gone. Constable Anna Olmstead spotted and ran to Tara. She embraced her friend and whispered, "Hold on, Tara. It'll be ok!"

The words registered but made no sense to Tara. Then through her tear-stained eyes Eugee's mom, Mrs. Lamont and Eugee's twins appeared followed by a familiar face. Tara shouted in glee, "Yes! Oh My God! Yes! Our Eugee is back home!"

All eyes turned to Tara. Her face glowed with elation. Anna Olmstead embraced her friend in a loving hug. She whispered, "See. I told ya."

Tara's stare locked onto her coworkers who were answering the constant array of questions posed by news media. Their actions drew attention away from the officer in charge. On numerous occasions Sergeant Stratford cut in and asserted his authority over the nature of the questions. For Tara, time stood still. Internal shivers and angst passed as the event unfolded. Tara had never lost a loved one or friend to death's call. Her heartbeat relaxed with each moment that slipped past. Quicker than the room had filled, it emptied. Eugette stooped down, hugged her twins, then stood and raced over to Tara and embraced her mate. Both sobbed and laughed, relieved to be reunited. Oh, but isn't life a treasure best shared with one's loved and cherished co-travelers through its journey?

CHAPTER 36

Later that day street parking vanished in the neighbourhood of the Lamont house. Well-wishers and elated friends and neighbours stopped in to welcome Eugette back home. They did not come alone. Everyone arrived bearing offerings of food and an abundance of treats. Gilbert lost himself in friendly chatter with the ladies who arrived bearing sweet treat trays. Recipes were discussed in detail including several secret ingredients and preparation tips sworn to secrecy in the presence of family members now passed on. A number of the ladies savored the moments shared in companionship with their former schoolmate and present-day Dalhousie Professor of English Literature, Gilbert McClaken. The same Gilbert McClaken they'd ogled over in their long passed teenaged romantic fantasies. None had bought into the beliefs of parents that the McClakens, especially Jeffery McClaken, aka Bugshit McClaken, had been cursed and touched by Satan's claw. They knew Gilbert, a widower, was unattached. AKA available. However, a late arrival set them all to scurrying away from Gilbert's side. Anya, on arrival, claimed her man with a passionate kiss that lingered. Disappointment painted itself on all their faces except Anya's. She displayed an air of confidence standing at, Gilbert's side.

Several guests commented on the side to trusted acquaintances that they'd seen a vehicle of local repute cruising the streets surrounding their present gathering. All felt the vehicle's driver's presence raised personal concerns. Auntie Lila glowed on reconnecting up with two former coworkers. Maternity nurses from back in the day. On hearing a name mentioned none of the reconnected workers dared to mention a recollection they'd been party to on a work shift buried in their pasts. Others questioned why the driver had failed to put in an appearance at the news update that afternoon. The coworkers ignored the questions.

The gathering broke up shortly after 10:00 pm at Mom's insistence Eugette and John were allocated to overnighting at the Ramsay homestead. Neither one objected. Gilbert, Hope, Lyndsey, Anya and Richard set off for East River in John's rental SUV. John and Eugette followed in Gilbert's truck. Parker drove Harley over to his parent's home in Chester. Once the visitors had all parted Maria and Auntie Lila set about cleaning up the gathering's leftovers along with the assorted dishware, trays, mugs and glasses. It gave the two a quality stretch of catchup time they eagerly shared.

Out in the living-room, the twins kept Grampa Jeffy occupied until he slipped off into a light nap on the sofa. His light often rumoured snorts ignited short bouts of laughter and giggles from Megan and Taylor who lost themselves in entertaining their unexpected overnight guest, Bailey. A bonus initiated by Jeffery. Who thought being separated from mom would be easier if there were a distraction. The hour grew later and company joined Grampa Jeffy on the sofa as Megan, Taylor and Bailey snuggled up and quickly joined Jeffery in dreamland.

Auntie Lila made two peppermint teas and delivered them to the kitchen table. She passed one to Maria. She repeated her often repeated thanks for the Christmas invite to come back home. Auntie Lila boasted, "I knew she were yours de minute the young lass walked up to me in the airport. You've got good cause ta be a proud mom. And her man. I likes him I does."

Maria chuckled. She replied, "Yes. And when she really needed him, he was there. My baby had to get away and without hesitation she knew where she had to go. The Ramsays are good people, here's and off in Ontario. Fine people."

"Pray tell me girl. Your man out there a' snoring on the sofa, any chance he's be the one you had wrapped right around yer little finger back in de day? Gads, but he was a sweetheart!"

"Yes, he is, Auntie."

"Don't be letting him get away a second time. He's a keeper."

Maria sighed, "He is that! Wish dad had seen his potential back in the day."

Lila smiled boldly, "Iff'in I recall, back in the day your mom and dad had a time of it raising their sweet blossoming teenaged daughter. Probably thought "Oh my God! What did we do to deserve this? Our baby is a spitting image of Delilah!"

"No!" Maria declared.

"Afraid so, sweetheart. Your auntie, like you fer a stretch, put her momma and poppa through hell. Boy was I a wild thing or what. The eldest. But definitely not the wisest. But, to their chagrin my Joshua set me strait, he did. Miss him and still loves my man. He got called home ta heaven way too soon."

Maria chuckled, "I've gotta confess, Auntie. On several occasions I got called Delilah."

"No way!"

"Oh Yes! And don't I know it. And, Auntie, back in the day I was rebellious and proud to refresh mom and dad's recollections of my Auntie Delilah. But life is strange at times. My Martin stepped in and we married. We had a good life. Then it really hurt losing him. It hurt more with my Eugette losing her Rusty at the same time. Two good men who respected and loved their women."

"Yes. I never met Rusty but believe he was a keeper too. Now, your Martin, he went well beyond the cause didn't he, girl? Stepped up when he was needed. No questions asked."

Maria buried herself in deep thought. Lila added, "Did he ever know the truth?"

The glow vanished off Maria face. Her cheeks sank, touched by a truth out of the past. "No." Maria answered. She added, "He never asked. Just stood by me. Loved me truly and raised our daughter at my side. It ripped my heart out when I learned our men were gone. We had a unique love."

Lila smiled. She replied, "Your mom and dad, they never knew the truth, did they?"

"No, Auntie. Martin was their son-in-law and father of their granddaughter. And mom, dad I can't thank them enough for all they did for me, for us. And, mom, dad I know you're listening, your granddaughter and great grandbabies are totally awesome and lovable!"

Lila nodded her agreement. She yawned then asked, "Where should I put myself down fer the night sweetheart. If I don't hit the bed soon, I'll be spending the night right where's I am at this very minute."

Maria emptied her mug of tea. She stood and Lila joined her. They walked into the living-room. There they shared a chuckle and decided to leave the dreaming in dreamland. A comforter was retrieved and placed over the dreamers. Maria set Lila up in Eugette's bedroom. Then she turned herself in for the night. Sleep came quickly to both Auntie Lila and Maria. A ton of stress and tension had been lifted off their hearts over the last few days. Actually, throughout Chester, East River and the surrounding area most folks slept much better. Knowing a missing daughter was back home and safe.

……..

Bailey stirred. A noise outside rousted him from the Sandman's grasp. He glanced around the room. Its subtle differences were starting to grow on him. However, a vaguely familiar odor out of his pass leaped forward and stirred feelings of fear enhanced with thoughts of a past master. He gazed about his surroundings. The fear overpowered thoughts out of the past. Bailey stood. A scent with a smoky tinge set him on edge. Instinct overpowered him. Megan gasped then turned over, pulling the comforter from under Bailey's feet. Reacting to the comforter's movement, Bailey flipped through the air then landed safely. He scooted to Megan's face. A tap, tap, tap of his paw on her face drew no response beyond her rubbing away the touch of Bailey's paw. Frustrated, Bailey called out, "Meow, meeow!" The living-room fell silent following his call out to Megan. The smoky air in the room grew stronger. Repeated actions on Jeffery and Taylor both failed to awaken Bailey's targets. Bailey made a call. He leapt off the sofa and ran down the hall in search of a woman he'd grown attached to, Maria, Megan's mother. There he batted at a closed door with his paw. It popped open. Bailey disappeared through its opening. Once inside her bedroom the determined feline leaped straight up onto Maria's bed. Thump. He landed on her stomach. Maria gasped in response to the force of Bailey's landing. She reacted and attempted to push Bailey away. The attempt failed. Bailey slipped past her waving arms. Poised on Maria's chest he slapped her face with a paw. Its claws were partially exposed. He followed up with a loud meow highlighted by a series of load fierce hissing. To Bailey's relief Maria's eyes flashed open. She frowned in response to seeing Bailey's hissing face shouting out at her.

A snapping crackling noise cast that frown aside. She shouted, "Bailey, what's wrong?" Bailey slapped Maria anew. She sat upright in bed free of the deep sleep Bailey had disturbed. A deep breath exposed her to the building's smoke-filled air. Maria coughed in reaction to the smoke. She panicked covered her mouth and gasped in search of fresh air. It alluded her search, Maria then rubbed her eyes attempting to relieve the burning itchy sensation that was alerting her to the nightmare reality Bailey's awakening had drawn her into. A glance at the alarm clock set the hour at 4:17 AM. The acrid taste of smoke in her breath confirmed the gravity of the situation. Fear and panic hastened Maria's leap free of the bed. Slipped into her slippers then grabbed a housecoat off the bedroom door hanger. In slipping it on she shivered on feeling its warmth. Maria followed Bailey out through the bedroom door. She did not feel any intense heat. Images of wee Megan and Taylor popped into her head. Adrenalin raced through her body. Smoke flowed unabated past Maria into her bedroom. Maria ran down the hallway to Eugette's bedroom. Bailey followed. The snapping and crackling of the fire's flames had not gained entry into the house. At the bedroom door she touched it. The door's coolness relieved her. Maria pushed the door it opened up, she then stepped into the bedroom. The room had not filled with heavy smoke. Maria ran over to the bed. She shook Lila hard but gently. Lila grumbled and fought Maria's attempted disruption of her dreamland adventures. She mumbled, "Maria, Sweetheart let me sleep."

Maria pulled Lila free of her bedcovers. She shouted, "Slippers, no shoes. Grab a housecoat. We have to get out of the house. It's on fire! Lila stared at Maria in panicked disbelief.

"No! No, Maria it can't be!"

"Now Lila, move it, Auntie, I'll get the others!"

Lila stepped out of bed onto the floor. She spotted whiffs of smoke floating into the bedroom through its doorway. "We're goanna die. Don't let me die, Maria!"

"Follow me Auntie. Head to the front door. I'll get the grandbabies and Jeffery in the living-room. We'll be ok!" In the living-room Maria madly shook Jeffery. He awoke and took to choking with the thickening smoke hitting him full force. She ripped the comforter off the sofa. Disoriented the twins rubbed their faces as the smoke hit their eyes.

Maria shouted, "Jeff, git up. Help me please. The house is on fire!"

Jeffery stared at Maria in disbelief. He coughed anew as the smoke thickened. Reality hit Jeffery full force. He picked up Taylor. Maria secured Megan in her arms. Megan hugged Grammie in fear. With Jeffery leading, they headed to the front door. Megan watched Jeffery feeling the door. Fear shouted out silently from her smoke blackened cheeks. Taylor tried to escape from Jeffery's grasp but failed. Jeffery withstood the test. The smoke grew thicker. Taylor rubbed his eyes. A glance over at Megan revealed her fears to him. Frightened, he wrapped his arms around Jeffery's neck and sobbed.

Jeffery stared at the others. He shouted, "I'm going to open the door. The fire appears to be at the back of the house. The minute the door opens, stick with me. We'll run outside and get clear and safe of the house. On two, one, two. The door flew open. Cold air greeted them. Auntie Lila and Maria followed Jeffery as they ran outside onto the front porch. Taylor escaped Jeffery's grasp and ran with Maria and Auntie Lila down towards the driveway. All breathed sighs of relief and sucked in the fresh cold air. Jeffery felt relieved that he'd parked at the street's end. They walked across the street. Safely free of the fire they turned and stared back at the house. Flames shot up over the back roof, lighting up the night sky. Embers landed on the front roof quickly setting it afire. All five stared horrified at the raging flames secure in the grasp of each other's arms. Lights in the homes of neighbours flipped on. The occupants, on catching sight of the expanding flames, ran to Maria, Megan, Taylor, Auntie Lila and Jeffery's sides.

Phyllis and Charlie embraced Maria and the twins. Jeffery hugged, Lila. Charlie released them. With cell phone in hand, he keyed 911 and hit send. Three rings sang out at the call center's end of the line. The call picked up, "911, what is the nature of your emergency?"

"Fire! House fire!"

"Where sir? Where's the fire? Are the occupan…"

"Maria, where's Eugette? Is she safe?"

Maria nodded, "Yes. She's away. She's safe!"

Charlie shouted, "Everyone is safe. The fire is in Chester at…"

"Thank you, sir! I've dispatched fire and police. They're on their way."

In the distance the screaming sirens rose up into the night sky. Charlie slipped his cell phone into a chest pocket. He rejoined the group hug. The sobbing continued unabated and tearless. Heat from the expanding fire cast all tears aside. Charlie nudged and shuffled their group over towards his home's driveway. Firefighters arrived, followed by two police vehicles. In moments fire and police vehicles filled the street, followed by an ambulance. The firefighters quickly attacked the house fire. The flames rose hungrily into the night sky. Several hoses were directed onto the neighbouring homes, working to prevent any spread of the fire. Maria hugged Megan and Taylor tight to her body. She crouched down onto her knees and kissed each on their foreheads. She whispered, "We're safe, sweethearts. We're safe. That's all that matters. The house can be replaced."

Phyllis joined Maria in a crouched stance. She asked, "Can we call anyone?"

"Oh please, can Jeffery call his home?"

Phyllis retrieved the cell phone from Charlie's pocket. She passed the phone to Jeffery. Neighbours, attracted by the flames and sirens, had gathered in Charlie's driveway, on the street and on neighbouring properties. Police officers worked to keep the fire gazers a safe distance from the inflamed house and out of the firefighters' ways. Elise, a neighbour from across the street, arrived with a tray of hot chocolate. She offered them up to Megan and Taylor. Maria attempted in vain to decline the offer. She failed. Jeffery held the phone to his ear and listened anxiously to the line ringing at his home. Please, John, Eugette, wake up, we need you now!"

Elise's husband George joined the group. He wrapped Megan and Taylor in blankets, then offered one to Maria. She attempted to decline the offer.

On hearing lines connect, Jeffery shouted into the cell phone, "John, John, we need you. The house is a blazing inferno. Everything is burning. Please come! Pleas…"

"Oh my God. Jeffery. I'm there!"

Eugette shouted, "What's wrong John?"

"We'll be there. Tell me you, Maria, Megan, Taylor and Auntie are safe?"

"Yes. We're safe."

"We're outside. See you soon."

John grasped Eugette and their eyes locked. He explained, "It's Jeffery. Everybody's safe. The house is ablaze."

Eugette dropped to her knees trembling. She shouted, "The Bastard tried to kill us. Barnie is a Dead Man!"

John crouched down and embraced Eugette. Then they stood up. John said, "Dress, we'd best get dressed and get the hell over there." They raced through the house, dressed quickly then ran out to Gilbert's truck. He started the engine, shifted it into gear and headed out the driveway. At Gilbert's he hit the brake in the driveway and laid on the horn. A quick hot key on his cell phone connected him to and aroused Gilbert's cell phone. "Jeffery called, Gil. Maria's house is an inferno. They are all safe! See you there." He disconnected the call tossed the cell phone to Eugette in the passenger seat and drove with abandon out onto the road.

Gilbert stared unbelievingly at the phone held in his hand. He dressed then raced downstairs. Hope joined him. She shouted, "What's going on, Dad? What's the panic?"

"He shouted up the stairs to her, "It's John. He's headed over to Maria's. Their house is on fire. It's a blazing inferno."

Hope froze a second, then two, in her tracks. She shouted back, "Wait for me. I'm coming!" She ran into the bedroom and quickly dressed. She ran to meet up with Gilbert. On the first step she slipped and fell. She shouted, "Shit!"

Gilbert did not comment. Richard poked his head out through the ajar bedroom door. He called out, "What's up?"

Hope regained her footing. She turned towards Richard and answered, "Jeffery called. Maria's house is on fire. Everyone's safe. We've gotta make tracks, gotta go. We'll call once we get there!" Hope stood and leaped with abandon down the stairs. She shouted, "Dad what about Rich and Lynds..."

Gilbert disconnected his cell call and pocketed the phone. He shouted out. "Richard, Lyndsey you'd best stay here. I just rousted Pappy and Lenny. They're going to head into the city and hit a clothing shop, get some outfits for the twins. The women and Jeffery will be ok. Stay here. Pappy, Lenny and their ladies will stop in on their return."

"But!"

Gilbert called back, "Sorry, Rich. No buts. We gotta go. Trust me, you'll be overloaded once everyone gets here." He ran out the kitchen door. A flip of the hand slammed the door shut as he quickly joined Hope in the SUV. They headed off towards Chester, Jeffery, Maria, the twins and Auntie. Back in Chester, George seized the moment and wrapped Maria in the last blanket. She nodded thanks and acceptance. She whispered, "John and Eugette are on their way." Maria tugged both children closer to her. They watched in awe as the roof collapsed into the burning remains of their home. The police officers walked up to Maria and the group surrounding her. They had already asked other fire gazers to head home. Maria stood up. She stared at the burnt remains of her home. Officer Johnson addressed her, "So sorry Maria. I'm so very sorry."

"We're safe. Our babies and I are safe, Eric. We're safe."

Phyllis suggested, "Let's step into our home Maria. It will be more comforting for Meg and Taylor and Auntie Lila."

"But, but, John and Eugette are on their way!"

"I'll stay outside and show them inside once they arrive." Charlie offered.

Eric added, "Thanks. It would be best. Let the firefighters take care of their business."

Maria nodded her approval. She stared in silence at the inflamed remains of her home. An icon leaped to the forefront of her mind. The safe, Martin's safe. Will it survive the fire?

Phyllis walked the children towards her house. She called to Maria, "Please, Maria. Let's get inside."

Maria took a step towards the house. She stopped. Staring directly at Eric she pleaded, "Martin's safe. It was always in the basement in his office. I need it!"

Eric nodded back. He assured her, "I'll tell the team to search it out." He smiled at Maria.

"Thanks, Eric. Thanks for all you do." Maria gazed once more into the flames that were starting to recede. She bit her lips then gazed around her surroundings in search of their savior. She uttered, "Bailey? Has anyone seen Bailey? He's a fluffy bundle of yellow fur and woke me up. He saved us from the fire!"

CHAPTER 37

Fear pasted itself on Megan's face. She pulled free of Maria and stepped off towards the burning home. Eric grabbed Megan restraining her movement. She shouting out, "Bailey, Bailey where are you? Please, you gotta save our Bailey. He saved us!"

Eric grabbed and pulled Megan into a hug. He said, "We'll find Bailey, Megan. Trust me, we'll find Bailey." He released Megan to Maria.

Maria's eyes locked on Megan's. She boldly assured Megan, "Trust Officer Eric and his team, sweetheart. They'll leave no stone unturned. They will find our Bailey."

Taylor shuffled over to Megan's side. He stared through a blank face at Maria and Eric. He asked in a pleading voice, "Is that a double, triple hope to die promise, Grammie?"

"Yes, sweetheart. It is! Let's allow Eric to go find our Bailey and we'll go with Phyllis to her house."

Taylor's eyes locked on Eric's. He asked, "Do you promise too?"

"Yes Taylor, Megan. I'll tell my team and we'll find Bailey. I promise."

Maria followed Phyllis's lead and walked off towards Phyllis and Charlie's house. On spotting Lila standing off to the side, gazing at the blacken remains of the house, Charlie nudged her and with effort convinced her to join the others inside. Eric watched her walk away then turned and walked off to join his fellow officers. A thought hit him. Eric retrieved his cell phone and called out to his contact Inspector Harley Kingston. On terminating his call Eric's eyes scanned the grounds in search of a fluffy ball of yellowy-orange fur. Silently he prayed for a successful search. He loved his work in law enforcement. However, the tears never failed to touch his inner soul at times like this. Seeing the reality of the pain and devastation in the eyes and faces of people connected to his life never failed to open the flood gates of compassion. He bit his lips, and cast aside all questioning doubts that had briefly arisen, it being best to maintain a composed look amongst his team's members.

John hit Hwy 3 leaving a strip of rubber from his tires on the pavement. Images of Maria, Megan. Taylor, Jeffery and Auntie Lila sang out inside his head. An image of the house, Maria's home, painted itself in his mind. Jeffery's words drove ice picks into his heart, *John, John, we need you. The house is a blazing inferno. Everything is burning. Please come! Pleas...'* He flew past the turnoff to Graves Island Provincial Park. On entering Chester, fumes from the fire hit John's nostrils. He did not slow to the reduced speed limits. A glance at Eugette ripped at his heartstrings. In her, he captured images of himself at the scene of his parents and grandparents' deaths. Thoughts of Eugette suffering the hurt he had endured cast a volley of knives into his heart. John pressed the accelerator down hard against the floorboards. Following a quick left turn the truck broke into a loud skid. John released the accelerator and touched the brake. Two more turns placed him on Maria's Street. Ahead of him he spotted three fire trucks, two police vehicles and an ambulance. John hit the brake then stopped directly in front of Charlie and Phyllis Mattock's house. The truck's doors flew open. John jumped out of the truck. He stared in shock at the remains of Maria's home and the flumes of acrid burnt wood smoke rising skyward from its ashes. Charlie spotted John and Eugette and ran to their sides. He embraced Eugette and John, while nudging them away towards his house and said, "Come with me, Eugette. Maria, Jeffery, the young ones and your Auntie are in our house with Phyllis." At Charlie's driveway, they all turned towards the SUV and Honda Civic skidding to a stop behind Gilbert's truck. Their doors flew open. Harley raced over to Constable Eric Johnston, who updated him. They joined the search for Bailey. Gilbert and Hope ran to John and Eugette's side. Hope embraced

Eugette in a bear hug. She stared past her at the burnt remains of the house. Emotionally, she cracked. She'd spent endless hours in that house with, Eugette. Frozen she stared in shock at the flames eating away at what remained of Maria's house. Her body shivered as the reality of the moment hit full force. Gilbert ran to their side. He stared in disbelief at the blackened remains. He wondered, what caused this? Could Eugette's fears have been true? Could Barnie have acted on the threats he'd made to Eugette? The smoky air threw Hope into a coughing spree. Hope tightened her embrace on Eugette. Then she released her from the embrace, and lovingly rubbed her back. Together Eugette, John, Hope, and Gilbert stared in disbelief at the scene of the fire.

Charlie broke the silence, "Let's get inside. Maria, Megan and Taylor, Jeffery and your aunt are inside with Phyllis."

Gilbert turned to John, Eugette and Hope and a trademark Gilbert hug ensued. A moment, then two, slipped past. Eugette sighed on feeling Gilbert release them from his embrace. The foursome held hands and followed Charlie up to the front door. They separated and nodded thanks to Charlie who stood holding the door open. Inside, they headed to the kitchen. Maria spotted Eugette and leaped out of the chair and ran to her. The two embraced. Tears flowed down their faces. Their embrace intensified with each tear drop. Hope spotted Megan and Taylor poking their heads out of the main floor bathroom. She raced over and the pair vanished in her hug. A glance into the sink revealed a messy black sudsy mix of soap, water and blackened smoke trailing's the twins had washed themselves free of.

Proudly, Taylor looked up into Hope's eyes. He boasted, "Sure glad Papa Jeffery let Bailey spend the night with us. He woke up Grammie. He saved us from the fire."

Hope smiled. She planted a string of kisses on Taylor's cheeks and forehead. He exerted a serious attempt at escaping from Hope's embrace. Success rewarded him with Megan returning Hope's hug and inadvertently releasing Taylor. Megan's eyes closed. Her body sobbed. She returned Hope's embrace tenfold.

Taylor turned to Charlie he asked, "Did Eric find our Bailey? He's gotta find Bailey! He promised!"

"He will find him, Taylor. You do know that cats have nine lives."

The kettle shouted out in the kitchen. Phyllis asked, "Anyone else up for a hot chocolate, tea, or would coffee be best?" Gilbert's face lit up on the mention of coffee. She took that as a positive and set about firing up the drip coffee machine for the new arrivals. Once the mugs had been passed out, she looked over at Maria and said, "Come with me, girl. Shake loose a pound or two and we're about the same size. Let's get you out'ta them bedclothes and properly attired."

After she'd shared one more lingering kiss with Jeffery, Maria turned to Phyllis. Phyllis led her and Lila off in search of a change of attire. Hope carried Megan over to a chair. She sat with Megan on her lap.

Megan whispered, "I think Bailey tried to wake me up first. Dumb me! I pushed him away. I should have listened to his call. If not fer Jeffery letting Bailey visit us overnight..." Megan stuttered, "I...I... wouldn't be here now. Grammie, Jeffery, Taylor, Auntie and I would be dead..."

Hope hugged the stuttering, sobbing Megan in a loving embrace. Like Megan, tears freely flowed down her cheeks. Megan's sobs eased with each rub of Hope's loving hand on her back. Minutes slipped past in silence. Sleep embraced Megan and she snuggled into Hope's arms. Running water broke the silence. Charlie walked to Hope's side. He stooped down and whispered, "Sounds like my Philly has convinced Maria to hit the shower. Please take the young ones and have a lay down on the bed in our guest room."

"Thanks. I will. They're not the only ones with sleepy eyes."

Charlie stood up he smiled at Hope and Eugette. "I'll get Taylor. He's losing his battle with the Sandman and will likely fall off that chair any second now." Taylor's eyes popped open on being picked up by Charlie.

He fought off the touch of sleep that he'd slipped into. "No! No, I gotta stay awake until Officer Eric brings Bailey to me!"

"Hush, Taylor, trust me I'll bring Bailey to you the minute he arrives."

"Promise?"

"Double dog dare promise." Taylor relaxed in Charlie's arms. Hope stood and followed Charlie to the guest bedroom. There Hope kicked off her shoes. Eugette followed her lead. They laid down on the bed, Megan snuggled to her mom's bosom. Charlie laid Taylor down beside Hope. He took the folded quilt off the foot of the bed and covered the bed's guests. He smiled then walked back to the kitchen after he'd closed the bedroom door.

Gilbert looked to Charlie. He asked, "Any thoughts bouncing about on how or where the fire started? Thank God everyone is safe."

Jeffery trembled on hearing Gilbert's comment. Maria had been his childhood sweetheart. Then the island had cursed him and he'd lost her companionship. The thought of losing her anew terrified Jeffery. Charlie fired up the coffee machine with a second brew. Nobody objected. The men chatted over their oft refilled mugs. No comment arose when the running water stopped. Charlie assumed his Philly had convinced Maria and Lila to lay down on their bed and catch a couple hours of much needed sleep.

Phyllis rejoined the men in the kitchen. "They're ok. Maria and Lila grabbed quick showers. They're now turned in on our bed. Thanks, Love for getting Megan and Taylor setup in the guest room with Eugette and Hope." She moved towards the coffee machine. Charlie intercepted her and poured out a fresh mug of coffee. Phyllis accepted it and they exchanged a kiss.

CHAPTER 38

Barnie sneered holding the phone to his ear. On its fifth ring Slick answered. He caught the incoming number on the caller ID display and had hesitated in answering the call. The caller shouted into his ear, "Did it work? Deja git them? Did you send the bitch a message?"

Slick shuddered. Envy arose in his heart. Maybe Ned was right and that Jesus guy wasn't so bad. He definitely seemed to be helping Ned Stone escape the clutches of Barnie's evil ways. Silently Slick cursed himself straight to hell's gates. Why, he pondered, did I stumble back under that bastard's controls. He'd felt redeemed. Saved, if one embraced Pastor Mikie's words. He sighed, engulfed in regrets. Slick shouted back into the phone, "Maybe? I don't know! I'm not stupid Barn... I didn't stick around to watch the fireworks!"

"You stupid son of a bitch, what did I tell you to do?"

"They're just kids and Euggie's Mom. I'm not a murderer..."

"Right, care to explain away the island happenings?"

Slick fell silent. He rued over the day he'd fallen under the clutches of Barnie's evil ways. In his mind, the island scene echoed in vivid detail. Bam! Bam! Followed by two, or was it three, more-gun shots that rang out. Barnie stood at his side. This time Slick had seen Barnie wipe the revolver clean of his fingerprints. With angst he recalled how he'd taken the revolver out of Barnie's hand as it had been offered to him. Images of Lamont and his dead son-in-law burned laments of regret in Slick's mind and heart. He recalled tossing the gun onto the island's beach. Then Barnie had ordered Ned to retrieve the gun. A fool like Slick,

Ned had fallen into Barnie's trap. In his mind, Slick watched Barnie accept the revolver from the second patsy, Ned, using a handkerchief. In two sly moves the bastard had added Ned Stone to the frame that had cast Slick and Ned into the roles of a murderer. Why, he pondered, hadn't he aimed the revolver at Barnie that day and fired a bullet into the bastard's heart? Slick knew the answer. He wasn't a murderer. Just a fool framed into being held prisoner and a patsy to a double murder he'd witnessed.

"Well? Care to share a thought or two?"

"You BASTARD!"

"Thanks, I'm honoured to be held so esteemed in your mind!"

"I'll not take the fall. Jesus will save me!"

"Right! Tell that to the judge. It'll git you and Ned life in the big house. I still have the prove of your murdering ways safely stowed away. Cross me and it's sure to resurface!"

Slick slammed the receiver down into its cradle. In frustration he strutted nervously around his living room. The phone sang out anew to Slick's ears. Ring, ring, ring... Slick ignored it. In front of the coffee table, he dropped down onto his knees and started to pray. "Our Father who art in..." The words drilled into him throughout his childhood slipped out and caressed his remorseful soul. Slick ignored the on off again series of summons from his phone. He prayed in honesty pleading that Eugette, her kids and Mom were safe.

Barnie cursed uttering an endless string of foul language. He hungered to get a look at the burnt out remains of the Lamont house. To inhale the stench of burnt bodies would be a reward. It would also deliver a message to Eugette if the fire hadn't taken her off to be with her husband, Rusty. A deserved destiny earned by the stupid bitch whose nosey prying had triggered the need to send a message. A message that Barnie ached to know it been delivered. Or at least confirmed with a stench akin to that of burnt bodies at the fire scene. Pissed, Barnie grabbed a beer can from the fridge, popped its pull tab then relieved the can of its contents. He sighed and tossed the can into the sink. Resolve set in. Barnie decided to overlook the wayward reactions of Slick. He stomped out the door and pulled the driver's door of his Buick open. Once inside he brought its engine to a roaring start. Barnie drove off towards the Lobster Pot. A morning gathering spot for locals and a guaranteed source of news focused on the tragic fire that had burst to life and ignited the early morning's sky. Yes, Barnie whispered. Our locals will be spreading the news I need to hear. The Buick ground to a stop in the Pot's parking lot. At the main door Barnie smiled on seeing the tables filled with breakfast diners. He stepped inside. Staff raced to greet him. Through tear-stained eyes they blabbered together giving each one's version of the night's tragedy. Barnie hushed them. "Girls, girls, please one at a time. A fire you say? I trust there were no injuries? God, please let everyone be safe."

Connie blurted out, "The house is burnt to the ground. Nothing remains but ashes and a few blackened burnt studs from the walls. The street is blocked off by the police and fire department!"

"Debbie added, "Gerry called me on my cell. They're safe. Everyone is safe!"

"Safe...who? Whose house?" Barnie asked.

"Eugette's Mom's house, it's been destroyed."

Barnie's hands grasped his cheeks. He shook his head in mock disbelief,

Debbie added, "We offered to send breakfast packs off to the fire-fighters and cops at the scene. But diners shouted out in protest. They insisted we do it and add the meals to their bills. Jack left ten minutes ago to deliver them!"

Barnie pulled his hands free of his face. He raised his face and glanced over at the diners at the Pot's tables. He fought off an urge to discipline the girls for having suggested freebee meals for the town's heroes of the moment. Instead, he smiled at them and nodded his support of their actions. He walked out into the dining area. With a wave of his hand and a loud shout out, "Good morning, friends!" He caught everyone's attention. "Our town has been hit by a tragedy. A family's home has been destroyed! The home of our Eugette's Mom burnt to the ground. Friends, many of you have offered to cover the cost of breakfast for our town's heroes who attempted to save the home."

Many shouted out in response, "Yes! We're there! It's the least we can do."

Barnie replied, "No! I will cover the cost. You've supported me over the years. This town has supported me. Debbie tells me they're safe. Thank God. Friends, enjoy your meals, your meals and our town's heroes are dining on my tab!"

A hardy round of applause broke out in the Pot. Barnie nodded his appreciation to the diners. He turned about and walked off to his office. Once there he paced about, silently gloating on having risen to hero status in the eyes of the Pot's diners. He pondered, had Slick succeeded and secured Martin Lamont's house safe? Had they succeeded and secured the evidence Martin had boasted and claimed to possess? The hero status felt good. It would feel great to know Eugette knew about the morning's tragedy. Barnie felt it would send a signal to her of the risk she'd face if she didn't shut up and toe the line. Toe Barnie's line! The image of Slick's face fluttered in Barnie's mind. It stoked angry fires in his heart. Curiosity energized Barnie. He walked out of the office back to the Pot's bar, there he told the girls, "Take care of business. I'm heading over to catch a glimpse of the tragedy. I'll be back." Walking out to his Buick, Barnie added a trip to Slick's abode to his TODO list.

....

The Mattock's kitchen fell silent. The four occupants felt the effects of their interrupted sleep. Feeling assured that all was in hand Gilbert suggested, "Jeff, John, let's head home. Charlie will call the minute Maria and Auntie awaken. Hope is a God sent blessing. She'll tend to the wee ones and their mom."

"I don't want to lose her, Gil. I need my Maria."

"We all do, Jeff." Charlie added. "I'll call like Gilbert suggested."

Jeffery frowned. He did not want to walk away from Maria. With reluctance, he stood and followed Gilbert's lead. At the kitchen, counter

Gilbert tossed the keys to his truck on the counter. "Charlie, they are for Hope."

Charlie nodded confirmation to Gilbert. Once outside, they stared in renewed disbelief at the blackened remains of Maria's home. Eric ran over to their side. He asked, "Are Maria and the young ones, OK?"

"They're sleeping." Gilbert answered.

"Good. Still no sign of that cat Taylor was going on about."

"Bailey!" Jeffery recalled how he'd agreed to allowing Bailey to overnight with Megan and Taylor.

Eric added, "Taylor claims the fur ball saved their lives. He woke them up."

Jeffery smiled a feeling of relief embraced him. He pondered how their mom had steadfastly claimed over the years that, 'Every action, every step taken in life has an intended purpose.' He sighed then followed Gilbert over to his truck. He recalled how Gil had dropped his keys on the counter for Hope. He glanced down the road at his truck. Its keys were somewhere in the blacken remains of Maria's home. "Guess I'll tag along, Gilbert. My keys were on the coffee table in the house."

Gilbert and Jeffery drove back home with John in his rental SUV. Gilbert insisted they go to Jeffery's home, the family's homestead. Inside Jeffery and John followed the lead the women had taken back at Charlie and Phyllis's. Jeffery hit his bed while John claimed Poppa's vacant bed. Once on the beds, both men slipped into the Sandman's grasp. However, dreamland eluded them. Gilbert walked back over to his house and updated Richard and Lyndsey on the tragedy.

CHAPTER 39

Lyndsey sipped on her tea gazing out the kitchen window at Gilbert's house. On spotting him walking briskly across the yard she called, "Here comes Gilbert. He's alone. I sure hope everyone is ok."

Richard abandoned his coffee and rushed to the kitchen door. He opened it and shouted out, "Everyone's OK right?"

Gilbert quickened his pace on spotting Richard at the door. He nodded a positive response and followed Richard into the kitchen. "Everyone's safe. Phyllis and Charlie Mattock, Maria's neighbour across and two doors down, has taken them in. Maria, Eugette, the twins, Hope and Auntie Lila are bedded down and catching some much-needed rest. John and Jeffery are bunked out at the homestead. The police, a few firefighters, Harley and neighbours are searching high and low for Bailey. Thank God he was there. He rousted Maria and saved their lives.

"What can we do to help out?" Lyndsey asked.

"We'll get everyone over here and to Jeffery's once they've rested up. My God! It's almost Christmas. The house is destroyed burnt to the ground. We gotta make Christmas right for everyone. Especially Maria, Eugette, Megan and Taylor. I can't imagine the hurt they're feeling. The loses they've suffered." Seated around the table all three clasped each other's hands. Their emotions painted clearly on each face. Gilbert whispered, "First a stretch back they lost Martin and Rusty. Now all their worldly possessions savored over their lifetimes gone. No family should have to suffer as they have been forced to. We gotta make it right for them. We gotta make this a Christmas that restores love and life's passions into their lives. We just gotta!"

"And we will, Gilbert. We will." Richard stated. Lyndsey released Richard's hand. She embraced and pulled him tight to her body. All three fell silent and broke free of the emotions ripping at their hearts. Gilbert accepted Lyndsey's offer to brew a tea. He felt coffee logged with the mugs of java he'd sloshed back over at Charlie's. The trio committed themselves to making Christmas a blessing for the Lamont family. After a stretch the sounds of crushed gravel outside alerted them to an arrival.

Gilbert jumped up. He ran to the door and opened it. On watching Charlie and Phyllis drive into the yard in their SUV with Hope in his truck close behind, he shouted, "They're here. All of them are here!"

Hope led the way. She walked the twins up to the house with a hand of theirs in each of hers. Megan stared up at Gilbert. She stated, "Our house is gone Mister Gilbert."

Before he could react, Taylor boasted, "We're here cuz Bailey saved our lives! Sure, hope they finds him. Bailey's our hero."

Gilbert dropped to his knees and embraced both twins. On a nudging from Hope, Gilbert released the twins and stepped away from the doorway. With Auntie Lila at her side, Hope led everyone into the kitchen. A glance at the kitchen clock revealed the hour to be 11:14 am. Slowly they made their way into the living-room. Hope held back and, with, Lyndsey the grilling and production of McClaken Grilled Cheese Sandwiches got underway. A glance out the window caught Jeffery and John running across the yard. On arriving, Hope pointed to the living-room. She said, "Straight ahead."

On hearing their men, Maria and Eugette ran into the kitchen. Warm embraces ensued. Charlie and Phyllis tried to slide away. Their attempt failed. In the kitchen Phyllis pulled Eugette aside. They embraced. Eugette listened with a questioning mind to Phyllis's words, "So glad we were able to lend a hand today. In chatting with your mom today I wanted to hug her to the ends of de earth. Charlie and I have seen your mom, you and your wee ones grow up right before our eyes. Your mom, the silly woman, is too much of a giver and struggles to accept a helping hand. Reassure her we're there for her, you and the wee ones."

"Don't be fretting Philly, you and Charlie are like family. You've both just been there for us throughout everything. And now today. Who steps up when a need arose? We know and to me and my babies you're both a second set of grandparents."

"That we are. And proud to be so. I'm just saying, your mom sometimes can be a stubborn lass."

"And I can't?" Eugette asked afresh and hugged Phyllis anew before the women separated and fast stepped it back into the living-room with others in tow. A typical Nova Scotian Jabber Party quickly ensued. Hope and Lyndsey kept the jabbers energized with a steady feeding of Gilbert's grilled cheese sandwiches along with liquid refreshments to the diner's expressed wants. Just as things started to mellow down a lively foursome reignited the gathering. Pappy, Lenny and the Wright sisters arrived bearing a shopping bag or was it three? Auntie Lila who'd taken a shine to the wee ones joined Hope and Eugette upstairs with the shopping bags in hand. The late arrivals declined offers of food but joined in the party following Pappy's visit to the cabinet to retrieve some of its golden nectars. The twins returned and received applause as they strutted about in their brand new, off the shelf, clothing that Pappy's crew had delivered. The afternoon quickly slipped away. Visitors arrived and departed throughout the day. Word had hit the street in Chester and East River, and Gilbert's home was designated the drop off point for donations to the Lamont family.

Once the house emptied itself of guests, sleeping arrangements were set in place. Hope ceded her room to Lila and claimed the den's loveseat. John held tight to Eugette's side and the twins. Jeffrey and Maria joined them over in Jeffery's home. The long day and its tragedy had exerted a toll on everyone. The twins claimed Pappy's bedroom, John and Eugette ended up in Jeffery's. He willingly reserved the sunroom for Maria and himself. He stared out into a star filled sky through the sunroom's windows. Quietly, he reflected on the day just passed. Gentle footsteps drew his ears then eyes to their source. He got rewarded with a view of Maria attired in one of Hope's nightgowns. He raised a hand and she accepted it into hers. They snuggled up to each other covered under the quilt on the loveseat.

Maria savoured the security of Jeffery's arms. His body warmly embraced her and with eyes closed she slipped back in time. Back to where a nightmare had destroyed her youth. Jeffery kissed her neck and hair. The touch of his lips rescued her from the icy grasp of the nightmare. The moment and the day's happenings diverted Maria from revealing to Jeffery the news that she wanted and needed to share with him. Earlier in the day she'd sensed Phyllis had clued into her current condition. Those thoughts quickly vanished. Once their lips touched temperatures soared. Their lips parted. Maria explored and caressed the body she craved until it was naked. Stoking its thighs confirmed its readiness. With ease Maria slipped free of her nightgown. Easing her body atop Jeffery, she sighed on feeling him enter her, ready and eager passion. The day's miseries vanished in a heartbeat. Time vanished in beat to their thrusting bodies. Each worked to please the other more with each movement. Jeffrey took Maria's breast into his hands. In touching them his fingertips energized his thrusts. A final drive triggered both their sexual pleasures into fulfilled states. Their bodies shivered and their lips sought out more from each other's. Snuggled together, sexually gratified, each drifted off into dreamland secure in the other's grasp.

....

Their awakening came bright and early. The twins raced into the sunroom and rescued Grammie and Grampa Jeffy from the Sandman's grasp. They shouted gleefully, "Grammie, Grammie, Grampa Jeffy! Looks outside! It snowed! We're all set fer Christmas and Santa Claus."

Grammie and Grampa Jeffy peeked out from under the quilt. Both admired the fresh snow-covered trees and ground outside the sunroom windows. Jeffery rescued Grammie. He replied, "Its beautiful. And yer right. It set everything up for a perfect Christmas." He yawned then added, "Give us a minute or two and we'll join you in the kitchen. Ok?"

Megan giggled and Taylor ran to catch up to her in the kitchen. A good morning kiss lingered longer than expected. It ended. Maria slipped back into the nightgown. Jeffery retrieved his clothing and got dressed. On standing up he joined Maria and both gazed longingly at the snow-covered vista laid out before their eyes. The chattering of the twins with their mom and John in the kitchen distracted them from the view. Together they folded up the quilt and reset the loveseats cushions. Both eyed it with a hunger for more of what they'd shared in the loveseat's comforts. However, a new day called out with fresh possibilities afoot. Jeffery joined the crowd in the kitchen. Maria wrapped herself in a crocheted shawl, slipped into Jeffery's bedroom, and got dressed. On returning to the kitchen, she learned they'd all been summoned to Gilbert's for breakfast and an update on the day's planned adventure. Jeffery, on following the others outside, locked the homestead's door. A practice he swore to abide by following yesterday's tragedy in Chester. He joined everyone in John's SUV and they headed over to Gilbert's for breakfast.

On driving towards Gilbert's driveway, a police vehicle drove by them towards the highway. Taylor shouted out, "Looks! It's officer Eric. I bet ya he found our Bailey. Said he would. I betcha he did too!"

Maria cautioned Taylor, "He did Tay. But let's hold off a bit before we get too excited."

"But he saved our lives, Grammie. He's gotta be OK!"

John turned in at Gilbert's. The SUV stopped beside Gilbert's truck. Taylor and Megan unbuckled their seatbelts then jumped out after Megan popped the door open. They raced each other up to the kitchen door then ran inside as the door opened with Richard greeting them.

They shouted together, "We saw officer Eric! Where's Bailey? Where's our Hero Bailey? Everyone is safe our hero just gotta be safe. Bailey!"

Megan spotted the yellowy-orange greyish sooty furry bundle Gilbert was massaging in the sink with a sudsy watery mix. She ran over to the counter. Taylor followed on her heels. She shouted, "Can I wash him? Oh, please Mister Gilbert. Can I wash our hero?"

"Me too. Me too!" Shouted Taylor. "He saved our lives."

Gilbert nodded to Hope, "Get us a couple of stools, no chairs will do. I'll assist. I promise."

Hope quickly returned with two kitchen chairs. Once set in place Gilbert's aides assisted in the cleansing of our hero Bailey. Once again, he'd achieved celebrity status amongst his admirers. Maria, Eugette and Jeffery walked into the kitchen. John followed on their heels. A bubbly spray of soapy bubbles floating through the kitchen greeted them. Good morning greetings were exchanged by all. Lyndsey stood and offered up breakfast. "Is everyone good with a batch of scrambled eggs and bacon?"

Jeffery called out, "Does it comes with a batch of buttered up toast?"

Hope answered, "Iff'in yer offering to do the toasting then it's a deal, Uncle Jeffery!"

"It's a deal! Get me some bread, girl."

"Girl? I'm a woman, Uncle Dearest!" Hope shouted back at Jeffery.

The kitchen door flew open and Anya and Norman stepped inside. He ran to Hope and embraced her. A lingering kiss ensued. Jeffery took to banging a kitchen pot with a wooden spoon.

He shouted out. "We'll be having none of that. There's wee ones abouts!"

The kiss ended and personal greetings were exchanged. Anya and Maria embraced. She whispered. "Sorry I wasn't in town yesterday. Thank God everyone is ok. Norman drove me by the house. Maria, our house is open to you and yours. It's the least we can do. I have some outfits that'll fit you perfect. They're yours." They released each other and followed the crowd being herded off into the dining room. Breakfast passed quickly without a hitch. That is if one overlooked the tussle to hold Bailey on their own lap and not share him by the twins. Before anyone attempted to leave the dining room, Gilbert stood up and announced the day's planned outing. "Maria, Auntie Lila, Eugette, Megan, Taylor, John, Anya, Norman and of course our Jeffery! In view of all that's beset our loved ones, everyone has agreed that a short change of venue could prove to be a blessing. And we all need and want to make this a Perfect Seaside Christmas for everyone. Sadly, there's something missing from this house and Christmas is rapidly approaching. I fear Santa Claus could miss our house becaus…"

"It doesn't have a Christmas Tree!" Shouted Megan and Taylor.

Gilbert grinned ear to ear. He boasted, "You're absolutely right." He paused a second or two then continued. "Therefore, we're all going to head up to Buzzard Mountain and make things right! Right?"

"Where's that, Mister Gilbert" Megan asked.

Gilbert puffed up his chest then bragged, "Buzzard Mountain is the absolute tallest mountain peak on the mainland of Nova Scotia. It's where Alpho…"

Jeffery jumped in, "Alphonso Buzzard and *'The Legend of Buzzard's Mountain and How Alpho…'*"

Gilbert cut Jeffery short, "Jeff, stop. We'll not be letting the cat out'ta de bag before we hit the road. To this day, Alphonso's children and their children's children still live up on Buzzard Mountain."

Chuckling broke out throughout the house. Outside Pappy, and Lenny drove into the yard. Lenny in his SUV, Pappy in a huge van, a Wright sister at each of their sides. Quickly they made their way into the house. Both men passed their keys over to Gilbert. Pappy announced, "We're here and set to keep things safe. Ye'd best be hitting de road and heading on up ta Buzzard Mountain! There could be more snow on the way."

Auntie Lila announced, "Maybe I should hang out here and chaperone the goings on with these young ones that's staying at the house?"

Hope called out, "Maybe we shouldn't go…"

Gilbert cut her off. "We're going. Everyone please gets yourselves dressed. We're heading out to Buzzard Mountain. OK! And, Auntie, it just wouldn't be right leaving you back here with this pair of loaf abouts. You'd best give in and join the party."

Auntie Lila shrugged then accepted her coat that Eugette offered up with a smile.

Eugette boasted, "Iff'in you've never been, then you just gotta go. Come with John, me and the twins. We're heading out in class in Lenny's SUV. It's loaded. You gotta go, Auntie. It'll be a blast. I haven't been since Hope and I were seventeen or was it eighteen?"

Gilbert shouted out. "Let's move it the experience of a lifetime awaits you up on Buzzard Mountain. You'll love it, Auntie Lila!"

CHAPTER 40

Everyone slipped into their warmest winterwear. The youthful ones took the lead. Hope, then Norman, Eugette, John and the twins led the parade out to the vehicles. Auntie Lila tried to hold back but Maria nudged her towards the adventure. She boasted, Auntie you'll love it. My first trip was with the McClakens. I was but knee high to a hedgehog. Dad took us once. You must've gone at least once?"

Lila wagged her head sideways a negative response. She declared, "Momma wanted to. But Daddy was just like your dad. Steadfast and logical." She paused and savoured the thought. Then added, "Guessing that's why we butted heads so back in the day." Maria nudged Lila closer to the door. The flow outside gained momentum. The last two out were Lyndsey followed by Gilbert. Jeffery stood beside the huge van, bundled to the nth degree in his winter's comfiest set of outdoorsman clothing. He appeared ready to stare down the worse nor'easter and its kinship that had ever painted East River into a perfect storm and wintery wonderland.

Hope grinned sheepishly. She puckered up her lips and leaned over sideways and kissed a receptive Norman. Everyone had boarded Lenny's SUV. John idled it while waiting for the others to load up the van.

"Hello!" Jeffery shouted. "Git yourselves onboard. The first bench is reserved. Come-on, Love. That seat's reserved for you and Anya. Move it! Move it! We ain't got all day, ladies." Maria accepted Jeffery's helping hand in boarding, after treating herself to a kiss. Anya followed in her footsteps, less the kiss. Hope led Norman and they claimed the wide back bench seat.

Lyndsey stopped on reaching the van door. She smiled in reaction to a series of energized thumps inside her baby bump, she hugged her belly. "She, he kicked me, Honey. Our baby kicked its Mommy!"

Richard ran to Lyndsey. He hugged her in his arms. A thump sang out silently again to the elated Mom-to-be anew. Richard slid a hand inside Lyndsey's overcoat. A series of thumps connected with his hand; he broke out in giggles." He kicked me! He kicked me … sweetheart."

"He, not she, kicked you?" Lyndsey asked in jest.

Richard kissed Lyndsey's forehead. She twisted free and sought out Richard's lips. They kissed. Applause and cheering broke out. The kiss ended.

"OK, let's get moving!" Gilbert called out. "The perfect Christmas Tree is calling out to us high up on Buzzard Mountain."

Jeffery walked around the multi-passenger rental van and claimed the driver's seat. A twist of the ignition key started the engine. Lyndsey climbed aboard with Richard and Gilbert's assistance. She claimed the middle bench seat and Richard followed her lead. The last to board the van, true to tradition, was Gilbert. He eyed the van's interior. Everyone appeared ready to hit the highway. The Christmas tree harvesters inside all gave him a thumbs up and waved him towards getting on board. He turned and smiled over to Eugette and the twins in Lenny's SUV. She rolled down her window.

Gilbert called out to her, "We'll see you guys and gals up on the mountain. It's a perfect day to embrace the Magic of Christmas."

Eugette replied, "It is Gilbert. We could all use a little magic in our lives. Can't wait. Haven't been up there in years!"

Nobody, including Gilbert, caught sight of the true last arrival. A fluffy orange fur ball slipped out the door before Gilbert locked it up. Focused on its goal, the flash raced off the doorstep then across the yard to the van. A silent leap and an accompanying left … right-shift landed Bailey under the bench seat occupied by Hope and Norman. He relaxed. Warm air flowing out of the van's heating ducts treating Bailey to a massage caressed with a warmth that humans and felines craved on the approach of Christmas's icy and snow kissed greetings. Music danced in the air. The radio's station sang out, airing a full slate of Christmas melodies.

A loud whoosh sang out! Standing outside the van Gilbert had grabbed the sliding side door and eased it along its tracks until, thump. It closed completely, engaging its locks. Gilbert opened the passenger door and claimed the front passenger seat. Thud, the door locked into place with Gilbert's tug on its armrest. Jeffery called out, "All aboard the Buzzard Mountain Christmas Tree Express."

Richard grinned and asked, "Buzzard Mountain, really, Uncle Jeffery, you're not pulling my leg? We're kin folk beyond a doubt. But Buzzard Mountain, where do Nova Scotians come up with the names of their towns and local places? Really … Buzzard Mountain, McKinney's Reach, Mushaboom, Meat Cove, Sober Island? I suspect it is a never-ending list buried in legends out of the past."

The van fell silent. Richard and Lyndsey awaited Jeffery's reply. Once he got the all set wave from John in Lenny's SUV, Jeffery pondered Richard's question while driving out onto the road. His pondering lingered. Richard did not press for an answer. Everyone settled in for their drive up to the mountain. Ten minutes, later the van turned and headed towards the highway on ramp. Their speed accelerated up the ramp to Hwy 103. Its signal light flashed, then Jeffery eased them into the flow of traffic. He eyed the rear-view mirror often confirming John was following close at hand. Several moments of silence flew past without a response. Richard grinned. He suspected the posed question required more time to weave together a believable response. A response that Come from Aways would actually take in as truths straight out of the good book.

Finally, Jeffery answered Richard, "Nova Scotians claiming true Bluenosers' status know the truth. The names our forefathers assigned to our lands are simple ways to preserve our history and heritage. Right, Gilbert?" Jeffery did not hold back awaiting Gilbert's endorsement. His explanation flowed onward, "You chuckled, laughed and questioned the naming of Buzzard Mountain. You'll have to be a patient lad in awaiting the revelation of Buzzard Mountain's history. For it is a history born of its forefathers' visions of undisputable legend."

Richard questioned, "Lyndsey, you're a newly discovered, reclaimed local. Not a CFA like me. Your thoughts, is Uncle Jeffery pulling my leg?"

Silence befell the van. Uncle Jeffery saved her from answering. "Richard, in just over an hour no closer to one and a half, we'll all be greeted by descendants of those after whom the mountain got it name. Relax, enjoy our ride. A unique experience awaits you. Savor its moments. Save them for, come Christmas Eve, those descendants I'm told will be joining up with us in East River. Come midnight on Christmas Eve our Gillie will once again share the truth behind the tale, or should Moses do the honours, Gilbert?"

Richard chuckled then answered, "Away with you! Away with you. Moses, you say? So, Moses will be descending the mountain come Christmas Eve? Could it be your Christmas Eves out of the past have left you an expert on the tale. For a tale it must truly be!?"

"Not a tale, my son. Simply 'The Legend of Buzzard Mountain and How Alpho...'"

Gilbert cut Jeffery short, "Jeff, stop. We'll not be letting the cat out'ta de bag before Christmas Eve." He tumbled into a fit of laughter.

Anya jumped into the conversation. She asked, "I've been there at least once. No, twice. Right, Gillie? Back in the day, Pappy and your mom drove all of us up onto Buzzard Mountain. It was a ball. The slides. Do they still have them? Karyn, lands alive, oh how she loved the slides. The owner was a total riot. Moses, just like Jeff said. If he wasn't running things up on the mountain, he'd be a stand-up comedian for sure!"

Richard grinned boldly. After a glance into Lyndsey's eyes, he declared, "Yes Uncle Jeffery. You'd best cut yourself off short. We sure don't want to let de cat out'ta de bag!"

Gilbert recovered first. While the laugher subsided, he clarified his viewpoint, "On my call booking this adventure and search for a Perfect

Christmas Tree and Christmas Turkey up on the mountain, our dear friends the Buzzards, Moses and Mary invited themselves to our East River Christmas Gathering of kin folk."

"Then the mountain's name is actually tied to a family's forefathers?"

Gilbert grew serious. He answered, "Not just tied, Richard. The mountain is named in honour of Moses' great-great and greater than great grandparents. Back aways it was a wild, unsettled forested mountain. Today, generations of Buzzards have added their mark and enhancements to the land." He paused then added, "Relax! We'll be there in the twist of a turkey buzzard's tail."

Anya shouted out gleefully, "That's it. That line you just call out, Gilbert. It was Moses', opening line to anyone asking how far it was to Buzzard Mountain. *'Relax you'll be here in the twist of a turkey buzzard's tail.'* He was a total riot. I almost peed myself reacting to his antics."

"Mom, really!" Norman chirped in response.

"But it's true." Anya replied. She added, "And the turkeys. Are they still shooting to hit the Guinness World Record for the biggest tur..."

Gilbert cut in, "Aye. And that would be a yes. But no letting the cat out'ta de bag. We got us some first timers on board this Christmas Express to Buzzard Mountain!"

"My lips are sealed", Anya replied with a smile.

Laugher ensued throughout the van. Richard turned to Norman, "Being a true local who once escaped the Chester and East River that connects to East River's McClakens years past, are they crazier today than you recall, Norman?" Richard watched Norman's eyes skitter around the van reading the faces and eyes of everyone.

Norman's eyes locked on Hope's. Richard caught it. He boasted, "It's a tough one, Normie. Our Hope, she's a sweetie. Will you risk it all and reveal the truth?"

Hope reached out and embraced Norman. On releasing him she said, "There's no risk Richie. Back in the day I was simply infatuated with an older man in my life. His storytelling and schoolyard eyes are what hooked me. And yes, I must have been a pain in his arse!" Norman chuckled on recalling the days past. Hope continued, "If it must be known then I must confess I had a crush on the poor lad. Fact is I've silently rued the day Normie and his mom vanished out'ta my life. I must 'a told him a thousand times I LOVED HIM. But he never heard me once. All the older girls were hanging off 'my man and I never stood a chance."

"Did so!" Norman frowned and protested. "Well not in the way you're talking it up. But I kind of liked watching over you and the story-telling when our families got together." He sniffled. After we moved, I really struggle for a stretch with writing class essays. But eventually I got back on track."

Hope cut in, "It's ok, Norman. I'm just glad I bumped into you at work."

Anya cut in, "That's a given, Normie. I love how you bragged and told me, 'Mom my coworkers think I rock. They saw a hot babe hit on me!'"

"Mom!" Chuckling floated around the van.

"Sorry!" Anya answered. "But moving back home was a tough call. Hearing you boasting it up. What can I say. It made me feel good!"

Hope wrapped an arm around Norman. She snuggled up and they kissed.

Gilbert reached back and took Anya's hands in his. The touching of hands relieved Anya of the guilt she felt. Richard glanced over at Lyndsey. He reflected on memories out of his childhood and they warmed his heart. Memories of Christmases past and images of loved ones floated through his head. The reality of loved ones lost hit him like a bullet. Lyndsey reached over with a tissue in hand. She dabbed away the tears on Richard's cheeks. Throughout the van everyone appeared lost in a fog of treasured moments out of their pasts. He recovered and asked, "Gilbert, Anya mentioned the Buzzards in raising turkeys were shooting to hit the Guinness World Record for the world's biggest turkey. How big is the turkey you've got your eye set on?"

The word turkey painted a delightful and tasty image in the stow-away Bailey's mind. He almost sneezed on catching a passing recollection of the taste of brussels sprouts. Recovered, Bailey locked himself on a memory out of his youth. In it he was secure under a Ramsay's Christmas dining table. The aromas totally relaxed his mind. A hand appeared. It clutched at Bailey's heartstrings. The attraction proved irresistible. Bailey's eyes followed his nose rising up to the beautiful white turkey meat envisioned in his mind. Gravy dripped off the meat. A cramp suddenly clutched at his belly. It signaled an intestinal eruption. Bailey did not react to the signals. The alluring turkey images captivated Bailey's mind. 'Phhffoop...oop.' Bailey grimaced. His eyes closed in anticipating the pending stench.

The van fell silent on hearing the robust Phhffoop...oop. Lyndsey and Hope frowned in disgust. Jeffery chimed in with the first denial, "It weren't me! It wasn't me!"

Lyndsey turned to Richard. She did not speak. Richard's puzzled look pasted doubt in her mind. She pondered, could the first denial tag the guilty party? Up front, Jeffery and Gilbert cast knowing looks at each other. Nobody seated in the van claimed ownership of the disturbance.

"Not me!" Jeffery shouted. An encore of male denials ensued.

"Nor I!" Gilbert declared, as he frantically rubbed at his watered-up eyes.

"What's with the look, Lynds? It wasn't me." Richard cried in affirming his innocence.

All eyes turned but Jeffery's turned and stared at the last known male in the van, Hope's Norman. He stumbled his denial, "I...I... would never. It's not me!"

The guilty party grimaced in anticipation of the pending side effects. His wait time was short! The putrid odor had hit everyone in one foul swoop. Jeffery's eyes burned in reaction to the foul stench that had hit the happy band on their Christmas Express to Buzzard Mountain. He reacted with ease. The van slowed on the release of its accelerator. Its signal light flashed, warning other drivers of Jeffery's intentions. He worked the brake pedal and steered the van safely off the highway and onto the curb. The van came to a complete stop. He shifted the van's transmission into park. Driver, passenger windows front and rear slid open. Fresh but cold air flowed freely into the van. Nobody uttered a word. Suddenly an encore 'Phhffoop...oop' broke the silence. An anguished gasp followed.

Just as suddenly Hope stared down at her feet. An orangey-yellow tail flopped guiltily back and forth, up and down. She shouted, "OH MY GOD ... IT'S BAILEY! It's Bailey! What did you guys feed him?"

"He's at home at Gillie's," Jeffery declared. "I saw him in the livingroom on the sofa jest before we left."

"I locked up the house. I was the last one out!" Gilbert stated confidently. "Bailey is back home in East River"

Hope wiped away at her burning eyes. She added, "Then pray tell whose orangey-yellow tail am I staring at?" A sour frown pinched her face and Hope's dimples popped out. With hesitance Hope released her seatbelt. She then stooped down and retrieved a guilt-ridden Bailey. She then held him up for everyone to see and declared, "Does this look like Bailey is back home? Bailey ... Bailey ... Oh my Gads, Bailey, you are a stinker!"

Refrained humorous chatter filled the van. Hope continued to hold Bailey. She rubbed and massaged his head, neck and back.

Jeffery broke the silence, "Looks like we're stuck with stinky till we get home. We're almost there. The mountain and its tree farm are not more than fifteen, twenty minutes away. We'll leave two windows open a crack or two and get back on the road. Do you really want to hold on to old stinky, Hope?" He turned and faced John who had stepped out of Lenny's SUV to see why Jeffery had pulled off the road. He explained their situation to John. A fresh round of laughter ensued.

John caught sight of the contented culprit seated on Hope's lap. He chuckled and asked, "How close are we to the mountain, Jeffery?"

"A mere skip and a hop away. Fifteen, maybe twenty minutes. We'd best get a move on. The weather can get iffy up on the mountain." John nodded agreement then turned and walked back to the SUV. The laughter abated and quickly both vehicles were ready to go back on the road. Jeffery shifted the van back into drive. Highway traffic cleared and he drove the van onto the roadway. John followed his lead.

CHAPTER 41

Jeffery piped up, "Sure hope it don't git much worse than it has. Let's try closing those windows. We should be good if you know who doesn't strike again!"

"Don't be so mean, Uncle Jeffery. Bailey just didn't want to stay home all by himself."

"But he had Pappy, Lenny and their ladies to keep him entertained." Hope simply smirked and continued to pat and massage Bailey and his wounded ego. She did not comment but smiled on Norman massaging a now contented Bailey in a way only veterinarians knew how. A loud purring expressed Bailey's pleasures. The last leg of their adventure flew by with only a minor repeat performance by Bailey. Jeffery caught sight of the Buzzard Mountain Free Range Turkey Ranch and its sister entities' signs. Driving up to the turn-off he signaled his intentions and the van slowed under his guiding hands. Once off the highway, their drive up the mountain passed in excited chatting.

Hope boasted, "We saw Moses' new World Record Turkey Challengers last week on the TV News updates. My God! They're huge. I didn't think turkeys grew that big. And don't get carried away, Dad. We need a turkey that will fit into our oven. We don't want a Turkey-Sorus-Dino-Rexious to be our Christmas Feasting Beast!" She paused. I hope you brought an appetite with you, along with stretchy pants and belts! You'll be needing them for sure comes our Christmas Day feasting."

Jeffery slowed anew and made the standard two right turns followed by the sharp upward left that set them on the road up to Moses

Buzzard's Buzzard Mountain Ranch. The locals chuckled at the expressions on both Lyndsey and Richard's faces. Hope pondered, if that bedazzles you, Sis, wait till you meet the Lord of de Mountain … Moses de Buzzard Man, then toss in a gander at his WRTCs. Store bought turkeys will never look the same. Jeffery guided the van into an open parking spot near the trail to the Christmas Tree Farm. John followed his lead.

Gilbert opened his door and stepped out into the fresh mountain air. Moses spotted him. Before Gilbert could complete his bends and stretches, he heard the shop door slam shut and watched Moses excitedly race towards him. Both men came together in a Buzzard's Mountain how's you 'a doing's greeting. Moses stepped back from Gilbert he boasted, "Lordie, I is a truly blessed. I gits to see you and yers not once buts twice comes Christmas. Why when's Mary and's I heard ya were inviting us on down yer ways fer Christmas it most melted me heart me, son! It'll be three times in'ta a month that's we'll have been down into the civilized world. Anyways, it sure Tis good ta sees ya agin me son."

Moses looked past Gilbert into the van. "Lordy! He shouted. You brought your Lassies and Jeffery and a bunch of others ups with ya."

"No Moses. Actually, Jeff brought us. He did the driving this time out."

"And it's good to see you, Moses. You're looking good." Gilbert turned and slid the van's sliding side door open.

Moses stared into the van. He walked to its side. "Gillie…Gillie is 'in that our newly-weds?"

"That it is. Lyndsey and Richard, they're Ramsays. Connected bang on direct right to our forefathers."

Moses strutted up to the van. He peeked inside, Excited, he started to dance a mountain jig and sing, "Two of them. Ye brought both of the gals up to de mount… a 'long with their men. Git yerselves out here ladies. Why, they almost be twins excepting fer Hope's hair and de other's ting. What's do they call them today?"

"Baby bumps." Gilbert answered.

Suddenly a blazing orangey-yellow fur ball leaped to freedom off Hope's lap. Moses frowned and dodged the flying freedom seeker. A grin broke out anew on his face. Everyone watched Bailey land on the snow slip and slide to a stop, then race off towards the barn door. Hope jumped out of the van. Her eyes followed Bailey running to the barn. She managed one, no two steps, then stopped dead in her tracks, locked in a Mountain Man's greeting. Her attempts to escape failed.

"But...but, our Bailey. He's never..."

"Relax, Hope. We'll not lets any harms come ta yer Bailey."

Hope fought in vain to twist free from Moses' greeting. Resigned to her situation, she groaned, "He's never been up on the mountain. Bailey has no sense of where he's at!"

Richard grinned ear to ear staring at Moses dressed in Christmas regalia beyond any he'd ever seen before. He stepped out of the van and helped Lyndsey join him. Then all the others followed his lead with Norman offering a helping hand. Richard's eyes followed Moses' and watched on with Hope and the East River-Christmas tree and turkey hunters, as Bailey reached the barn, then slipped inside through its opening door. A family walked out of the barn having completed their tour of the Turkey Farm's facility. Moses released Hope. She ran off in pursuit of Bailey. All eyes followed her every step. Suddenly Bailey raced back out of the barn. Hope stooped down looking to draw Bailey into her extended arms. A loud attention grabbing, 'Gobble, gobble, gobble,' broke the silence. Its source strutted out of the barn. With wings flapping and head flying up, down, left, then right and jowls flopping everywhere; a massive turkey stepped off in pursuit of Bailey. A second, then third, massive turkey strutted out of the barn to freedom, 'Gobble, gobble, gobble … Gobble, gobble, gobble.' The family's father hoisted up their child and together they raced to safety towards the Turkey Farm's Restaurant and Gift Shop door. The mother slipped and fell on the snow-covered parking lot. She looked up pleadingly and watched her husband disappear through the gift shop's door. Richard moved to assist the woman. He held up on seeing two closer couples run to her side. Bailey eluded Hope's arms. He raced towards the van. Jeffery ran to Hope's side. He scoped his niece up into his arms then ran to the van. Hope tumbled into the van out of Jeffery's arms.

'Gobble, gobble, gobble ... Gobble.' The lead beast strutted, hot on the trail of Bailey. Lyndsey eyes popped wide open. She'd never seen a turkey outside the safety of a kitchen. Her jaw dropped in response to her stunned state. These creatures couldn't possibly be to related to the turkeys that had filled festive kitchens with dining delights and alluring aromas over the years. Hope's Turkey-Sorus-Dino-Rexiouses were more akin to monsters out of every child's worst nightmare. Lyndsey remained frozen in awe of the actions unfolding. Maria, Anya and Norman shocked, stayed, by her side.

Outside, the fallen mother regained her footing with the help of a gathering of rescue volunteers and Mary Buzzard. Gingerly, she walked with them towards the shop's door. Inside her head a vision of hubby racing off with Ariana in hand replayed itself nonstop. Bruised buttocks and a throbbing elbow did not abide warm feelings towards hubby. Moses also received a scowl or two from Mary. He reacted quickly. A glance northward caught sight of Bailey racing up the Christmas Tree trail, pursued by the three escaped Turkey-Sorus-Dino-Rexiouses, Moses' new crop of World Record Turkey Challengers, on his tail. The jingling bells and carolling of a returning horse drawn wagon filled with Christmas Trees and their new families drew everyone's eyes and hearts to their arrival. Images that had terrified them earlier vanished. The horses drew to a halt on a command sung out by their driver a young man dressed akin to Moses himself. Gilbert eyed the unloading of the Christmas Trees and their new families. He suggested, "Perhaps we should be looking at setting off in pursuit of our Christmas Tree?"

Hope blurted out, "What about our Bailey? The poor frightened dear will perish out there all alone. And what iff'in those beasts catch up to our Bailey?"

Moses' piped out, "Don't ya be a fretting, sweetheart. They only eat grains. They're vegetarians by nature!"

"Really?" Hope asked.

"Really!" Moses replied. He added, "I'll chase me lads up there after the wee ting. Your Bailey is safe. I guarantee it, sweetheart."

Hope nibbled at her lower lips. The commotion and activities in the yard died down. With the assurances of Moses in hand everyone made their way over towards the empty wagon. Lyndsey held herself back from the group initially. However, under the guiding hand and assurances of Moses she joined up with them. The wagon loaded up quickly. Its elfin driver called out, "Are we all aboard de 'Buzzard Mountain Christmas Tree Express'?"

"Yes! Yes, we are!" Megan, Taylor and their accompanying young tree hunters sang out together.

Their driver shouted out, "Giddy up, giddy up, Willow and Sarah, we're off to Buzzard Mountain's Christmas Tree Wonderland, where's every tree is touched and nurtured under Santa's watchful eye."

"Really?" Taylor shouted out.

"No!" Megan stated with conviction. "He's up in the North Pole. He can't see these trees."

"Oyez! Yes, he can young lady. Why Santa Claus sees everything and everyone all year round, and especially comes Christmas Eve. Why he even keeps a list."

The wagon fell silent for a short spell of pondering. Then it burst into song led by its elfin driver. *"Jingly, jingly here's we come. Jingly jinglier, looking to find the perfect Christmas Trees fer everyone's homes. Giddy up, giddy up, Sweet Willow and Sarah!"* Everyone, young and mature, joined in on the robust carolling their faces aglow in wishful anticipation. The carolling shifted time into fast mode. Suddenly their driver howled out, "Whoa, whoa Sweet Willow and Sarah. Ye have delivered us again safely into Buzzard Mountain's Christmas Tree Wonderland. The wagon drew up to a stop. Its driver, aided by the men onboard, helped everyone climb down onto a snow-covered ground. In every direction Christmas Trees, groomed to perfection, appeared. The driver issued long brilliant red plastic tapes with wooden numbered disks attached to each group of tree hunters. Then each group strolled off at their own pace in search of their perfect Christmas Tree.

The East River gang allowed Megan and Taylor to take the lead. Each tree passed called eagerly out to them. Both their faces were aglow in wonderment, kissed by the Magic of Christmas. Suddenly, they both stopped side by side in front of a tree. The air filled itself with huge white fluffy snowflakes. It felt like Santa's hand had reached down and touched Megan and Taylor's hearts. Together they shouted out, "This one. This one, Mommy. It's a perfect Christmas Tree."

Gilbert handed the disked red tape to Megan. He said, "Here you go sweetheart. Tie our claim tag to our tree. And you're both right. It is a perfect Christmas Tree."

John stood at Eugette's side an arm about her waist. Both were embraced by Maria, Jeffery and Auntie Lila. Gilbert, Anya, Hope and Norman copied their led. A feeling of family touched their souls. Richard stood at Lyndsey's side, each embracing the other. In eying Megan and Taylor, a joyful essence filled both their hearts. A series of kicks tapped agreement with their thoughts on Lyndsey's belly. Her face lit up tenfold and pending motherhood embraced her from within. With the tag attached, they waved out to their driver and his assistant. In short order everyone's tagged tree was cut down and delivered back to the wagon where it was loaded on. The snow continued to fall gently out of the sky. Children stuck out their tongues eagerly gathering falling snowflakes on their tongue tips. The successful tree hunters climbed back onboard the wagon. Its driver called out anew, "Giddy up, giddy up, Willow and Sarah, we're off back home with another haul of perfect Christmas Trees. Giddy ya selves up, come Willow and Sarah, let's get ourselves back home." Each child on board sang out echoing their driver's words. Willow and Sarah followed their orders to perfection. Song broke out anew, *"Oh Wonderland in Buzzard Mountain's Wonderland how glorious thy bounty be. Our Christmas Trees, Our Christmas Trees will soon bedazzle our homes. Oh, Wonderland, Buzzard Mountain's Wonderland how glorious thy bounty be."* All adults joined in and sang along.

....

The ride back to Buzzards Mountain landing passed much quicker than the ride out to Christmas Tree Wonderland. On arrival, everyone disembarked and followed their Christmas Trees back to their vehicles. Lenny's SUV had built on roof racks. It was assigned the task of delivering the perfect Christmas Tree back home to Gilbert's in East River. The staff willingly took on the task of securely attaching the tree to the roof racks. Once the task was completed, Gilbert slipped a healthy tip to the workers. Moses popped out of the shop door. On greeting everyone at the SUV, he stepped up to Hope and embraced her. On releasing her he spotted her worried look. Panic did not embrace him. He looked Hope in the eye and announced, "Don't ya be a fretting sweetheart. Old Moses here has rescued yer Bailey and he's over in the gift shop resting up."

Hope leaped forward and wrapped Moses in a loving forgiving embrace. On releasing him she shouted, "Oh! Thank you, thank you Moses. I thought we might have lost our charming Bailey."

"No! We'd never have let that happen. Never ever." Moses proclaimed. He contacted everyone by eye then asked, "Would anyone like to be taking a tour of the turkey barn? My beauties are back inside and secure in their facilities."

All the ladies and Megan declined along with Gilbert. Jeffery nodded a positive response along with John, Richard, Norman and Taylor. The two groups separated. Gilbert and the ladies headed to the shop. Jeffery led the way up to the turkey barn. Inside a worker greeted them and led them on a guided tour of the turkey barn and its operations. John and Richard were impressed with the modern equipment and state of the barn and its operations. Norman focused his attention on the barn's residents. The area called home for the current WRTC, World Record Turkey Challengers drew and held his full attention. The birds if one could call them birds, were huge. Thomas, Norman reconned, would tip the scales at sixty-five pounds or more. The tally board mounted above the pen areas surprised Norman. It listed Thomas at seventy-one pounds. It also listed the World Record Holder at an amazing eighty-six pounds. All the men joined Norman in discussing the stated numbers. Taylor focused himself on feeding Thomas. An open feed bucket filled to its brim provided plenty of food for the purpose. Shortly their guided tour drew to a close. Loud exchanges of opinions followed the men over to the gift shop.

Inside they joined up with Gilbert and the ladies. Jeffery boasted up their tour. "Thomas, the biggest contender for the world record tips the scales at seventy-one pounds. He was the big one that chased Bailey up de hill!"

"A monster for sure." Hope declared. She added, "What would anyone want a seventy-one-pound turkey for?"

Norman boasted, "The world record is eight-six pounds! Can you imagine?"

"No!" Hope declared. "What on earth would you do with an eighty-six-pound turkey? And no! Don't even think it, Dad!"

Laughter broke out amongst the group. Gilbert recovered first. He announced, "Not my call, sweetheart. I invited Moses and Mary down the mountain to join us for Christmas in East River. They've accepted and are going to provide and fire up the turkey for our Christmas Feast!"

"Really?" Hope asked.

"Yup! And I'll be arriving dressed fer de event. Jest like I is now." Moses shouted over to their tables. He paused then asked, "I'm open to taking orders. The meals are on me. Gentlemen, could I tempt you with a Monster of a Burger? A Buzzard Mountain Turkey Burger, dressed to yer likings?"

All the men except Taylor nodded then shouted, "Yes! I'm in fer de burger!"

Moses signaled a positive with a thumbs up. He asked, "Ladies, might I tempt you with a serving of our world-renowned turkey soup or turkey stew? Or would a slice of our famous crispy turkey pie be more to your liking?"

Hope did a survey. She responded with, "We're good with six turkey soups, one stew for Auntie Lila and a slice of the pie for me."

"Coming right up." Moses shouted back to Hope. "Help yourself to more coffee or tea ladies, and soda pops are in de cooler. Gentlemen, help yourself to the refreshment of yer choice."

Jeffery and Richard took the lead. They topped up the mugs of their ladies as asked and then delivered refreshments for everyone else. Quickly, the soups, stew and slice of pie were delivered. Everyone's eyes popped out on seeing the men's monster turkey burgers delivered on platters with overflowing sides of home fries. Their tables fell silent. The eating possessed everyone's full attention. Most of the men cleaned their platters while Mary, understandably, packed a take-out package to hold Taylor's left overs. Even the child sized burger overwhelmed the lad. Several ladies requested take home soup bowls. Hope cleared her plate of its turkey pie. Payment was adroitly refused by Moses and Mary. Hearty partings were exchanged. The East River crew departed and headed back to East River. The weather cleared and their return trip passed without any disruptions. That is, if one disregarded the gaseous discharges from the monster burger diners. Both Megan and Taylor quickly drifted off into dreamland. In the SUV, John got treated to a chorus of snorts and grumbles after Eugette and Auntie Lila joined the twins in dreamland. Each mile driven at his lady's side drew him closer to her.

Sleep in the van claimed Richard and Norman first, followed by Jeffery. Gilbert claimed the wheel the entire trip home. He ignored the ladies on their cracking several van windows partially open. At times he appreciated their action and its reasoning. On arriving home at Gilbert's, Lenny and Pappy assisted Gilbert and they freed up their Christmas Tree. Working together, it was carried through to the livingroom. John's group shifted out of Lenny's SUV and into John's rental SUV. They headed off to the old homestead for the night, along with Maria and Jeffery. John tossed the keys to Lenny on leaving and thanked him for its use. Next, Pappy and Lenny teamed up and set the tree up in a tree stand. It was left to settle overnight. Pappy advised that young Eric Johnson had stopped in and picked up the spare keys to Jeffery's truck.

Then with his Ginni as back-up, had delivered the truck to Gilbert's. The keys were on the kitchen hooks. Pappy boasted, "That lad's Ginni is quiet the gal. She drove him home. Imagine that!"

Janella jumped up off the sofa. She declared, "Get me Lenny's keys. I'll show you some driving skills you'll beg me ta teach ya!"

Lenny burst into laughter. He retrieved the keys from his pocket and tossed them over to a smiling Janella. He chided, "Robert! I'll pay to watch Janella running ya through de paces. Lordie! Your Helene was a trooper to put up wit ya. Trouble is she done spoilt ya rotten with her loving." The truth struck home. Pappy simply smirked and followed the others outside. Pappy, Lenny and the Wright sisters then headed home with Janella at the wheel.

Back inside, everyone opted to turn themselves in after Norman headed home to Chester with his mom in tow. It started to snow again shortly after midnight.

CHAPTER 42

Sunrise on December 21st kissed East River's Winter Wonderland with a sweetness that energized the Magic of Christmas that was unfolding and embracing each soul on its awaking into a new day. Over in the homestead, Maria had arisen before sunrise. Alone in the kitchen, she whipped up several batches of huge muffins and set them aside to be dressed up later. She then cleaned up the kitchen and returned to Jeffery's side in the sunroom.

Later, an excited Megan and Taylor awoke and quickly chased everyone else free of dreamland with their choruses of "Happy Birthday, Mommy, Happy Birthday, Mommy. Oh, how we love you so. Oh, how we love you so."

John embraced Eugette and kissed the birthday lady at his side. The twins giggled nonstop until Maria, Jeffery and Auntie Lila joined them and everyone sang out, "Happy Birthday, Eugette, Happy Birthday, Eugette Happy Birthday to you!"

The twins wrapped it up adding, "Happy Birthday, Mommy. Oh, how we love you so. Oh, how we love you so."

All but John was then shooed out of the bedroom. Once dressed, they joined everyone in the kitchen. Then Maria and Eugette claimed the kitchen. Together, they whipped up a buffet breakfast that would shortly sate their men's hungers. The twins begged off and settled on a breakfast of crunchy flaked cereals. Auntie Lila sided with the ladies and joined them in making short work of a flavorful fruit salad. Drawn into the kitchen by its powerful aroma of freshly brewed coffee, John and Jeffery sat gazing at their women as they prepared breakfast. The wait passed quickly. Maria and Eugette strolled over to the table and presented breakfast to their men. Jeffery rightfully rewarded Maria with an embrace. On hearing the twins chiding him for not kissing Grammie, Jeffery released Maria and put the chiding to rest. Catching Eugette's face light up in a glow on catching Jeffery's actions, John simply followed Jeffery's lead.

Megan called out, "Grammie, Mommie, really! Their breakfast is getting cold!" The couples pulled apart. A short folly of cheek pecks ensued, then the men set to work on their breakfast. Megan glowed in gazing over at mom and grammie. Taylor coyly hid his emotions. A relief bubbled up inside of him and he sensed home taking on a good feel. Being the man of the house was cool. But Taylor had recently slipped downward into the dumps. He'd wrongly taken on the blame for the loss of their family home to the blazing inferno that had burnt the house to the ground. In glancing over at Jeffery and John, Taylor felt the burden of guilt lifting from his shoulders. His dad's words, often overheard by Taylor, echoed in the young lad's heart, *'Promise me love. If something happens? Promise you'll love anew. Our babies need to be touched constantly by love's treasured touch.'* Those treasured words in Taylor's heart reinforced the glow in his heart. He felt alive again. A treasured piece of a family embracing love anew.

Megan broke Taylor free of his inner thoughts. She asked, "Will Santa know where to come? If he goes to our old house, what will he think?"

Jeffery leaped off his chair. He embraced Megan and shouted, "Santa knows sweetheart. He knows everything! But thanks for the reminder. Grampa Jeffy needs some help with his Christmas shopping!" He set Megan back down on her chair.

In a blur she leaped back up and kissed his cheek. She boasted, "We will! Taylor and me, we would love to go Christmas shopping! Besides, I know what mom and grammie want for Christmas!"

"Really?" Jeffery asked.

"Really!" Taylor joyfully boasted. He added, "I'd get it. But my shoebox savings all got burnt up in the fire."

John joined Jeffery at the twin's side. He pleaded, "Can I go too? With all my travels I haven't had a chance to get all my shopping done." Four sets of eyes turned towards Maria and Eugette and Lila. The women simply nodded a positive response back across the table. Megan and Taylor raced off in search of their outer clothing. They were sold on the option of heading out Christmas shopping with the men. Maria set to work clearing and cleaning up after everyone's hearty breakfasts. Eugette headed off and helped the twins get ready to head out. The front door flew open and the twins ran outside. The women retained their men for a partying PDA then released them to join Megan and Taylor. Jeffery closed the door on stepping outside behind John. Minutes later the sounds of John's SUV's engine and the crunching of snow signalled their departure. Maria and Eugette headed back to the sunroom and relaxed. An inner peace eased away thoughts of uncertainty surrounding the loss of their home. Mother and daughter set their minds free and lost themselves in a robust mother-daughter jam session. Auntie Lila joined them. Time stood still yet raced forward like a lightning bolt. Time's speed accelerated with each memory shared.

....

Over at Gilbert's, breakfast also reenergized everyone. With Christmas mere days away, each TODO list was fully itemized and committed to. Hope insisted that she'd oversee the cleanup, freeing all to tackle their lists. Determined to shoo Lyndsey and Richard out the door, she retrieved Lyndsey's coat and Richard's jacket. Once Lyndsey had slipped both arms into her coat, Hope passed Richard his jacket. She chided, "Enjoy your carrot cake, Richie."

"What?"

"Enjoy it!" Hope replied.

A twinkle leaped out of Lyndsey's eye. He asked, "You told her?"

"She's, my Sis. Sisters know all!"

Hoped hugged them both then shooed them out the door. Gilbert glanced over at Hope. She boasted, "It's a man thing...He'll learn in time." He chuckled having learned himself decades past. He savored the moment recalling how he and Karyn had held Hope in their arms and how it had been their turning point in life. Outside, Richard opened the passenger door of Jeffery's truck. They'd been offered its use for the day. Lyndsey accepted his hand offered in assistance. Once seated behind the steering wheel and buckled in, Richard turned to Lyndsey. He embraced her warmly. They kissed; it was a kiss that reinforced in Richard the sweetness of the treasure held that moment in his arms.

The drive through to Bridgewater passed quickly. Scenery and recalled landmarks triggered long shared conversations that recalled their first drive to meet the McClakens. The road taken followed the sea, its icy blue waters rekindled a flood of memories in both their hearts. Stopped at a traffic light in Bridgewater, Lyndsey shocked Richard as she leaned over and kissed him with passion. He tried to pull away, however, a chuckle and joy cast the effort aside. Lyndsey ended her kiss. A honk behind them sang out. The light had turned green. Other drivers had places to be and things that needed doing. They lacked the patience Richard and Lyndsey felt in their lost moment of pleasure. Following the traffic signs pointing towards LaHave, their destination appeared up ahead. In passing the ferry ramp. Lyndsey shouted, "Look, Richie. There's our ferry. Oh, we so have to take it on heading home."

Richard reached over and hugged Lyndsey. The hug signaled approval of their return route. The truck glided into an open parking spot effortlessly. Once parked, both stepped eagerly out of the vehicle and walked across the road to their destination. A myriad of pleasant memories embraced both their hearts and minds. The LaHave Bakery, its alluring aromas called out passionately to them. Richard savored the essence of carrot cake melting in his mouth. Lost in a recollection from their previous visit, Lyndsey gazed lovingly across the street into the bakery's window at the table they'd once shared. She relived the moment. In it, her eyes were locked onto the baby blues of her lover and husband-to-be at the time. Richard opened the door. Lyndsey walked inside. She eyed the dining area off to the right. A sigh energized Lyndsey's step. Their original table was unoccupied. She walked straight to the counter.

"Welcome to LaHave Bakery, we have some delightful specials of the Season. Would a bl…"

"We'll have two teas and two slabs of your amazing carrot cake."

"They're big, our slabs that is. Perhaps you'd rather share one between you and hubby?"

Lyndsey smiled at the hostess. "We've traveled over twenty-four hours on a train. They served us carrot cake in the dining car. It was a tad slimmer than the ones we enjoyed here on our first visit. We're back. And I want, no I'm dying, to sit down and ravish a slab of your famous carrot cake."

"Then two slabs of carrot cake and tea it shall be. Take a seat in our dining area and I'll bring it to your table."

Lyndsey stepped away from the counter. She caught sight of the carrot cake display. Her finger popped up and pointed out the two largest slabs. "We'll have that one and the one next to it!"

The hostess smiled warmly. "They're yours. Will there be anything to go?"

Lyndsey glanced over at Richard. She giggled. "My hubby has that under control. I believe we'll be loading up with more than just carrot cake." Richard waved to Lyndsey. She made her way over to the dining area and their table. Seated, a flood of treasured memories raced through her mind. Silently her fingers twitched, calculating her due date against the magic day. In Lyndsey's heart a group of soaring sea gulls sang their lonesome song of love and the sea. Love embraced her being. A glance down at the table revealed their order had been delivered. Whiffs of steam floated up from the tea pots. Hungry, Lyndsey swapped the slabs of carrot cake. She opted to take the largest one for herself. That same hunger made Lyndsey the first to feel a bite of carrot cake melt delightfully in her mouth. She felt totally in her Zen moment. The scrapping of a chair's legs over the floor returned her to reality.

"I see somebody just couldn't wait." Richard sat down across the table from Lyndsey. A staff member walked over to their table. He handled Richard a set of keys, "Everything is tucked away in the back of your truck sir."

Richard nodded then handed him an assorted handful of change in thanks. He then eyed Lyndsey. A glance down at her plate revealed only a scattering of cake crumbs remained on it. "Hungry, I see?"

"A little, what's that you have? Don't you want your cake?"

"It's a monstrous blueberry cinnamon roll, I couldn't resist its call. Want to try some?"

"No, I'm full. I couldn't handle anymore after my little sampling of their carrot cake."

"OK!" Richard set to work on his roll. It vanished in short order. He wiped his lips and chin clear of the bun's sugary coating and blue berries with a napkin. He then reached over with his fork to sample some of his carrot cake. The fork struck an empty plate. He smiled across the table at Lyndsey. She gazed lovingly back at him. Richard did not question the missing cake. Instead, he wisely asked, "Would my lady be ready to head home?"

"Only if we get to stop in Mahone Bay. Hope and Zerli told me the shops are to die for with their Christmas offerings."

Again, Richard did not question Lyndsey's comment. They walked through the bakery and exchanged Christmas greetings with the staff. The ferry carried them swiftly across the LaHave River. The drive to Mahone Bay passed quickly since Lyndsey had fallen asleep on the ferry. Richard entertained himself by listening to Christmas melodies on the radio. Parking in Mahone Bay was at a premium. However, Richard lucked out. He pulled into a spot being vacated by a vehicle with Maine plates. Once stopped, Richard gazed lovingly over at Lyndsey. She was crunched up and snuggly against the passenger door, secure in her seatbelt. An aura sang out from Lyndsey's face. He pondered, was it the aura Mom and Grandmother had so often alluded to in referring to women with child? He reached over to tap Lyndsey's shoulder. She whispered in a seductive tone, "Richie, oh I love you. I love you."

He opted to kiss her lips. She responded on their lips touching. The kiss lingered a moment then ended. Richard whispered, "Wakie, wakie. Time to wake up, sweetheart. We're in the Bay."

Lyndsey freed herself from the Sandman's fading grasp. Her eyes flickered, then locked on the image discovered on opening. Richard's baby blue eyes and his warm breath touched her senses. Desires arose within her being. Slowly she became aware of her surroundings. A warm, alluring smile touched her face. She inhaled Richard's breath. A reality kicked it. And a calendar flashed up in Lyndsey's mind. Boldly highlighted was December 21 ... She shouted, "It's almost Christmas Eve. I gotta git my shopping done!"

Richard wisely kissed her cheek and retreated. Lyndsey fought with her seat belt release. After several frustrated failed attempts, the release triggered and her belt released. "Where are we?"

"Relax, we're in the Mahone Bay parking lot across from the churches and shops."

"I gotta go, the clock is a ticking. What am I goanna git Moses and Mary?"

"Relax sweetheart. I'm sure the shop keepers will have gifts for everyone along with a couple to spare." Richard opened the driver's door and stepped out of the SUV. A walk about found him at Lyndsey's door. He opened it and a composed Lyndsey stepped out of the vehicle, purse in hand. Time never stands idle. It's always on the move. Time flew by in mere moments. The last stop provided a break and a treat. Over teas in a Mahone Bay café, Lyndsey enjoyed a cherry scone while Richard waivered over two of the same. A glance out the shop's window alerted both of time's passage. Dusk and sunset were sliding into place. A spectacular display awaited those out and about in Mahone Bay. Richard grabbed the bags they had amassed on their visits to the many town shops. Lyndsey stood and he took her hand in his. Their eyes caught a glitter in the eyes of the other. Both stole a quick kiss. Outside the shop they crossed the road at a crosswalk then followed the pathway along the waterfront. An amazing sunset stopped them dead in their tracks. They stood in awe, watching Mother Nature's amazing display unfold before their eyes. The dying moments before sunset appeared to linger forever. Then, in the blink of an eye, it vanished. They walked on towards the SUV. In turning to cross the parking lot another amazing view unfolded. Mahone Bay's famed three churches were framed in fading bluish sky. A glittering low moon highlighted the evening sky. Both their cell phone cameras clicked off a series of photos. The last ones caught the photographers together in selfies. Following the last click they returned to the vehicle. Both remained silent on the drive home. Lyndsey's mind flicked through images of their captured sunset and moonlit photos. Richard focused on the road while allowing an occasional picture to pop up in his mind, reminding him of their shared magical moments.

On turning into the driveway to Gilbert's home, they discovered the parking area had expanded over the snow-covered lawn. Richard picked an open spot by Grammie Ramsay's beloved rose hedge. On the deck, Richard stomped his boots free of snow then removed his jacket and passed it to Jeffery who stood in the opened doorway. He followed Lyndsey inside. Hope raced into the kitchen. She spotted Lyndsey and stole her from Richard's side. She embraced Lyndsey in a sisterly hug. On releasing Lyndsey, she freed Richard of their shopping loot in the bags amassed in their last-minute Christmas shopping spree in Mahone Bay. She then fled the kitchen with Lyndsey in hand. Lyndsey's slower pace restrained Hope's energy. Gilbert waved Richard through the kitchen then passed him an ice topped seasonal liquid refreshment. On entering the living-room Richard stopped dead in his tracks. He gazed in wonder at the Christmas tree standing in the room's far corner. It had fully opened up on embracing the warmth of the house. Gilbert walked up to his side and placed his arm on Richard's shoulder. He boasted, "She's a beauty. But then she's a Buzzard's Mountain Tree and anything less than perfection just doesn't make the cut."

Richard nodded in agreement. The tree was huge. Many branches called out to him, all claiming to be the prefect spots to place the assorted special ornaments they'd brought along from back home in Newmarket. Special ornaments that would connect them to family back home that they'd lost. Family that had put in place the steps needed to reconnect them in moving forward to reconnect with their families' heritage and descendants they'd bonded with in moving forward from their losses. They acknowledged that their family of three; Richard, John and Lyndsey was no longer merely a family of three. A myriad of past Christmas Eves flashed through his mind. He embraced the recalled memories bonding them with those yet to be.

Gilbert buried him in a trademark Gilbert hug. He boasted, "Isn't she's a beauty. Just what's needed to bond us all together in our Seaside Christmas, my son." He released Richard then raised his glass in a toast, "To family and loved ones gathered by our side. To this Christmas and those that have been and those yet to be."

Richard joined Gilbert and raised his glass. Quickly the glasses touched their owner's lips. The nectars of the glasses revealed themselves to be rum based. If any doubt remained a glance under the coffee table confirmed the fact. A dozy eyed Bailey stared back at Richard while emptying a saucer of its contents. The reality of their Christmas by the Seaside finally took hold. The adage that *'Home is Where the Heart Is'* sealed the deal. Richard relaxed and savored the moment. They were truly home for Christmas.

CHAPTER 43

Hours later, the kitchen door flew open and the house lost its silence. Jeffery's crew flowed into the house bearing an array of over-stuffed Christmas shopping bags. Hunger pangs called out on catching a hint of the seafood chowder's aromatic callings wafting throughout the kitchen. Gilbert turned away from the stove and raced over to the ladies. Each received a welcoming embrace and peck or two on the cheek. Hope and Lyndsey freed the new arrivals of their shopping bags. She shouted out, "Details later. And us women folk will tend to the wrapping! Meanwhile, we have a bigger task at hand. One that will add the finishing touches to Christmas at the McClakens household."

"But I'm starving!" Jeffery protested.

"Me too!" John added.

"Then get into the living-room and help us get our tree decorated!" Hope answered boldly. Nobody challenged her lead. In the living-room the women and the twins claimed ownership of the bins filled with Christmas decorations and regalia. Lyndsey slipped away briefly. She returned with a special metal box covered in seasonal décor that placed its vintage back in time. Only Hope noticed her sister's short disappearance and return. She smiled coyly at Lyndsey on catching her return. They'd toyed with the box's treasured contents into the wee hours of morning. In simple terms, some treasures are best appreciated seen through the eye of a woman. The men, blind to the sisters' connection, opted to join Bailey in their tasks at hand. Quickly all their glasses were topped up. They almost got to occupy the sofas and loveseat, but were ceremonially summoned to the tree. There they were assigned lighting duties. Under the directions of their attentive ladies the men quickly strung a multitude of varied stringed Christmas tree lights on the huge tree. The tree took on a unique aura. Its lights displaying the evolution of Christmas tree lighting history over the years. An array of glass painted, clear coloured and bubbly candlestick lights covered the movement of tree lights toward the new age LED phenomenon. The LED lighting in turn added many strings of variously shaped and sized LED Christmas tree lights. On adding the last string Jeffery moved to plug the stringed lights into a powered extension cord. He shouted, "Are we ready?" No one answered. He shouted out the countdown, "Five, four, three, two, one, whoosh ... let there be lights!"

A blast of coloured lights lit up the tree. Everyone stared at it in awe. Jeffery broke the silence, "I'd be saying, sure, looks like Santa Claus will have no problem finding this house. Wow! Isn't she a beauty!"

Quickly the boxes of vintage and modern-day Christmas tree decorations made their way onto tree branches eager to add a touch of glitter. Megan and Taylor busied themselves in attaching decorations to the lower branches. Time almost stood still for those adorning the tree with treasures gathered over the years. Maria pulled the twins aside. She handed them each a box of newly acquired ornaments. All of theirs had been lost in the fire. On opening each of their boxes both of their jaws dropped. Jeffery had succeeded in fulfilling Maria's request. He'd visited the much treasured *'Christmas by the Sea'* shop in Halifax and picked up an array of replicas of tree ornaments from out of the past. The glow on Megan and Taylor's faces added drew tears to Jeffery's eyes. Maria hugged then kissed him. She then assisted both of her grandchildren in adding their newly acquired treasures to the tree's branches. Lyndsey joined them. On spotting her actions, both Richard and John raced to her sides. Together they added treasures from Lyndsey's decorated seasonal tin box of ornaments. Richard and John focused on those connected to their past. Lyndsey eyed each one retrieved from her childhood treasures and hung them on the tree. The last one she attached to a hook and followed Richard's eyes to the branch he'd selected. It was a beautiful Christmas ball with Mahone Bay's three churches painted in a snowy seaside scene. John sighed on spotting it. On visiting Mahone Bay with Eugette he'd taken a shine to its unique friendly atmosphere. He turned towards the men but Eugette intercepted him. Together they added an ornament Eugette had taken a fancy to in Newmarket. It reflected their coming together as a couple. Gilbert flick on the stereo and Christmas music filled the air. He then ushered everyone into the dining-room.

Jeffery followed Hope's lead. Together they set up the dining-room table. With everyone seated, Gilbert wheeled in a trolley cart that held a covered pot of his seafood chowder. Its aromatic callings wafted the essence of the seafood chowder throughout the room. At each setting he topped up the diner's bowl as directed. On reaching his own setting, Gilbert topped up his bowl to near overflowing. Jeffery glanced at him with questioning eyes. The look rewarded him with a hearty topping up of his own bowl. He then awaited Hope's return from the kitchen. The wait was short. Applause greeted her return with a platter of home baked rolls. Jeffery waited for Hope to sit. He then assumed an honoured role and delivered the Meal's Blessing, "Lord we truly thanks ye. All these fine folks; family, friends and family soon ta be. Yes, we are a bonded gathering richly blessed by Ye and most certainly by my Brother Gillie's cooking. I truly hates ta cut Ye off short, me Lord, but dang it all I'm a starving lad, I truly am. So, thanks Ye Lord and Blessing to all, Amen. Now let's all chow down."

A quick round of amens flew around the table. Everyone lost themselves in the task at hand. Hope made several runs to replenish the supply of rolls that disappeared with the speed of lightening. Following a loud belch, Jeffery excused himself then raced into the kitchen and retrieved the dessert he'd provided. Laughter and joy flowed freely amongst those gathered together. Hope glanced at Gilbert; she caught him lost in deep thought. In truth, she knew where his thoughts and heart were focused. Her Norman and his mom's absence from their Christmas festivities prevented them from freefalling into the magical connections unfolding in their midst. The room's joyful energy freed

Hope of the doubtful thoughts that had tried to catch and control her thoughts. Normie had broken down on their last date, no Hope corrected herself they were beyond the dating stage and into outings. He'd revealed the truth behind why they'd fled from Chester years past. A mere child, he'd been in grade six at the time. Norman had witnessed the assault of his mom in their home. He'd managed to block it, hide it deep in the depths of his mind for years. However, the death, a suicide of his baby sister August had released the truth from the depths. To protect his mom, he had hidden his recollection from her. She'd suffered too much pain. Hope shivered on recalling how on learning the truth and why August's dad never arose in conversation. She pondered maybe he should have? After all, at times knowledge can be a powerful healing tool. The joy playing out about the dining-room shielded her from the pain in her heart. On discovering the truth, August had faltered, lost her positivity and will to live. The truth, once revealed, had triggered her suicide. In a state of abject sorrow concealed by the seasonal joy surrounding her, Hope edged her way over to Gilbert's side. She stooped down and embraced him in a loving hug. Into his ear she whispered, "Love you to pieces, Dad and a ton more. It's ok. They'll be ok. Trust me, my Normie knows the truth. They need to be where they're at right this minute. Just like us, father-daughter. My Normie, your Anya, mother and son, they're where they need to be to fully heal. It hurts to think of the loss they suffered so close to Christmas. I trust visiting August in her place of rest will aid them in healing and open their hearts to us. God, Dad, I'm so blessed to have you in my life."

Gilbert broke free of his trance. He gazed into the eyes of Hope. A joy glowed off his face. Hope sighed on spotting it. She whispered anew, "They'll be back tomorrow and ready to embrace our love."

Gilbert stood and buried Hope in a loving parental embrace. Eager to shake free of the feelings raging inside he shouted out, "Hello! I say it's time to shake up this roof and git some hips swaying and dancing underway. What say you all?"

Jeffery jumped up from the table. He shouted out, "I'm with ya, Brother. Jest let me clear off the table and I'll be teaching these young ones a new dance step or two!"

"Don't ya dare Jeff! Cleanup can wait till morning. Let's get some high stepping music on that old stereo," Hope shouted out to Jeffery.

Auntie Lila jumped up and led the race into the living-room. She playfully nudged Gilbert at her side. Everyone followed their lead. The sweetest dancers on the floor turned out to be the twins, Megan and Taylor. They swayed and jigged through the fast-paced seasonal tunes blasting out of the stereo. The only dissention coming during the waltzes when they fought to win their mom, Eugette, as their dance partner. John gracefully ceded his lady to her pursuers. He was not long unattended. Auntie Lila made a lovely dance partner. Towards midnight, the twins and Lyndsey started to show signs of burn out. However, reluctant to turn in, Lyndsey treated herself to a waltz in John's arms. With ease she rested her head on John's chest. No fear arose. Their lives had raced through a gauntlet of emotional and physical twists and turns through the year drawing to an end. The newness that now embraced both their lives caressed Lyndsey's heartstrings and allowed her to forgive John's past transgressions, easing both forward into worlds filled with possibilities. The twins shared a final dance with each other. Jeffery ended up with Hope and Maria waltzed about the floor in Eugette's arms. Gilbert and Richard watched the action wind down from the sidelines. The stereo fell silent. Everyone cued in on its lead. The gala Christmas gathering slowly broke up. The homestead crew headed out after biding everyone a goodnight. Gilbert and Richard headed upstairs to bed. The sisters held back from following the men. They chatted briefly over the evenings good times shared until they heard robust signs that the men were off in dreamland. Both giggled on hearing robust snorts echoing out of the bedrooms above them. They cleared the dining-room and loaded the dishwasher. With the cleanup completed they headed upstairs to bed. Quickly both answered the Sandman's beckoning calls.

Outside, winter's reality kicked into action with gusts of snow-filled winds that howled with a strengthening fury against the house's exterior. A forecasted nor'easter embraced East River. Inside, the silence vanished. A harmonized snoring duet attempted to entertain Hope and Lyndsey. Gilbert's robust snorts along with Richard's accompaniments while competing with the nor'easter succeeded and chased the ladies out of their beds. They donned housecoats and ended up in the living-room snuggled up side by side under a knitted Afghan as they stared at the Christmas tree. They shared recollections of the special Christmas Tree decorating party that had unfolded earlier with everyone gathered together in the house. The house fell silent with them seated side by side.

Its assorted ornaments echoed a mural of memories in Hope's mind and heart. Their vintage spanned decades and beyond of her family's Christmas treasures. Several glittering balls held her spellbound. Grammie had gifted unique ornaments to her each Christmas. The two were the last ones gifted. No words were spoken. Lyndsey blinked on spotting a unique ornament out of her past. She gazed at it attempting to age its origin. She settled on aging herself at ten the year her parents had gifted it to her. Lyndsey lost herself in the magic of her recaptured memory.

Hope lost herself focused on grammie's last two gifted ornaments. They almost slipped her back off into dreamland. Each one possessed special moments out of her past. Some, she confessed silently, were downright comical. However, each one easily triggered recollections of memories created with loved ones now passed on and special ones that continued to enriched her life on a daily basis. Outside, the howling winds sent a shiver racing through both sisters' bodies. A glance around the room solidified the feelings of security they felt. Captivated, Lyndsey stared at the tree and listened intently as Hope shared memories of the two ornaments and the memories they ignited in her heart. Lyndsey turned and caught Hope focused on the gifted ornaments out of her past. She reached over and pulled Hope closer in a loving sisterly embrace. Their warmth carried both off into Christmases of their youth. Christmases where both recalled treasured moments in the companionship of imaginary sisters. Reality won out. Both pulled each-other closer they turned and smiled, then sighed, in recalling the moment they'd discovered the reality of their relationship. Both savored the moment they'd spotted the other's dimples pop out. Both turned and looked back at the tree. The ornament on the right twitched as its hook slipped free of its branch. It tumbled softly downward bouncing off a series of branches in its downward path. Finally with grace it came to rest on a saving branch. Lyndsey and Hope's jaws dropped and they gasped. They tossed the Afghan off in reacting to the ornament's tumble to safety on the lower branch.

Hope jumped up off the loveseat. She raced to the wall and flicked on the light switch. Lyndsey stared at the tree. Hope walked over to the tree quickly joined by Lyndsey. Hope stooped down and picked up the ornament from its resting place. She whispered, "It's Grammie's nineteen eighty-seven. Oh, Grammie thank you for saving it." Hope turned to Lyndsey, "I'm so glad it didn't break. I'll set it aside to be reattached to the tree later. So, so glad. It's an irreplaceable treasure." They hugged. "I'm OK. Dad would really have missed it had it broken. It's from nineteen eighty-seven, a very special year. Let's turn in. Hopefully the Harmonizers have performed their encore and shut down for the night."

Lyndsey stood and joined Hope who switched off the lights. They headed back upstairs in search of a peaceful night's sleep. Upstairs in the hall, silence prevailed. At the door to her room Lyndsey said, "Hope I'm so glad that ornament didn't break?"

"Yes, me too. It is special."

"We'd best turn in. Get a good night's rest." They hugged. "Nighty night, Lyndsey. Love you, Sis."

"And I love you too, Sis. Nighty night!" Lyndsey said, walking into her room. Hope watched the door close then headed off to bed. A memory of a late night shared with Lyndsey on her first visit flowed through her head. Hope tossed the thought aside. She crawled under the blankets and embraced the sandman. He carried her off aboard Uncle Jeffery's Rose Bud. A past adventure called out, welcoming Hope to a rerun that had cemented the sisters' bond.

CHAPTER 44

The magic hour quickly approached. Suddenly it was Christmas Eve morning. Time had vanished quicker than a honey bee slurping up spilt molasses. Ring-a-ding-a-ling, detecting no movement inside the house, Moses pressed enthusiastically anew on the door bell. Ring-a-ding-a-ling, Moses strutted impatiently to and fro on the doorstep. Silence continued to be his sole greeter. He pondered. What's the deal with these lowlanders? The day be half over and I kin nae hear a soul up and abouts, let alone a mouse's footsteps mak'in ready to greets us. Lordie...Lordie, gits your selves out'ta bed. Frustrated, Moses took to knocking loudly on the door. Bang...bang...bang! 'Squeak...squeak.' The first sign of life hit Moses' highly tuned and alert ears. He waved over to Mary sitting patiently in the truck. A glance back into the kitchen caught movement. A smile broke out on Moses' face. He watched Lyndsey waddle sleepily across the kitchen floor. He waved a top of de morning greeting to her.

Lyndsey caught sight of the disturbance. Moses' smiling face and trademark nose...schnozzle identified their visitor. She flipped open the deadbolt lock and twisted open the door handle. She stepped back from the door and a simple tug on the door handle pulled it open. Moses stepped inside. He stooped down and embraced Lyndsey in his arms. A stolen kiss on Lyndsey's cheek ended the greeting.

"Burr... she's a might nippy out thar," Moses boasted. "Sure, wouldn't want 'a be a brass monkey." He released her and stepped to

Lyndsey's side then turned and waved to Mary. "Hurry on up, girlie, you're gett'in slower with every year!"

Mary ran with caution over the heavily drifted snow-covered yard to the deck. On spotting Lyndsey and her baby bump, she stopped and smiled lovingly at their welcoming hostess. Moses waved frantically at Mary. "Moves it, girlie, we ain't aiming ta heat the neighbourhood."

Mary entered the house and embraced Lyndsey in a loving hug. Cheek kisses were exchanged. She paused and gently placed her hands on Lyndsey's baby bump. She smiled and said, "Boy ... girl. Oya ye have such a beautiful glow." Moses closed the door.

"Thanks, Mary. I love it when I can feel a heartbeat or gentle twitch or two."

"It is a precious gift reserved for expectant Moms. Seeing you, girl, rolls my biological clock back a decade or two, well truth be told almost three, or is it four?"

Lyndsey smirked, "And I'll admit a time or two I've sworn if I get any fatter my beach ball bump will explode." Mary glowed on hearing Lyndsey share her thoughts and feelings. She watched Lyndsey walk over to the kitchen counter and start to set up the drip coffee maker. Mary slipped out of her coat, then shooed Lyndsey away from the counter. "You'd best head upstairs and freshen up. Sorry we arrived so early. My Moses is an early morning pain ... I mean man."

Lyndsey glanced at her wrist watch then peaked outside through the kitchen window. Sunrise had started to embrace the new day. Spotting warm pinkish hues in the sky, she pondered was that saying *'Pink or is it a red sky in the morning ... sailors take, warning?'* "Thanks, Mary. I will head up and freshen up. My shower should chase a few more out of slumber-land." Lyndsey walked away from the counter.

Mary called out, "Coffee, where will I find the coffee?"

Without turning to face Mary, Lyndsey called out, "In the pantry over by the fridge."

"Thanks, if your shower doesn't get them up and about, my coffee should do the trick. See you in a bit."

Up in the bedroom, Richard rolled over and reached out seeking Lyndsey. His efforts failed. He rubbed sleepiness out of his eyes. On catching a glimpse of Lyndsey, he motioned over towards the bed. Standing bedside in her housecoat with fresh clothes in hand she relented. They kissed. He attempted to tug her back into bed. Coyly, Lyndsey twisted about and avoided the attempt. They smirked at each other and exchanged a volley of, "I love you toos," Then she sashayed off to the bathroom calling back, "Sorry, Love. Company has arrived. Mary and Moses, the Buzzards from up on the mountain."

"Aah! What time is it?"

"It's seven forty-eight. Time all good boys and men were up and about."

"If I have too, what time did they head out?"

"Real early. Mary says he's an early riser. Now move it."

The shower felt great. It relaxed Lyndsey's muscles and joints. Her mind lost itself in recalled memories of their recent Christmas tree adventure up on the mountain. Life back home in Newmarket had become too routine and predictable. Since they'd first connected with the McClakens, every day embraced new adventures and opportunities. Lyndsey pondered silently the year ahead and motherhood the thrill of holding and caressing their baby and not just feeling a heartbeat and pining for the real thing. The bathroom door opened then closed. On Richard lifting then dropping the toilet seat Lyndsey was jarred free of her wandering mind's travels. The steady trickle then heavy flow into the toilet sealed her return. Satisfied and feeling clean and refreshed. She twisted the water lever off. A quick reach retrieved the bath towel from the shower curtain rack. Lyndsey toweled herself dry. A hand grabbed the shower curtain and pulled it open. Its naked owner smiled teasingly at Lyndsey. She took the offered assisting hand and stepped out of the tub. Richard's assistance was rewarded with a kiss.

"Thanks, Sweetheart. No time to spare. It's a wasting. You'd best shower and join us down in the kitchen. I've got a hunger pang calling out."

Richard eyed Lyndsey up and down. His smile was rewarded. "Hit the shower."

"But...but I'm hungry for yo..."

"Shower now! Breakfast in ten no fifteen minutes downstairs in the kitchen."

They kissed. Richard obeyed. The shower curtain closed and the shower fired up anew. Lyndsey finished drying herself off then tossed her towel in the laundry basket. Standing in front of the mirror, memories of a mirror visit out of the past resurfaced. She chuckled then cast aside her recalled memory of searching her body for confirmation that a magical moment had triggered a conception in her body. There was no doubt of her condition. Touching both hands on her bump, Lyndsey shivered on feeling four rapid but gentle kicks. She sighed then dressed and returned to their bedroom. Along the way Lyndsey smiled on hearing Gilbert's voice singing out joyfully from his shower. Once the bed had been returned to a made-up state, Lyndsey set off back to the kitchen. In the hall Hope joined up with her. The aroma of coffee greeted them on the staircase. Both sighed.

"Oh, I so need a shot of caffeine to kick start my day," Hope confessed.

"Lately I've been avoiding coffee. The gas it churns up inside is getting worse."

"Tea, I'll assume, works?"

"Green tea yes, but black tea can trigger a bad session."

"Then green tea it will be." Hope added. They arrived in the kitchen. Moses jumped up and raced over with morning greetings for Hope and a repeat greeting for Lyndsey. They survived.

Mary called over from the stove, "Don't mind my old fool. He sees young ones liken you two and he jest goes stir crazy." Hope joined Mary at the stove. A warm greeting hug was shared.

"Do I have enough on the go?" Mary asked. "If yer men eat like my Moses, I suspect we'll be firing up a second batch of everything."

Hope eyed the stove and sizzling grill. "We're good, Mary. Jeffery and John are with Maria, Eugette, the twins and Auntie Lila over at the homestead. I imaging Maria and Eugette will take care of that bunch. Megan and Taylor will be wired to the nth degree it being Christmas Eve."

"Then step aside and yer Mary will treat you to breakfast."

"No. Lynds and I will go with a fruit salad. I'll get it along with Lyndsey's green tea. Care to try one?"

"Green tea no, fruit salad sure. I'd love one and thanks for the offer, Hope."

The kitchen doorway darkened on Gilbert and Richard's arrival. Gilbert called out, "Mary, lassie, git yourself over here and give me a proper greeting."

Mary's face burst out in a joyful smile. She ran over and wrapped Gilbert in a loving hug. It barely extended past his sides. She tried to break free, but Gilbert had locked Mary in his welcoming hug. Once released, Mary kissed Gilbert's chin. She declared, "Lordie, laddie, yer getting taller and, Lord forbid it yer losing weight." She frowned. You're OK. Not sick or nothing?"

"Healthier than I've been in years. I decided to slim down in sympathy with Bailey. He's not taking well to the cut back in his rations of late."

"Send him back up with us. Thomas will gladly give chase and add a strut-gobble-gobble-strut to the feline's daily exercise."

"We don't mention the T-Turkey word around Bailey since he met Thomas. It's taken on a new meaning."

Moses shouted out in boast, "Gads, yes. My Tommie shore did git yer kitty cat moving. Bet kitty is still having nightmares."

Gilbert shook his head. He asked, "Speaking of Thomas and his mates, what's the latest weigh in? Is there a challenge afoot?"

"Seventy-four pounds and no we're still a stretch away from challenging the world record for turkeys." Moses boasted and bemoaned."

Hope created and delivered three fruit salads along with Lyndsey's green tea. Mary delivered plates overflowing with pancakes and eggs along with loads of crispy bacon to the men. After refilling everyone's coffee mugs she joined the table gathering.

Meow...meow. Bailey strutted into the kitchen. Moses called out, "Comes a here, kitty, kitty. Yer buddy Moses has brought cha a greeting from Thomas de Turkey...Gobble...Gobble, Gobble and how's a ya a doing pretty kitty?"

Bailey stopped dead in his tracks. His face snarled, his back ached upwards like a Halloween Cat leaping over the moon. He snarled out a series of high-pitched squeals. Mrrreow...Meeooow!

Everyone twisted to catch a glimpse of Bailey. Their eyes locked on Bailey. Then Moses broke the pattern. He stood walked towards Bailey. Three feet away he stooped down onto the floor. Bailey eyed Moses' every movement. Flashbacks to a mountainside visit added tension to Bailey's posture.

"Oh, but Thomas be a sending Bailey a greeting and apologies. Why he didn't mean ta scares ya on yer visit. Liken you, whys Thomas is Mary and a Moses, that's be me ... our pet. Jest likes you bees ta Hope and Gillie." Moses' hand reached out to Bailey. Mrrreow! Moses flipped over his hand and revealed two, no three crisp strips of bacon. Bailey eyed the offering amorously. His body language and earlier tension melted like butter on a skillet. Moses waved the bacon strips at Bailey. The snarl vanished. Bacon had been sliced from Bailey dining options. Savory memories of past bacon delights ignited and tortured Bailey's taste buds. Moses smiled warmly into Bailey eyes. Something in the smile attracted Bailey. Memories of his encounter with Thomas the monstrous mountain turkey faded. Bailey inched himself closer to Moses and the offered bacon. Only one other temptation had ever held Bailey in a similar grasp. His mouth watered. Bailey's journey ended. He had arrived at his destination. Sniffing the bacon ignited dining memories past. Crunch, snap, crumble the crispy bacon tumbled freely inside Bailey's mouth. One bite was all it took. Bailey smiled warmly over into the eyes of Moses. All tension in the kitchen vanished. Moses returned to his chair and sat. Bailey snuggled up on Moses' lap. He chewed away contentedly on the strips of bacon. Each one vanished in short order. Moses patted Bailey's head and massaged his new found companion's back and chest.

"Why, I believe old Bailey here was connected with me. Bet 'cha, he smells traces of old Shelby on me. Does ya want 'a meets our Shelby, Bailey? She's sure one sassy kitty cat."

"No. No, Moses," Hope offered up. "We will keep our treasured bundle of fury cheer right here in East River."

Breakfast filled the kitchen with laughter along with the sharing of everyone's Christmas plans. Most centered on last minute shopping adventures. Lyndsey felt ready to embrace a laid-back lazy day after just one quick last-minute go at Christmas shopping. Richard stood contented with a fully sated belly and complemented their chef. "Mary, your kitchen magic is amazing. Would you be related to the McClakens? The dining we've been treated to on our visits has been amazing."

"Thanks, Richie, I've never been one to turn down da complements. Related, beyond de tag of Bluenosers in crime, no, there's no direct connections."

"Then you and Uncle Gilbert should look into opening a restaurant. They'd be lined up outside pining to taste your offerings."

Moses jumped into the bantered-up compliments. He boasted, "Don 'cha be tempt' in me Mary ta be a running aways from de mountain, lad. I'd be naught but skin and bones, in less dan a week."

Mary walked over to Moses and planted a kiss on his lips. Moses rewarded her with an all-encompassing hug. A round of applause ensued. Released, Mary rewarded Moses with a second kiss that lingered to the delight of Moses. Their lips parted. Mary poked her man in the chest. "You'd best be gett'in our Mountain Turkey Blaster a set up and readied up fer tomorrows' beast feast."

Richard walked over to the kitchen window. He looked outside eying up Moses' truck and the huge shiny black trailer attached to its hitch. A black pickup truck with artistic renderings of mountains covering its sides caught his eye. Unlike Uncle Gilbert's truck, Moses' truck had obviously been professionally painted. The wording declared, 'Visit Buzzard's Mountain ... Home of the Legendary Thomas de Turkey'. A twinkle added sparkle to Richard's eyes. He recalled his first encounter with Gilbert McClaken's truck. The image in his mind and the truck parked outside confirmed his emerging view of Nova Scotians and their story telling finesse. He could not recall having seen the truck on their Christmas tree visit with Moses on the mountain. He assumed it had been off-mountain or parked out of sight. A glance behind the truck added a broad smile to his face.

Lyndsey interrupted his attention from the window, "Rich…Richard, time is a wasting. We need to head out if we're to be the early birds out and back home!" The words sailed straight over Richard's head. Lyndsey sighed. Only six months past a single word spoken drew him to her side with the bonus of a tender kiss or two. She gazed down at her baby bump. Doubts arose. Could her fat beach ball body be chasing her man's attentions elsewhere? Determined to head out and put the finishing touches on their Christmas shopping she tried to avoid Richard's diversion tactics. Lyndsey stood up. She walked towards the window and Richard. "Rich…"

"Look Lynds! Look at Moses' Mountain Turkey Blaster. It must be in that trailer."

Lyndsey glanced out the window. She sighed on spotting the trailer's massive skewered turkey painted on its side. She pondered does he really find that, oh my god. I look like that greased up buttery beast on that trailer. In the bathroom this morning that's what he saw. Me fat, obese and ugly!"

Richard broke Lyndsey's train of thought. "Look Lyndsey. That rig is amazing! The red-yellow tipped flames reaching out to embrace that beast. Look at the words the beast is calling out."

Lyndsey locked onto the words, above the beast *'Buzzard's Mountain Free Range Turkey Ranch,'* and below *'Turkey Cooked to Perfection by Buzzard Mountain's … Turkey Masters Best of the Best.'* The turkey took on the essence in Lyndsey's mind. In Lyndsey's eye she stared in angst at herself … fat, obese and ugly. Nervously she nibbled on her lower lip. A glance down to the last words confirmed her inner thought, 'Home to the Future World's Biggest Turkey.'

Moses stepped up behind Lyndsey. He embraced her in a Mountain Man's hug and broke her train of thought. He boasted, "Ain't she a beauty! Me and my boys built her. Our Faith done did all de painting. A talented one our gal be!"

Lyndsey whispered, only Moses heard, "If your Faith had used me as her model, that turkey' would be twice as big."

Moses tightened his hug on Lyndsey. He whispered back, "Ah, yer naught but a wee lassie abouts to be a mom. In a blink off's yer eye you'll be hold 'in de most beautiful wee thing in dis world…yer baby."

Lyndsey caved with joy into Moses' hug. Moses caught the moment pulled Lyndsey closer then quickly released her and tapped Richard on the shoulder. "Me, son, times a wasting. Don't ya have somewhere ta be going with yer beautiful wife?" Hearing no reply, he tapped Richard once more.

Richard responded, "Sorry, Lyndsey, I just got caught up in the beauty of the artwork. Moses your Faith is one talented lady."

Lyndsey frowned. Inside, she resolved to check out local art classes once they arrived back home. In her mind she felt her man connecting to Faith and her artistic talents. Moses walked over to Mary kissed then hugged her with passion. Richard turned to Lyndsey pecked her on the cheek and chirped, "Let's get going, Lynds. A busy day awaits us. Remember, we're headed into Halifax."

Hope had watched the whole scene play out. She'd caught sight of Moses' tender side. The man's statue had soared tenfold in her heart. Determined to add a smile back on Lyndsey's face, she retrieved Lyndsey coat and Richard's jacket. Once Lyndsey had slipped both arms into her coat, Hope passed Richard his jacket. She chided, "Enjoy your twosome time together, Richie."

"What?"

"Enjoy it!" Hope replied. She added, "Soon you'll treasure every snippet of alone time that comes your way."

The discussion between Lyndsey and Moses caught Gilbert in its vibrant criss-cross revelations centered on the huge BBQ Turkey Blaster Trailer parked outside. An eye cast towards Moses revealed a touch of envy on Gilbert's face. He briefly joined the others in sending Lyndsey and Richard off on their way. Though in truth his focus was elsewhere.

Spotting the look on Gilbert's face Moses chirped up, "Oya she be a one and only. Our youngsters are an amazing asset to their ma and pa. The boys conceived it and then they built it on their own. The devils wouldn't let their pappy see it till after our little Faith had finished adding her touches to it. She sure be a beauty me son. Wait till I fire her up Christmas Day and cranks out the best Christmas Feast you've ever chowed down on. Why my Buzzard Mountain Turkey Blaster sets a glimmer and then some of envy off in every chef's eye."

Gilbert stared in awe at the Blaster. Moses chuckled, "Grab a jacket, me son. We gotta haul in tomorrow's star attraction ta git him thawed out and ready fer de Blaster."

Hope tossed a jacket over to Gilbert. He hesitated at first then quickly slipped his arms into the jacket and zipped it up. He followed Moses outside, where Moses opened his truck's door and started its engine. He rejoined Gilbert explaining, "Me Turkey Blaster needs an assist from de truck's electrical do-higgies. Don't be asking me what fer. Those questions are best left fer me lads to answer." Moses dusted snow off a Blaster panel then popped it open. He depressed a button and the Turkey Blaster came to life on its own. The painted side opened up. Moses stepped towards the Blaster's end and opened a door. He retrieved a huge frozen block then rejoined Gilbert. "You'd best take the beast inside ta git defrosted. Then I'll demo my amazing toy."

Gilbert stared in awe. He almost dropped the frozen beast as Moses passed it to him. He gasped.

"Watch it, laddie. This one tipped de scales at fifty-eight pounds defrosted, gutted and defeathered. Showed no hope of beefing it up and taking a run at the world record like our Thomas is a doing. But even Thomas has a stretch to go before he's in competition with the world's best. Seventy-four pounds and counting the wee lad were yesterday."

Gilbert chuckled then turned and headed inside. He set the beast down in the sink then raced back outside. Moses and his Turkey Blaster had captured his full imagination. Back outside, he stared in awe. Moses twisted a brass handle and pulled open the Blaster's huge oven with the twist of a knob and the touch of a button the Blaster fired up. Moses toyed with the knob adjusting the gas levels up and down. He savoured the envy pasted on Gilbert's face. Both men moved closer to the open oven. The flames killed the icy chill in the air. Satisfied the Blaster was set to go with its Christmas Day assignment, Moses shut it down. Once it cooled off, he hit the control-panel button and the Blaster's panels closed. He killed the truck's engine and headed back inside.

Later in the living-room with Mary and Moses, Gilbert accepted the coffee mug offered by Hope. Finished serving everyone Hope joined Mary on the sofa. Moses buddied up with Gilbert. The two men lost themselves in a detailed discussion centered on the Turkey Blaster. Each detail and feature revealed heightened Gilbert's boy toy dream list. Across the room Mary and Hope shared precious moments both women had shared with Helen McClaken before her passing. Occasional tears were quickly swept away by robust bursts of laughter. Both savoured each shared memory out of their past. A heavy series of knocks on the kitchen door ended their chat. Hope jumped up and ran off into the kitchen. Staring through the door's window she spotted Norman with his mom in tow. A gleeful smile greeted the new arrivals. She yanked the door open then claimed Noman in a loving embrace. Their accompanying kiss lingered. Parental interference cut the kiss short.

Anya smirked and shouted, "Coming through, coming through. Don't mind me but it's a tad chilly out here."

Norman released Hope and she stepped outside giving Anya clearance to get inside the house. He winked at his mom and whispered, "Thanks mom. We needed it." He followed Hope inside and closed the door.

Anya shouted out, "Anyone else here? Sorry we're late. The weather is a touch iffy out on the roads."

Gilbert sighed on hearing Anya call out. He stood and trotted off sharply into the kitchen. On spotting Anya, he froze and gazed at her with an unspoken joy leaping off his face. Anya ran over and wrapped Gilbert in her arms. Their lips touched igniting wants and needs in the bodies and hearts. Staring across the kitchen, Norman sighed with a joy racing through his body. Hope followed his lead. They walked over and embraced their parents in a loving hug. It lingered until Moses stepped into the kitchen. He called out, "Whoa me laddies and lassies what do we have going on here. Not that I disapprove. But introductions might be appropriate. No, not needed. Lassie you were up on de mountain the other day with this McClaken lad, right? Well with all the commotion going on that day we never did get properly introduced."

Anya nodded her head with a positive motion. She released Gilbert from her embrace. Anya and Gilbert licked their lips and eyed each other amorously. Mary joined them in the kitchen. Moses eyed Anya up and down then coyly asked, "Lassie, would ya be that wee Trinity lass that used' a hang out with much younger Gillie McClaken and his Karyn back in the day?" A smirking grin burst out on everyone's face. Without hesitation Moses skittered over and wrapped Anya in his arms. Two no three cheek kisses ensued then Moses released Anya from his grasp. He nodded, "You sure has blossomed into one beautiful young woman, lassie."

Anya smiled back. She replied, "Maybe if I could just lose the jiggly extras off' a me butt I'd agree. Judging from the truck and its attachment outside, you must be Moses and Mary Buzzard from up on Buzzard Mountain. God, I loved those trips up onto the mountain way back in the days of my youth! You haven't changed a bit, well a touch sassier maybe! Mary, you look great. I loved that turkey soup we had the other day."

Mary chuckled joyfully, "I wish! But I will confess keeping my man in line has kept me in shape. You must have been fifteen, maybe sixteen the last time we saw you up on the mountain back in the day. And talk about looking great. Let's just say my generation on catching sight of yours, we simply sigh and not even in our wildest dreams did we ever have bods like yours, girl!" Anya blushed. Mary walked to Moses' side. She poked him in the ribs then chided, "We hit the road early, Love. This old doll could use a quick nap and recharge."

Before Moses could protest Gilbert nodded his agreement. He said, "Upstairs. End of the hall on the left. Take my room and catch some reenergizing shut eye."

Mary took Moses' hand and led him off towards Gilbert's bedroom. Moses simply followed Mary, his silence confirmed Mary's appraisal of their condition. Once they had started up the stairs Hope smiled at Gilbert and hinted at their intentions. "Dad, Norman and I would like to head over to Jeffery's for a bit. We won't be long."

"Ok. You'd best drive. Take my truck and we'll see you in a bit."

Hope rushed over to Gilbert and hugged him. She whispered, "Thanks Dad. Love you."

"Me too." Gilbert answered and jovially hugged Hope. They separated and Hope, rejoined Norman. Once the kitchen door closed the house fell silent.

CHAPTER 45

Gilbert eyed the sofa chair and Anya glanced at the loveseat. She won out. Both admired the Christmas tree. A myriad of seasonal memories raced through their minds. He spotted the heirloom ornament Hope had set aside after its tumble off a branch to safety below on another branch. A walk over to the tree and he secured it to a new branch. In turning back to Anya, he said, "It's one of mom's favorites. Don't know why it never made its way onto our tree." He joined her on the loveseat and they eagerly snuggled up together. Anya pressed her face to Gilbert's chest. The scent of his body aroused her. Determined to open a door into her life to Gilbert, she nibbled on her lower lip, fighting off a rising insecurity. Could the boy she'd once wanted to be the first to touch his lips to hers still be convinced a magical experience awaited him? After all, she reasoned, truths once revealed too often ended budding romances.

Gilbert broke into her train of thought. He asked, "Are you Ok, Anya? I sense a dash of hesitation."

Gilbert's hand vanished on Anya taking it up to her lips and gently kissing each knuckle and finger in turn. She clutched the hand to her bosom. She whispered, "I assume you know the truth behind my past. That bastard viciously raped and beat me. I never told mom or dad. But in time they picked up on my condition. I was too far down the trail. Abortion was not an option. Mom and dad totally supported me. I hated the bastard but my baby was a total sweetheart. I loved him then and will till the day I'm gone."

Gilbert embraced Anya in a loving embrace. He kissed the top of her head. Both relaxed. Somehow their togetherness in the moment just seemed right.

Anya continued, "Mom and dad loved little Normie to pieces. Then the bastard returned. They were out on a dinner date. God, they loved each other. He knew I was alone. They were at the Lobster Pot Pub & Eatery. I had dozed off and my little Normie was asleep in his room." She hesitated. Then admitted the truth to the man she'd once been totally infatuated with. "In all honesty mom and dad suspected their daughter had surrendered her body while infatuated with one of the fictional beaus I had claimed to have. And yes Gillie, you were one of my fictional beaus. God! I was totally infatuated with you; it took a stretch of pleading and convincing before they believed my version of what had happened. The town never really bought into the storyline. After all, I was a woman of colour. In hindsight, Karyn was the perfect match for you. We were like sisters. She stood by me and never tolerated the slurs and racial bias others tossed my way. We were buds! And damn it all. In the end I wasn't there for her! Some bud I turned out to be."

Gilbert felt Anya's tears dampening his top and chest. He pulled her closer then treated her to an array of never-ending kisses that warmed her cheeks and energized her self-confidence. Anya pulled free of Gilbert's embrace. She whispered, "Please let me continue. I've never felt so right sharing the truth out of my past. Most times it was tough growing up, basically, most shunned me and my family. Pretty much like they did with Jeffery. Seeing him with Maria and feeling the love radiating between the two, I envied what they had and wanted it."

A lingering kiss ensued. Anya pulled away and added, "Mom and dad, to their dying days, stood by me with love and without question. The decision to move back home? It was a tough one. I almost bailed and listed the house for sale. My precious August is at rest with mom and dad, her grandparents and our forefathers, mothers. I can't thank you enough for allowing Norman and I time to visit with them, chat with them, and ask permission to move on in life and finally savour the love I once hungered over but never really tasted." Anya fell silent.

She almost froze fearing love would once again be denied her. The old grandfather clock in the corner sang out its chimes. Both almost leaped out of their skin. Throughout time lovers create precious moments and memories together.

Gilbert broke the silence. Coyly he played with his hands. Once he had retrieved the object of his efforts, he kissed Anya. Both sighed on its ending. Their eyes locked and the silence was tentatively broken creating a hope in the air. With Anya's hand in his, Gilbert whispered, "I too envy the love Jeffery and Maria have rediscovered and joyfully embrace. Karyn loved me beyond expectations. I miss that loving feeling of belonging to another whose feelings replicate my own deepest longings. Cancer robbed me and our Hope of Karyn's love."

Anya spotted the gold ring in Gilbert's hand. She sighed. It represented a world she'd wished for throughout life. A world she'd failed to give her precious August. Hunger pasted itself on Anya face. Reflected rays of light from Christmas tree ornaments bounced off the ring onto Anya eyes. On spotting the glow Gilbert whispered anew, "Anya, I'm ready. I promise to love you with every breath I take. Will you marry me? I need and want you in my life."

Silence took possession of the room and its occupants. Time almost stood still. It did for Gilbert. Fear slowly touched his heart, had he pushed too hard and too soon for too much?

Anya's hands reached out and touched Gilbert's face. They pulled him towards hers. They kissed. She pulled back away from Gilbert. Fear of rejection rose up anew in Gilbert.

She whispered, "Oh, I want 'a so bad I can taste it. But would I be betraying our Karyn and the love you two shared throughout your lives together?"

"But?"

"But who abandoned her best friend in the greatest hours of need? Gilbert our Karyn never once abandoned me. Grade one, no it must have been grade two, we connected early in life. Recess out in the schoolyard we saw the Madison gang of bullies walk up to us. Their leader stared me down. Then he berated me boldly, flinging N words at me. I was what, six, maybe seven. Spit flew off his lips in shouting those words at me." Anya cringed. Compelled to totally open up she held a hand up to silence Gilbert and continued, "Karyn stared him down. Then she let loose a left hook. It landed with a crushing bam! Broke the bastard's nose. Blood flew everywhere." Anya smirked in self-satisfaction then said, "Little Rotten Barnie Madison dropped flat on his back and cried like a baby. We got called to the principal's office, so yes, I know who abandoned her best friend in her hours of need. Never mind, no need to answer, I know who. It was me."

Gilbert stared with amazement into Anya's eyes. He answered, "With good reason. I now know the whys and the who that tore you out of our lives back then. You were right in fleeing after the horrors suffered. Karyn never shared the words you just shared. Had she chosen to it would not have surprised me. She was beyond special to both of us, Anya. Like you, I've visited loved one's graves often. And I don't feel morbid in confessing my actions. I enjoy visiting Karyn's grave. Our shared time in life is and was very special. Yes, at times my faith has stumbled but its's never failed me. I believe she's up there in heaven embracing the rewards earned throughout life. We talked often about what. my future might be after she passed on. Karyn pleaded with me to allow love back into my life when it came calling. Holding you this moment, I know it's calling out to me. I want it, sweetheart."

Anya snuggled up into Gilbert's renewed embrace. She whispered, "I want to, Gillie. I really do! Can I say yes, but not tell the world just yet? Savor the moment and those to be and let our reality sink in? But more importantly let Maria and Jeffery have their…"

"Yes!"

"And a double yes!" Anya shouted, "Oh my God, Gillie, without a doubt Yes! I'll marry you. Just give me…" A passionate kiss ensued and the newly betrothed bodies bonded. Tongues touched tongues, feeding the wants of their aroused bodies. They froze on hearing the kitchen door fly open. A gusty wintry breeze blew through into the living-room. Gilbert and Anya pulled apart and made their clothing respectful. Anya slipped the ring out of Gilbert's hand and placed it on her finger. The fitting was loose. She smiled with confidence, reached up and unclasped her necklace. In a slick move she added the ring to the necklace then reclasped it.

"Dad, we're back." Hope shouted out.

"In the living-room sweetheart. We're just relaxing. Prepping ourselves for our Christmas Eve gathering and sharing of memories out of our past whilst savoring those yet to be."

Hope entered the living-room with Norman at her side. They missed Anya slipping the necklace and its ring under her sweater. She did not miss Anya's smeared lipstick. That knowledge added a smile to Hope's face. Could it be that love had come calling and embraced her dad? Coyly, Hope led Norman over to the sofa. Once seated they shared their visit to the homestead. She expressed concern over both twins and their fears Santa Claus might not find them come Christmas Eve. Footsteps on the stairs caught their attention. Moses joined them in the living-room. Mary called out, "Can I interest anyone in a tea or coffee? I'm having a tea." On hearing three calls for coffee and two for teas, Mary shouted back, "Got it. With my tea it's three coffee and three teas. Right?" Hearing no objections, she set herself to work in the kitchen. Hope joined her and tended to each mug's finishing touches. She also retrieved a cookie tin from the pantry. Once served everyone engaged in a lively Christmas focused on the sharing of personal memories out of their past. The unfolding future did not arise in the conversations. Although two of the women present quickly picked up on vibes that something was definitely afoot.

CHAPTER 46

    Lights in the yard signaled someone's arrival. On stepping through the kitchen door, the aromas of Gilbert's lasagna filled the McClaken household. Lyndsey and Richard's taste buds watered with recollections of their first sampling of Gilbert's Lobster Lasagna. Richard, popped the door closed and stood with the twenty or was it twenty-one shopping bags he held in both hands. On shedding her coat Lyndsey walked over to her hubby. She relieved him of one hand's burden then rewarded him with a kiss. Hope joined them and repeated her sister's actions to a T, or was it a K? Together, the sisters vanished upstairs. Vehicle lights bounced off the kitchen windows. On hanging up his jacket Richard greeted the new arrivals. The first arrival Inspector Harley Kingston, deposited his contribution, a huge container of Caesar Salad, on the counter. Then he greeted the hosts with handshakes and hugs. He then followed Richard's cues and, once free of his outerwear, headed into the living-room. Next up, the twins, their mom and John greeted Richard. From all outward appearances both Megan and Taylor were wired and ready for Jolly old Saint Nick's scheduled visits. Seeing them ignited childhood recollections in Richard's heart. He received John's firm handshake and brotherly hug. The twins dashed off into the living-room. Eugette rewarded Richard with a kiss and joyful hug. Jeffery and Maria brought up the rear with Auntie Lila in tow. After they placed their meal offering of garlic bread and four homemade pies on the table, both rewarded Richard anew then freed Auntie Lila of her burden, three huge plastic tubs of ice cream. Maria rescued the ice cream by stowing it safely in the freezer. They then all joined the gathering in the living-room.

There was a lively buzz and energy shared by all gathered together on Christmas Eve. Without fail, on catching a glimpse of Megan and Taylor wishfully eyeing the Christmas tree and casting hopeful glances out the window into a wintery wonderland, each adult relived in their hearts a myriad of Christmas Eve memories out of their pasts. A number of rumbling stomachs called out on this special occasion. However, Gilbert held off getting supper underway. Although difficult to fathom how the room could accommodate more guests, he awaited their arrival. Lyndsey and Hope rejoined the gathering. On their stepping off the last stair the kitchen door flew open and a chilling wind raced inside behind the last arrivals.

Freed of their outerwear, Pappy and Lenny shouted out, "Comes over here you, sweet young lassies, we need our Christmas hugs!"

Hope sashayed into the kitchen and rewarded both of them. Lyndsey followed suit. She did not sashay, but did walk with eager anticipation in each step. On hugging, and then releasing both Pappy then Lenny, the Wright sisters stepped forward and embraced their hosts. Aimee whispered, "Pappy had us stop in at the homestead and drop off our Santa offerings fer de wee ones. My, my what a beautiful tree Jeffery has set up over there. I bet 'cha he had a little help from those wee ones, I does."

Properly greeted everyone headed into the living-room. There, a lively fresh round of greetings and introductions ensued. Hope and Jeffery pick up on Gilbert's cue. They headed off and, with John and Richard's help, added the kitchen table to the dining-room table's end. In completing the settings, a second set of seasonal chinaware was used. It hadn't seen a table in decades. We will not name names and their sitting ordering at the tables. Suffice to say the McClakens hadn't seen such a joyful and energized gathering since Pappy's sweet Helen had passed on. That truth echoed warmly in all their hearts. Gilbert, Jeffery and Hope delivered all the food to the tables. Once they'd completed the tasks, they joined the dining-room gathering.

Gilbert cast an eye over the length of the table. He stopped on connecting eyes with his target. Both nodded their readiness. He announced, "On special request I call on Lyndsey to present grace."

All eyes did not lock on Lyndsey's, they closed and their heads tipped forward in a bowed position. A moment passed then Lyndsey spoke, "Lord, less than a year ago we Ramsays suffered a horrendous loss. We were reduced to a family of three. Being an only child, I managed to slowly accept fate's hand. However, true to my faith, I quickly rediscovered and embraced the fact that you, our Lord, tends to work in strange ways. You brought our family back, reuniting us with our roots. You did not stop there. You gave me back my baby sister and an amazing life. A life that embraces a family that continuously expands beyond my mind and heart's wildest imaginations." Lyndsey paused. The room remained silent. She continued, "Not all family is connected by bloodlines but they are beyond the reality of love and its gifts You so willingly offer up to all of us gathered together in celebration of your son's birth, Lord. For that, Dear Lord, I truly thank you and say Amen ... Let's eat!"

A loud round of amens echoed throughout the room. Actually, they made several rounds around the tables. Richard leaned over and hugged Lyndsey. On releasing her they kissed. The action played out around the tables. Megan and Taylor shrugged on catching each other's eyes. However, in the blink of an eye they too hugged.

Next, a healthy round of serious chowing down got underway. Not everyone out there has had the pleasure of savoring a feed of Lobster Lasagna. Some may have other favourites they prefer to set out at family gatherings come Christmas Eve. Being a technical Come-From-Away, I can relate and savor memories of Tourtiere Pie on a Christmas Eve at my baby brother's in-laws' in Gatineau, Quebec years past. Lordie, I can almost taste it this very moment. Having relocated to Nova Scotia years past, I've easily come to more than savor a good feed of seafood.

Enough about me, your author savoring past Christmas Eve feasts, we'd best get back into the action playing out at Gilbert's in East River, Nova Scotia.

Laughter and good-times possessed the gathering. In a rarely seen maneuver, the men took control of the after meal clean up. The women and twins retreated into the living-room where a lively chat session broke loose. Each shared a favorite Christmas memory out of their past. Off in the kitchen and dining-room, the cleanup wrapped up much quicker than all the men anticipated. In truth, it was accelerated by the potent workings of the working crew's digestive systems. Several, at times, sought out refuge on the deck outside where a fresh winter air quickly aided in their recovery. Although cold, the winter wonderland presented to the eye kept more than one lingering longer than needed outside. The last one to step back inside hesitated a stretch. It had started to snow. The snowflakes were huge and, once one caught an eye, if almost hypnotized the viewer. Following one last lingering gaze that viewer turned to walk back inside. His action was thwarted.

Maria stepped outside and joined Jeffery at the deck's railing. They embraced. Snuggled up to Jeffery's chest, Maria whispered, "Jeffery, I never thought I could love anew. Now I just can't get enough of you and your gentle loving ways."

"Me too! And to think I almost didn't make it to the wedding. Losing you to life's twists and turns broke my heart way back in the day. Lordie, that first dance with you in my arms. Thought I'd died and gone to heaven."

"I know, sweetheart. At Gilbert's when you and Pappy walked into the kitchen on the eve of the wedding. Would you listen to me? I'm babbling on to the man I love and avoiding what I really need to say."

Jeffery frowned. He replied, "There's no need to hold back. Come tomorrow our new beginnings will be singing love's serenade."

Maria stretched up and touched her lips to Jeffery's. The kiss lingered then ended with two sighs then Maria bit the bullet. She pulled their bodies closer together then said, "I never thought I missed the physical loving after I lost Martin. I was wrong and simply want more of you with each passing day sweetheart."

"Me too, honey. You're the best."

"You too. But I wasn't careful, if you know what I mean? I should have realized my body's clock was still ticking."

Jeffery grinned, "Sure glad your heart is ticking sweetie. I want and needs more of you with each new dawning."

"Me too! But trust me, my heart is ticking just fine and it's not lonely." Maria sighed, "It's my body's clock, love. Call me stupid, call me Grammie but in the end, you'd best call me pregnant cause I am and we're going to have a baby."

Their eyes locked and lips bonded. Together they savored the truth just revealed. They separated then, holding extended hands, started to strut and dance about the deck's snowy surface. On Maria slipping, Jeffery secured her body to his. Together they landed on the deck. Jeffery's body softened Maria's tumble. They giggled with abandon. Gazing into her eyes he asked, "Then I'll take it come tomorrow your gift will come with, a yes that I'll savor throughout our lives together?"

They kissed anew sealing tomorrow's new beginnings they'd be embracing. The kiss lingered. It ended on Eugette shouting out onto the deck, "Mom, Jeffery what are you two up to? You'd best be acting your age and not giving your daughter any ideas. Besides, the storytelling is about to get underway. It's the best part of any Christmas Eve! Move it. Git inside."

Neither replied. They simply smiled stood up and walked back into the house knowing the best story had just been shared. A story both felt would go onward as a never-ending love story long overdue.

....

Each storyteller if the truth were to be told did embellish their storyline and memories shared with their transfixed audience. A mood shift took place on Gilbert passing honours of Christmas Eve's last tale over to Moses Buzzard. No objections arose. After all, the man had clearly won the title of ugliest Christmas Sweater. In the eyes of Megan and Taylor he looked to be on a first name basis with Jolly old Saint Nick. He just had to be! Yes, the sweater was an ugly. However, the rest of his apparel almost raised the man up to Elf status in both the youngster's eyes and hearts.

Moses did not disappoint Megan, Taylor or their accompanying guests. All their eyes and ears were locked onto Moses. With a quick dusting off of his person, Moses prepared to spin his tale. The dusting action set in motion the jingly, ringing of the assorted bells attached to his apparel and elfin like hat. He then crouched down on his knees and gazed out over his admirers. The gaze did not stop there because it sidled over to the window and stared out over a snowy winter wonderland. The huge snowflakes held Moses in awe a minute, no it must have been two.

On breaking free, Moses set the mood and whisked all present off to Buzzard Mountain. "Friends and believers in the Magic of Christmas, come along with me and I'll share a tale of wonderment straight out of my family's past. For it truly was my great-great-great and somewhat greater grandpappy, Alphonso Buzzard, that first settled atop of what is now known as Buzzard Mountain. And yes, dear friends, I am named in honour of his son, Moses Buzzard. Times were tough back in the day. All those techie conveniences you take for granted, why, they did not exist. Communications, you say. If Alphonso needed to call someone like my great-great-great and somewhat greater grandma, he'd curl his hands about his mouth and take in a deep, deep breath."

Moses demonstrated the move with his hands. "Then he'd hollered out, 'MARY, MY MARY ... WHERE's YA AT MARY?' with a loud booming voice." Everyone almost jumped off their chairs, or the laps they sat on. Mary Buzzard simply frowned and covered her ears. Moses ignored her move. He was in a world of his own making.

Satisfied with the effects he'd garnered, Moses continued, "Grandpappy Alphonso, a hard worker, searched out ways he could make a living and survive on the mountain. A glance about and he discovered himself surrounded by trees. What do you suppose was the first thing that popped up in his head?" Moses paused. He glanced about the room and stopped on catching sight of the living-room's Christmas Tree.

Megan and Taylor both shouted out, "CHRISTMAS TREES, MISTER MOSES! CHRISTMAS TREES POPPED UP IN ALPONSO'S HEAD!" Laughter broke out throughout the room.

"YOU'RE BOTH ABSOLUTELY RIGHT, SWEETHEARTS! Christmas Trees popped up in Alphonso's head. And that very day he became a Christmas Tree Farmer. A proud tradition that I carry on to this very day. If you're looking for a Perfect Christmas Tree then you'd best be headed up onto Buzzard Mountain."

Megan looked over to Taylor she boasted, "That's where Mister Gilbert got his Christmas Tree, Tay. Remember we were there?"

"Yup! I remember. And that's where Bailey met Thomas!" Taylor replied.

Moses nodded his agreement. "Bailey sure did meet my Thomas."

Taylor asked, "Is Thomas really a turkey, Mister Buzzard? Auntie Hope called him a 'Turkey-Sorus-Dino-Rexious.'"

Moses chuckled aloud. The bells on his hat jingle, jingled. "Agreed, Taylor. But he's only seventy-four pounds. The wee lad has a stretch to go before he can challenge the World's Record for the Biggest Turkey to ever trot fancy footed across the land."

Taylor stared open eyed, "Gads how much bigger does he have to get?"

"Eighty-six pounds is the current world record."

Smirking Taylor answered, "Gosh! I bet Bailey is glad Thomas is just a wee lad and not eighty-six pounds."

Moses broke into uncontrolled laughter. On recovering he continued his storyline. "My great-great-great and somewhat greater grandpappy, Alphonso Buzzard, was never a man who could stand still very long..."

"And yer jest like him!" Mary injected.

"I confess, Love. I am a Doer." Moses answered. Then he set off anew. "Alphonso couldn't keep himself busy just being a Christmas Tree Farmer. Sitting still just wasn't to his liking. On a trip down the mountain to gather up a few of the groceries they didn't have available, he bought not one but several big geese and four turkeys. A fellow farmer bumped into Alphonso on recognizing him from a trip up to the Christmas Tree Farm. He asked, 'Those birds ya got looks good. But I could do you much better. How'd you like to take up Turkey Farming?' Alphonso eyed his fellow farmer with questions in his eyes. Spotting a potential business cohort the farmer asked, 'I'm looking to expand my operation. However, I'm of limited resources unlike you up there on that mountain.' Alphonso nodded a willingness to listen to the man's words. 'I'll sell you ten, no twenty baby turkeys. No, on second thought I'd best make them fryers. They're sixteen weeks old and would be best to start you up with. I'll toss in some hens, and a young Jenny, no five would be best. What do ya say kind sir?'

Grandpappy Alphonso had a sharp eye for business opportunities. He shook hands and sealed the offer with Ralph Goodman that day. And I thank the Lord every day for Grandpappy Alphonso's wisdom."

Moses paused just to catch his breath then carried on, "The handshake worked out best for grandpappy. In the long run he bought out Ralph and hired him on to oversee his turkey operations. Both men took kindly to each other and challenged each other to achieve more. Ralph suggested they raise gobblers that could challenge to be the world's biggest turkey. Try as they did a world champion never surfaced from all their efforts over the years. However, they did raise many contenders. And it was one of those very contenders that one night rose up and led a group of his fellow gobblers, rafters into flight and saved Santa Claus! Oh! I'd best advise in a group of turkeys are called rafters. Thought you'd best be in the know."

The room fell silent. Both Megan and Taylor's jaws dropped open in disbelief. In their minds they struggled to believe Santa Claus would ever need anyone's help, let alone the help of a flight of rafters. Wait a minute, could turkeys really fly? The youngsters and several adults struggled with that one. In the end they all bought into Moses' storyline. After all, it was a tale unfolding under the Magic of a Christmas Eve gathering of family and friends.

Moses carried on. "That Christmas Eve a terrible Nor'easter hit Nova Scotia hard. In truth, Buzzard Mountain bore the brunt of the storm. Santa Claus survived it because of Alphonso's prized challenger for the world's title, Thomas. A wise and humongous Gobbler of fame that my Thomas works towards emulating. Santa Claus was bang on schedule as he flew into Nova Scotia that Christmas Eve long, long ago.

The stars were ablaze guiding him on his merry way. Suddenly, a fierce swirling wind hit Santa's sled and reindeer. They battled it hard and, sadly, Santa Claus quickly came to realize the winds were tossing them off course. Santa blinked and tumbled out of his sled. His reindeer panicked. With Rudolph in the lead, they searched to find their Holly Jolly, red clad driver. Doubts hit them quickly. Could they find Santa in time to complete their night's work? The disturbance up in the night sky awoke everyone down below in Alphonso's barn. Awakened on hearing desperate calls for help, Thomas responded. He led the way. First one, then two gobblers followed their leader. Their barn door flew open and Santa's rescuers-to-be made their breakaway and set off to rescue the one calling out to them in need. Outside the barn, they strutted boldly forward. Suddenly a gust of wind hit them head on. Madly flapping their wings, a lightness overtook their bodies. In that very moment Thomas and his supporting rafters took flight. Airborne, they soared over Buzzard's Mountain.

In close formation they focused on the Ho, Ho, ho, ho calling out to them in the darkness of the night. The wind and heavy snow hampered their search. A glowing red light drew their them towards its light. Suddenly a loud kerplunk, thump and thud ensued. A rollie-polly, jiggly, wiggly, jolly ball landed atop of Thomas and his crew. A volley of gobble, gobble, gobbles sang out into the cold snow blown night air."

Moses paused. In catching his breath, he gazed about the room. All eyes and ears were locked onto Moses. He continued, "A robust, "Ho, ho, ho, ho and who do we have here shouted out?" Without hesitation Thomas and his rafters answered Santa's shout. "Tis I," Thomas declared. "Me Gideon", "Isaac here sire", "Linus," "Patrick," "And me, Timothy." Each gobbler shouted out back to Santa. With Santa safely rolling about upon their backs they veered eastward aligning with the glowing red light. The two flights, reindeer and gobblers, approached each other. Rudolph took the lead dropping low below Santa and the gobblers. A hearty "Ho, ho, ho, ho," "Gobble, gobble, gobble," and, "Santa truly thanks ye' lads," sang out. Then with a rollie-polly, jiggly wiggly leap, Santa jumped free of his rescuers and landed safely back in his trusted sled. Thomas and his rafters circled about and followed the sled and its Jolly Ho, ho, ho's that sang out with renewed vigor and energy. Seeing their mission completed Thomas and his team of gobblers waved off a silent adieu then followed a swift Nor'easter gust, gliding with ease through the chilly night's air. In truth, they'd been told turkeys couldn't fly. But on that Christmas Eve to Santa Claus's total joy, Thomas, Gideon, Isaac, Linus, Patrick and Timothy proved everyone wrong. Because in the Magical World of Christmas's Winter Wonderland turkeys can fly. That night, afraid their flurry of loop de loops, spiraling star bound whooshes and careening left, right maneuvers might only be a figment of their feathered imaginations, Thomas and his rafters seized their moment of glory entertaining all lucky enough to catch a glimpse of the Santa Claus rescue and his rescuers' amazing starlit air show. On a final dip and twist, Thomas and his rafter felt a rumble and a grumble call out from their stomachs, for you see, unlike us, turkeys have two stomachs. A gizzard that uses the grit they eat to grind their food up. And a glandular stomach that uses juices to process their food and soften it up. Hungry Thomas and the boys glided downward and completed a quick circular flight of the barnyard. Below them their gals skittered about gazing upward at their Toms. Their eyes aglitter on hearing the boys call out, "Gobble, gobble, gobble." A joyful sound to each Jenny gazing skyward. The sounds echoing sweetly in their ears as only Toms can gobble, gobble, gobble. Whish adee doo, with the smooth twist of a turkey's tail they landed back down onto the barnyard. Proudly they strutted back inside the barn's door. A gust of wind slammed the door shut. In short order, Thomas, Gideon, Isaac, Linus, Patrick and Timothy sang out, "Gobble, gobble, gobble," to the many a skittering Jenny striving to catch their eyes. And that, my fine friends, is how the Legend of Buzzard's Mountain came to be as Thomas and his brave gobblers once upon a time saved Santa Claus."

Moses took a bow. His many bells jingled and jangled. Taylor and Megan jumped up and raced over to Moses. Together they buried him in a volley of hugs and kisses. A loud boisterous round of applause sang out. Released by the twins, Moses bowed anew to his audience. A glance at the grandfather clock revealed the midnight hour was close at hand. Jeffery and Maria rounded up their crew and headed off to the homestead. Anya and Norman bid all a goodnight, reserving hugs and kisses for their special ones. Pappy and Lenny set off with the Wright sisters in hand. Those remaining headed off to various hiding spots throughout the house. The busiest were Hope and Lyndsey, however, the men also visited their secreted stashes of Christmas gifts. On meeting up in front of the Christmas Tree, they delivered all the gifts they'd retrieved. Simply stated, Santa Claus had received a bountiful helping hand. Everyone savored a special image of loved one's and treasured companion's faces as they would be opening their gifts come Christmas morning. A second round of hugs and kisses extended the excited elves sharing their excitement. The old grandfather clock struck one a.m. and chased everyone off to bed where they turned in for the night. Visions of sugar plums and turkeys in flight filled their dreamland adventures through to an early dawn arising on Christmas morning.

CHAPTER 47

A frosty Christmas morning unfolded in East River bright and early. The morning sunrise had barely caressed the eastern horizon along the highways, byways and cozy lanes where excited youngsters awoke, excited beyond their wildest imaginations. Some found stockings stuffed beyond capacity and got tied up in the moment by exploring each sock's rewards. Apples and tangerines quickly fell onto bedcovers. Sweets and treats energized the bodies whose mouths and faces soon vanished under a painting of chocolate marvels. Taylor offered Megan a second peppermint candy. She willingly accepted and popped it into her mouth. Taste buds exploded in both siblings. Taylor cautiously asked, "Do you think he found us, Meg? What if he went to Chester first and saw our house was gone.?"

Megan lost herself in thought for a moment. A smirk twisted into a smile. She calmed Taylor's worried heart. "I think we're ok, Tay. I heard mom and grampa Jeffie talking after you fell asleep. They sounded pretty confident that you know who would find us before morning's light hit."

"Really? I want to check out the tree but I'm really scared 'a what I might not see."

Megan led and Taylor followed. They slipped out'ta bed. "I think we're good, Tay. After the house fell silent, I heard footsteps out in the living-room..."

Taylor smiled with confidence. Fears that Santa Claus had missed them faded. He chirped, "I sure hope so, Megan. All our stuff burned with the house. We need lots and lots of Santa stuff and other stuff. You know clothes." Together they tip toed side by side out to the livingroom through the unlit house.

Off in the sunroom Maria snuggled up to Jeffery. They kissed then listened intently to the footsteps in the hallway. Images of Megan and Taylor inching cautiously towards the Christmas tree warmed both their hearts. More footsteps called out. Maria counted them silently. She signaled to Jeffery a five count, Megan, Taylor, Eugette, John and Auntie Lila. A second kiss sealed their fate. Together they tossed off the covers and crawled off the loveseat.

"Santa came, Meg, oh look at all the presents. He found us!"

All the adults huddled up together in the kitchen. Each leaped into the hearts of one of the twins and relived countless Christmas mornings out of their youth.

"Look, Meg, there's one for you. Do you want to open it?"

"No! We gotta wait for mom and grammie."

"But they're still sleeping. I can't wait for them ta git up."

"No! Go get mom." Megan answered firmly.

Taylor twisted about to go wake up mom. Mom reached out and embraced a shocked Taylor. He squealed with delight. Megan joined him and hugged mom, who called out, "Auntie Lila, care to play Mrs. Claus and hand out the gifts? Oh! Megan, please switch on the tree's lights. I love Christmas trees when their lights are all aglow."

Once Mrs. Claus was set up on the sofa chair, the twins took turns delivering gift wrapped presents to Auntie, who in turn passed them out. Jeffery broke away and quickly the aroma of the drip coffee machine's coffee filled the air. Two special requests for teas were hand delivered. John joined Jeffery and together they bagged up all the loose wrapping paper. Santa had come through bigtime with the twins' coming out on top.

Auntie called out, "Wow! Santa sure did come through. Look at all those gifts. I thought I'd be here all day passing them out. But my helpers were amazing. How about some breakfast?"

"But Auntie, there still one more present under the tree. Look there by the tree stand it's a little box."

Auntie gazed under the tree and spotted the present. She said, "You're right Megan. Bring it to me please."

Megan obeyed. On placing it in Auntie's hand everyone waited to heard a name called out.

Auntie toyed with the box. Coyly she called out, "Maria. Is there a Maria in the room?"

Timidly Maria walked over to Auntie and accepted the gift. Everyone watched as she slowly opened the gift. On dropping the wrapping paper, a black box was revealed. Maria eyed it in silence.

Megan shouted out, "Come-on grammie show us what you got!"

Jeffery edged his way over to Maria's side. She flipped the box open and the tree lights bounced excitedly off the exposed ring's diamond setting. A flurry of awes raced through the room. Jeffery dropped down onto his knee and faced Maria. He looked up into her eyes and asked, "Maria together we've rediscovered the lost passions and love of our youth. Say yes, you'll marry me and make our lives complete."

Silence befell the room. Eugette jumped up and shouted, "Mom! You love the man. It's plastered all over your face. Just say YES!"

Maria dropped down on her knees. Holding the box out to Jeffery she reached out and kissed him with a hunger both savored as the kiss lingered onward. Finally, it ended and, as they pulled apart, Maria whispered, "Yes. I'll marry you, my love."

Eugette and the twins shouted, "Louder, we didn't hear you!"

Maria smiled and called out to Jeffery and his supporting cast, "Yes. I'll marry you, my love."

Applause filled the room. Once it died down, Maria snuggled up to Jeffery. She eyed everyone in the room then announced, "Thank you. On losing Martin I swore I'd never love again. But fate dealt me, us, a hand I couldn't resist." She paused and looked skyward then added, "Sorry, mom, dad, I just couldn't say no and, well, you know the deal!"

Eugette shouted out, "Mom! You're not!"

Bang, bang a series of loud knocks hit the front door. Taylor and Megan raced over to the door. Maria shouted out don't answer it, Tay, Grammie will get it. Taylor stopped just as his hand touched the door handle. He released it on hearing Grammie step up behind him. Grammie opened the door. She froze on spotting their visitor. A tall heavyset police officer stood in the doorway. "Good morning, madam. I am Sergeant Stratford, Robert Stratford. Would Maria Lamont reside in this residence?"

"I am Maria Lamont. Is there a problem officer?"

"Madam, I need you come with me for questioning."

Maria froze then caved to a series of shivers ripping through her body. Her eyes tilted skyward and she dropped to the floor. The twins dropped down next to their Grammie sobbing. Sergeant Stratford attempted to enter the old Ramsey Homestead. Taylor jumped up and blocked his entry. He shouted, "Stay away from my Grammie. Get out or I'll kill you!"

Robert Stratford froze in his tracks. Taylor stared him down. Jeffery, Eugette, John and Auntie Lila gathered by Maria who had started to stir. A minute, then two, passed in silence as nobody moved an inch. Maria's face twitched nervously then both eyes popped open. She inhaled a series of deep breaths and her eyes glanced upward and randomly about her surroundings. Maria sat upright on the floor. Sergeant Stratford stepped inside the house. Taylor wrapped his arms frantically around the officer's right thigh.

Megan shouted, "Grammie, Grammie, are you ok?"

Maria attempted to stand up. Eugette stopped her, embracing her mom. Jeffery addressed the officer and asked, "Is there a problem, what prompted you to destroy our Christmas morning? I don't understand why you're here." Nervously he chewed on his lower lip.

Sergeant Stratford replied, "Perhaps we should all drive down to the Chester Detachment together. Questions have arisen surrounding the fire that destroyed Maria Lamont's home. I apologize for being so blunt with my words and for upsetting your Christmas morning. I'm sure everything can easily be cleared up at the station."

Maria, with Eugette's help, stood. She smiled warmly at her supporters "It's OK, we will drive down to the police station with the officer and everything will be ok."

Jeffery ran into the kitchen and grabbed his cell phone off the table then rejoined the gathering at Maria's side. He frowned on her asking, "Please give me a moment to get dressed officer. The sooner we get going the sooner we'll get everything cleared up."

Jeffery shouted, "You're not going anywhere, Love." He speed-dialed Gilbert's house. The phone line called out. Maria stared nervously down at her feet.

"Hello."

"Hope! It's Uncle Jeffery. I need Inspector Kingston, is he up and about.

Sergeant Stratford uttered a grunt and said, "Shit, what's he doing at the McClakens?"

Jeffery stared down the officer then said, "Inspector Kingston will be taking care of my Maria and setting you in your proper place!"

"No. It's best I go and clear this mess up." Maria injected. She added, "We've done nothing wrong."

Jeffery sighed on hearing, "Harley here. How can I help, Jeff? What's happening?"

Sergeant Stratford shook his head with a negative nod. He looked to Maria and said, "Look, you're right. It's Christmas morning. Day after tomorrow come to the Chester Detachment. It's just a few questions to clear up loose ends surrounding that horrible fire that destroyed your home."

Jeffery sneered and shouted, "No. We'll clear it up right now. Just as soon as Inspector Harley Kingston gets here from Gilbert's."

Sergeant Stratford looked to Maria and repeated, "Maria, anytime that's convenient for you. Day after tomorrow drop in at the Detachment." He then turned and walked back outside. The door closed behind him. Maria sighed. Word on the street said the Fire Marshall had concluded arson was the cause of the fire. She had concluded the same the night of the fire. Why had it taken them so long? Why come calling

Christmas morning and disrupt our joyful gathering? A glance at Eugette and she knew who really needed to be questioned and charged?

....

A slower wakeup unfolded over at Gilbert's. The early risers had frowned on hearing the phone sing out. Hope answered the phone. Her frown deepened on hearing Jeffery's call out for Harley. Hope shouted out to Harley as he sat down at the kitchen table, "Inspector, please. It's my Uncle Jeffery!"

Harley stood walked over and took the receiver. He listened then said, "I'll be right over. Jeff. We'll get this mess straightened out. Enough is enough." He hung up the receiver. Silently he rued, *'What is the bastard up to? Why did he have Stratford crash the homestead on Christmas morning? Why did the bastard send his dirty cop calling?'*

Hope approached Harley. He said, "Not to worry. I'll straighten this mess out right now."

"Call if we can help. Please!"

Harley donned his outer wear then stepped outside. He waved back to Hope, confirming he'd heard her plea. A quick arm-hand brushing partially cleared his vehicle of snow. No warmup time was taken. He headed straight over to Jeffery's.

Meanwhile, Sergeant Stratford headed back towards the road. He frowned as he passed a vehicle headed to the homestead. On spotting Harley Kingston behind the wheel his frown deepened. Once out on the highway he speed-dialed a number on his cell phone. A phone rang in the home of Chester's notorious Barnie Madison.

Harley parked beside John's SUV and exited the vehicle. Then he walked briskly over to the homestead's front door. He knocked three times. Footsteps were heard. Jeffery opened the door. On seeing Harley, he reached out and embraced the man. They parted and Harley stepped inside. He sang out a hearty Merry Christmas greeting then asked, "What's up, Jeff. How can I help?"

All eyes turned to Harley. Jeffery standing beside Maria wrapped her in a loving embrace. He replied, "Stratford came calling this morning.

Headed out the minute I mentioned your name to Hope on my cellphone. He claimed Maria had to accompany him to the Chester Detachment for questioning regarding the fire that destroyed her home. On Christmas morning for, God's sake. He destroyed our Merry Christmas awakening. What was he thinking? Oh! She's been asked to head over to the Detachment the day after tomorrow. At her convenience, I must add."

Harley sighed in disgust. He walked over to Jeffery and Maria and took Maria's hands into his. He said with confidence, "Maria, I apologize. I've been a police officer, detective throughout my working career. If one of my men or women officers pulled off the stunt Stratford did this morning, as their Inspector, I would have them up on charge and under review. And no, I would not treat their indiscretion with a slap of the hand." Harley paused then added, "I'm here for the holidays with Gillie. Parker Rose, a seasoned attorney, is committed to working with us. We will take you to the Detachment at your convenience and represent you. Don't fret. I know Stratford and will handle him."

Maria broke free of Jeffrey. She freed her hand from Harley's and wrapped him in a grateful embrace uttering, "Oh thank you, Mister Kingston, thank you."

Harley pulled free of Maria's embrace after he'd returned one of his own. Their eyes locked and Harley's assured her he would be there for her. She reached over and rewarded him with a quick kiss on the cheek. Harley blushed then said, "We'd best head over to Gillie's. From what I saw this morning Santa Claus stopped in over there after he visited your house, Jeffery."

"Really?" Megan and Taylor asked spontaneously. Their wildest Christmas expectations had already been exceeded.

"Really!" Harley replied. He added, "If you haven't set down to breakfast, Mary and Hope have an amazing one underway over at Gillie's. I suggest everyone get dressed and we head over there. I can take anyone in a rush to get there to check out Santa's deliveries? Just saying."

Taylor bounced up and down, totally energized. He squealed, I'll go Inspector, I'll go. You coming with me Meg?"

Before Megan could answer Eugette spoke for her, "OK, Tay and Meg, get yourselves dressed and you can go with Inspector Kingston."

Taylor and Megan raced off to get dressed. Harley shouted out, "Just call me Harley. It works for me."

Short Christmas greetings were exchanged while they awaited the twin's return. Harley spotted a glow on Maria hand. He asked, "Is that sparkle on your hand something new? Sorry. I had to ask. I didn't see it yesterday over at Gillie's"

"It is something new. Something very special. My man asked and I said yes."

Harley wrapped Maria in an embrace. He quickly released her and grabbed a short kiss. He smiled at the newly betrothed and said, "Congratulations, you two love birds. Congratulations!"

The twins bolted back into the living-room. They'd donned their outerwear and shouted, "We're ready, Mister Harley, we're ready. Let's go!" Each one grabbed one of Harley's hands and dragged him towards the door. He willingly followed their lead and they headed over to Gilbert's.

Eugette sighed and said, "We sure are lucky to be connected to the McClakens. We'll be ok, mom. We'll be ok! Let's get dressed. I'm hungry and I suspect somebody has an announcement or two they're itching to proclaim." Smiles were exchanged and everyone headed off to get dressed. In short order they climbed into John's SUV and headed over to Gilbert's.

…….

Back at Gilbert's, strangely, Lyndsey was the last of the women to arise. On arriving downstairs, a magnificent bright sunny Christmas morning greeted her. Along with a bout of chiding from Hope and Mary. Together they laughed off their morning greetings. Snickers broke out as another robust round of male bonding with loud snoring roared out greetings throughout the house. A contest emerged amongst the women. In the end, Moses won out and his seasoned snoring abilities were declared the game winner, or loser, depending on one's point of view. The kitchen filled itself with jovial Christmas morning greetings. Moses willingly took a bow in recognition of the title bestowed on him. It was asserted that gift exchanges would await the arrival of the homestead gang. Mary and Hope fired up the grills and prepared to get breakfast underway.

....

Eugette entered the kitchen first. On spotting Hope, she ran to her and they embraced. She whispered, "Ya gotta check out mom's ring finger!"

"Really?"

John held back, allowing Jeffery and Maria to step inside ahead on him. Their news had proceeded them. On entering Gilbert's kitchen, Maria was accosted by the women. They all sought out her hand and ring finger. "It's beautiful, Maria. It's beautiful and you're so deserving. Oh! You too Uncle Jeffery! Congratulations you lovebirds!" Hope shouted out. Mary slipped over to the counter and shut down the grills. Breakfast was once again put on hold.

Jeffery quickly vanished, surrounded by a vocal round of congratulations and backslaps by all the men folk including Taylor. Gilbert saved a special hugging embrace for his brother. Jeffery almost lost his breath. Gilbert released him on hearing Eugette shout out, "And that's not all folks! That's not all. My Mom's pregnant!"

The congratulations leaped into a repeat performance. Mary shouted out, "I knew it. I knew it!"

Hearty laughter ensued. Eugette joined in with them. Quickly the action shifted into the living-room where Moses assumed the role of Santa's Head Elf and handed out gifts delivered to him by Megan and Taylor. Breaks ensued each time they discovered gifts tagged with their names. The breaks were frequent. Taylor took favor to a plush stuffed replica of Thomas de Turkey that Santa had tagged with his name. Everywhere Taylor went Thomas tagged along. Megan faded away from gift delivery duties. Sitting by the tree she casually worked her way repeatedly through each new piece of clothing she'd been gifted. A silent joy and confidence added a positive glow to the young lady's face. Most Christmas mornings five or six new pieces of clothing topped her gifts most treasured. And that included underwear. In sniffing a pretty pink sweater she savored a thought, *'Batchas Esther Morgan and her bullying ninnies never got nothing as nice as this.'* All this while her mind calculated that it would be close to Easter before she had to wear a piece of used clothing. It just felt great. And friends having grown up in a family of limited means, I can totally relate to little Megan's feelings that Christmas morning.

The room's energy took on an upswing on Anya and Norman's arrival. Hope easily occupied Norman's attention. Anya and Maria bonded on the loveseat and lost themselves in conversation. To most adults, the magic of Christmas is best viewed and captured in the eyes and excitement of children. The twins delivered beyond everyone's expectation. Gilbert laid low. Seeing Maria and Anya bonding across the room warmed his heart. He did not plan to double up on Jeffery's great news and knew Anya would follow his lead. Richard and John took on the cleanup duties. They gathered up all the loose wrapping paper. In the end they collected four blue bags of it. With his task completed, Santa's elf arose and headed off in search of more coffee. In time, Mary and Hope jumped back into full breakfast mode.

Energize by chocolate overload both Megan and Taylor never showed up at the breakfast table. They kept themselves entertained by exploring their second Santa delivery of the day. Having arisen early, both quickly answered the Sandman's callings and fell asleep under the Christmas tree. Breakfast ended up in the dining-room. Nobody walked away with a hunger pang calling out. The men actually demonstrated the failings of their digestive systems compared to the average woman's as they gathered together in the living-room. Those demonstrations quickly chased all the ladies out of the living-room.

……..

Moses excused himself on glancing at his watch. The morning had vanished. He moved to take on his self-appointed duties. A

Turkey-Sorus-Dino-Rexious awaited its date with the Turkey Blaster. Mary halted Moses on his attempt to step outside without outerwear. He gave in and headed off to their bedroom. Shortly, he reappeared in an outfit that Mary simply shrugged at after so many years of seeing him decked out in matching apparel. Fifty-five years of marriage had seasoned her tolerance. Once outside, Moses fired up the Turkey Blaster then stepped back inside.

In the kitchen, he shuffled all but Hope into the living-room. Laughter and friendly chatter flowed out of the living-room adding energy throughout the house. Hope joined the gathering as coached before starting to prepare the stuffing. On her return she had Maria at her side and Moses' mastery of the kitchen was called into question. The master's gentler side agreed to listen to the proposal that Hope suggested would amaze him. He smiled and nodded to the women, giving them the green light to amaze the master with Maria's proposal.

Nervously, Maria nibbled on her lower lip. Hope hugged Maria and nudged her to proceed. "I'd never question your mastery of the kitchen Mo...Moses." Their eyes connected and Maria's confidence soared. She continued. "It's only a suggestion to add my Gramma's magic to the bird's stuffing." A smile burst out on Moses' face. He nodded his approval. Maria nodded back then added, "The inner workings of men and women are unique beyond the wonders of their creative powers. Our Lobster Lasagna supper the other night is a prime example. Like the McClakens, my family is connected heart and soul to the sea. I was raised by a fisherman, even married one." She paused. Memories of a loved one lost and her daughter's lost love touched her deeply. "Yes! At times I was sent outside to eat my school lunch. Only poor folk and fishermen's kids ate lobster sandwiches. But let's get to the point. That Lobster Lasagna supper the other night. I can't speak for you, bu..."

Hope jumped in, "Trust me, it hit Dad too!" Moses smirked, attempting to supress a chuckle.

Maria continued, "Just like it hit Jeffrey and Bailey. It's a man thing. However! Let me add my Gramma's magic to this bird's stuffing and the damsels in your midst will sing your praises."

Moses' face revealed him to be lost in deep thought. He'd heard rumours of Gramma Lamont's magical bird stuffing in the past. If rumour proved to bear truths, Moses wanted access it its magical ingredients. Moses eyed Maria with ah in his gaze. Recollections of days long past captured his thoughts. In his heart, he eyed two toddlers Helen Ramsay had boasted about walking hand in hand towards the school bus stop. He blinked and the image of a youthful Maria at Jeffery's side vanished. Ages and life's entanglements had torn the childhood sweethearts apart. Moses sighed in reflection. He stepped over to Hope with zest and lovingly nudged her out of the kitchen. On returning he walked up to Maria and buried her in a trade mark Moses hug. Akin to the one Gilbert had learned from Moses. In that moment he assured Maria her presence was welcomed in his kitchen. Especially if her Gramma's recipe proved effective as claimed. Maria sighed on being released. Moses pleaded, "Hope has prepared the basic stuffing. I ascend to your wishes, fair damsel. However, I beg of you, let me add your Gramma's magic to Gramma Buzzards' treasure trove of recipes gathered over the ages and entrusted to me."

Maria smiled then nodded agreement. Moses released his kitchen to Maria pleasures. Together they worked and quickly finished the big bird's preparations. Once Maria stepped away from the beast, Moses declared the beast was ready for the Blaster and took charge after asking, "Would it augment the recipe's powers if a sampling were added to de gravy?"

Maria face glowed and Moses took that as a positive response. He grabbed a notepad and pencil which he passed to Maria. She accepted Moses' pencil and wrote on the notepad her Gramma Lamont's magical secret recipe. The pencil was returned to its owner and the treasure was tucked into one of Moses' shirt's pockets. Maria felt like a princess having been allowed to work in the kitchen at a master's side. Together they prepared the veggies and sides then cleaned up the kitchen and themselves. The passions shared with Jeffery the previous night had bonded two hearts. The morning's treasured gift added a glow to Maria's persona. Maria glowed with pride. Together they walked out of the kitchen and joined everyone in the living-room. She walked to Jeffery's side and stole a hug. Moses flashed a thumbs up towards Gilbert. The two quickly exited the living-room.

In the kitchen Gilbert tried to slip into his jacket. Moses deflected Gilbert's actions by assigning him veggie duty. In Hope's humble opinion it was the quickest veggie detail she'd ever seen her dad complete. She stood aside and watched Gilbert as he donned his jacket. His duties entailed carrying a huge bake pan ladened with veggies outside to the Turkey Blaster. Moses followed Gilbert outside. He did not follow suit and his jacket remained on its closet hook. Once the veggies were loaded into the blaster's oven they returned to the kitchen. Moses snickered on directing Gilbert towards the feast's beast and aided him in hoisting up the stuffed beast. Moses quickly abandoned Gilbert. He opened the door and followed the beast and its conveyer outside. A warmth flowed off the Turkey Blaster. On opening the Turkey Blaster's oven Moses cued Gilbert and the two worked the stuffed Turkey-Sorus-Dino-Rexious into place in the Blaster's cook chamber. He closed the door. Both stared through the glass door at the beast. Moses grinned and pulled out a cigar from a hidden shirt pocket. He nodded to Gilbert an offer. It was declined, Anya had clearly stated her views on smoking. In truth Gilbert agreed. The two men remained outside gazing at the Blaster. Aromatic wafts of sizzling beast rose up off the Blaster. It easily overpowered the smoke from Moses' cigar. Inside Mary and Hope gazed out the window at the pair who every male except Taylor had gathered around. Only Gilbert wore a winter jacket. They shook their heads in disbelief on seeing Moses' exposed legs. A chill ran through them. Moses after all was clad in a favorite pair of elfin beach shorts. He appeared to be totally oblivious to his wintery surroundings. After watching all the men step outside and gather around the Blaster's Master Mary chuckled aloud. The scene confirmed the greatest drawing card for most men was a boy's toy regardless of its complexity. Provided it was mechanically driven not many men could withstand the call. Mary turned away from the window and Hope followed her lead. They returned to the living-room and its lively chitter-chatter flowing throughout.

Curled up at her mom's side Eugette vocally shared her thoughts on Maria's condition. "Mom, it would be so awesome to actually have a sister. A baby sister if you catch my drift. And Meg and Tay would get another auntie. But I'd never turn a cold shoulder towards having a brother. That actually might be sort of neat."

Maria reached over and embraced her daughter. Just having her safely back home elated her beyond comprehension. In thinking back to the moments that had led to her condition she shivered in embracing the joy embracing her heart. A bonus, this time the father was one that owned her heart, body and soul. The other she simply blocked out of her thoughts. In doing so she avoided anew the fear of telling Eugette the truth and revealing the real biological father. She pondered whether Norman hinted at his roots. Maria closed her eyes and sighed. In that moment she relived the moment she'd revealed the truth about her first pregnancy to Jeffery. The joy of her current condition overpowered Jeffery's anger over a shame Maria had hidden too long. Willingly she embraced the freedom her soul savored on being relieved of the guilt neither had ever deserved. Joy did not embrace her heart for Maria knew Eugette's reaction to the truth would not be akin to Jeffery's

Anya drew up to Maria's side and Eugette set off in search of John. Her journey pulled her towards the kitchen door and the man scene painted outside on the deck. In full blast mode, aromatic wafts of turkey called out to her while it held all the men in a transfixed state. Rather than attempting to break into a male bonding session Eugette headed off in search of her twins who had awakened and joined Bailey upstairs.

Back in the living-room Anya, and Maria quietly admitted the truth to each other, Anya had already faced the jury in confessing it to her son and daughter. Norman had admitted to having witnessed the second rape Anya had endured. Poor sweet August learned on asking an inquisitive mother-daughter question after she's heard her mom shout out the truth from a deep deprived sleep induced state. Words Anya knew she'd regret through to the day of her death, Sweet August had been unable to cope. The racial bigotry cast her way coupled with the newly learned knowledge had led quickly to August committing suicide and breaking Anya heart. In truth Anya could feel and relate to Maria's reluctance to speak openly about a past both had opted to leave buried deep down in the neverlands of their souls and memories. However, at this point in life, Anya felt a need to know. Should they become future in-laws the truth would bond them best if shared between them.

Maria spoke softly. "I sense you've shared your past with Norman, I can see it in his eyes on connecting with him, I'm terrified. On my Eugee's fleeing, her disappearance terrified me. You'd already shared your loss. I feared if she learned of August's actions and my shame, she'd follow in her footsteps. How are you coping with such a tragic loss?"

Anya wrapped Maria in a loving embrace that only they grasped the depth of honesty it contained. Maria whispered the words she'd buried deep within since the night of her assault. "Barnie Madison broke into our home. I was only thirteen and clueless to the reality of sex and its complications. Besides I felt safe. To me kissing was doing it. If you grasp my meaning. I felt safe. I'd really pushed the limits of safe sex with the beaus of my day back then. Needless to say, the bastard opened my eyes to the reality of sexual relations. It totally broke my spirit."

Anya kissed Maria's forehead. Then replied, "I was sixteen, sweet sixteen and had no beau. God how I wanted one. Like you, Madison broke into our home. My parents stood by me and my little bundle. But I did get shipped off to a distant relative for the duration of my pregnancy. On returning, Gillie and Karyn were a committed item. It hurt not having a man at my side. But I accepted it. Mom and dad totally supported me. I finally graduated a year after my peers. Then, in the blink of an eye, school started for my Normie. Thank God, Karyn and Gilbert still wanted me in their lives. Both so supportive. Then they were blessed with Hope. Life was truly good back then. So truly ironic. Then mom and dad headed out on one of their Friday night dates. God love them. Married life never stopped them from dating. They headed out to the Lobster Pot Pub & Eatery. The bastard saw them and knew I was home alone with my Normie. He came calling and broke into the house. I'll spare you the details. I prayed that little Normie hadn't witnessed my assault and beating. That hope was dashed when he revealed the truth on our Christmas Eve visit to Sweet August's grave. On a positive Normie reassured me he was ok."

"But?"

"No buts!" Anya reassured. "I look at your Eugette and I see a strong determined young woman and loving mother."

"That my girl is! Definitely determined and blessed with a giving caring heart."

Anya sighed, "Yes, we suffered that bastard's assaults. But love triumphed in my case and yours. Our bloodlines were strong. The values our blessings were raised with overpowered the evil that conceived them within our bodies."

Maria pulled Anya closer in a reassuring hug. "Yes, and I will admit the bastard's mother was a good woman. Auntie tells me she tried. But like us an evil befell the poor woman."

They pulled apart. The twins raced into the living-room in pursuit of a fleeing Bailey. Eugette followed on their tails. Quickly the living-room conversations drew all the women together. They lost themselves in idle Christmas memory reflections. To nobody's surprise, Auntie Lila led the conversation's flow.

·······

Mary's gaze caught sight of activity underway off in the dining-room. Jeffery raced about with John and Richard in tow setting up the dishes and cutlery for their feast about to get under way. She spotted Moses walking into the living-room and acknowledged his nod. The nod signaled the feast was about to get underway.

Mary announced, "Ladies! We're about to be treated to a Christmas feast that'll have you hankering for second and third servings. Leftovers are a rarity I assure you. Oh! Rumour has it we womenfolk will be treated to an experience beyond your collective imaginations. We'd best rise up and get ourselves seated." Maria edged past Mary first. She smiled on hearing Mary whisper, "If your Gramma's recipe delivers, missy, we could be looking into filing for trademark and patent rights. Women of the world will be clamoring to our door." Maria simply smiled in return. In view of her recent personal setbacks' success was definitely not a contender on her list. Excepting of course the glitter that bounced off her ring finger since this morning's gift exchange and the joy exploding inside her body.

Quickly, everyone was seated. Gilbert passed hosting honours over to Moses who stood and grace proceeded. "Lordie, here's we all be gathered together in celebration of yer son's birth and, iff'in I may declare, my fine cooking. Tis an honour me, Lord. A gaze about and I sees myself seated amongst true believers in your ways. An extra blessing fer me Mary. The wee lass has tolerated and loved me beyond all expectations. And wee Hope fer guiding me your humble servant into the hand of another who assisted in this feast's preparations and shared a gift you'd once bestowed on her Gramma. Blessing to those who've lived the joys of motherhood and those about to relive it and of course the wee ones that Santa Claus visited not once but twice I've been told..." Moses caught sight of a look shining off Mary's face, He grasped its meaning and intent. He wrapped up his grace oration, "And, Lordie, bless all those gathered with us along with our loved ones at home with you. Amen." A volley of *'Amens'* rotated quickly about the tables. Then Moses excused himself and set off to get the feast underway. In no time at all the feast's maestro returned to the dining-room wheeling a cart with a huge stockpot soup brewer. On closer inspection its label was revealed *'Buzzards' Mountain Crock Inc. 4-gallon Soup Master.'* Moses wheeled it around the tables stopping at each setting. A warm inviting aroma ignited the diners. One in particular glowed in anticipation of the soup's contents. Lyndsey chirped out, "Carrots I detect carrots and a hearty sprinkle of ginger along with just a tiny touch of cinnamon. Right, Moses?"

Moses ladled an extra scoop into Lyndsey's bowl. Their eyes locked and Lyndsey had her answer. Since her condition had fast tracked into a real baby bump, carrots had become a insatiable menu item. Although hers leaned towards raw carrots, in Lyndsey's mind, a carrot was a carrot regardless of its state. And enough could never be enough to sate her taste buds. Moses nodded confirming her thoughts. He then set off, serving up his carrot, ginger-cinnamon soup to each diner. On Richard's first sampling he turned to Lyndsey and boasted, "Guess what, love? Carrots! It's got carrots." He did not question the joy on Lyndsey's face. But did relax in the knowledge the carrots were not raw.

Lyndsey replied by dipping and retrieving a full spoon of soup and popping it into her mouth. An ecstatic glow appeared on her face. It bounced off Richard's. He frowned with concern. Their paternity doctor had advised against Lyndsey's passion for carrots. The frown vanished on Lyndsey firing a look back his way. Only Mary caught sight of the exchange.

Chit-chatting accelerated with each new bowl emptied by its diner. Only one called out for more … Lyndsey. Her need was quickly filled. Jeffery cleared away the empty bowls. Gilbert joined up with the maestro. Together they retrieved the feast's main course from the Turkey Blaster. Moses wheeled in the veggie offerings in their Fine China serving bowls that were seated on another cart. Gilbert followed behind him. He approached the table's cleared area and, with strain, set down Georgio, the Feast's main Guest of Honour. Moses' Buzzards' Mountain Free Range Turkey Ranch contribution. Most eyes stared in wonderment at the beast. Jeffery nervously shouted out, "I want a drumstick, I think. Or is it a Turkey-Sorus-Dino-Rexious thigh?" He stared in awe at the beast sitting atop its plater on the table.

Veggie options were passed around the tables and everyone loaded up their plates. Eugette assisted Megan and Taylor in their selections. Moses took on the slicing and dicing of the beast. Women and children received healthy potions of tender white meat. Their dining pleasures barely made a mark on the beast. The men were next on Moses' serving priority. Gilbert followed the white meat trend that had topped off the served plates. Jeffery eyed the beast on hearing Moses call out his name. His plate stood towered high with veggies. Tradition proved to be too great a calling card. Jeffery shouted out, "Maybe? No definitely I'll take one of those Turkey-Sorus-Dino-Rexious thighs, if you think it'll fit on my plate?"

Moses eyed the beast over closely. After a pause he nodded approval of Jeffery's dining request. A touch of the blade to the thigh base, followed up with a twist of the leg and the selected choice broke free of the beast. Moses nodded to Jeffery to leave his plate on the table. He obeyed. On landing on the plate Jeffery's veggies were squashed sideways. He eyed his plate with a hunger driving him to dig in which he did. Everyone added a healthy scoop and more of stuffing to their plates. Most of the men opted to add extra gravy to their plates. Moses helped himself to the other thigh. Then he turned to the hungry companion rubbing with anxiety against his leg. A glance downward and their eyes locked Moses got the message Bailey eagerly projected concerning his wants and needs. He took up an empty bread plate from the table. 'Meow, meeow, meow!' Bailey eagerly sang out. Moses loaded the plate up with a heathy serving of white beast meat, then added a scoop of stuffing topped off with two mini ladles of gravy. Bailey almost leaped up and knocked the plate out of Moses' hand. On Moses stooping down and serving up Bailey's Christmas chow, down the old feline focused his attention on the task at hand, emptying the plate and calling out for more. Moses eyed Bailey and grinned at the feline's enthusiastic dining mannerisms. He then sat down and started to work on clearing his plate. The dining-room fell silent with everyone focused on their plates. With each bite Hope, Maria and Moses eyed the others and inhaled with a cautiousness the others did not notice. Maria gazed over at Jeffery's plate. The beast's thigh had vanished. She pondered; would Gramma's recipe prove effective as momma had so often claimed it to be? She returned her focus to the plate that called out to her. In doing so Maria caught sight of Moses and his nod of approval. Dinner started to wind down. Mary silently snickered on spotting several men loosening their belts a notch or two. A questioning look appeared on her face. Why, she wondered, is there no male belly-grumbles calling out? The room filled to overcapacity continued to display an alluring aura in its air of roasted Turkey-Sorus-Dino-Rexious augmented by its supporting veggie cast. Thoughts cast back to sessions in their Buzzard's Mountain Gift Shop

Restaurant's dining-room reminded her of the foul stench that tested the endurance and tolerance of staff and new arrivals. Mary watched Moses stand then strut over to Maria's side. She eyed him closer on him leaning down and embracing Maria in a generous hug. Her ears reached out to capture a glimpse of the words being exchanged. They failed.

Moses whispered into Maria's ear, "Lassie, I believe we have us a winner here. One we'd best patent."

"Really?" Maria answered.

"Really!"

"But it's only Gramma's recipe. Nothing special really." Maria added.

"Really, Lassie. We got us a winner." He quickly kissed her cheek then stood and walked back to his chair with a strut in his step. Dollar signs danced willie nellie in his head. Offerings of coffee, tea and desserts were quickly declined. Satisfied the women headed off into the living-room. The twins followed. Then the men worked the cleanup with Jeffery in the lead. On the second loading of the dishwasher, Harley begged off further participation. He claimed he had a duty to perform but promised he'd only be gone a short time. He departed after offering up a cover story that explained his plans.

CHAPTER 48

Harley drove to the local café and met up with Parker. He'd called him earlier and set up the meeting. He updated Parker on the details surrounding Barnie's history and the interference he believed Robert Stratford had worked on Barnie's behalf. Parker's career had opened years past with a focus on criminal law. Recent years had seen him shifting over to family law centered on marital breakdown and paternity. On hearing Parker reveal these pointers Harley lightened up. He sensed a backdoor opening up to assist them in nailing the bastard that to date had successfully thwarted Harley's efforts to break his nemesis circle of protection. Harley updated Parker on Stratford's attempt to drag Maria Lamont off to be questioned earlier that morning. Parker grinned on hearing repeat mention of Robert Stratford's name. He updated Harley on his involvement in Stratford's divorce. Harley filed that pointer away for future reference. With both their coffees cold, they stood and headed off to the Chester RCMP Detachment office. Parker followed Harley in his vehicle. On arrival they both parked beside the one police vehicle in the parking lot alongside a dark charcoal grey coloured sedan. The door was lock. Harley pressed the buzzer to announce their presence. On seeing officer Eric Johnson walking towards the door, Harley breathed a sigh of relief. He wasn't really up to confronting Sergeant Stratford on his earlier actions at the old McClaken homestead. The door opened and Harley greeted Eric with a hearty handshake. He then introduced Parker to Constable Eric Johnson, Harley's connection to the Chester

RCMP Detachment. Inside, they exchanged hearty Christmas greetings then walked down the hallway into Eric's office.

Harley asked, "Where's Stratford? Taking a vacation day off. Escaping the stresses of the working environment?"

"Actually, he is Inspector. Visiting family as a matter of fact." Eric answered.

"Really?" Harley replied. He then asked, "Are there any new updates on the Lamont house fire? A terrible loss for that family given the time of the year."

"That is true, Inspector. The Fire Marshall is calling it arson. Thanks to God and their furry friend no lives were lost. The twins are sweethearts. I went to school with their mom, Eugee. A sad situation given the losses Eugee and her mom have suffered recently."

"Have any new leads surfaced?"

"No. Not to my knowledge. Hold on I'll grab the file." Eric answered with an offer Harley greeted with a nod of approval. After Stratford's morning antics and on learning of his vacation status, Harley really wanted to get his eyes and mind into the fire's case file. Eric stepped away then quickly returned with a file folder in his hand. He sat then flipped through the folder's contents. A frown surfaced on his face. He started to speak then stopped.

Harley asked, "Is there an issue? Something closed to outside eyes?"

"Not really." Eric replied. He added, "There's something added then scribbled out with heavy ink. I can't really make it out."

"Can I give it a go?" Harley asked.

Eric squinted, giving it another go but failed to catch the drift of the original writing. Frustrated he handed the file over to Harley and added, "Bottom right of the last page, Inspector."

Harley took the file and eyeballed the scribbled-out entry. The marks scribbling out the entry were very heavy. However, the original ink was black and the scribbly-out marks were in blue ink. To the other's surprise, Harley reach into his sports jacket pocket and withdrew a magnifying glass. On applying it to the scribbled off area he squinted staring through the lens. The focused stare's duration stretched out longer than the others expected. Finally, Harley set the folder down on his lap. He pulled out a notepad and jotted down a notation. Eric and Parker almost stopped breathing, waiting for an update from Harley. He stretched out their wait time flipping through and reading the entire file. Finally, he spoke, "Looks like Leon Log... reported seeing someone outside the house. Does the name ring a bell, Eric?"

"Actually, it does. Eric answered. He added, "That would be Leon Logan. A local lobsterman and rumoured cohort of Barnie Madison. I've heard they go back years. Old school buds."

Harley asked, "Can I see a sample of the Sergeant's handwriting?"

Eric answered, "First five pages are in my hand. Check out pages six through nine. Robert did those while reviewing my write up."

Harley flipped back to page six and eyed the writing with interest. Pages seven, eight and nine received the same treatment. Eric looked away as Harley flipped slowly through all the pages snapping cell phone photos of each page in the folder. He then flipped the file closing it. Harley asked, "Just one more favour, could I get a colour copy of pages six through nine, the Sergeant's?" Eric nodded a positive response then took the folder and disappeared. On his return with the requested copies, he passed them to Harley. A silent thanks was exchanged. Harley folded the copies and stuffed them in his jacket pocket. He stood and said, "You never saw us today. And my eyes never scanned the pages of this file. Right?"

Eric replied, "Absolutely, inspector. And give the Café a visit tomorrow. No, you'd best go there the day after. Ask for Ginni, Virginia, she's my gal and works there. Leon hangs out there often. You can trust my Ginni."

"I will." Harley replied. He asked, "Is there any reason you can think of that would put Leon out in the middle of the night close enough to the Lamont house that he could..."

Eric cut in, "Absolutely none Inspector. It's in a residential area away from the waterfront. Maybe if he was..."

Harley cut in, "Maybe if he was standing guard. Keeping an eye out for the safety of the real arsonist?"

"Yes. That could be."

Harley stood up. Parker followed his lead. Parting exchanges took place and they headed back over to East River and Gilbert's house. Harley stowed the file copies in his glove compartment. On stepped out of their vehicles Parker injected, "Just my thoughts. But if the Detachment's sergeant is running interference on the main suspect, well I'd say your chances of busting him are slim to non-existent."

"Agreed." Harley answered with anger in his voice. Years past he'd encountered a similar situation in the rape cases of several young Chester women. A fact that riled Harley on each new dawning he awakened to.

Parker offered up an alternative solution, "What if there was another way to break the bastard? A fail-safe way in this modern day of new edge technologies?"

Harley laughed aloud, "If you're talking DNA-RNA there's no evidence that'll stand up in court. It got conveniently misplaced over the years."

"Then hear me out my friend. The evidence we need does exist. You sat down and shared a fantastic Christmas Feast in its company earlier today. If you catch my drif…"

Harley slammed the roof of his vehicle and hollered, "Son of a Bitch! We've got the bastard. At least two if not more of his offspring are alive and walking the streets of Chester and East River. And sadly, another is buried in a local cemetery."

"We'll need to get their DNA and officially get it tested without you know who gaining knowledge of our activities." Parker added.

Harley nodded agreement. He committed, "We'll need to talk with Anya and Maria. He asked, "In your early days of criminal defense practice, friend, our paths crossed on a number of occasions. You were one of the defense attorneys I hated going up against in cases that got to the courts. However, at this moment I'm elated to have you on my side, friend. Why did you step away from criminal law and step into family law?"

Parker grimaced then answered, "The likes of Robert Stratford for a starter. A bad dude, my friend. I felt vindicated on nailing him on behalf of his ex-wife. She's recovered from the past abuses and remarried. Yes! It's cases like that one that make my work so rewarding."

Harley embraced Parker. He released Parker and they walked across Gilbert's yard. Parker eyeballed the truck and trailer parked next to the side deck. Harley grinned while watching Parker's reactions to the truck and its trailer's painted exteriors. Loud Christmas music called out to them from inside the house. They stepped inside and rejoined an ongoing Christmas gala celebration. Easily they blended in. Nobody mentioned Harley's short absence or Parker's arrival.

Harley quickly found himself on the dance floor being passed partner to partner non-stop. Even Megan gave him a twirl about the floor to a hyped-up Christmas Rap number he'd never heard before. But given the age factor it could be considered a given. With grace, he escaped the dance floor. On leaving, Harley's heart skipped a beat. He'd spotted Megan and Taylor on the dance floor moving and jiving with an energy he often savored in dancing with his wife Bev. He savored the recollection as the twins launched his spirits skyward. It became obvious to Harley the siblings were elated with the brand-new clothes they'd discovered early that Christmas morning and the Christmas cheer that embraced everyone in the house. Then Parker caught his eye. He'd quickly found himself a sought-out dance partner. Or did that partner find him? Auntie Lila definitely was the mover and shaker on the floor. And Parker, to his credit, was keeping pace with her moves. Laughter off in the den caught Harley's attention. He followed its call. On stepping into the den, Bailey drew his attention. Stretched out in what appeared to be a semi-comatose state, the fisty old feline appeared to have just burped then his tail rose up erratically off the floor only to drop back down again. A half empty saucer of golden liquid sat on the floor, inches from Bailey's nose. Harley shook his head in wonderment. Bailey confirmed his suspicions and let rip a sharp raspy series of snorts. Jeffery jumped off his chair and ran to Harley's side. He asked, "Did ya see that? Bailey farted and there wasn't any kick to it? It's incredible. The scary thing bees it's the same ting fer us men!"

Harley stared at Jeffery with a questioning look in his eye. He answered, "No. I can't say I've noticed."

Jeffery shouted over to Moses, "Git yer arse over here, Moses. We got ourselves a situation!" Moses strolled over and joined the pair. Jeffery stated, "Moses, you ate one of them Turkey-Sorus-Dino-Rexious thighs right. I knows I sure did. It was delicious. But there's something wrong."

"And what would that be?" Moses asked. He added before Jeffery could answer, "Didn't you like the meal? I'm not complaining. But you'd be the absolute first to raise an issue."

Jeffery frowned then replied. "I absolutely loved it. Every last bite. Best turkey I've ever had to be honest."

"Then, what's the problem?"

Jeffery smirked then stated, "I can't fart. Well, no I can pass wind. But there's absolutely no kick to it! If you catch my drift? Same ting holds true for all us old farts and youngsters gathered together for a good after dinner rum and a good chat. We just can't fart like we should be! I'm concerned!"

"Why are you concerned, me son. I take it to be you can still fart, you're firing off rounds like never before. Right?" Moses declared.

Jeffery frowned then replied, "I just got me life together. Engaged to the love of my life and I'm going to be a daddy! I don't want' a die!"

Moses stared at Jeffery in total disbelief. Before he could reply Jeffery added, "Women and men are different. Their innards I means. They're more refined and don't fart. Or if they do, their innards process it better than a man's can. If you catch my drift. Gilbert, Pappy and me, why, before today on stepping away from the Christmas table, mom and Gillie's Karyn would boot the lot of us out'ta de dining-room before our innards started to kick into high gear. Boys we sure could clear a room in no time flat! So, you can see why I'm so concerned. It's obvious. I can't fart like I used to fart. And there's no kick to my farts!"

Moses gazed at Jeffery in wonderment. Could it be that the recipe deployed in today's stuffing and gravy could be a flop? In reflection he pondered, could odorless farting drive men's stress levels skyward through the roof. Expose them to higher risk of stroke and heart attacks. He swore in contemplating the failure of a potential mega-million-dollar royalty generator. Ideas flashed through his head. How can I sell the lad on the benefits of odorless farts? Suddenly, it hit Moses full force. He broke into a joyous smile and boasted, "Fear not, young laddie. It's a known fact in ninety-eight percent of relationships the women live longer. Their farts don't stink. Right?"

"Absolutely!" Jeffery replied with confidence.

"Then relax my son. If the symptoms you've encountered today hold true. Your life-line has just been extended." Moses declared with assertion.

"Oh, thanks ye, Lordie, fer working this miracle today. We men have been truly blessed in celebrating your son's birth." Jeffery boasted in replying. He then abandoned Moses and walked off to refill his glass with more rum. Moses downed his glass of rum in one shot. Then slipped off down the hall, pulled out his cell phone and speed dialed his son. The call went into voice mail. Moses posted a message after the beep, "Son calls me first chance ya gits. I got us a winner. Odorless farts. No! I'm not kidding it'll be the winner we been searching fer. Catch ya later. Love Pop."

Richard sought out Moses. On seeing him disconnect his cell call he approached and asked, "That Turkey Blaster it did an amazing job on the beast of a turkey you fired up in it!"

Oya That the Blaster does thanks to our son. The boy is an engineer and mechanical genius to say the least."

The den's occupants, on hearing Moses' comments, formed a close circle around him. He continued. "Great Granddaddy's wood fired oven died off while the lad was off in university. But that never stopped me, son, from coming through fer his daddy. Granddaddy's stove had an oven that could handle two of our heavyweight birds. Winter was approaching and our Christmas season would 'a been a total disaster if it weren't fer me oldest lad. Made our need his major dissertation or whatever. Anyways, once he'd solidified his theories with de blessing of his professor, he took a leave of absence. The three of us - him, junior and me - brought his ideas ta life, we dun did. The first test runs needed a touch of fine tuning but, in the end, we had us a winner. Then our daughter Faith stepped in and added de finishing touches. She sure is the artistic one in our clan. A real sharp artist she be. Jest peek outside at the Blaster's paint job. It's a wonder fer sure." Moses ended with a proud grin pasted ear to ear across his face.

John asked, "That beast on the plater or should I say blaster tray, how do you get them to the size you do? I've never seen a turkey, if that's what you call them, that big! Its taste was amazing. Two or three could feed an entire army."

"If and only iff'in they had themselves a Turkey Blaster me son." Moses answered. He added, "Our patent is still pending approval. And size? Why the one we fed off 'a Georgio were but a wee lad. We ween the small ones off fer use in our Buzzard's Mountain Gift Shop Restaurant. The three we're working towards becoming challengers fer the world title of de world's record AKA de largest turkey ever? Day before we left home our biggest Tom, Thomas, tipped de scales at seventy-four pounds, he did!"

"Away with you!" Harley shouted out. Then asked, "What's the record right now?"

Moses grinned boldly then announced, "Current record holder tipped de scales at eighty-six pounds. But given time our Thomas will be hitting that and a touch more early in de new year!"

Richard, John and Norman kept Moses busy with a barrage of questions centered on the mechanics behind the Turkey Blaster. Norman's questions on the other hand centered on the birds and how their abnormal sizes were achieved along with the birds' health. Their ability to handle the abnormal weights they bore. On that question Moses simply grinned with pride and said, "Lad you'd best ask Bailey that question. The kitty got chased off with a batch of our birds in pursuit of de poor kitty cat. Gotta says, our Thomas sure did us proud. Why, he flittered and ran so fast I dun near thought de bugger would take flight. Now that would 'a been a sight to see." Moses' audience flew into fits of laughter and partial disbelief in the tale been spun.

Until Richard claimed, "It's true. I was there and saw Thomas and his buds chasing poor Bailey. My God, they were fast. You were there, Norman."

"That I was, Rich. I'm a veterinarian approaching graduation but, trust me, I'll not raise the tale on returning to class in the new year. I'd be the brunt of a ton of jibbing for sure." Their grouping chuckled loudly amongst themselves.

Harley and Parker paused briefly on passing them and hearing the laughter. They then waved back in stepping out of the den. In a private discussion they'd come to the conclusion it was time to chat with Anya and Maria off to the side. Back in the living-room they smiled on seeing the twins lost in entertaining themselves with the many toys and games under the Christmas tree with Auntie Lila and Mary in their company. Hope, Eugette, and Lyndsey were together chatting away with occasional bursts of laughter rising up highlighting their topics of discussion. Spotting Anya and Maria together on the loveseat, Harley led the way over to their side. He stooped down and cut into their chat. "Excuse me, ladies. Could we have a conversation in private."

Maria paled. She gazed at Harley then turned back to Anya with a frightened look painted on her face. Anya took Maria's hands in hers. She said, "Maybe it would be best if we did, Maria. With everything that's been unfolding I'm thinking we should."

Maria nibbled on her lower lip nervously. Anya stood up and motioned Maria to follow her lead. She did and together they followed Harley and Parker out of the room. In the kitchen Harley took the lead. He suggested, "Could we take our chat over to the homestead? It would be best I'm thinking."

Anya nodded approval. She embraced Maria and whispered, "I'm here with you, girl. We can do this." She then retrieved their outerwear. The men grabbed theirs. Outside, Harley led the way to his vehicle. A short drive landed them over at Jeffery's. Maria pulled out her key and unlocked the door. She'd finally, with Auntie Lila's backing, convinced Jeffery to lock the door when the house was unoccupied. She led them off into the sunroom. Everyone slipped out of their coats and jackets.

Seated Harley opened the conversation. "First, ladies, I apologize for my failure to slam the door shut on the bastard that raped you. He was protected by forces beyond my resources. However, I intend no, I will, with Parker's assistance, deliver a form of justice to you both before I retire."

Maria stared blankly at Harley. In total fear she asked, "Will my baby, my Eugee have to know the truth?" A silence befell the sunroom. Anya wrapped Maria in her arms. She pulled her tightly to her body and whispered, "Maria. We've suffered too long undeservedly. My August suffered more. Let's work together and make everything right." Anya released Maria.

Maria whispered, "But my baby, her babies will hate me!" Anya reached out and embraced Maria. Their hug each extolled deep emotions. Maria pleaded, "Did your August hate you Any…"

"No. She loved me with every breath she took. Every beat of her heart. Just like you have loved your Eugette and her babies. You did what had to be done. We survived and are living in a different world. Today's world is so much more accommodating to women living through the circumstances we survived. Trust me, Maria. Sadly, my August suffered the added horror and hatred that racial bigotry cast upon her."

"Really?" Maria pleaded.

"Yes. Really. Like you, I love and cherish the love of my children. Without them, would life been kinder? I'd never have felt his or her heartbeat within my body. Never felt their eagerly sought and treasured thumps bouncing off the inner walls of my baby belly. We gave them birth. We held them in our arms and nursed them, loved them beyond all physical and emotional comprehension. We're mothers. Your Eugette's a mother. Like us, she knows the passions motherhood encompasses."

Maria's eyes locked into Anya's. She asked, "Does your Norman know? Does he…"

"Yes, like I said earlier, my Norman knows. Memories out of the past resurfaced on our moving back home. To my horror, Norman confessed he'd witnessed my second sexual assault and beating. Trust me, my Normie loves his mom to the moon and back. Just like your Eugette and her amazing babies love you, their grammie, beyond the moon and back."

Maria pulled herself back together. Anya dabbed away the watery remnants of Maria's tears. She looked over to Harley and Parker and stated, "I'm ready. Let's make things right. But please give me a little time to process the truth I've hidden behind far too long before forcing me to confess it to my baby. My Eugette."

Harley knelt down at Maria's side. He reassured her, "Maria! That bastard needs to feel the consequences of his long past actions. He believes himself invincible and beyond the reach of justice's arm. He is my nemesis. He's thwarted my career. If anyone failed you ladies, you're looking at him. It's me. But on my word, and with Parker's assistance, we're goanna nail the Bastard where it'll hurt the most."

Parker joined Harley kneeling down at Anya's side. He reassured Maria, "Take the time you need to process and deal with what we're asking. To some the actions we are asking could appear simple. They're not. And those thinking that way have not walked in your shoes or lived the consequences life has dealt you. He believes he's untouchable. He's not. Take some time. We're here for you and yours. Hear me out. Take some time. Then, when ready, tell us what to do. Meanwhile, we'll be working to bring it all together if that becomes your chosen path."

Maria nodded her head in agreement. Anya stated, "I'm there with you, Maria. Where do we go from here, Inspector Kingston?"

"Please, call me Harley."

"And call me Parker. And where's the coffee? I could use one," Parker added.

Maria pulled free of Anya, stood and walked into the kitchen. She busied herself setting a brew of drip coffee in motion. The others joined her in the kitchen. On serving a round of coffee to everyone, Maria joined them sitting at the kitchen table. She grinned and said, "Fire away. I'm ready to listen."

Harley stated, "He's connected. Filth like him survive because of connections. And he definitely has some big ones."

Parker jumped in, "Not to worry ladies." He added, "I suspect you've caught an odd crime show on the telly once or twice. Connections can open doors for the guilty to walk free. However, science has progressed light years with new developments surfacing almost daily. Forensic Science does not lie. And it will nail the bastard for his past actions."

Anya injected, "But my second assault failed when all the evidence vanished!"

"True!" Harley responded. "But the truth is living proof. Alive and ready to deliver its knock-out TKO punch on your behalf, ladies."

"My Eugette's DNA?" Maria blurted out.

Parker added, "And Anya's Norman, and August if needed."

The kitchen fell silent. The ladies stared into each other's eyes. A moment then two slipped by. Maria broke the silence. She firmly replied. "I'll need a little time. My Jeffery's involved, we're engaged, I'm pregnant. He knows my hidden past, but in moving forward he has to buy in. Will my pregnancy go against us?"

"No! Definitely no." Parker replied with firm conviction.

Anya interrupted, "Inspector…"

"Please, Harley works."

"Ok. Harley. In chatting with Gilbert the other day, a memory popped up. I recalled how back in our early school days Madison and his trolls were schoolyard bullies we all feared. One day he let loose with a barrage of racial slurs and yes, the N word flew unimpeded. Karyn, Gilbert's to be wife took a stand. She stared him down and let loose a vicious left hook. It landed and broke Madison's nose. He landed flat on his back crying like a baby. Then, and I just remembered it, Kiki, well Kimberly Tobias burst into laughter and we all joined in."

"Interesting." Harley said.

"More interesting!" Anya said then added, "Kiki, if you recall Maria, also ended up like us.

Everyone stared intently at Anya. Parker asked, "Is she still a local? We should contact her. Madison's actions, could it be revenge?"

Maria answered, "Local if Lunenburg is local. I've bumped into her while in Lunenburg on occasion. Never married still a Tobias."

Harley eagerly jotted down notations in his notepad. He raised his coffee mug and emptied it in one final sampling of its java contents. Parker followed his lead. Parker suggested, "Take the time needed. We're here and can be easily contacted. And yes, we definitely will track down Kimberly. Now I suggest we head back to Gilbert's before we're missed." Nobody disagreed. Maria and Anya cleared the table, then they all grabbed their outerwear and stepped outside. Harley drove them all back to Gilbert's. Along the way, Harley asked Maria for names of neighbours that kept late night hours and may have witnessed something or someone out and about the night of the fire. Maria fell silent in deep thought. On their arrival at Gilbert's, she fired off a list of six names. Harley pulled out his pen and notepad and asked Maria to repeat the names. She did and glanced at Harley's notepad as he held it out for her to confirm. She nodded a yes and the pad and pen disappeared back into Harley's jacket. Together they rejoined the Christmas celebrations still in full swing at Gilbert's

....

Christmas in East River stretches out well beyond the constraints placed on it in big cities and large towns. Work commitments along with scheduled travel plans force many to escape the relaxation offered up by the holiday season and leap eagerly right back into the work-a-day reality life offers up to most adults. School and educational commitments treat its participants to a similar ending to their holiday seasons.

Harley sensing victory over his career's nemesis extended his stay with one simple call into his office. Retirement incentives had on numerous occasions been dangled in attempts to ease him out of active duty. A widower, Harley's life focused totally on work. And on specific cases that he'd failed to close during a storied career. A chance encounter with Gilbert and a working lunch had drawn him back home to East

River. With Parker Rose' services backing him, Harley could almost taste his retirement. Life in Chester quickly shifted out of festive mode. He slipped away and first headed over to Maria's old neighbourhood. There he spent the better part of the morning knocking on doors and interviewing Maria's old neighbours. The process got dragged out longer than expected when he encountered friends and old schoolmates out of his past. Harley Kingston was a good old Chester boy. Born and raised in the Southshore town years past. Several commitments were made to meet up and chat about the good old days. The commitments and encounters energized Harley's day.

Satisfied, he headed over to the local RCMP Detachment. He'd called Constable Eric Johnson earlier and confirmed that Robert Stratford was manning the Detachment's operations solo. A traffic incident had pulled all the junior officers out to the scene. The scenario fit Harley's plans to a T. On arrival he parked and headed into the detachment. An icy cold exchange unfolded between the two seasoned police officers.

Harley asked, "Enjoy your time off over the holidays, Stratford? Your family must have been elated you'd been able to join their Christmas gathering."

Robert Stratford's icy glare deepened its intensity. Harley fired a second volley, "Your exes' new man must have been overjoyed having you join their seasonal celebration!"

"Fuck you, Kingston. My personal time is my time."

"Not when you go calling on good people Christmas morning, making unjustified allegations, attempting to drag them off to be interrogated on unfounded charges. The Lamont family has suffered enough due to your incompetence!"

"I have a witness. A witness that places one of your innocents at the scene of the arson. A reliable witness, I'll have you know. Not that you're familiar with that term!"

Harley stared down Stratford then challenged him, "Bring your reliable witness in. I'm still working the Martin Lamont and Russel Walker murder case."

"Fuck you! That case is closed. A tragic loss of two men to a raging sea."

"Not in my books. In my books the arson case and young Eugette's reasons for fleeing Chester tie in nicely with the murder!"

Stratford slid his hand down towards his holster and its pistol. Harley chuckled aloud. He sneered and boasted, "Go for it, fool. You never could best me on the firing range." The two men starred each other down. It ended on Harley twisting about and walking towards the exit door. There he shouted, "I have three upstanding citizens of Chester willing to swear your witness was seen fleeing the arson scene in the company of a well-known felon. Their testimony, I assure you, will influence any jury they testify before in court!" With that said, Harley open the detachment's door and stepped outside. Back in his vehicle a feeling of victory energized his spirits. A twist of the key started the engine.

In heading back towards East River and Gilbert's, Harley drove over to the arson scene. He stopped and stared in anger at the vacant lot. White snow covered most of the burnt remains of the Lamont house. Four heavily burnt studs reached skyward, marking where the house once stood. A home that Harley knew had suffered far too much heartache and tragedy. The seasoned inspector drove off, determined to deliver the justice that circumstance and ill placed connections had denied him in the past. In passing the entrance to Jeffery's and the old McClaken homestead, Harley's determination took on a new intensity. He arrived at Gilbert's and parked next to a familiar purple pickup truck. The memories it rekindled relieved Harley of his built-up tensions. Once up on the deck, he glanced through the kitchen door's window and spotted Gilbert and Parker at the table playing a lively game of cribbage. A loud rap on the door drew their attention to him. The cribbage players waved him inside. Gilbert stood and ran off, returning quickly with an empty rum glass in hand. He filled it to Harley's standard. Then a threesome cribbage match got underway. Loud, boastful pegging points were declared around the table. An occasional cry for a refill rose up from beneath the table. Meow...meeow! The cribbage combatants took turns topping up all the glasses in play along with Bailey's saucer. Around midnight Bailey's calls for refills vanished and he slipped away beckoned off into dreamland by the Sandman.

....

Back in Chester, Sergeant Robert Stratford's shift ended with backup from the Lunenburg Detachment. The accident scene had cleared earlier but in normal fashion the paperwork extended everyone's day. Robert twisted the ignition key of his personal vehicle then drove away from the detachment to an isolated location that he knew would display coverage bars on the cell phone he'd absconded from the evidence room. The call he was about to make required an element of untraceable privacy. The cell had never been registered as evidence. Hence it could not be traced back to him. On hitting the last number, the line's other end sang out. "Barnie here."

Robert barked out, "We have a problem, my son!"

"You got a problem, my son. You crossed the line. Nothing is traceable back to the Barnster! Asshole."

Robert sneered shouting back, "Your old nemesis is back in town. I will assume the name Harley Kingston rings a bell? If not for certain favours you'd be nothing today. Actually, you'd be in a six by twelve cell snivelling for protection from those who've been doing your dirty work."

Barnie shouted back "Son of a bitch. Take the bastard down. I'll pay whatever it takes."

"Not going to happen. I've got issues with the bastard. But I'll not be doing your dirty work this time around. Now Jives and Logan, That's a different story. Kingston's got witnesses willing to swear your boys were in the neighbourhood the night of the fire. And they'll swear on a stack of bibles that they weren't witnesses to the Lamont bitch torching her own house!"

"Son of a BITCH. Jives and Logan gotta be dealt with take them out. I can't afford to have those idiots being interrogated and shooting off their mouths about town. Round them up! I'll get Arnie to make things happen. But get it done A.S.A.P., ok? You know the drill."

Robert pondered the options. First check box would see his nemesis on the other end of the line taken down. Eliminated! But without access to the records and dirt the son of a bitch had stashed away that option was a definite no go. Option number two would work. But only if its action figure was also taken out. Robert knew he'd crossed the line gone dirty and that more than just his pension and service time were at risk. If he failed to handle it right he could end up the one doing time in the big house. And that was not an option he was willing to risk seeing himself caught up in. He shouted back into the cell phone, "OK! Get a hold of Arnie. I'm on board. Call back on this number and I'll round up Jives and Logan."

Barnie snickered into his receiver's mouthpiece. He loved it when a plan of action fell smoothly into place. He recovered from the snickering and answered, "Not a problem. Besides, they were actually a little stupid in taking care of the business that had been put in their hands. The idiots told Chad that they suspected they'd been seen by a neighbour of the Lamont bitch while they were getting the action underway. Make things go away and I'll get you the standard ten,"

Robert fired back, "Best make it twenty grand. This mess is just too screwed up!"

Barnie growled, "OK! But you'd best take care of it quickly." He then slammed the receiver down. Anger seethed through his entire body. He strutted over to the fridge and yanked the door open. On retrieving a cold beer in one hand, Barnie slammed the door shut with his other hand, A pull on the can's tab exposed its contents. In one simple thrust of the can to his lips followed by a backwards tilt of his head emptied the can. The action ended with a robust belch and firing of the empty can across the room. Barnie grabbed his nontraceable cell phone and retrieved Arnie's cell number. The simple press of a button activated the ringer at the line's other end.

....

Anticipation energized itself with Christmas fading into the background. The driveway looked empty with the departure of Moses and Mary with the Turkey Blaster in tow. Their visit down off Buzzard Mountain to Gilbert's home and East River had set a new Christmas Tradition in motion. That being the year store bought turkey's vanished from the McClaken grocery lists. Before Christmas totally fell from sight, it ignited thoughts of New Year's Eve celebrations and the frequent short lifespan of planned New Year's Resolutions. To that end, Harley dragged his newfound sidekick off to the local café. There, over coffees, he started to updated Parker on a new lead in their case. Ginni cut him off short before the two men could chat.

"Excuse me, sir, you stopped in the other day asking about Rene Jives and Leon Logan and I thought you should know that they've vanished."

Harley connected eye to eye with Ginni. He picked up on her nervous edge. "Yes, Ginni, I did stop in. And thanks for the information you shared, it's helped. Is it unusual for Jives and Logan to drop out of sight?"

Ginni frowned then answered. "Actually, I don't mind the fact that they've vanished. Of the two, Rene creeps me out the most. But don't tell my Eric. Rene is creepy and he's constantly hitting on me. Well, need I say more?"

"No, Ginni, and I won't go blabbing to Eric. When were they last here at the café?"

"The day after you stopped in to chat. I wouldn't know had the girls not updated me. They know how much Rene creeps me out. Sally mentioned he'd tried to hit, no he actually did hit on her and a customer broke it up. Rene fled the café with Leon on his tail. The strange thing being they have not returned since that incident. Sally is off shift today. But I could give her your card. If you have another to spare?"

Harley reached into his sports jacket and retrieved a business card holder. He passed a card to Ginni. She smiled and said, "Could I have a few? Sally and I aren't the only ones. And I hesitate to tell Eric. You know he might..."

Harley frowned this time. He slipped several more business cards out of the holder and passed them to Ginni. He took on a solid good cop, fatherly look and said, "Ginni, what I'm hearing is wrong. And should not be happening. How often are we talking about?"

"I'd best get back to my counter. It's getting busy."

"Ginni?" Harley said with conviction.

"Let's just say only my Eric gets to touch what that pair and their cohorts are grabbing." With that Ginni twisted about and walked back to the counter. She slipped Harley's cards into a pocket then assisted a co-worker in filling customer orders. Back at the booth she'd just left Harley's disposition expressed itself all over his face.

Parker rapped twice on the table to interrupt Harley's thoughts. He succeeded. Harley spoke his deep thoughts, "Friend it's cutting too deep. But this time, thank God the victims are ready and willing to walk the line."

"Meaning Anya Trinity and Maria Lamont?"

Harley grimaced then replied, "No. There's more. One I always suspected was also victimized back in the day. Anya's comment the other day jogged my memory. That's why I felt nudged to drag you out'ta the house over here to chat it up, my friend." Harley paused. He took a casual glance about the café. Nobody was seated near them. He lowered his voice and said, "I suspected a third highschooler had been victimized back in the day. Anya's recollection the other day. The name spoken aloud jogged my memory. Kimberly Tobias. I tracked her down, And, yes, she's living in Lunenburg as Maria mentioned. I've arranged for us to meet up with her and talk. She's ready to do what she couldn't do back then.

Parker grinned then replied, "Ok. When and where?"

Harley sipped his coffee; He frowned since it had gone cold. He stood and said, "In the vehicle, Parker. And I think I need a refill." Both men stood then walked towards the counter.

A smiling Ginni greeted them, "Thank for stopping in, Mister Kingston. Have a nice day."

Harley smiled back, "I will, Ginni. But our mugs went cold. Could I have two refills to go?"

"Absolutely!" Ginni busied herself putting together Harley's two refills then placed them on the counter in front of him. Harley reached for his wallet. Ginni blushed and said, "My treat, Mister Kingston. Catch you later."

Harley picked up both coffees, turned and joined Parker at the door. On stepping outside, he passed Parker his coffee. Back in the vehicle Harley updated Parker on his newest informant's details. "Today Kimberly Tobias would be a respected member in any community. Back in the day she was different." Parker nodded signalling that he read the message being conveyed. Harley continued, "She was basically an outcast. Schoolmates, the community and sadly her parents. Only her brother stood by her side. A true sibling. Had the officer in charge deployed common sense he'd have quickly realized that a young lesbian highschooler was highly unlikely to be on the make or looking to go for a roll in the hay with the likes of her main source of berating bully Barnabas aka Barnie Madison. Yes, like his other victims she ended up pregnant and had a child. A son. With the support of several partners and her brother that son is now a happily married man and a father. He knows the storyline. The family is behind her and ready to back Anya and Maria in moving forward."

Parker injected, "We'll be needing paternity testing to certify the facts through the son and mother's DNA."

"Not a question." Harley replied. "They are on board and ready. Been to Lunenburg lately, my son?"

"Actually, it's been years since I last visited Lunenburg."

"Then you're in for a treat. It's a beautiful town," Harley answered. Throughout the drive to Lunenburg conversation drifted off the case and back onto Harley's recollections of the Christmas Feast at Gilbert's. Many bouts of hearty laughter erupted throughout the drive. Harley asked, "Did Jeffery question you about farts with no kick?"

"Oh my God! Yes, and more than once. The look on the poor bewildered lad's face. It was priceless! Then the storyteller Moses stepped in and set the lad at ease. Can't help thinking old Moses had an ulterior motive up his sleeve in setting Jeffery's mind at ease."

Harley chuckled aloud confirming he aligned with Parker's train of thought. Up ahead signage announced their approach to the Town of Lunenburg. The vehicle fell silent. Harley savored the memories triggered into the moment by the bright vibrant colours of the houses and businesses they drove past. Beverley had been a Lunenburg gal, born and bred. The recollections eased some of the tensions arising as their case moved forward. Parker, on the other hand liked the towns look, but couldn't imagine painting his home in any of the colours jumping out at him. In reflection he suspected his neighbour Otto, would report him to local authorities in short order if he painted his house a 'la Lunenburg.

The vehicle stopped in front of a century home painted in vibrant yellows with blue trim. The men stepped out of the vehicle. On walking up to the door, they noticed a woman glancing out the window at them. Harley pressed the doorbell twice. Footsteps were heard approaching the door. It opened.

"Inspector? Inspector Kingston?"

"Yes. That is me." Harley answered. He added, "Harley works for me just fine. And you are Kimberly?"

"Yes, I am. Is your companion the lawyer you mentioned?"

"He is, Kimberly. Let me introduce Parker Rose, Attorney. We're working together on this case."

"Please come in." Kimberly answered and stepped aside while her guest entered the house. She led them off into the kitchen. "Take a chair, please. May I offer you a tea or would you prefer a coffee?"

Parker answered, "Actually a tea would be good."

Harley added, "Yes, please make that two teas."

Once the kettle had boiled and the tea set to steeping Kimberly joined them at the table. She sighed then spoke, "I love my son and his family more than life itself. But not the shunning and outcastings, my what can I say? Sexual leanings exposed me to back in high school. Well no. I'd best confess I was different right from the get-go." Kimberly paused and poured three cups of tea. Parker accepted her offer to add a dash of cream. Harley kept his black. Both men nodded and Kimberly continued. "My parent and most of the community never took to who I was, who I am. Paul, my brother Paul, has backed me throughout life. But you really want to know about my history. Right?"

Harley answered, "In your time Kimberly. We're working to close out..."

"Then I'd best just keep on talking." Kimberly injected. She continued, "That Madison, Barnie. If you weren't in his circle or were different then the Lord best have mercy on you. Today kids like me have a shot at being accepted. Back then, for the most part I didn't have a hope in hell. Yes, the bastard raped me. Claimed he was going to cure me. Give me more than the average woman could handle. And yes. He knocked me up. I believe that was the term my condition was listed under. Right up until I started to show, the bastard would taunt me. *'Want some more sweet cheeks.'*"

Harley injected, "We are truly sorry for everything you were forced to endure."

"Thank you, Harley, Parker. Where do we go from here? I am ready to make him pay for his actions."

Parker started to answer, "We'll need a..."

"A DNA test from me and my son Keith. Consider it done. Keith is in Halifax. Where would I go?"

Harley pulled out several business card and passed them over to Kimberly. Parker followed his lead. He said, "Have Keith call me and I'll get it set up. We will contact you with details for your testing." He looked over to Kimberly and said, "Thank you for agreeing to take action. We need your participation. And Kimberly, we will make him pay."

Everyone stood and handshakes were exchanged. Harley and Parker set off back to East River. On return, they found the house and driveway empty. Parker accepted an invitation to join Harley in a visit with his parents in Chester. A satisfying day drew to a quiet conclusion.

CHAPTER 49

    Gilbert felt strange driving away from the house with it in darkness beyond the entry lighting and interior lamps on timers. However, Anya had extended an invitation that received a welcomed embrace. Hope, he recalled, had chided him into giving Anya an opportunity to open her home up to some lingering seasonal cheer. All it took had been a simple smile and glance at his daughter's dimples. On arriving he grinned on spotting Jeffery's truck and John's SUV. He'd anticipated an evening out with Hope, hosted by Anya and Norman. On stepping up onto the front porch the door swung open. Anya stood there with her arms extended in a welcoming greeting, one Gilbert quickly embraced. Hope slipped past them and headed off in search of Norman. She found him in the kitchen overseeing their meal's final preparations. Anya released Gilbert and together they joined the guests gathered in the living-room.
    In the kitchen, Hope grinned watching Norman's adroit maneuvers in the kitchen. On sensing her presence Norman twisted about and a physical greeting ensued. It ended on Anya returning with Gilbert in tow. The youngsters were shooed off into the living-room to join the main gathering. They found the twins gazing in awe at a sepia portrait of a beautiful young teenaged girl. Megan twisted about and on spotting Norman asked, "Who is she, Normie? She's so pretty."
    Norman smiled and walked over to the portrait. He raised a hand to it after having kissed its fingers. The fingers touched the girl's cheek. Gazing at the photo he said, "She's my baby sister, August. And yes, she is beautiful."

Taylor asked, "Will she be joining us for supper?"

Norman bit his lower lip. Then said, "August is with us in our hearts. But she won't be joining us for supper Taylor. She's gone home to be with Gramma and Grampa."

Lighthearted conversations floated around the room. Norman stepped away then returned shortly with a bundle of board games in hand. Chinese Checkers ended up the game of choice. Play quickly got underway. Richard and Lyndsey joined the game. The leader took quick control of the game.

On hearing Anya call out, "Come and get it. Supper's ready." Megan was declared the winner. Everyone arose and headed into the dining-room. There, a huge crockpot called out with its alluring aromas. Norman took on serving duties. Once everyone had been served, he sat.

Anya said grace, "Lord thank you for drawing Norman and me back home. I fought your will at first. But your gentle nudges through our August succeeded and here we are gathered together with good friends and companions. We thank you for your love and caring ways, and the good food we are about to eat. Blessings to all and welcome to our home. Amen."

Everyone reached out with fork in hand eager to taste the aromas wafting about the dining-room. Lyndsey quickly called out, "Wow! Anya your Mac and Cheese is great. And the scallops and bacon are absolutely divine!"

Anya replied, "Thanks, Lyndsey. There's one more key ingredient you missed. Care to guess?"

Everyone sampled a new bite in earnest. To everyone's surprise John called out first, "It's clams. Right Anya?"

"Absolutely right, John. It's an old family tradition that I grew up with back in the day. At times I'd give mom a frown on seeing it served up at mealtime. But in hindsight, I confess, I love it!" Complements flew about the table. Quickly the crockpot emptied. Post meal refreshments were served along with Tea Towel Peach Pie. Then Richard and Lyndsey cleared the table and loaded up the dishwasher. Once its start button was hit a new round of Chinese Checkers got underway in the dining-room. Maria and Eugette held back, taking on observer roles.

Maria led Eugette off into the living-room. Their hands touched in a mother-daughter bond. Eugette tensed up on seeing Maria's eyes water up. She asked, "What's wrong mom?"

Maria released her lips from the nervous bite that had possessed them momentarily. She whispered, "I have a confession that…"

"I know mom. You're pregnant."

"Yes. But there's something else. There's a lie I've been living and it's been too long. The truth must be spoken."

Eugette shuddered then whispered in fear, "Tell, me you're ok Mom. You just gotta be ok!"

Unnoticed, two supporters slowly and quietly made their way into the living-room. A supportive halfmoon separated the pair from the dining-room. Maria pulled her daughter's hands up to her lips. "Sweetheart, I love you more than life itself. Years ago. Math doesn't lie, sweetheart. I was thirteen and I was raped."

Eugette stared in shock at her mom. She demanded, "Who mom? Who raped you? Was it dad? That's ok, you loved each other. To the moon and back. I get it."

"No sweetheart. It was not your dad."

"Then who mom. Who raped you?"

Maria shivered uncontrollably. With tears streamed down her cheeks, she confessed, "Barnie Madison."

Shock hit Eugette full force. Ashamed, she whispered his name in anger on breaking free of the horror that raced through her body unimpeded. She stared with questioning eyes at her mom. Then blurted, "But dad loved me. He raised me by your side. It cannot be, mom. I won't let it." A silent anger flashed across the room. Shivers raced throughout her body. Recollection of the beating she'd been subjected to raced violently through her mind. A horrifying reality struck a chord. Eugette sobbed, "That bastard's blood is in me. It's in my babies!"

Maria stared at Eugette through watery eyes. She stepped forward but Eugette cringed and inched away from Maria. In desperation she pleaded, "I was thirteen, barely a teenager. I was home alone. The bastard broke into our home and raped me. Not once, not twice but three times! I was totally naïve. To me sex was kissing." She dropped down onto her knees. Eugette flew down and embraced her mother. The embraced intensified. Maria whispered, "Your dad was my teen-aged heartthrob. God! Oh, how I loved him. We'd pledged our love a thousand times over. My mom, my dad. They were loving parents. They were strict and, yes, they walked the line and held me to the same standards that ruled their lives. I started to show. Mom knew my condition before I had a clue. She told dad that I did not have the flu." Maria vigorously wiped away her tear-stained cheeks. She pulled away from Eugette. Words she'd suppressed throughout life continued to flow, "They shipped me off to be with family and spoke to your dad's parents. Sweetheart, they went to their graves believing your dad was your biological father. The love he doted on us reinforced those beliefs in their eyes. It was a topic he never asked me to explain. We tried but failed to rekindle the cycle of life within my body. Again, I failed! Your dad simply loved us. Then along came your precious babies. Our grandbabies. It was like we'd died and gone to heaven. Honey, your dad, your father, raised you and loved you over the moon. He worshiped the gift entrusted to him, you. I could not bring my shame to bear on the love of my life. The essence that arose within you over the years. Simply stated, we believed our love had succeeded. Your self-confidence, your persona reinforced our beliefs. Rusty worshipped the ground you walked on, each and every breath you took. If we, if I was wrong. Then go ahead and hate me, sweetheart. You have every reason to hate me. Maybe I should have sided with my dad and gifted you to a proper loving family!"

Eugette reached out to Maria. Each buried the other in an all-encompassing embrace. Their bodies melted in to one. Mother and daughter. Shivers raced through their reconnected souls. Stuttering Eugette declared, "No no...no I could never hate you mom. You're my life. Please, love me. I love you." Both stood up.

John nudged up and embraced Eugette. She turned to him and they kissed. Quietly Norman, with Hope in hand, inched closer to Maria and Eugette and the embrace expanded. Jeffery walked up to Maria and they snuggled up comfortably to each other. Eugette gazed over at Jeffery and whispered, "You'd best be loving my momma, we need you in our lives." The words went unanswered since none was needed. Jeffery wrapped Maria tighter in a loving embrace. They kissed. It lingered. Eugette welcomed Megan and Taylor, her twins, her babies, who had skittered over and joined them. She smirked and chided, "Really, mom. Control yourself. Our babies are watching!"

Megan and Taylor shouted out. "It's OK, Grammie. We love your kisses too!" They snuggled up to grammie and embraced her lovingly. Jeffery sighed as they shifted over and added him to the embrace. Quietly, Richard, Lyndsey and Auntie Lila joined the gathering.

Anya, with Gilbert at her side, inched in closer to Eugette while nudging Norman. He got

the message and pulled Anya tighter into the group hug. She sighed and said, "Me too! What does that make me, my own Grandmother?"

Eugette frowned. "Say what?"

"Your mom wasn't the only one."

"Really?" Eugette asked.

"Really! Anya answered. I was raped twice. My Norman and my sweet August are blessings I cherish. I'm guessing that makes you and Norman half siblings or whatever. Fear not like you love embraces his body and my sweet August's soul. The half siblings embraced and families expanded their horizons. Drawing everyone physically and emotionally closer together.

CHAPTER 50

Robert's fist slammed down hard on the car's dash. Logan and his cohort Jives had disappeared off the landscape. They were all that stood between him and an easy twenty-thousand tax free loonies. Where could the bastards be? Frustrated he drove over to the café. On stepping inside business appeared slow. Only three booths were occupied. At the counter he accepted the takeout coffee set before him. Staring down Virginia, Constable Johnson's squeeze, Robert asked, "Kind 'a quiet tonight, Virginia. Have you seen Leon or Rene hanging out the last few days?"

Ginni smirked and replied, "Can't say I have, Sergeant. Since the fire across town, they've not been around much."

On picking up his coffee Robert turned and walked towards the door. No payment offer had been made. He called back, "Should they show up, don't mention that I inquired about them."

"I won't," Ginni called back to the Sergeant. On seeing him step outside she wondered, should I call Eric? He had asked her to call if any sightings or inquiries of Leon or Rene occurred. Just thinking about Jives made her skin crawl. Leah joined her at the counter. Ginni asked, "Please cover for me. Gotta hit the room." Leah nodded she was good to cover off the counter. Ginni headed off to the washroom. Once inside a quick speed dial connected her to Eric. On learning the sergeant had stopped in asking questions, thanks and telephone kisses were exchanged. Then Ginni headed back out to the counter.

Later that night, just past midnight Robert cruised slowly past Chester's newest house of worship. It stood in darkness if one ignored the lights reflecting off the snow drifts in its backyard. Robert did not. They caught his eye and perked his curiosity. He pondered what could *Chester's Jesus* be doing up and about at this hour of the night? The only water he'd be walking on would definitely be of the frozen ilk. Parked across from the Slivers Residence he noted the driveway was unoccupied. Robert worked his way back towards the backyard. There he positioned himself behind a cluster of three pine trees. They provided him with cover. Gazing into the room through its sheer white curtains he spotted his quarry with the reborn Slivers woman. She appeared to be pleading with both Jives and Logan. Robert pondered, wasn't your man enough for you, lady? Curious, he creeped up to the back wall of the house. Tessa's voice came through clearly. A snicker hit Robert's face. She wasn't looking to get laid. The stupid bitch was looking for passage out to the so called ominous floating islands.

"Listen up you idiots, Pastor Mikie ain't goanna save your sorry arses from the wrath of Barnie, or gain you forgiveness for your deeds." Tessa boasted. She added, "Besides, get me back out there and your trouble will be gone. I've got proof of what is out there waiting to pave our paths to freedom. Financial and physical freedom. With the money waiting for us out there we will live buried in wealth beyond your wildest imaginations."

Jives injected, "But Mikie said with his blessing and word spoken on our behalf that our souls would be sav..."

"Bullshit!" Tessa shot back at a shocked Jives. Logan stood dumbfounded at his mate's side. Together Robert gave their combined gene pool rating a failing grade. The woman? Dye the hair and dress her up... Robert saw a potential for some hot action. He listened intently to the sales pitch the lady was tossing at the two losers on his hit list.

Logan snarled, "You're that bitch that let Mikie feel yer tits at the Pot. What yer going on abouts makes no sense. There's no money out there. Jest a gateway ta Satan's Hell Hole. Mikie said so. Said he stared the Hooved Demon down eye to eye and scared the bejesus out'ta him.

He did! We'll just wait till Mikie gets back from that Soul Revival he's heading up with his Pappy and Ned Stone."

Tessa stared the pair down in frustration. She walked over to Jives, reached out and grabbed his crotch. He dropped to his knees in agony. Tessa had grabbed his balls and crushed them in a vise-like grip. She released him as he dropped, squealing like a male boar staring down a castrator with knife in hand. Tessa sneered, "Just as I thought. I'd be better off sticking it out with the Pastor. He's been blessed, iff'in you grasp the meaning. You're a pathetic pai..."

BAM, bam, bam! Three gunshots sang out into the night. The patio door glass shattered and crumbled. Robert stepped through the opening. Tessa, Leon and Jives froze as they stared at the gun in Robert's hand. "Good evening, gentlemen, and your ladyship? What's all this bullshit talk about wealth beyond my wildest imagination? I've heard the local crap making the rounds. I'm not a loser like some in this room. Work your sales pitch on me, bitch, work it hard I've heard you fast talking Barnie and local lobstermen at the Pot. I'm all ears!" Jives made a move to bolt towards the glassless patio door. Bam! Robert, fired a shot at his feet. Jives froze where he stood. A wave of the revolver returned Jives to Leon's side.

Sensing she had an open ear, Tessa called out, "I'm Italian! Tesoro Kalpesh? Immenso Tesoro, a huge treasure is out there waiting to be claimed! Kalpesh? Rosener, my second husband. Thankfully dead. Couldn't give me what, I needed. That being wealth and the drive to handle my needs. My maiden name, 'Marchesi', Pappa's Italian roots. Tesoro Immenso, an enormous treasure that could be yours and mine, sweet cheeks. If you get me out to that island. Great wealth awaits us!"

Robert barked back, "Right, just like that other island gold mine that keeps its treasure seekers at bay through a series of engineered, tunneled waterways. I've heard some mighty good lines over the years, lady. The name is Robert, Sergeant Robert Stratford, it's not Duffus! Take a closer look! I'm no spring chicken. Ain't got a lifetime to twitter away digging holes to uncover buried treasures."

"Go the distance with me and time will cease to be a factor."

"Right! First off, I've worked the game. I can spot scammers or con artist a mile away. Let's just move it bitch, and we'll bring your idiots with us. Delivering them will fill my pockets nicely." Robert shot back.

Tessa snagged her jacket off a chair. Both Jives and Logan froze but on seeing the revolver raised and pointed at them they followed Tessa through the glassless door. At the side of the house a beep released the trunk of Robert's vehicle. He motioned Tessa. "Put the jacket on, go to the trunk, and return with the bag of police restraints. Now move it! Shut the trunk then get your ass back here."

Tessa obeyed. She retrieved the restraints and returned. The Jives and Leon took on a sickly pallor. Both ended up with their hands bound with the restraints as Tessa followed Robert's instructions. He then yanked both of their restrains, then headed over to the vehicle. Under duress Jives and Logan slid into the back seat. Tessa took the front passenger seat. Robert took the wheel. A click locked all the doors. Engaged, the child restraint sealed the back doors.

Robert drove off to meet Arnie and a guaranteed twenty thousand. That did not stop Tessa from pitching her line to Robert. She blurted out a final line, "Look I've skimmed the parishioners' donations. Would ten, or twelve grand twist your arm?"

"Keep talking," Robert answered. "I'm listening."

"Tessa sensed an opening and worked it. "I've got my bank card in this jacket pocket along with keys to my man's boat. Head over to the dock and once we land out on Tesoro Island the card and its pin is yours. What you do with the two losers in back is no concern of mine."

Robert liked the option. He changed plans and headed towards the bank's 24-hour atm. There, Tessa inserted the card and punched in her pin, concealing it from Robert. The balance flashed up seventeen thousand, six hundred and ten dollars, twenty-seven cents. It sealed the deal. Tessa removed her card. Robert grabbed the card and pocketed it. They returned to the vehicle. Jives tumbled off the back of the front seats on spotting Robert returning. He was rewarded with a fist driven into his face, The drive over to the dock where Mikie and Ned's lobster boat, Total Satisfaction was docked passed quickly. Once they were all aboard, Robert checked the fuel tanks. They were full. He nudged then booted both Jives and Logan into the hold under the bow. Tessa had convinced him they'd make good Tesoro diggers. She pointed out an axe and shovel in the vessel's tool box. He held a hand out and she passed the keys over to him. With priming and coaxing the engine came to life. Robert allowed it time to idle up. Then motioned Tessa to release the docking lines. She obeyed and they headed out to their destination. He had a concept of their location from the tales that had circulated about town over the years. Robert figured, worse case, he'd off the bitch and her companions out on the island, pocket her bank stash along with Barnie's twenty thousand and head out'ta town to a new life. If the longshot paid off, other options would present themselves. Tessa stood at his side. He eyed her up and down and smiled as another short-term option aroused feelings within him. After a stretch run, Tancook Islands appeared on the horizon.

....

The Midnight Revival wound down. Pastor Mikie Slivers, Pappy Slivers and Ned Stone arrived back home at the Chapel. A cold chilly air filled the house. Mikie cursed, believing the furnace had bit the dust. He called out but nobody answered. Strutting through the main floor he failed to find their house guests or Tessa. At the basement entrance icy air greeted him. He flipped the light switch on then Mikie and Ned rushed down into the basement. They discovered the shattered patio door. In the shattered glass the shell from Robert's revolver caught Ned's eye. He swore, "Son of a bitch! That fucking Barnie is behind this somehow! I just know it's his workings.

They stepped outside and followed a trail of footsteps in the snow. They ended across the street from the house. All neighbouring houses were unlit. Frustrated, Mikie headed back inside. He grabbed the house phone and dialed Barnie's home number from memory.

On the fourth ring, Barnie answered. "Whoa, who do we have here? Could it be the Lord's ways ain't paying de bills? What's up Mikie, me son?"

"Don't be fucking with me, Barnie. What did ya do with my woman?"

Barnie snickered. It felt good to hear the old Mikie Slivers back in town. He answered, "I ain't done nothing wit your sweet young silver haired bitch. What's happened? Should I call the cops?"

"Don't breathe! Don't move an inch. We're headed over your way now! And you'd best have answers. I know she's been asking about fer passage back out to that fucking island. If you've arranged it, you're a dead man!" Mikie slammed the phone back down onto its cradle. Pappy and Ned followed him back out to the vehicle. Back on the road they raced over snow-covered roads. On arriving at Barnie's, he instructed Pappy and Ned to stay put in the vehicle. He opened the glove compartment and retrieved a thirty-eight Weston and shoved it in a jacket pocket. At the front door to Barnie's, he knocked hard five times.

The door opened. Barnie smiled in greeting his guest. "Welcome to my humble home, Pastor Mikie. Or should I be calling you Jesus?"

Angered, Mikie whipped out his Weston and thrust it in Barnie's face. "Move it, asshole! Drove past our dock on the way over! Total Satisfaction Is gone and Stratford's car is parked there by the dock."

"Mikie! Believe me, I never touched your lady. Or arrang…"

"I said move it, asshole. Now! We're heading out in the Devil's Mistress, your boat." Mikie shouted out!

"But Mikie. Let's talk."

"Get the fucking keys, asshole!"

Barnie obeyed. He grabbed a jacket and his boat's keys off the kitchen key board. At Mikie's vehicle he tried the back door. Mikie waved him over to the front passenger's door. He opened it and claimed the seat. Mikie got in behind the wheel. All the time he was waving his revolver at Barnie. A short drive landed them at Barnie's dock. On board the Devil's Mistress he took Barnie's keys and waved them at Ned and Pappy, both standing on the dock. Pappy obeyed his son's directions. He stepped off the dock with Ned, and returned to the vehicle. Pappy claimed the driver's seat. Mikie eyed Barnie. He quickly fired up the boat's engine. Barnie followed directions shouted out and released the docking lines. The Devil's Mistress headed out onto Mahone Bay. Nobody onboard uttered a word. Pappy and Ned watched the Devil's Mistress head out, then they drove off back home.

CHAPTER 51

Over in East River, Richard awoke. He stared in shock at Lyndsey who shouted at him. "Richie, please help me somethings wrong. My belly hurts. Help me, I don't want to lose our baby!"

Richard tried to embrace Lyndsey. She pushed him away and screamed, "I need help, Ritchie! Please help me!"

Terrified Richard leaped out of bed. He ran to Hope's bedroom pounded on the door then entered. Hope awoke to his pounding. He screamed, "Help me, Hope. It's Lyndsey, she's in severe pain. In terrible pain. Her stomach. Please help us!"

Hope jumped out of bed. She grabbed her cell phone and hit 911. Together they raced back to Lyndsey's side. Gilbert, awakened, ran to their sides.

Lyndsey, grief stricken, cried out in pain, "It's my belly. It hurts like hell!"

"911, How can we help?"

"It's my sister. She's pregnant and awoke screaming in severe agony!"

"Are there any signs of bleeding"

Lyndsey stared terrified into Hope's eyes. Hope pulled the covers off Lyndsey. There were no signs of bleeding. Hope shouted into the phone "No. There's no bleeding!"

"Good. You're calling on a cell phone. Where are you located ma'am?"

"I'm Hope, Hope McDonald. My sister is Lyndsey Ramsay and they're visiting from Ontario. We're in East River down Chester way. The address is off Hwy 329, 6 Aspo..."

"Got it ma'am, sorry, Hope. We've dispatched ambulance and police. Some emergency volunteers will also show up. Please stay on the line. Could you have someone call 911 on a landline?"

"Yes!"

Gilbert flew out of the room and down the stairs. In the living-room he dialed 911. On connecting he identified himself and stated his connection to Hope's 911 cell call. Flashing red and blue lights lit up the house interior. Gilbert shouted police are here. "I'll open the door."

On flipping the kitchen door locks, Constable Eric Johnson entered, Gilbert pointed to the stairs. He shouted, "First room on your right. Where's the ambulance?"

Eric shouted back to Gilbert, "It's on its way. I heard its siren on the way here!"

Two emergency responders, arrived followed closely by the ambulance. The EMTs entered and raced upstairs. Quickly they accessed Lyndsey's condition. On being asked if she had any allergies Lyndsey nodded no and answered, "Not that I'm aware of, sir."

Richard frowned and asked, "Did you hit the raw carrot bowl?"

Lyndsey's face displayed anger on her passion for raw carrots being questioned. On connecting to the Emergency on Call Doctor a series of tests and instructions were carried out. A condition suffered by a co-worker an ER Nurse popped up in the lead EMT's mind. He asked Lyndsey do you eat many raw carrots?"

She frowned, then admitted, "Only baby carrots. They're easier to chew."

The EMT asked the doctor on the line, "Does nurse Suzanne Quinn's situation ring a bell?" He nodded on hearing a positive response. Lyndsey relaxed a little. She sensed the raw carrot question had been resolved. Hope cradled Lyndsey's head on her lap and continuously chatted in a soft supportive voice to Lyndsey. The other EMT instructed the emergency volunteers to retrieve the ambulance gurney and bring it up to the room. On its arrival, Lyndsey was quickly transferred onto the gurney and secured. Everyone stood aside watching in shock as the EMTs moved Lyndsey out to the ambulance. They called back to their shocked observers. "Give us an hour. We'll call the minute we have answers."

Richard shouted out to them, "I'm her husband. Can I go with you"

"Yes sir. Please hurry!"

Richard scrambled into jeans and a top, then ran downstairs. With his boots on he slipped into his jacket and ran out to the ambulance. On boarding it, the doors were shut and the ambulance sped off into the night.

Jeffery's truck raced into the driveway as the ambulance headed out. The glowing lights and sirens had awakened everyone at the homestead. On stopping he jumped out of the truck and stared with questioning eyes at Gilbert and Hope. They waved him inside and walked back into the house. Hope looked to Jeffery and said, "Lyndsey woke up with severe stomach pain. We called 911 and..."

One of the emergency responders turned to Hope and stated. "She's stabilized and in good hands. You will be called once they arrive at the hospital." They chatted briefly with Eric then headed out. Eric joined Gilbert, Hope and Jeffery at the table. Talk centered on the positives the EMTs had mentioned before heading out. Eric turned down Hope's offer of a coffee and headed off back to the detachment shortly after 4:08 am.

Jeffery looked at Hope and said, "I'd best call Maria. She woke me up and I suspect is worried sick. Those lights were some bright viewed out'ta the sunroom." Jeffery pulled out his cell phone. A speed dial connected him to Maria on the first ring.

"What's happened Jeff? Is everyone ok?" Maria pleaded.

"Lyndsey awoke with severe stomach pains. She's headed to the hospital in the ambulance. Richard is with her."

"Oh My God! Her baby? Is her baby, ok?"

"Yes, sweetheart. They stabilized her before leaving. She's in good hands."

Maria paused then replied, "Thank be ta God."

Jeffery answered Maria, "Are the other's awake?"

"Yes."

"It's best they know. Looks like we'll grab a coffee and wait for Richard to call with an update. Don't hang up. I'd best talk to John."

"Ok, Sweetheart. Here's John." Maria passed John the cellphone and led Eugette and Lila off into the kitchen there they grabbed chairs and sat at the kitchen table while Maria updated them.

Back over at Gilbert's very little conversation flowed. Both Hope and Gilbert were buried in a mountain of "what if"" thoughts. Hope headed to the counter and set the coffee machine in motion. She listened to Jeffery update John on the phone, then poured out three mugs of black coffee. Back at the table, once served, the mugs were played with in a distracted manner. Very little coffee was consumed. Headlights outside announced John's arrival. On entering the house, the phone called out. Hope leaped out of her chair. She grabbed the phone and called out, "How's our Lyndsey, Rich? Tell me she's ok. The baby is ok? Please!"

"Relax, Hope. Our Lyndsey is in good hands. I haven't seen her yet. But her nurse has kept me up to date."

"And she's ok? What triggered the attack?" Gilbert and the others stood by Hope's side. Their ears glued to the receiver at Hope's ear.

"It's an intestinal blockage. She's been stabilized and they've put her on a pump."

"A pump? What kind of pump is she on?"

Richard answered, "A stomach pump. Looks like our lady's obsession with raw carrots caused a blockage in her intestine. I'm told both Lyndsey and our babies are ok."

"Babies? Did I hear you right Richard?"

"Yes! We haven't done any testing to determine our baby's sex. Besides the old swinging needle tricks. Guess we won't have to go that route anymore. There's two of them and they're both healthy. A boy and a girl, I'm told. And yes, both are healthy. And Lyndsey's stabilized."

"Yahoo! Yahoo! She's OK and I'm goanna be a double Auntie! Can we come and see our mom-to-be?"

"Best hold off Hope, Lyndsey is stabilized and is sleeping. We'd best give her some time."

"Ok," Hope answered. Then added, "You're at the Fisherman's Memorial Hospital in Lunenburg. Right?"

"Yes." Richard answered.

"Ok. It's 5:38 am We'll wait a bit before we head out to Lunenburg. Is there anything we can bring?"

"A coffee? The coffee in the machine here sucks."

Hope answered, "Coffee, can we do anything else?"

"No. I'm good and relieved that Lyndsey is getting the care she needs."

"We're with you on that one Rich. Love ya. Give our love to Lyndsey when they let you in to see her."

"I will, Hope, see you soo..."

Hope shouted into the phone. "John's here with us. You'd best update him."

"Ok. Put John on. And Hope, bye and thanks for being there for us."

She passed the phone to John then returned to the kitchen table. The conversation was boosted over the news Richard had given. It struck a chord in the hearts of Hope, Gilbert, and Jeffery. On hanging up, John joined the table conversation. He refused the offer of a coffee. Time definitely stood still. Most state that to be an impossibility. Ask anyone awaiting word on the condition of a loved one and they'd set you straight in a hurry.

Each tick of the clock raised the kitchen's anxiety levels. Finally, it passed the point of no return. Waiting no longer stood as a viable option. Both Hope and Gilbert scooted upstairs and quickly traded bedclothes for casual dress. Back downstairs they slipped into their outerwear and boots. Jeffery and John exchanged keys. Then he watched the three drive off towards the hospital in Jeffery's truck. He locked up the house then drove John's SUV back over to the homestead. On arrival he updated the anxious ears on Richard's phone call and its news. Lively chatter was exchanged over breakfast prepared by Maria and Eugette.

....

On arriving at the Fisherman's Memorial Hospital, after parking the truck, the anxious trio made their way in through the Emergency entrance. With no sign of Richard, Gilbert inquired at the desk, "Excuse me. My niece was rushed in here early this morning by ambulance."

"Her name, sir?"

Gilbert smiled, "Lyndsey Ramsay. Richard, her husband, is with her."

"One minute sir and I'll check. Oh, here she is. Your niece was treated in emergency and is stabilized. She's waiting to be assigned a room. But I'll call to see if there's any updates." The receptionist's phone connected with the emergency room staff. She inquired about Lyndsey's status. Once disconnected she said, "Your niece is stabilized and currently sleeping. I suggest you sit down and relax. Mister Ramsay has been advised of your presence."

"Thank you," Gilbert replied. Together Gilbert, Hope and John followed her suggestion Gilbert eyed the coffee machine with caution. He opted to heed Richard's earlier warnings. They claimed chairs and sat down. Gilbert toyed with his cell phone but quickly pocketed it on spotting Richard walking towards them. A round of welcoming embraces were exchanged.

"She's sleeping and all appears good." Richard commented. He apologized, "Sorry I didn't call, I fell asleep in a chair by Lyndsey's bed."

"But our Lyndsey is ok, no complications?" Gilbert asked.

Richard hesitated. Hope picked up on it immediately. She said, "Ok. What haven't you told us, Rich? Lyndsey and our babies are good. Right? Don't spare me the truth, I gotta know"

Everyone stared anxiously at Richard. Finally, he caved, "Everything is ok. Lyndsey has stabilized. Both babies are good. She's still on the stomach pump. She's being constantly attended to. The wait is to see the blockage breaks free and clears itself out. If, and only if, that fails to take place, surgery may become an option. But only a last-ditch option. There were others but I'm not medically up on what they explained."

A group hug ensued. John offered to make a breakfast run. Everyone submitted their order then John headed out to find a restaurant. The others each shared time solo with Lyndsey who was awake and ready for visitors.

CHAPTER 52

The winds abated once they were out beyond the Tancook Islands, Iron Bound and Pearl Islands. Total Satisfaction gained speed racing towards Tessa's destination. She looked over at Robert. Their eyes locked. She asked, "You're a local sort 'a! Have you ever been out to the islands"

Robert snarled back, "Why would I? I'm a seasoned police officer. I deal in facts!"

"And graft I'd dare to say!"

"Watch your tongue, lady. I assume return passage is on your wish list?"

Tessa fired back, "My recollection of directions is vague. However, I know from chatting with hubby that Jives and Logan are familiar with their location."

Robert pondered the options, a one eighty twist about popped up first. Doubts had started to arise in his mind. Money talked legions in the mind and twisted heart of an officer who'd crossed the line. He answered, "Ok. Get Jives out here. He's the least likely to pull off a Mutiny on Total Satisfaction."

Tessa stooped down and called out to Jives, "Git yer sorry arse out here, boy! It's your chance to earn some brownie points."

Jives hesitated then obeyed. He crawled out from under the boat's bow. On standing he gazed around at their surroundings. The only thing in sight was water, water and more water. He asked, "Are we out past East Iron Bound and Pearl Islands?"

Tessa answered, "If you're talking about those two piles of rocks with a tree or two clinging to life on them, then yes. They're fifteen minutes back that away." Tessa pointed back towards the vessel's stern.

Jives, mulling over the opportunity to earn his captives trust, nodded seaward and off to their starboard side. Tessa caught the motion. She shouted over to Robert, "No Fool! Off to your other starboard." Robert twisted the wheel and corrected their course and motioned for Jives to crawl back under the bow.

Tessa overruled the motion. She asked Jives, "How far and no bullshit?"

Jives answered, "Thirty, no closer to forty-five minutes at most. If you plan to pull up on the island's leeward side"

Tessa nodded her approval. Conversation onboard vanished, if one excluded Logan's frequent digs fired at his captors and Jives. Those fired at Jives held a personal vendetta in their deliveries. Twenty minutes later the air warmed slightly. Tessa unzipped her jacket. A good feeling started to arise within.

....

Off to the south easterly on the island of their destination an uneasy feeling arose in Wilbert Enid's soul. Mere months had slipped past since he's opened his soul's heart to Grace Ramsay's spirit. To Wilbert it felt like a lifetime. The years, no almost two centuries, spent in total isolation felt like a mere speck of time on the evolution of time's passage. He glanced over at Grace and silently whispered the Lord's Prayer in gratitude for the gift received in Grace's treasured presence. In that glance recollections of soul-searching discussions, they'd shared arose. Wilbert pondered their agreed conclusions. *John Ramsay, Grace's father merited no forgiveness. He had abandoned his family and fled with gems stolen from the treasure Wilbert had been left to stand guard over. Grace rued the day she set out in search of the island to gain forgiveness on her father's behalf, she had failed and broken her mother, Sarah's, heart. They agreed true forgiveness and joy had come on her arrival on the island with Selby's treasured rosary in hand. The gift had erased all memory of the years of isolation Wilbert had spent on the island alone. In so many ways Grace reminded Wilbert of his younger sister. A sister he'd left behind on setting out to sail the oceans of the world on a ship manned by a questionable captain and crew. He believed he'd been granted redemption on touching and blessing the souls and bodies of the descendants of both Grace's father and mother who'd brought her to his side mere seconds past in times endless passage.'* Wilbert rued over the possibility of safe passage arriving at their island that would possibly carry them both back into Grace's world. He savoured the thought. Knowing that, if it were to be, the sparkle would once again glow in Grace's eyes and spirit.

Wilbert frowned on spotting questioning look on Grace's face. He asked, 'What is it my love?'

'A presence approaches dearest Wilbert. It somehow feels familiar. Connected to my past, possibly our future?' Together their souls arose and glided towards their island's western shore. Gazing outward both spotted the lights of Total Satisfaction as she approached their island. An unease arose within Wilbert, whilst an excitement arose within Grace. Those feelings strengthened on Total Satisfaction drawing close and closer to their island.

…….

Through a light dissipating misty fog Tessa, then Jives, caught site of the island. She shouted out, "Yes! We're about to grasp our destiny."

Robert frowned on hearing Tessa's excited outburst. He knew return passage did not include Jives and Logan. Tessa's passage remained open to discussion. Guided by moonlight and the glow of a starlit night Robert glided Total Satisfaction into a shoreline cove revealed to his eyes. Tessa reacted and tossed the vessels bumpers over both sides. They bumped up against the grassy treed shore of the cove. Robert grabbed Tessa, picked her up and tossed her onto the island. She sneered back at Robert in anger. He ignored her and tossed a docking line over to where she stood. Without directions Tessa secured the line to a weathered old shore pine tree.

She shouted out, "Toss the axe and shovel over my way."

Robert followed orders. Both items landed with a bounce and thud at Tessa's feet. She nodded thanks back to Robert. Then called out, "Our diggers. Send them ashore!"

Robert nudged Logan out from under the bow with a wave of his revolver. Both men stared with questioning looks in their eyes at the island. They'd grown up living under the local lore that had been assigned to the island and its past. Robert shouted out in anger, "Now! Jump before I fire a warning shot to your destiny."

Jives stepped onto the vessel's gunnel. Robert's boot landed on Jive's butt and he flew onto the island. Logan bit the bullet and simply opted to jump over and joined Tessa and Jives. Robert joined them. He eyed Tessa and the tools at her feet. She shot back at him, "Free up Jive's hands. He's the least likely to try anything."

With his hands released, Jives picked up the axe and shovel. The treasure hunters set off in search of Tessa's obsession, buried treasure. No one caught sight of their observers. Quickly, they arrived at the abandoned hole Tessa had once overseen while Ramsays and McClakens dug it out. She shivered on spotting the skull that had once hit her and denied her of the wealth about to be unburied. Robert sent Jives into the hole. Abandoned implements were tossed out of the hole. Robert handed Jives a pickaxe and work got underway.

....

The Devil's Mistress followed the course taken by Total Satisfaction. With hesitation, Barnie jumped ashore. He grabbed the line tossed to him by Mikie and secured it to a shoreline tree. Mikie eyed his vessel resting up against the shoreline. Feeling blessed by the Heavenly forces of his new calling, Mikie joined Barnie on the island. With Barnie in the lead and a gun pointed at his back, the pair set off in search of Total Satisfaction's crew. On entering a clearing, they spotted activity at the far end. Two people were crouched down and hands reaching out of the ground were exchanging something.

Barnie stopped and twisted around. He asked, "Could your Tessa be right? Could there actually be buried treasure on this island?"

Mikie frowned. He'd not really been supportive of Tessa's obsession with the island and its rumoured treasures. They continued on towards the action.

Thirty feet away Barnie shouted out, "What in hell are you doing out here on my island?"

Robert twisted around and stood up. An assortment of rocks flew out of his hand. Angry, he hoisted his revolver and fired a shot at Barnie. He shouted. "Fuck you, Madison. These gems are mine!"

Barnie and Mikie ran towards Robert. Logan and Jives attempted to climb out of the hole. Four, no five rapid gunshots sang out. Both Logan and Jives dropped down into the hole. Thirty, forty seconds later both men lay dead at the bottom of the hole. Blood flowed freely from their bodies muddying the earth they lay on. An armed standoff ensued. Neither side appeared willing to cede ground to the other.

A blazing red haze soared up out of Tessa's Tesoro Pit. Its eyes fired out greenish blue laser darts. Mikie recognized their adversary from his last trip out to the island. Images of Tessa swimming in a panic towards him aboard Total Satisfaction raced through his head. The reality of the moment vanished in a heartbeat. He watched Robert scooping up gems off the ground and pocketing them. The haze reached out towards him through Tessa. In a panic he fired off a rapid series of gunshots. Tessa's body tumbled down into the hole. She landed atop the bodies of Jives and Logan. Her blood flowed freely, mingling with the blood of the lifeless corpses beneath her. Robert twisted round then dashed off. Younger, fitter and more agile than the older Barnie and Mikie, he quickly passed them as he ran off towards the boat that had carried him to the island.

Barnie stared in disbelief at the thing roaring out in anger and reaching towards him. A man of questionable ethics, Barnie did not stand his ground. He raced off following in Robert's footsteps. Mikie followed suit. On approaching the cove, Barnie stared in disbelief at his boat the Devil's Mistress racing off with Robert at its helm. Determined to seek his form of justice he headed to Total Satisfaction's line and freed it from the tree. A glance back into the woods revealed Mikie close on his heels. There was no sign of the roaring flaming beast that had been pursuing them. Barnie pulled on the line and Total Satisfaction bumped up against the shore. Mikie reached his side. Together they jumped aboard. Mikie ran to the helm and fired up the engine. Barnie retrieved the vessel's docking line. Mikie shifted into gear and Total Satisfaction raced off towards the Tancook Islands, Mahone Bay and Chester. Neither Barnie or Mikie had seen those that had preceded them in boarding Total Satisfaction. No conversation arose throughout the run back to Chester.

Below the bow, Wilbert Enid felt a freedom he'd not experienced since his teenaged years growing up rebelliously on the streets of France. Huddled up at his side, Grace Ramsay sighed, embracing an inner peace. She was headed home. Home to her family with her man at her side. A joy she'd envisioned often in life, but never experienced until this day, this moment of joy.

CHAPTER 53

Several days slipped past. Lyndsey's body had recovered from its ordeal. Convinced their patient no longer posed a threat to her person and her babies, Doctor Tyne and nurse Quinn signed off on Lyndsey's release from hospital. To both Richard and Lyndsey's surprise they found themselves setup in the old Ramsay/McClaken homestead. They quickly settled in to their new living quarters. Relaxed sitting in the sunroom's loveseat, its footrests extended, Lyndsey tensed up on hearing the roar of sirens calling out into the night. Richard reached over and embraced Lyndsey. Soft kisses and neck rubs gradually erased the short-lived tensions that had arisen. Curiosity and a woman's need to know led to Richard getting up and grabbing his cell phone off the coffee table. He speed-dialed Gilbert's home phone.

On the second ring Hope answered, "Hi, Hope here. What's up, Rich? How's my Sis?"

"She's fine. Relaxed, stretched out on the loveseat and tuned into the *'Beatles'* on her headset. Those sirens that blasted down the road. Any idea what they're all about?"

The kitchen door at Gilbert's swung open before Hope could answer. Hope stared over at Gilbert and sniffed. The aroma of burnt wood floated off him. Hope frowned. In response to Gilbert's questioning signals, she held the phone out to Gilbert and said, "It's Richard. Asking about the sirens. You reek of the acrid stench of burning wood. You'd best talk with Rich."

Gilbert took the phone. "Hi Richard just got in. The sirens? On my way home I got close to the fire but got detoured. From what I could see it looked serious. Hopefully nobody's been hurt. I'll call Eric Johnson and get an update. How's our mom-to-be doing? Relaxing, I hope?"

Richard sighed and gazed over at Lyndsey. She'd dozed off to sleep. "Lyndsey's fine, Gilbert. Actually, she's off in slumberland as we chat. I better let you go."

"Take care, Rich. I'll call once I get an update. Catch you later." With that said, Gilbert disconnected the call.

Back over at the homestead, Richard crawled under the covers with Lyndsey. Just having her safe at his side eased Richard's mind. He gazed over at Lyndsey; her peaceful relaxed aura triggered a recall of their hospital adventure. *Their nurse Suzanne had walked out of the emergency room. On drawing closer she'd said, "Lyndsey is stabilized and holding her own. Doctor Tyne sent me out to update you on your wife's condition. Once she clears her for transfer to a room, she will give you a complete update. Perhaps we could step over into a private room and chat. Trust me..."*

"Trust, I need to touch my Lynds. I lost he..."

"Trust me Mr. Ramsay ... Richard, the worst is now over. Lyndsey's blockage has cleared. We're now into stabilizing and recovery mode. You spent hours at Lyndsey's bedside throughout her ordeal. You're tired. I saw you crashed out in the chair next to her bed. I'm a mom. I survived the battle Lyndsey has overcome. Like her, my recovery took time. That's why they assigned me to your wife's case. My Nathan, like you, survived a terrifying ordeal. He never left my side without a battle royal. Please let's go to that private room." Suzanne took Richard's hand and started to walk out of the waiting room. Hope took Richard's other hand. Gilbert followed their lead. Together they walked down the hallway then into a private unoccupied room. Suzanne switched on the room's lights. Richard sat on a bed's edge. Suzanne stood facing him. Gilbert nudged himself up next to Richard's side and sat down on the bed. A trademark Gilbert series of hugs ensued. Once they abated, Hope claimed Richard's free side, she took Richard's hands in hers. Grateful for Suzanne's personal connection and

commitment they waited for her update. Questions had swirled through their minds. What had triggered Lyndsey's sudden attack? What had zapped her of her bodily strength?

"What happened?" Richard asked. "We did everything step by step as coached ... instructed to anticipate and embrace." He pulled free of Hope's hands as uncontrollable sobbing embraced him. Again, he asked, "What happened?"

"Just like I did Richard, Lyndsey became obsessed with carrots. Raw carrots. Yes, carrots are a healthy food choice. But they're not the be all of healthy foods if not balanced with other healthy choices. Like me, your Lyndsey concealed her obsession from you and others. My God! My Nathan never had a clue! I believe the same held true for you. She wanted to enrich her body throughout her pregnancy."

Richard nodded agreement with Suzanne's words. But still felt helpless not being in there at Lyndsey's bedside. Suzanne looked over at the door. It had swung open.

Dr. Tyne walked into the room smiling. "Raw carrots, did I just hear the boasting up of raw carrots and their benefits?"

Suzanne nodded her head in agreement.

Dr. Tyne looked to Richard and said, "No more raw carrots for our mom-to-be. Shall I repeat my prescription? Richard, Lyndsey's over indulgence of carrots, raw carrots triggered a bowel blockage. Carrots are an excellent piece of a healthy balanced diet. However, I cannot stress it enough. Eaten in moderation yes, however they are not a stand-alone one at a time cure all for what ails one's body. Suzanne here can relate all the detailed effects and root causes of blockages. Like your Lyndsey she is a survivor of the same scenario.'" The recollection faded. A glance over at Lyndsey fired up a want-need to pull her body to his in a loving embrace. Richard opted for a cheek kiss instead and freed Lyndsey of her headphones. He snuggled up and slowly drifted off towards sleep.

Richard mulled over the chats shared with Lyndsey both at the hospital and since being set up in the old Ramsay Homestead on her release from hospital. Their talks had been soul searching and with each revisit and mulling over of the developing wants they worked, he felt pulled towards walking the new path opening up before him that Lyndsey was nurturing and nudging him towards. Off in dreamland those possibilities quickly turned into a reality. He willingly accepted the new home that greeted his family with open arms. The salty tang of Nova Scotia's air quietly called Richard Ramsay home. Home to Nova Scotia.

....

Earlier an angry Robert Stratford had walked away from his vehicle towards Barnie Madison's residence. On arriving there and finding the mini-home in total darkness Robert set his two gas containers down on the ground. He'd not been able to confirm whether Barnie had escaped the island or whether his corpse had been embraced by an earned and deserved destiny and lay dead on the accursed island he'd managed to escape? Could it be justice had finally been delivered and Satan had stepped up and dragged a deserving soul screaming in agony off into the depths of hell? Robert did not dwell long on either option. On spotting his nemesis's Buick parked in the driveway he decided to put the plan afoot into action. First, he approached the door and knocked. No response came. He quickly applied his skills and tools to the locked door. It popped open. A quick runabout inside confirmed it was empty. Robert rifled through all the normal hiding places felons normally favored. No sign of the records was uncovered. He bumped into the freezer door. It popped open. A glance inside revealed it stuffed full of bundled up paper money. Robert dug into it, stuffing bundles of large domination bills into all his pockets. On running out of pocket space he searched the cupboards and found garbage bags. He quickly stuffed one with many bundles of the frozen cash. Satisfied with his newfound wealth, Robert hoisted the bag over his shoulder and stepped outside.

There he removed the gas caps off both containers. He carried them into the mini-house, then proceeded to douse the mini-home inside and outside with gasoline. Other than a persistent hooting owl the night stood eerily silent. He tossed both empty gas cans under the Buick's gas tank after he'd drained the last of their contents into the car through a partially open window. With a snarling face, Robert lit a series of matches and tossed them at the gas sodded ground. It ignited and

Robert fled on foot back to his vehicle. Night breezes carried the scent of the mini-home, engulfed in flames, to Robert seated in his vehicle. A glance at the back seat and the stuffed garbage bag elated him. Satisfied, he hit the gas and raced off towards Chester. In driving past the Lobster Pot Pub & Eatery he spotted another nemesis, Inspector Harley Kingston and his Legal Side-Kick walking across the Pot's parking lot towards a vehicle. Robert drove off, avoiding any possible contract with a feared nemesis. Sirens roared off into the night towards Barnie's mini-home.

On arriving at his house, Robert packed a quick overnight travel bag, stuffing the money from Barnie's freezer in the bag. A dig deep down into his jean pockets iced Robert's long-term plans. He retrieved and eyed a fistful of gems. Snickering, Robert repocketed his island loot. He then headed back to the Pot, his intension being to wait out its closing, then break in and check out Barnie's office for the items he needed. Turning his back on a career of policing had not been his first choice. But in crossing the line he'd made that choice years past. An hour later the lights at the Lobster Pot Pub & Eatery went out. The last staffer stepped outside, locked the door and headed to her vehicle. Robert watched her drive out of the parking lot. In reflection, Robert savored the satisfaction he'd tasted on docking Barnie's vessel, the Devil's Mistress, and then setting her on a blind course back out over the darkened waters of Mahone Bay and beyond. Rubbing his face sweetened the taste on smelling the gasoline on his hands. The flames had consumed his foe's mini-home in mere minutes. The only regret centered on the lack of burning flesh in the flames that had engulfed Barnie's house.

He waited ten minutes then worked his magic on the back door's lock. Inside, he disabled the alarm by entering the passkey numbers, a privilege gained through his working arrangement with Barnie. At Barnie's office, he tried the door it was locked. That did not stop Robert and in short order he stepped into the office. In running about the office, he rifled through all accessible desk drawers and file cabinets. Success did not reward him.

A voice in the dark called out, "Looking for this, asshole?"

On hearing Barnie's voice, Robert froze. Their eyes connected. Survival drove both men forward. Barnie won the night. Clutching his revolver in hand he fired off three rapid gunshots in the dark office. Robert dropped to the floor clutching his gut and chest. Barnie walked over to Robert's body. He kicked the dying man, driving rapid boot shots at his face. On stooping down, Barnie rifled through Robert's pockets. The island loot quickly changed hands, along with Robert's car keys. Satisfied, Barnie fired one last shot into Robert's head execution style. He then picked up his stuffed briefcase and pocketed his revolver. Back outside, Barnie claimed the wheel of Robert's car. Its engine roared to life and Barnie headed out of town to retrieve the monetary stash he'd safely stowed in the freezer of his refrigerator. On approaching his house, he slammed on the brakes. A round of cursing unfolded. Barnie had arrived home and found his mini-home burnt to the ground. His beloved Buick, a burnt-out skeleton of its past beauty. He made his way past the property and headed down the road. Other options called out to the town's nemesis. He smirked on savoring the option that called out paving a safe road to another life. Chester faded out of sight. With each notch added to the vehicle's odometer, Barnie closed the gap on the opportunity gaining momentum in his mind. Those who'd paved the road to the situations he now fled would, in time pay the price others once had for fucking with Barnie Madison's world.

....

Gilbert woke to the summons of a ringing house phone. "Gilbert here. How can I…"

"Mister McClaken, it's Eric, Eric Johnson here. Inspector Kingston said I should call. There's been a murder at the Lobster Pot Pub & Eatery!"

"A what? Are you sure Eric? This is Chester. Not exactly a crime mecca."

Eric paused then answered, "Afraid to say we're giving the city folk a run for their money. First Eugette's family home was torched, then yesterday evening Barnie Madison's house was torched. Burnt to the ground."

"Really Eric? Another fire?"

"Yes sir. And a topper to that, my superior, Sergeant Robert Stratford's, body was discovered at the Lobster Pot Pub & Eatery in Mister Madison's office. Shot four times. Thought I'd end up retired and never have fired a shot. Sure, glad the Inspector is in town."

Gilbert asked, "Is he there with you now. The inspector, that is?"

"Yes. Hold on a second, Mister McClaken. I'll get him."

Gilbert held the phone to his ear as his thoughts and reasoning powers raced wildly inside his head. He escaped his thoughts on hearing Harley shout into the phone, "Gilbert! Are you there?"

"I'm here, Harley. What the hell has hit our town? Arsons and now a murder?"

"You nailed it there, my friend. My gut is pointing me towards Madison. But I'd best walk the line and let the facts and evidence do the talking. There's an APB out on Madison. Go ahead, ask me. Am I happy? We got the bastard, Gillie. We got him this time. He won't be walking away from this one cuddled in the safety of his vile network of supporters. Gil, I believe he's fled the local scene. But don't drop your guard. After what's unfolded the last couple of days, just be aware he's armed and dangerous."

Gilbert replied, "I read you loud and clear, friend. Just keep us in the know of any updates. And, friend, take care. That retirement you're savoring could be close at hand. Don't expose it to unnecessary risks."

"That's a given. Later, friend. The forensic team is asking questions and I best go. Trust me we will track him down and close this one out. Have a good one." With that said, Harley disconnected the call. At the call's other end Gilbert pocketed his cell phone. Although he'd never developed a connection with Robert Stratford, Gilbert refused to savor ill thoughts of the dead. The man's career in law enforcement spanned many years. Not being privy to the details of his death Gilbert gave him the benefit of the doubt. Anya walked into the kitchen. Showered and refreshed, her presence stirred up wants in Gilbert's body. The couple shared a lingering kiss. Christmas had bestowed gifts on Gilbert that he'd never imaged possible. Their lips parted. Anya's face snuggled up to

Gilbert's chest. Deep within him an invigorated heart skipped a beat, or was it two, no, three. Its heartstrings echoed with joy on being touched by the lips of a spirit releasing Gilbert from the bonds of love once shared in life at Gilbert's side. On sensing the departure of Karyn's lips, Gilbert shivered and allowed a new love to caress his soul, Anya's.

On pulling apart, a series of short kisses sealed their bond. In truth, Gilbert felt surreal with the new living arrangements that had unfolded. Jeffery and Maria were setting up house in the Trinity house. Richard and Lyndsey were set up in the old Ramsay-McClaken homestead, with Auntie Lila, a retired nurse supporting the mom-to-be. Hope had joined Norman who'd returned to PEI, focused on closing out the last term of his veterinarian's degree. John, Eugette and the twins were with Maria and Jeffery in Chester. They were in a holding pattern awaiting a decision in the hands of those at the old homestead.

Freed from the guilt he'd embraced on Karyn's passing, Gilbert nudged Anya back towards the stairs. Together they walked back upstairs into the master bedroom. All guilt vanished as Anya slipped out of her housecoat and straddled Gilbert on the bed. Naked, she played with Gilbert's clothing. The clothing quickly vanished. Both their wants soared. In coming together their bodies swayed in tune with each other. Each upward sway pulled their bodies apart then rewarded them as each downward thrust drove Gilbert deep within Anya raising both their sexual passions. Glancing up, Gilbert's eyes locked on Anya's He struggled to suppress an early ending to their lovemaking. He spotted the golden glitter bouncing off Anya's breasts aglow in the droplets of sweat racing downward to her belly and their bonded union below. Lost in the pleasures of their sexual connection they sighed as one final thrust bonded their bodies in an explosion that bonded them together. Anya collapsed onto Gilbert's chest. Electrical energies raced through their bodies. Gratified they sighed, signalling the state of their bodies and minds. They drifted off into a euphoric dreamland.

·······

Customers lined up outside the Café and out into the parking lot. The drive-through lineup extended down the road. Inside, Ginni and her coworkers were burning out. The buzz inside and throughout the town added unproven rumours to a rumour mill embracing each burning ember tossed on its blazing wildfire. Many of the booths and tables inside were occupied by staff from the Lobster Pot Pub & Eatery. The star attractions were those that had opened the Pot up that morning and discovered bloodied shoe prints exiting Barnie's unlocked office. The bloodied shoe prints exited the front door. Tara had dared to enter the office. She had screamed in terror on spotting Sergeant Robert Stratford's body on the floor. A floor covered in dark red congealing blood. All it took was ten seconds at most and she'd passed out. The kitchen staff rescued Tara and called 911.

The police had arrived in no time at all. Blaring sirens and bright flashing lights added to the action that had destroyed the routine shifts the Pot's staff had arrived expecting to work. Following preliminary police interviews Constable Eric Johnson had taken charge of the scene. Keys to the building had been ceded to Eric upon his request. The entire shift had headed over to the café after they'd been interviewed. They called coworkers who quickly joined up with them at the café. Customers turning up at the Pot expecting breakfast soon joined the rush to order breakfast and catch up on the latest gossip surrounding the murder investigation unfolding at Chester's Lobster Pot Pub & Eatery. On seeing Eugette's number flash up on her cell phone, Tara answered. Very few words were exchanged, then Tara left the café chatting into her cell with Anna at her side. Anna drove and shortly they arrived at the Trinity home where Eugette and her family had temporarily moved pending the rebuild of the Lamont home. Maria had approved the clearing of the rubble once Martin's safe had been recovered. Insurance roadblocks were tumbling with Parker Rose working on Maria's behalf. A sense of curious relief befell most in the town. Most felt secure while craving to learn more about the investigations underway in Chester and beyond.

CHAPTER 54

Three weeks into the new year Norman, Eugette and their mothers received confirmation that DNA testing had identified their biological father's identity. A third testing also identified the father of Kimberly Tobias's son. The Lobster Pot Pub & Eatery remained closed. Some of the former employees gained employment at existing restaurants and cafés where business had picked up with the Pot's closure. Most ended up applying for unemployment benefits and hoping the Pot would reopen under new ownership. Maria struggled to adapt to the absence of her grandbabies. Although Eugette had assured her it was a mere two hours away by air, the ache in Maria's heart placed it a million miles away. They, along with their mother, had accompanied John on his return to work in Newmarket. With no local closure on the location of Barnie Madison she felt her family was safer in Newmarket.

One's childhood quickly vanishes in the passage of life's timeline. On becoming parents, we quickly lose ourselves in the joys and occasional frustration of parenthood. On marching our youngsters off to school, we lose status as our children's teachers lead our gifts forward into an exciting world with each lesson taught. Then a sonic boom hits and we're grandparents. The true meaning of life hits us, blasting out joyous rewards that we embrace more with each day lived in companionship with our grandbabies. Some of us, due to life's circumstances, only get to spend time in the companionship of our grandbabies on visits that are far too rare and definitely always too short. That was the scenario Maria found herself in these days. Photographs are great but they can never replace the glow on the faces of loved ones coming together. The touching makes it all a reality. Basically, stated time and life's passage never stands idle, regardless of one's choices in life.

....

Discovering the stash of bills on the back seat of Robert's car, a jubilant Barnie exalted over how routinely the true downfall of those that tried to cross him always played out to the master's will. The money had aided Barnie's efforts to remain incognito and out of sight. Tracking down his prey had been difficult at first. However, he'd refused to abandon the game plan. Once discovered, the prey proved to be simple minded and locked into a predictable daily routine.

Sitting outside the home of his quarry the taste of revenge sweetened Barnie's state of mind. He'd uncovered his prey's residence easily via online searches and references to Momma's old diaries. He watched the man step out of his car and walk up to his house then through the front door into his home before his jubilant eyes. Convinced his plot would work, Barnie walked away from the house and its occupants. Back inside his temporary vehicle Barnie drove off to his place of seclusion after a quick drive through at a local fast-food restaurant. Drippings from a grotesque burger stained the pages of the newspaper he was flipping through. Three days had passed since the last writeup had appeared in the newspaper. A state of affairs he knew would soon change. Frontpage coverage and the beginnings of a new life stood mere hours away. Spit flew out of Barnie's mouth as he belched loudly into the night. He reached into his jeans pocket and fingered the keys to Robert Stratford's vehicle. A vehicle Robert no longer required, but one that would pave the way to Barnie's new life. A follow-up grunt freed a goober of mucus in his throat. It quickly followed the earlier spit onto the newspaper's pages. The night dragged on slowly. Sleep alluded Barnie. However, a supply of cigars eased the darkness on towards dawn.

With a new day dawning and a new life about to burst forth into reality Barnie twisted the ignition key and the engine started. Having tracked his quarry relentlessly the past three days Barnie drove directly to the man's place of employment. Like clockwork, the routine played itself out until Barnie greeted the man with a gun barrel thrust into his side. Shocked, the man stared at Barnie. He shouted, "My wallet. Take it please. Take my car but please let me live!"

"Right! Well, my friend, life comes with conditions. Move it. That blue compact, open the passenger door and get inside. Don't whisper a word! Get in now!" Terrified, the man fumbled with the car door's handle. Barnie reached out and yanked on the handle. The door flew open. Once the man had seated himself Barnie hit the passenger door. It closed with a resounding thud. He then raced around to the driver's door. He stared the man down until seated behind the wheel. Barnie flicked the door lock switch and started the engine. The man pulled out his wallet and threw it over at Barnie.

He pleaded! "Please. Take the wallet. I'll give you the pin numbers. But please don't kill me. I've got a wife and kids!"

The pleas went unanswered. Barnie headed off to the deserted country road behind the airport he'd previously chosen. Parked, he shouted, "See those clothes in that bag? Strip and get into them."

Sobbing, the man fumbled with his shirt's buttons. Frustrated, Barnie stepped outside and ran to the passenger door. He flipped the fob unlocking the passenger door, then shouted, "Git your sorry arse out here now. The man obeyed. Barnie sneered while watching him strip. He frowned on spotting the ugly birth mark on the man's right thigh. Determined to fast track his plan, Barnie grabbed the bag and shook its contents out onto the ground. He aimed the gun at the man. He demanded, "Now get dressed in those clothes. And move it. I ain't got all day. God! How could your wife do it with you. You're fucking ugly!"

Dressed, the man followed Barnie's demands. Barnie joined him back inside the car. He started the engine and locked the doors then drove off leaving the man's discarded clothes on the ground. All personal items had been retrieved by Barnie. He drove directly to the Halifax Airport's Park'N 'Fly lot. Once inside the lot he drove to the spot he'd parked Robert's vehicle. He parked in a spot two cars away from Robert's. A glance confirmed nobody was in the area. At gunpoint Barnie led the man over to Robert's vehicle. There he flicked its fob and unlocked the driver's door. First, he retrieved a wallet front a jacket pocket then tossed it inside the vehicle. It bounced then landed on the passenger seat. A poke with the gun barrel nudged the man inside behind the wheel. Tears streamed down the man's face. He turned and stared through watery eyes at Barnie and begged anew, "Please, sir just let me…"

"Let you live," Barnie snarled. "Not likely, Brian. Look at you, a sniveling snit. Oh! You've had a good life, we can't deny that. Look at your wife. She's aged nicely. Bet ya she's a hot one in de sack, Say what. But your fate is sealed. Your Momma, our Momma, sealed your fate years ago, my brother!"

Brian stared in shock at Barnie. He pondered the words he'd just heard, *'Your Momma, our Momma, sealed your fate years ago, my brother!'*

Barnie laughed heartily. Then snarled, "Ya! Our Momma had twins. But gave one away. That being you! And relentlessly throughout life at every turn she'd swear, *'Where were you, God? Why'd you let me give the good one away?'*"

Brian stared in disbelief at Barnie. In staring he slowly recognized their similarities. He cried out, "I'm sorry, but I never knew! I never knew!"

Barnie fired off four rounds into Brain's head. Brian collapsed onto the steering wheel. Blood and bone fragment flew onto the dash, door and seat. The horn blasted. Barnie shoved Brian off the steering wheel, He fired two more shots into Brian's face. Satisfied, he then ran off to his car. Quickly, he fired it up and drove off to the check-out gate. Driving out of the Airport's Park'N 'Fly, lot Barnie felt redeemed. He headed off into the new life he'd often imagined over the years. Silently he whispered, "Are we happy, Momma. No? So sad. But surprise your other baby me is fucking happy. Say hi to Brian! You stupid bitch! You fucked with the wrong son. Nobody fucks with Barnie!"

……..

Over in East River at the old homestead Richard eyed Lyndsey across the kitchen table from himself. The doctor had suggested their date with parenthood could come as early as mid-February. The thought both excited and scared him. That time would come faster than they could imagine. The thought amused Richard. He'd been reminded throughout life of his welcomed but premature arrival. Lyndsey smiled and her dimples popped out. Richard sighed. Once he'd bought into Lyndsey's expressed wishes, the reality of their new path in life excited him. He reached out and took Lyndsey's hands into his. Raising them up he kissed each fingertip and knuckle.

Lyndsey simply giggled in response and whispered, "Love ya, sweetheart. I know it's been a hard call to make. But I believe it's the right one for us."

In that moment Richard relived a moment shared with Lyndsey and John in grandfather's attic back in Newmarket. So much had unfolded and changed in their lives since then. Their family of three had reconnected with their biological roots. Their true beginnings. They no longer stood alone. In truth, Richard confessed to himself that he treasured the new world that had embraced him and his family into theirs. They both stood up. Lyndsey turned and walked towards their bedroom. Richard followed Lyndsey's lead. The aura flowing off Lyndsey's body sexually excited Richard. He fought off its urges. Together they crawled under the blankets. Lyndsey quickly drifted off into dreamland.

Richard mulled over the buy in he'd agreed to in accepting Lyndsey's wishes. He sighed in reflection over the research Lyndsey had put into place. She'd covered every plausible argument he would raise in discussing why it wouldn't work out. In the end, compromise had ruled the day. The workload over winter ran light. On being contacted, Bill, their de facto business manager, during John and Richard's travels over Christmas and beyond had agreed with the proposal suggested. In truth, Richard suspected Lyndsey had worked her will on Bill and suggested the staffing adjustments Bill agreed to implement. It all made perfect sense, which nudged responsibility out of Bill's hands into Lyndsey's. Richard glanced over at Lyndsey. Besides, he thought Lucas and Ivan were ready to take on more responsibilities. The early return from their seasonal layoffs would be a financial boost to their young families. Satisfied that the right move had been made, Richard relaxed and quickly fell asleep. Snuggled up to Lyndsey he offered no resistance to the Sandman's beckoning calls. Sunrise did not disturb the snuggled-up couple.

Auntie Lila enjoyed her early awakening and a peppermint tea while working away on a Sudoku puzzle. On retiring, she'd missed working the hospital wards back at Kings County Memorial Hospital in Montague. She'd quickly bonded with Lyndsey. Besides, Lila mused, she kind' a taken to being back home. Many old acquaintances frequently stopped in to chat and refresh old childhood friendships. Only one thing stood in the way of Lila overextending her stay, Timothy. In admitting a long-established truth, she missed her charming neighbour the man who'd quickly won her heart over the years. The phone rang and Lila jumped up and answered, "Hello Lila here."

....

Back in Chester, frustration filled Inspector Harley Kingston's efforts to track down Barnie Madison. Headquarters had assigned him to the Chester detachment pending the closeout of the case at hand. Freedom from the pressures of headquarters agreed with Harley and he enjoyed working with the Chester team.

Eric broke Harley free of his frustration. He shouted, "Inspector! There's been a shooting, an execution style murder at the Halifax Airport's Park'N 'Fly lot. And they've identified the victim!"

Harley frowned on hearing Eric's excited announcement. No connection to their case appeared in his mind. He asked, "Ok? Is the victim connected to our case in any way?"

Eric beamed, he nodded a positive response and boasted, "It's our man. It's Barnie Madison."

Harley jumped out'ta his chair. He stared at Eric and begged, "Don't be pulling my leg, son. It's Madison you say? And there's no doubts?"

"No. They found his wallet and ID in the vehicle. Forensics recovered fingerprints everywhere inside the vehicle and its exterior. The corpse has been removed and will undergo further testing. Yes! Inspector, your nemesis has met his end."

Harley savored the thought. He grabbed his cell phone and speed dialed headquarters. The line was answered in two short rings. "Inspector! Tammy here. You must be over the wall in jubilation. Your nemesis has finally been nailed. Congratulations! Hold on and I'll transfer you to the boss."

Harley answered, "Thanks, Tam. I want to scream and shout! Then dance a Chester Jig. But first I just gotta see the bastard stretched out on a slab in the morgue."

"Gott Cha, Inspector. Hold on and I'll connect you with the boss man."

Ring, ring, rin... "Superintendent Donaldson, how can I assist you?"

"Dan, you old fart. Have we really nailed that bastard to a morgue slab. Is the gig really up, my son?"

"Are ye dancing about the detachment hoisting that olde flask of yours higher than a soaring sea gull with a sore arse laddie?" You must be over the moon and back again twice over. Yes, looks like we, no, you've, finally nailed that bucket of anguish closed with no possibility of appeal!"

"Have they started the autopsy, Dan. I've gotta be there and see him sliced and diced before I can believe the bastard is really dead!"

"Then you'd best head up and sweet talk Doc into bumping the autopsy up the priority list. As you know, the old bugger is a stickler for protocol and procedure. Madison's face is a real mess, Harley. Fingerprint evidence is good. Real good. They've lifted great prints throughout the vehicle. But until we get the lab results back confirming a solid DNA match, we'll be holding off on slamming the door shut."

"Right. Procedure, I read you loud and clear boss. Could you twist an arm or two? Doc won't listen to my bemoaning's. But he just might respond to a nudge from you or from above!"

"I'll give it a shot, my Friend. No promises. But I'll give it a shot. There's a good team in place down Chester way. Put young Johnson in charge and get your arse on the road. Call me from the morgue. We'll do supper."

"I will, Dan. Shake a string or two and get things moving up the line. I'll call."

"You'd best call. I'll warn Kristin. It's been too long since we got together."

"Later. And thanks, Dan." Harley disconnected the call. A short conversation with Eric Johnson placed him in charge of the Chester Detachment. Back slaps and handshakes with staff extended their congratulations to Inspector Harley Kingston and sent him on his way up the road to Halifax. Along the way, Harley speed dialed Gilbert at the house and on his cell. Neither line answered. He followed up with Jeffery's home and cell numbers but met the same results. Short voice mail messages were left for Gilbert and Jeffery. He flipped though his cell's phonebook listing but no listing popped up for Trinity. Harley disconnected his cell and pocketed the phone. Resolve set in and he focused his attention on the road.

CHAPTER 55

Jeffery held the phone to his ear. A blank gaze passed between him and Maria. He spoke into the receiver, "Gilbert, please, I need to hear it again." Jeffery then motioned to Maria and she walked over to his side. He nudged Maria's ear up to his and repeated his pleas to Gilbert, "Maria's with me, Gil. Please repeat your news. We need to hear it together."

Gilbert responded, "Ok, Maria, Jeffery, Harley called from Halifax. Barnie is dead. Laid out on a slab at the morgue. But final confirmation is on hold. It will come with the forensic DNA test results. However, Harley believes it's a given."

Maria collapsed into Jeffery's arms. The receiver dropped down onto the floor. Jeffery called out, "Thanks, Gil. Fantastic news. Maria needs me. I'll call back in a bit." He then stooped down and scooped Maria up in his arms. A short walk across the room and he placed her on the sofa.

Maria held Jeffery in a loving embrace. She whispered, "Yes! Please Lord, let it be true. Let it be true. Oh my God. Please send the bastard straight to hell! Oh my God. I feel so free. So ready to really embrace love and not be in fear of that bastard!" Tears of joy streamed down Maria's cheeks. A joy that reassured her that her baby, her daughter Eugette, was safe. Her grandbabies, Megan and Taylor, were safe. Maria released Jeffery from her embrace. He reached to grab tissues from the box on the end table. Maria shook her head signalling the tissue wasn't needed. She broke out in sobs that shook her body. Jeffery stared into Maria's eyes questioning her state.

Maria whispered, "No, Love. I need these tears. They're tears of joy and freedom and not just mine. My family, Anya, Kimberly and their families. And God only knows how many more lives that bastard ripped to pieces over the years. Let me cry, Love. It feels fantastic! We're free! Everyone is free of his hateful ways! Give me a moment to savor the sweet taste embracing my heart."

Jeffery pulled Maria back into a warm loving embrace. Together they sobbed, sharing the tears that covered their faces in joy that freed both from a lifetime of abusive interactions with Barnie. No sorrow touched their hearts or souls in the joyful moments being shared.

Maria whispered, "Another moment or two please, sweetheart. Then I'll call my baby, my Eugette. She needs to feel and taste the sweetness that's caressing my heart and soul with joy beyond my wildest imagination."

Earlier, a similar scene had embraced Gilbert and Anya on answering Harley's call. And like Jeffery and Maria, the news bonded its recipients into their budding relationship. News quickly flowed throughout Chester, Easter River and the surrounding areas. A phone call by Harley to Lunenburg widened the area of celebration. Death is often followed by a celebration of the deceased's life. The opposite rang true in this case. Death was simply celebrated with rejoicing in the hearts of those the deceased had crushed and those of their families and connections.

....

A week slipped by almost unnoticed. Over in East River a panic set in on Monday morning. Auntie Lila caught sight of the first warning signs. Lyndsey had arisen early. Refreshed and energized from a great night's sleep, she'd taken to cleaning the old homestead top to bottom. Not a speck of dust was left unattended to. Lila had arisen to the sounds of Lyndsey's energized movements about the house. Dressed and sitting at the kitchen table with a fresh peppermint tea in hand, she eyed Lyndsey and her frantic nesting antics. The actions triggered memories experienced over years of nursing. Lila watched Lyndsey pause and rub her back sighing in the relief the rubbing delivered. The two ladies' eyes connected. Lila suggested, "Looks like a break in your cleaning routine is in order. Care for a tea, Lyndsey?"

Smiles were exchanged. Lila took that as a positive. She stood and set about preparing Lyndsey's tea. She soon returned to the table with Lyndsey's peppermint tea. Lila opened the conversation, "You're one early riser today. Did you have trouble sleeping?"

"No. Just woke up and had an urge to set things right. Do a little… Oh my God!" Lyndsey cringed and grasped her lower abdomen. Lila stood and raced around the table to Lyndsey's side.

She asked. "How far apart are they?"

"Oh! It's nothing. I just pushed myself a little too far in my cleaning."

Lila frowned. "That's the first one since I sat down. Were there any earlier ones?"

"One or two but it's nothing to worry about, Lila. I'm ok. Just some cramps."

"How's your plumbing running? Any loose stools?"

Lyndsey smirked then answered, "A little maybe. But I'm ok. Really. The doctor said I shouldn't go into labour before mid-February and then I'd be two weeks early."

Lila chuckled. First time moms. They read every book on pregnancy and labour. They had the routine down pat until premature labour hit them front and center. Lila gazed into Lyndsey's eyes and said, "Agreed. Lyndsey, please trust me, you're experiencing all the signs of premature labour."

Lyndsey tried to stand but failed. She shouted, "Please get Ritchie. We gotta get to the hospital!"

"No!" Lila responded. "I worked years in various maternity wards. You're experiencing the signs of premature labour. We'll wait it out and you, young lady are off household chores as of this minute."

Lyndsey smirked and asked, "Really?"

Lila answered, "Absolutely! You're under my care. And trust me, Auntie Lila will be calling all the shots."

Lyndsey chuckled then agreed, "Ok. Auntie, it's your call." The sound of running bathwater announced that Richard was up and about.

Auntie Lila, with a finger to her lips, whispered, "Not a word to him. Unless you want a non-productive round trip run to the hospital." Lila helped Lyndsey up into a chair. They embraced. Once released, Lila returned to her chair and sat. Conversation bounced around memories both eagerly shared. After a stretch Richard joined the ladies and exchanged good morning kisses and hugs with Lyndsey.

....

Locals driving past the cemetery only gave the activity casual glances. Most were not aware of any recent deaths in the community. The internment taking place had not drawn many to its graveside. The only vehicle was the black hearse whose occupants assisted the groundskeepers in positioning the coffin for burial. Once it was set in place the groundskeepers stepped aside allowing the service to take place. A brief reading followed by a recital of prayers followed. Then the coffin was lowered into the earth. The reciter scooped up a handful of earth then tossed it down onto the coffin. It landed with a deadened thud. They then retrieved their hardware and stowed it in the hearse. A glance over at the groundskeepers signalled the service had ended. Both men entered the hearse and it drove out of the cemetery. At the highway the hearse made a left turn and headed back towards Halifax. Conversation was non-existent. Both men knew who they'd interned. Words lost out to the contempt both felt towards the coffin's occupant. They'd followed the case and conversations with morgue staff had filled in any details they'd missed. Silently, they did question the propane powered hot air heater caressing the pile of soil beside the grave. Most times heavy equipment was deployed to fill in excavated graves in winter.

Back in the cemetery the groundskeepers walked back towards the graveside, each with a shovel in hand. In turn they scooped then tossed the first two shovels of dirt onto the coffin. On stepping off to the side both nodded to the long lineup of vehicles that had entered the cemetery. No words were exchanged with the newly arrived graveside visitors.

Each one carried their own shovel or shared their partner's. On walking by the excavated gravesite each in turn scooped up a shovel load of soil and tossed it down onto the coffin. It quickly vanished as the soil piled up over it. Throughout the procession a number of men paused and lingered staring down into the grave. Only after the sounds of trickling water stopped and whisps of mist arose out of the grave did they move on allowing the next in line their turn.

The grave slowly filled. Once it had been completely filled in and the graveside visitors had departed both groundskeepers stood briefly over the grave site. Disgust painted a reflection of their emotions on their faces. A moment then two slipped by then both men spit down onto the ground they stood on. Satisfied, they returned to the cemetery office, stowed away the propane air heater and locked the door. Both had once been school mates of the deceased. No sadness surfaced. Like many locals they'd suffered the bullying tactics of a once young Barnie Madison. In reflection, they gloated over the total lack of attendees that had arrived to express heartbreak on the man's death. The ones whose lives he'd bashed and destroyed had shown up after the graveside service had concluded. Together with them they'd conducted their own long overdue graveside celebration of Barnie Madison's death. The celebration of his death would still be in full swing had everyone the deceased crushed in one way or another shown up graveside. Many had fled their community over the years. Although many had been contacted and were celebrating the event in ways that gladdened their hearts and left them savouring feelings of satisfaction and embracing welcomed feelings of freedom. Nobody noticed the dark figure standing off at the cemetery's back edge amongst a cluster of trees.

....

Richard quickly adapted to working remotely through his laptop. Conversations with both John and Bill assured him that Lucas and Ivan were proving themselves and succeeding in the performance of their workloads. Each passing day provided Richard downtime to reflect on the career choices open to him. The constant exposure to sea air quickly freed Richard of the stress he'd feared would beset him in moving forward in life. Most nights, following exchanges of goodnight kisses, he'd quickly fallen into the grasp of the Sandman.

Lyndsey seldomly followed Richard off into dreamland. Reading had replaced her passion for raw carrots. Come bedtime each night she eagerly lost herself in the pages of the many books found in the old homestead's sunroom bookshelves. Many of the books carried her off into the highlands of Scotland. One book a personal favourite, rekindled many treasured moments along with moments out of a distant past relived in reading the words a young Grace Ramsay had once written into the pages of her 1796 Diary. A week before the big day, Lyndsey had actually fallen off to sleep with the diary in her hands.

The diary had tumbled down onto her baby bump. Responding thumps internally by the upset twins jarred Lyndsey out of slumberland. Awakened, she tried to retrieve the diary. She failed. A glance down towards the foot of the bed startled Lyndsey. She connected with an entity she'd thought had willingly moved on. Their eyes locked.

Grace Ramsay's spirit glowed. Its essence relaxed Lyndsey who listened to their returned houseguest. *'I did not find father out there on the island where we last chatted. I did however discover something sweeter. I came to be with the fabled beast. And I quickly discovered he was, in truth a lost soul cast aside by a group of blood thirsty pirates that had killed him and tossed his earthly body down atop their buried treasure in a grave you and the East River Clan attempted to dig up.'*

Lyndsey stared at Grace Ramsay in disbelief. Stuttering she declared, "You're dead. You're not really here. It's that double chocolate bar I had before bed. This is not really happening to me."

'Sorry lassie. It is and I'm here. Do not fear. The island was desolated and lonely. We, meaning me, Grace Ramsay and my beast, Wilbert Enid who is a gentle loving soul. We've bonded and in our bonded afterlife are experiencing the joyful love I once envied on seeing it shared between you and your man. Please allow us to embrace the joys we were both denied in life. We mean you no harm.'

Frozen in time's brief pause, Lyndsey stared at Grace Ramsay's spirit. On spotting the essence of mist-like tears on the spirit's cheeks, she nodded an affirmative reply to Grace Ramsay's spirit. Slowly, the essence of Wilbert Enid appeared at Grace's side. Lyndsey stared at the pair in shock and the twins she carried relaxed. The thumps of their feet abated. In awe, Lyndsey stared at the beautiful couple floating above the foot of her bed. Wilbert, she silently admitted was indeed a handsome dude. Youthful with a gentle kindness that radiated off of his essence.

Spotting the woman's kindness and gentle spirit, Wilbert whispered, *'Merci madam. We are so grateful of your willingness to accept our presence. We will not harm you or yours and promise to stay on our side of life's energy sphere.'*

Agape, Lyndsey stared at the foot of the bed. Slowly the images of Grace Ramsay and Wilbert Enid faded then completely vanished. With their disappearance, Lyndsey slowly relaxed and tumbled into slumberland. Sleep embraced and rejuvenated her body. Come morning she awoke totally reenergized and Auntie Lila's patience was tested to the max. However, in the end, Lila won the day.

....

A week later a convoy raced off towards the hospital. Richard led the way with Gilbert's truck close behind. On arrival in Lunenburg at the Fisherman's Memorial Hospital, Lyndsey was quickly seated in a wheel chair and whisked off to ER to be attended to. Richard attempted to accompany her but was restrained by Gilbert and Anya. Anya succeeded in getting Richard to relax. He refused offers of fresh coffee. Breathing deep energizing breaths Richard regained control of his body and mind. Images once viewed on various television screens flashed images of women in the midst of childbirth. He valiantly fought them off and savored the glance he'd stolen of a very pregnant Lyndsey seated at his side in their SUV on arriving at the hospital.

A nurse appeared at the ER entrance. She called out. "Richard, Richard Ramsay please come with me. Your wife is in the delivery room and wants you there at her side."

Richard jumped up. He ran to the nurse and pleaded, "Please! Can they come too? They're family an uncle and aunt! Please!"

The nurse frowned and the response was accepted. Gilbert then Anya hugged Richard and reluctantly released him. They both nodded their understanding. The nurse urged Richard to go with her. Together they headed off to the delivery room. Gilbert and Anya watched them go. Anya whispered, "I'm so excited for them. They're a beautiful couple. And soon will be parents, a mommy and a daddy."

Both Anya and Gilbert took into nervously pacing awaiting word from the delivery room.

Richard stared in awe at Lyndsey on arriving in the delivery room. On being cued he followed all instructions to a T. He even managed to exalt some of the tips picked up at their prenatal classes back in Newmarket. Lyndsey heard his prompts and ignored them as mere background noises. She screamed in responding to the doctors and nurses' instructions singing in her ears. "Oh! Oh my God! Mom, I'm goanna be a Mommie. Oh my God!"

A loud 'Wwwwwaaaaa, Wwwwwaaaaa' exploded into the room. Parenthood embraced Lyndsey and Richard. 'Wwwwwaaaaa, Wwwwwaaaaa'. Richard stared in awe at the baby in the doctor's hands though tear-stained watery eyes, Lyndsey's, their first born, a daughter. He clutched Lyndsey's hand in his. The doctor passed their daughter to a nurse then returned her attention to Lyndsey. Richard turned to Lyndsey. A surreal feeling embraced him. Background instructions sang out. Richard did not hear a word. A final sigh and Lyndsey relaxed. She stared through watery eyes at Doctor Tyne holding their son. Wwwwwaaaaa, Wwwwwaaaaas' echoed throughout the room. Once attended to sister and brother were ceremoniously presented to their mom and dad. Both glowed. Especially Lyndsey who cuddled her babies lovingly. Loud tears of joy flowed freely. Minutes later Richard was ushered away. On spotting Gilbert with Anya, he ran excitedly to their sides. A group hug ensued. On being released Richard boasted proudly announcing the birth of his twins, "I'm a daddy!"

Anya chided, "Who came first Richie?"

"Our daughter! Our daughter was the first."

Anya beamed and boasted, "I knew it. I knew it!"

Gilbert watched Anya chatter it up with Richard, digging for details. But Richard had none he could pass on to her.

Richard continued his boasting, "It was an amazing experience! I ended up enthralled and overjoyed having experienced the birth of two beautiful babies. Our babies! Lyndsey and me! We're parents!" Slowly he calmed down.

Their nurse reappeared and suggested they head to downtown Lunenburg to a restaurant and grab breakfast. Over breakfast congratulations continued to flow freely. Richard refused to announce the babies' names. Though during the delivery Lyndsey had shouted them loudly out to the world on each one's arrival. Richard diverted the official naming until everyone was back together with Lyndsey and her babies.

Gilbert called Jeffery. With the line ringing at Jeffery's end, he passed his cell phone to Richard.

"Hi Gil, Jeffery her…"

"Gilbert! Spill the beans. How'd it all go?" Maria shouted. She'd grabbed the phone out'ta Jeffery's hand.

"It was amazing Maria," Richard boasted. "Our daughter arrived first. Both are amazing. Beautiful babies. Hey! I'm a Daddy!"

Maria shouted, "We'll see you in a bit. Gotta hit the road! We're on our way!" She disconnected the line.

Richard grinned and announced, "We'd best head back to the hospital. That was Maria and the crew is headed our way."

Gilbert paid the bill and everyone headed out to his truck. On arrival back at the hospital they found Lyndsey in her assigned room. The babies were down in the maternity ward under the care of their nurses. All eyes turned to Lyndsey. Richard held both her hands in his. They kissed. Then Lyndsey announced, "Letitia Sandra Mary Ramsay seven pounds three ounces, William Richard Allan Ramsay seven pounds six ounces. Born 11:32 am and 11:48 am February 14th."

A loud round of applause erupted in the room. Anya had lost herself in extending congratulations to Lyndsey. Many parenting tips were bouncing around. Across the room, Gilbert chatted up a storm with

Richard. Richard stepped aside and pulled out his cell phone. He made several quick excited calls announcing the births of Letitia and William. Hope and Norman were the first two called. Richard actually set them up on a conference call to make his announcement. Once he connected John and Eugette, to the conference call both, ladies bombarded Richard with endless questions. What did they weigh, how long are they, what colour are their eyes, their hair. Richard escaped the answering phase by turning the phone over to Lyndsey.

The room's excitement exploded on the arrival of Jeffery, Maria and Auntie Lila. The ladies joined Anya bedside and Lyndsey basked in the outflow of congratulations. The new arrivals received full details without asking.

At that point the three men headed off to greet the babies in the maternity ward. They totally lost themselves in the antics of father and uncles greeting the new arrivals into their family. In truth, as is often the case, the most entertained were not the babies, but the jubilant nurses caught up in watching the parents, grandparents, uncles, aunts and family friends introducing themselves to the babies.

After a stretch, Lyndsey joined them in a wheel chair pushed by Maria and Anya. Time stood still and the greetings grew more animated. Both Letitia and William slept through the high energy welcome into the family. Shortly after, Gilbert, Anya, Jeffery, Maria and Lila headed back home. Richard stayed at the hospital either with Lyndsey, or down visiting Letitia and William. Time almost stood still but never does. It actually raced by unimpeded. Soon mom, dad, Letitia and William were back home at the old homestead.

Norman and Hope arrived for a short visit then reluctantly headed back to PEI for his studies. Auntie Lila declined Norman's offer of a ride back home to Murray River. She felt needed in supporting Lyndsey and Richard's entry into the world of parenthood. Richard and Lila questioned Lyndsey's refusal to place the twins in the master bedroom. Their attempts to convince her to give if a trial run fell on deaf ears. Until she walked into Lila's bedroom one overcast afternoon and caught Grace Ramsay and Wilbert Enid's spirits singing gentle lullabies to Letitia and William. Standing in the doorway she watched both babies cooing in response to the lullabies. That night both babies dropped off into slumberland charmed by a trio sharing their love with those in their care.

Following a week of never-ending phone chats, John, Eugette and the twins flew home to East River. The twins were ecstatic and bubbled with joy connecting with the new twins. Maria, needless to say, was constantly over the moon having Eugette and her grandbabies back home. However, that ended with reluctance on them flying back home to Newmarket. It had been a hard pill to swallow but Maria managed. The selling point was the joy and happiness she saw and sensed in her baby and grandbabies.

....

Harley stopped in to visit with Gilbert. Later they ended up at the homestead, where Harley met Letitia and William. The subject of his retirement arose. Harley shrugged and said, "Still awaiting the forensics confirmation. After a stretch Gilbert and Harley made ready to head out. Harley embraced Auntie Lila. Just before releasing her, he whispered, "Thanks Lila. Without you we may never have managed to closed out this debacle of a case in ten lifetimes. Now with Madison down and out of the picture many lives will be safer. All we need is the confirmations from forensics that the man tested, processed and now interned matches up to the DNA from the crime scene."

Lila smiled and stepped back. She replied, "And I'd bet those results can't come fast enough to erase the touch of anxiety I see in you, Inspector?"

"Agreed, Lila. My retirement is so close I can actually taste it!"

Puzzled, Lila stared at Harley in disbelief. Frowning she asked, "But surely you already know. You've seen him laid out on a slab in the morgue."

"True. I have seen his sorry corpse stretched out on a slab. Hell, Lila I suffered through his autopsy. All we need now is the forensics to nail the case down and then I'll submit my retirement papers! And trust me, Lila, I can taste it!"

"You suffered though the autopsy and still don't know?"

"Mere paperwork, Lila!"

Lila asked, "Back in the day I was an assisting nurse at his birth. My God. That poor woman suffered through the ordeal. No to mention a life of absolute hell in raising the lad. But surely the birthmark on his thigh. Surely to God you saw that? With that there's no need for the forensics. Besides it's best used in closing cases on television. Right?"

Harley boasted, "So he had a birthmark in the shape of a bird's talon. Lots of people have them."

Lila stared sternly at Harley. She asked was it on his left thigh and shaped more like a rat's claw?"

Harley chuckled, "No! It was on his right thigh and in the shape of a bird's talon. Why do you ask?"

Lila turned ashen. Richard ran to her side for fear she would pass out. Gilbert joined him in supporting Auntie Lila. She whispered in a trembling voice, "He's not dead. He's not dead! They were twins. His mom gave one up for adoption. Oh my God! The bastard's not dead. He murdered his twin brother!" Saliva trickled down Lila's chin. Her head collapsed on Richard's chest.

"Harley froze, then shouted in anguish, "Son of a bitch. The bastard's not dead!"

The End

EPILOGUE

Will Inspector Harley Kingston retire? Life is a pattern of constant change in a never-ending cycle. I believe we came together and celebrated a special Merry **Seaside Christmas**. Many lives were affected. Some in a positive manner. Others; Simply stated some are hard to satisfy and their preying natures and devious ways trend to cast them outside the web of decent society. That simply being my stated opinion. In moving forward, I see a potential Children's Book on the horizon. A reader has nudged suggesting a Mysterious Haunting would not be out of line. Meanwhile I look forward to meeting many readers and budding authors at future book signings and promotional events.

St Ignatius Bedford, NS Parish Photos

Wayne is happily retired from a working career that got underway with him serving in the Royal Canadian Navy at the Shearwater Air Base.

Next a career in computer hardware and software spanned the world of mainframe computers through to the first personal computers and beyond. Wayne's working career ended on his retirement from the Atlantic Lottery Corporation.

Retirement reignited Wayne's love of the written word. He published his first novel *Seaside Glitter* in 2017. Wayne enjoys getting out in public settings and chatting with avid readers and budding authors. It energized his writing and a return to his scribblers and keyboards. Nudges from readers urged Wayne to write a sequel and *Seaside Christmas* took flight. Should the opportunity arise at a book signing, stop and chat a minute or two. A good time awaits all stopping by to share a love of the written word.

CPSIA information can be obtained
at www.ICGtesting.com
Printed in the USA
LVHW010710081222
734771LV00001B/24